Affair at Boreland Springs

A novel by
Kay Meredith

Warren Publishing, Inc.

Text copyright © 2008 Kay Meredith
Warren Publishing, Inc.

All rights reserved. No part of this book may be reproduced or transmitted in any form by any means, electronic or mechanical, including photocopying, recording, or by any information storage system, without permission in writing from the Publisher.

www.Warrenpublishing.net

Affair At Boreland Springs

This is a work of fiction.
Any resemblance to persons living or dead is purely coincidental.

ISBN 978-1-886057-09-8

Manufactured in the United States of America
First Edition
17039 Kenton Dr.
Cornelius, NC 28031

Dedication

This book is for Cecil Arthur Huggins and Elma Sweeney Huggins, beloved parents who were adventurers in their own right and supported me in all my efforts to prove that a child of Appalachia could follow dreams that led me all over the world competing for my country with my horses.

Acknowledgements

I wish to thank Cathy Brophy, President of Warren Publishing who was willing to take a chance on a first novel by an unknown author, supported by her wonderful staff. They provided the editing and guidance needed by a neophyte writer.

There is so much appreciation in my heart for my long suffering friends, you know who you are, who faithfully read all my books and asked for more. I will forever be in your debt.

And to my mother, who lived long enough to relate to me how life went in that region and during the time of this novel.

PART ONE

Affair at Boreland Springs

PROLOGUE

Boreland Springs, West Virginia
August 1924

Will didn't like the sound of it. His younger brother, Millard, had brought a message from Wyatt saying the run was to be made on Tuesday; instead of Wednesday, the normal delivery day. According to Millard, who worked in the gardens at the Boreland Springs Resort, Wyatt had been acting strange. Late one night last week, he'd been seen down at the springhouse with a couple of strangers. He wasn't spending as much time with the young clientele, especially the girls, as usual. Millard had overheard Wyatt's father, John Mathieson, order Wyatt to do a better job of entertaining their customers.

Will reckoned Wyatt's surly attitude may have originated from the fact that he owed Vince Palmetto, owner of the Wheeling racetrack, a large amount of money on poor bets. The general consensus of opinion over at Satterfield's Saloon was that he could expect serious consequences if the debt wasn't paid soon. Vince wasn't someone to mess with, which must have had Wyatt sweating through his English-cut tweeds.

Thus it was with a great deal of misgivings that Will slid into the usual spot beside the springhouse on Tuesday just before midnight. With a suspicion innate to a bootlegger, he climbed out of the truck with shotgun in hand and leaned it against the doorjamb. Before he could say a word, Wyatt ran out of the darkened structure to meet him.

"Change in plans, Will. Hurry up, will you? I want this unloaded on the floor here. You don't have to put it behind the wall." His voice was shrill and full of air. "Another thing. You'll have to take 75 cents less on a crate. Got more overhead up in the kitchen than I'd expected. Have to make a profit somehow." He started to take the first crate from Eugene, another brother of Will's who helped him with these runs.

"Just a god-damned minute." Will intercepted the handover with a thrust into Wyatt's chest. "You wouldn't know overhead from cabbage rot. You've got someone comin' to pick up my load here, probably at 100% mark-up. Well, not on my 'shine' you won't." His powerful fist backed Wyatt into the springhouse where their words would be muffled. "Before you get one bottle, you'll hand over my cash at the usual price. Otherwise I leave now and my liquor goes with me. Understand?"

Wyatt's face flushed bright red. The last thing he needed was to be without moonshine for the guests – but he had to get it cheaper so he could get Vince off his back. "Listen hillbilly. I'm in charge here." As the words came out of his mouth, Wyatt pulled a small handgun from the side pocket of his hunting jacket and aimed it at Will's head. "Do as I say or that face of yours will look more like one of you Pa's hounds."

With an instinct honed by years of surviving in a dangerous business, Will's long right arm shoved Wyatt's hand to the side and his bone-hard chest hit Wyatt with the force of a maddened bull. Both men fell to the floor. Will landed on top. The gun was still clasped in Wyatt's hand. As the two scrambled on the damp stone floor, Will felt the muzzle of Wyatt's Colt sliding past his shoulder toward his heart.

Will pulled Wyatt into a standing position, trying frantically to wrestle the revolver from his assailant's clenched fist. Suddenly, the staccato sound of the Colt split the quiet air of the springhouse. Will fell to his knees, stunned by the impact. Desperation filled him with strength. He stood up and struggled backwards toward the twelve-gauge braced in the doorway. Through a haze of pain, he hoped Eugene could somehow get both of them into the truck. If he could hold Wyatt off with the shotgun they could escape with their lives and cargo. Wyatt, calm and deadly, was advancing, his gun aimed directly at Will's heart.

Suddenly a crazed yell from the darkness brought both men to instant attention. Eugene was running from the truck toward the two fighting men. Huge and strong as an ox, he was capable of dispatching Wyatt with his bare hands. Froth flew from his mouth. He looked like a demon from Hell. For an instant Wyatt stood frozen on the spot. Then he dropped his revolver and ran back into the springhouse.

"No, Eugene!" Will yelled frantically. They reached the shotgun at the same time. The impact threw them both off balance and knocked the gun into the dark interior. A blast ricocheted through the sullen summer night, reverberating in waves through the valley and up to the ridges beyond. The noise of so much power exploding in the small enclosure temporarily deafened Will and Eugene.

In the muffled echoes that followed, the world stood quiet as a hay meadow with no breeze. Then Will came to his senses. "Eugene! We've got to get out of here. Now!"

Eugene stood trancelike, peering into the interior of the springhouse. He looked at the bloody mass that had once been Wyatt Mathieson. Then he turned and stared at his brother. His eyes were glazed with fear.

Will heaved himself up out of the moist summer grass where his collision with Eugene had thrown him. He stuffed his handkerchief into the wound, trying to stop the blood that flowed from his left shoulder. Recognizing the stupor that claimed Eugene when his mind was befuddled beyond any comprehension, Will shook him with his good right hand bringing him to a semblance of awareness.

"Get the twelve-gauge and get in the truck, Eugene." Will's voice was quiet and persuasive. Eugene picked up the gun and walked meekly to his side of the truck and got in. Will took his place behind the wheel and with one arm incapacitated he manhandled the clumsy vehicle out of the meadow, spinning its wheels as he raced onto the gravel road that led to the ridge.

Keeping the truck on the road took several minutes of concentration. Eugene was huddled against the other door, his breath coming in heavy spurts. When the road smoothed out somewhat Will turned to his brother and once again spoke in a soothing voice.

"You can't talk to anyone except Pa about what happened tonight." Only the noise of the engine broke the air between them. Will leaned toward his brother. "You understand, don't you Eugene?"

Finally Eugene nodded. "Won't tell nobody, Will."

"That's a good fellow. We did what Wyatt made us do. He wanted to cheat us out of our money."

Eugene let the breath out of his tight chest and lapsed into silence. Will knew that in time his brother's childlike mind would block this unpleasantness from his memory. Will wished he could as well.

Kay Meredith

Affair at Boreland Springs

CHAPTER ONE

Three months earlier

A quarter-moon teased lovers and skulkers with its fickle rays filtering through the heavy layer of oak trees that covered the difficult foothills of the western edge of the Appalachians. To the west, it was only a hoot and a holler to the Ohio River. But the terrain that led to the imposing mountains in the east was hard to negotiate, easy to get lost in, and tricky enough to hide the whereabouts of anyone needing to cover his tracks for a spell.

It was Wednesday night. An old Ford panel truck eased into the meadow beneath the imposing Boreland Springs Hotel that was located in this wilderness. It was throttled down to quiet the engine. The lights were turned off. The driver, Will Hart, who could have done it blindfolded, slipped the vehicle close to the stone building that housed the famed springs. The springhouse door was ajar. Inside, elaborate gas lanterns lit the interior, casting mysterious shadows that glinted off the water, water that smelled like the bowels of the earth.

The length and breadth of West Virginia was contorted by mountains that sliced through the state like a butcher knife creating a maze of hollows, ridges, and creeks that could baffle experienced guides. It was not unusual for visitors to be swallowed up by this morass of chasms that could disorient even the best hounds.

Regarded as primitive by outsiders, West Virginians enjoyed these ravines that seemed to hold the mysteries of the world within its coal and oil rich soil. On most any morning the valleys were enveloped in soft swirling ground mists while the mountaintops were swathed in wet fog. The dwellers of this old land felt protected from an outside world that didn't value them. It was a place where the repetitive thrum of an oil well pump provided the heartbeat that made life understandable. Dependable.

Concealed by mountains and mist, where the state motto was 'mountaineers are always free', West Virginians grew up with a notion of remoteness. Through the years they developed a culture that clutched their thoughts and secrets close to the chest. They weren't a talkative lot, reckoning that folks who needed too many words to say something didn't know what they were talking about.

Underneath their taciturn manner was an appreciation for the surroundings in which they lived. Speech wasn't necessary when one felt the power of a tiny creek as it became a rushing wall of water during spring rains. Hillsides of redbud, dogwood, and rhododendron that looked like colorful quilts needed no human comment to confirm the beauty. It was rare to hear a mountain man complain about his lack of belongings or the hard labor needed to provide for his family. If there was a bed to sleep in, food for sustenance, plus liquor and hounds for entertainment, it was enough.

Another, more insidious trait had crept into the ways of these people as a result of having been secluded in this landscape for so long; distrust of the federal government. Washington was a far-off city full of politicians whose laws never affected them in a positive way. Mountaineers felt the needs of their state and its inhabitants were ignored by the administration in Washington. Therefore, they felt no loyalty to obey rules that had no effect on their lives. When it came to voting, it was more important to attend local elections. They supported men who would turn a blind eye to unpaid taxes and moonshine stills hunted by the United States Revenue Department.

Will switched off the ignition. The engine hiccupped twice; then was silent.

"Wait here, Eugene. I'll see if Mr. Mathieson is inside."

Eugene nodded, then tried hard to hear the hushed words being spoken in the springhouse. It sounded like there were more people than usual. He shrugged his shoulders and gazed at the moon instead, the single wonder of nature that had always fascinated him.

The side of the truck advertised 'Hart's Fresh Grown Vegetables, Reasonably Priced'. Several years ago that sign, professionally painted, had been the pride of the Hart family. When the glossy lettering had first been done, young Will had rubbed his fingers lovingly over the slightly raised words along the metal panel. Some said they were trying to look better than they were, and it *had* cost more than they could afford. But it was quality advertising that would bring enough business to pay for it in the long run. Town folks wouldn't buy unless the equipment looked expensive.

Will had been eleven then and could barely wait until the time when he could help his Pa drive their produce to the markets in Waverly, St. Marys, and Parkersburg. He always felt pride when he saw that truck with their name emblazoned in green, outlined in gold. He figured the Harts must be well known all over West Virginia and Ohio with such a fine bit of publicity.

When Will was sixteen, hard times had set in. A season of drought, followed by harsh spring rains, had diminished their crops for two seasons in a row. Vernon and Eleanor Hart had scraped every bit of produce from the unyielding clay but could barely grow enough for their own use. Their customers had had to go to other suppliers.

Thus the lucrative business of moonshine provided the next logical purpose for these crops. Will became part of the family's second commercial venture, albeit one that was not proudly noted on the side of their truck. He detested using the vehicle that still promoted vegetables, but was a front for the illegal moonshine instead. However, it brought in enough money to pull the Harts from the jaws of bankruptcy and put them on the road to better times. As long, of course, as the government men were unable to find the stills that manufactured their product. While the lettering faded with time, the business of bootlegging flourished like the vegetables had never done.

Making moonshine did not come without its perils. The work had to be done at night in hard-to-find places and one had to be certain of the loyalty of his associates. There was the constant worry that an undercover government agent might infiltrate the tight structure of the bootleggers. A complicated system of identification, which changed weekly, was always in place. Anyone unable to come up with the right code words was eliminated before ever getting close to the location of the actual distilling operation.

In the event of a shoot-out, with resultant injuries and deaths, it was imperative to have a hideaway to run to. The hills were riddled with hidden caves stocked with enough supplies to stay awhile. It was a line of business that required an impressive assortment of firearms, and demand for the illegal liquor always exceeded the supply. The moonshiners cooperated with each other, signaling when agents were around, regulating prices, and swapping products if necessary to keep the money flowing.

Eugene got tired of waiting. He didn't much like these late nights. He wanted to be home in his own bed. He walked over to the doorway and looked in. He was shy and rarely took it upon himself to try to hurry things on a bit. Will was talking with John Mathieson, the owner of the hotel. Standing beside him was his son, Wyatt, who'd recently come home from West Virginia University for the summer. Eugene frowned. He didn't care much for Wyatt and had never seen him at one of these midnight deliveries.

Finally, Will came through the door and motioned for Eugene to join them in the springhouse. Eugene plodded in after his brother. His eyes were downcast as though he was studying where to place each foot, in case he tripped in the darkness. At fifteen, he was clumsy and embarrassed whenever his big feet brought him to his knees. He'd gotten into the habit of watching every step he took, making certain not to walk in rough or muddy footing.

Mr. Mathieson came forward to greet him, thrusting his arm forward to shake hands. Eugene looked up briefly then clasped the hand offered in friendship.

"Eugene. Want you to meet Wyatt." John Mathieson spoke in undertones. "He'll be taking over for me this summer. He needs to learn the ropes, so he'll know what to do when he becomes owner one of these years." He chuckled self-consciously. "Needs to learn how and where all these crates are stashed and who can be trusted and who can't. That's as important as making our guests comfortable."

Eugene nodded but said nothing. Didn't even look up. At Will's whispered instruction, he went to the back of the truck, opened the doors, and began pulling off crates. He handed them to Will who carried them into the springhouse to John and Wyatt.

Will's lean, muscular body worked like a machine. He didn't even breathe hard at the exertion demanded during the hour it took to get the truck unloaded. His black hair fell over his forehead, making his dark brown eyes water at the intrusion. He was a tall man whose Irish ancestry was evident in skin so white that even a small amount of sun raised angry red blisters. The business of bootlegging had taught him to hide his thoughts behind a face that rarely smiled.

The load was counted, recorded in a ledger then stacked behind a false door in the wall. John paid Will in cash, leaving no traceable evidence that the prestigious John Mathieson was dealing in moonshine. Government authorities constantly roamed the hills searching for stills, offering rewards to anyone willing to give information about the bootleggers and their locations. However, it was a tight-lipped community and when questioned, the citizens of Boreland Springs professed ignorance of any such goings-on.

Throughout the operation, what little communication that occurred was done in low whispers and hand motions. When anyone spoke to Eugene, the words were short and the orders uncomplicated.

'Soft in the head', everyone said, but Will knew his younger brother was like a faithful puppy who had never learned how to hunt. From the time it was noticeable that Eugene wasn't quite right, Will had taken it upon himself to watch over the child, much to his parents' relief. With a brood of six, there was no time to spare for a child who needed extra attention just to get him dressed.

The community accepted Eugene the way God had made him. That was their way. No one questioned why the Almighty allowed children to be born who needed more help than others. They reckoned it was His way of testing them to see if they followed the rules of the Bible and took care of the weak among them. Reverend Leland Knox, of the Bull Run United Brethren Church, warned the fires of hell would be the legacy of any man who turned a blind eye to the lesser of God's children. When Eugene was lost, someone walked him back home; they offered a word when he had trouble talking; and the children played tag around his massive frame. He belonged to all the folks of Boreland Springs and without exception they took great pride in making him feel normal.

"Good man, that Will," John commented as he spat a stream of tobacco out the side of his mouth. It was a habit he indulged in on these Wednesday night forays. He'd rinse his mouth out with a bottle of the liquor before returning to bed and hope his wife Roberta was too sleepy to notice any stain on his mouth. In her mind it was a filthy habit that only low-life men practiced.

They watched the little truck lumber onto the rutted gravel road and begin its laborious climb out of the valley. "You'll never find a fairer or more dependable fellow for such a hazardous job." He looked pointedly at Wyatt. "That's the first lesson to learn, son. Only deal with reliable suppliers."

Wyatt nodded solemnly.

The rickety vehicle left as it had arrived: quiet and without lights. It coughed and sputtered as it pulled out of a deep rut or bumped over a rock on its way to the top of Horseneck Ridge.

"Gonna need a new truck one of these days, Eugene." Will's voice slipped every time they hit a hole.

"Yep. This'un's on her last legs." Eugene spoke slowly. Then he chuckled.

"What's funny?"

"She don't have legs, Will. She's got wheels." He slapped his thigh and laughed out loud.

Will joined in, then took his right hand off the steering wheel long enough to give his brother a companionable shove in the arm. It always made him happy to hear Eugene laugh. He seldom did. Guess he doesn't have much to laugh about, Will thought. Must be hard to be too slow to keep up with his buddies yet quick enough to know he's not quite the same as they are.

He looked fondly at Eugene. Shadows played over the strong planes of his face that was fringed with ragged black hair crawling down his neck and under the frayed collar of his old brown shirt. The threadbare bib of his overalls was held up with a rusty safety pin that was nearly pulled apart with the strain of the large boy's heavy chest. Eugene didn't look much different than all the other young boys who lived around Boreland Springs. Only his speech and ability to follow conversations revealed a deficiency in his mind.

Will knew that one of these days, he and Eugene wouldn't have to slink around during the night delivering moonshine to fancy places so wealthy customers could get a thrill while someone else took the chances. When he saved up enough, Will intended to leave these hills and make an honest living somewhere else.

Affair at Boreland Springs

His thoughts turned to Wyatt. Will had never been comfortable with the smooth-talking older son of the Mathiesons. Wyatt had a way of making the right words sound like a slur when he spoke to the locals. It wasn't anything you could put your finger on -- just a feeling that the innocent face and proper speech concealed a heart that was not always genuine.

Tonight was not the first time Will had seen Wyatt since his return from college. Just last Saturday, Will had watched Wyatt drinking and playing up to the women at Satterfields, a tavern in the little village of Waverly about five miles from Boreland Springs. As the beer loosened his tongue Wyatt had bragged about spending time and lots of money in Wheeling betting at the race track there. Will exhaled loudly, disgusted at the willful and thoughtless ways of the privileged.

The truck climbed steadily upward, laboring now and then through a ditch or over a rock. At the crest of the ridge huge oak and chestnut trees were silhouetted by the moon behind them. Far below, the soft swish of Bull Run Creek sloughed its way toward the Ohio. One would have expected the mournful call of an owl or distant howl of a hound, but not even a leaf moved on this windless night.

Will turned right and drove slowly to where the potted road intersected with Polecat Hollow that was little more than an obscure trail leading to the meadow where the Hart family lived. The house was protected on all sides by a heavy stand of pine and oak trees. Their father, Vernon, met them as they pulled into a shed that housed the farm vehicles. With little fuss and no noise, the firearms were stowed in a shallow well and vegetable bins replaced the crates that had carried the moonshine.

It was 2 am when the three men finally slipped inside the clapboard house to the smell of strong coffee. Eleanor Hart, long accustomed to this way of life that went against her Christian beliefs, hugged each one, thankful for their safe return. Will turned over the proceeds to his father who put the money in a metal box that was kept under the floor of his bed. When Vernon was assured that the delivery had gone without a hitch, Will and Eugene joined their two younger brothers in a crowded bedroom that was an extension of the front porch. Two daughters, Wilma and Imogene, shared a bedroom adjacent to their parents.

West Virginia was no stranger to bootlegging. It had been a booming business long before the Civil War, when there was no *West* Virginia, only Virginia.

The mountaineers, considered primitive by the standards of the coastal Virginians who lived in more arable land, had learned there was only one profitable way to haul their corn out of the coves and crevasses of the treacherous Appalachian Mountains. It was distilled, bottled, and hauled out in wagons as corn liquor. When the government of Virginia, run by those wealthy eastern plantation farmers, decided to tax the wagon loads of liquid gold, the hill people began their tradition of moonshining and bootlegging. It was a tried and true system, running full-tilt long before the U.S. government passed the Eighteenth Amendment in 1919 that initiated Prohibition.

In time, the cat-and-mouse game of eluding the 'revenuers' became bragging rights for every mountain man who spent long black nights 'coon' hunting with his buddies. While monitoring the agents under the pretense of hunting, they exchanged stories of great hunting dogs and listened to baying Blue ticks, Redbones, and any other combination that endowed a hound with a good nose and plenty of stamina.

Even before Prohibition illegal moonshine had an appeal far greater than the expensive imported wines and liqueurs offered in the menu of the fashionable Boreland Springs Hotel. It was a fairly safe way the affluent clientele could satisfy a strange need to outwit the law, have a taste of forbidden fruit, so to speak, and do it in a place the authorities seldom prowled. There were those of the religious community who thought official palms were being greased to omit the hotel during their surprise raids on places suspected of dealing in moonshine. However, no one was ever able to bring hard evidence to substantiate the charge.

When questioned, none of the regular churchgoers in the surrounding hills and valleys ever disclosed any suspicious transactions they might have seen at odd times of the night at the hotel. The resort was where young members of every family earned extra money during summers away from school. It provided steady year-round employment for many of the adult residents of the community. Those who did not work directly for the

Mathiesons sold farm produce to them for kitchen and stable needs. It was for their own good that the hotel stayed prosperous, (and anonymous concerning any purported presence of moonshine). In their minds, bootlegging was a minor crime that God wouldn't have time to note anyway, concerned as He was with wars, pestilence, and whores.

Therefore, when Preacher Knox admonished his flock to do God's will and inform the authorities of any wrongdoing they might see in the community, all eyes turned in the opposite direction. The Mathiesons were looked upon as generous neighbors who operated a business that benefited everyone who lived near Boreland Springs. They attended church almost every Sunday, sitting in their special pew close to the front so as not to miss any of the minister's lengthy sermons. They were the first to donate money for any unusual catastrophe that might have occurred: floods in the middle of the state or collapsed coal mines deep in the mountains. In addition, they contributed liberally to the countless missionaries world wide that were supported by this district of the United Brethren Church.

When it was all said and done, everyone trod carefully through the delicate process of embracing and avoiding the law. Boreland Springs was experiencing prosperity unknown by even the oldest dwellers of the region. No one wanted the status quo to change.

Kay Meredith

CHAPTER TWO

Amelia Sue Conroy stood on her front porch, shading her eyes from the bright morning sun. For fifteen minutes she'd been watching the path that wound its way from the top of Horseneck Ridge down to the valley. Her eyes and forehead were wrinkled and stiff from looking for the familiar figure of her best friend, Priscilla Lockhart.

Today would be their first day of employment. Last month the two girls had squealed with delight when they'd learned their application for a job at the Boreland Springs Resort had been accepted. Not that there were many others vying for the spots. The hotel employed as many of the young folks in the area as possible during the busy summer months. In especially hot years, when town folks wanted to get out of the city heat, it had been necessary to augment the staff from Waverly or St. Marys.

Amelia, or Melia as she was called, was the oldest of the four Conroy children. She would be sixteen in the fall and the only daughter of Silas and Maxine Conroy. They were proud of this girl who was a popular member of the church, always ready to take food to the sick, and especially fond of teaching bible classes to the children when the regular teacher was absent. She planned to contribute all but a few dollars of her earnings to add to the finances of her family. The Conroys were hard-pressed to cover all the costs of raising a family of fast-growing children.

Melia was lucky in one respect. Maxine, a superb seamstress, transformed the colorful sacks that had contained cattle feed into attractive creations that complimented Melia's lanky frame and fair coloring. She was blessed with thick chestnut-colored hair that glinted like gold when sunlight hit it in just the right light. Her hazel eyes, sprinkled with green specks, captivated every young fellow who'd ever come into contact with her. True to her strict Christian upbringing, however, all improper advances subjected the wayward lad to a stern lecture on correct moral conduct. She was taller than the other girls her age and often envied the shorter stature of some of her friends.

It was a hardship for Maxine and Silas to keep their children in school. Silas relied on the boys to help with the farming and Maxine needed Melia to assist with the heavy laundry, canning, and cleaning required of the active family. Many families living in Pleasants and Wood Counties could allow their offspring to attend school only long enough to learn to read and perform elementary arithmetic. Some never got to school at all.

When Melia was almost ready to go on alone, Sil rounded the bend and threw a wild wave in Melia's direction. Sil's full name was Priscilla Louise, but no one had time to say more than 'Sil'. She wasn't happy with the diminishment of 'Priscilla', which she considered elegant, but she was overruled by classmates and siblings too busy to mouth such a long name.

"What took you so long?" Melia shuffled her feet impatiently. "I was about to come looking."

Sil laughed. "Why are you so anxious to start working? It's just a summer job."

"How can you be so casual?" Melia sounded peeved. "We'll earn a bit of money and get to see some glamorous and rich people. They'll be sleeping in beds we've made and eating food we've served. Just think, to be able to rub elbows with folks who never have to worry about money at all." Her words spilled on top of one another faster than Sil had ever heard her talk.

"That's the point. We'll be working for them! They're rich and we're poor. I don't see what's great about being a servant to privileged people. I'm looking forward to the time when I can have a position that puts *me* in charge."

"For once I don't want to hear about your grand plans for the future, Sil. Today we'll begin something new in a place we've never been. Even if it's just working for pennies, at least it's a sign we're almost grown up."

"I was only kidding. You're right. I should look upon this as another step toward taking my place as an adult. The world will be a better place when we enter it with our expertise at being servants to the upper-class!"

"You're making fun of me." Melia shoved Sil to the side of the road then doubled over laughing as her friend tried to avoid stepping into a mud hole. "It would serve you right if you landed on your backside and had to explain to Mrs. Mathieson why you had to go home for a change of clothes."

After a few more minutes of thought, conversation ran to the more immediate reason for working during their summer vacation.

"What will you do with all the money you make, Sil?"

"Thought I'd get a new pair of shoes over at Clegg's. A white dress for church. The rest will go to Mama."

Melia was dumbfounded. "You could work all year and not earn enough to buy all that, let alone give any to your mother."

Sil reddened. "You're right. I was just dreaming. I've never seen a white dress at Clegg's anyway. Guess it could get dirty from all the feed, boots, tires, wagons, and farming equipment they sell there, too." She kicked a large rock out of her way. "What're you going to do with your money?"

"Buy a green hair ribbon and give the rest to Mama."

Sil asked nothing further. The Conroys had it hard to farm on the side of a hill without much bottomland to plant. It left them little produce to sell after they'd done the canning and butchering needed to feed their family through the winter. Mr. Conroy did as much logging as he could with only one horse. His two oldest sons, Harold and Troy, were learning to become blacksmiths. The youngest, Little Earl, was only eight, but determined not to spend his life as a farmer. He was a voracious reader and often borrowed books from Sil's mother, who'd been a schoolteacher before she got married. After beginning her own family, Ruth Lockhart taught youngsters who could not attend normal classes in the one-room schoolhouse at Pumpkin Knob. She could hold a babe on her hip, stir a pot of beans with the other hand, and correct reading mistakes at the same time. Earl Conroy was the most faithful of her students, often arriving after supper for corrections to his arithmetic problems and the next assignment.

They followed Bull Run Road to where it forked with Boreland Springs Road. Looking up at the impressive structure standing more than two hundred feet above them brought solemn expressions to their young faces. Few words were spoken as they walked up the graveled drive and then around to the back entrance. Before entering, they smoothed their sweaty hair and tucked in their blouses. When they pulled the screen door open, Mrs. MacIntosh, the morning cook, greeted their arrival with relief.

"Thank goodness you're here. We're running late." Mrs. Mac (as she was known in the community) gave a running set of instructions as she bustled about the kitchen, getting breakfast prepared for a very discerning clientele.

"Sil, help me here in the kitchen. Melia, report upstairs to Cricket Mathews. She's in charge of the east wing and will show you the ropes there." She motioned Melia up the side stairs, then turned to Sil and began introducing her to the others who performed kitchen and garden work.

The day moved too fast to overcome the confusion of learning their duties, hurrying to keep up with the orders that weren't always clear, and trying to stay out of the way of the rest of the staff in the same predicament. Before they knew it, it was time to go home.

At the edge of the evening the low-laying sun sent shafts of soft light through the forest leaves. Sil and Melia sat on the stone steps that led up to the porch that wrapped around the front of the hotel. It was lined with white columns that supported the roof and railing. Hanging pots overflowed with peonies, wild roses, ivy, and ferns. Wrought iron tables with hand-painted tops, surrounded by matching chairs provided a visiting place for guests enjoying the remote landscape. They sipped iced tea and made small talk. Waiters dressed in white shirts with black jackets and trousers stood discreetly in the background, ready to perform any service required. The guests' manners were faultless, their clothes expensive, the conversation dignified. They waited patiently for the night when music, dancing, and liquor would degrade the façade of gentility and high morality.

Sil and Melia wasted little time getting on their way home. The thrill of entering the world of wage earners was beginning to lose its luster. If Melia were to be honest, she no longer thought playing servant to domineering wealthy patrons a reasonable way to spend her life. She didn't intend to admit this to Sil.

For her part, Sil was too tired to notice Melia's change of attitude. She'd known it would be hard, but she hadn't counted on sore shoulders or her red and nicked hands from peeling endless potatoes.

Their shoulders rubbed together as they trudged home, providing support for each other. It had always been so. Born within months of one another, they'd attended church together as toddlers, developing an affinity and loyalty rarely seen at such an early age. Throughout childhood only sickness severe enough to put one to bed would separate them. They hid special keepsakes in the hollow of a rotted oak that had been hit by lightening when both were four. Inside this hallowed space, wrapped in oilcloth begged from Mr. Lockhart, lay dried flowers and butterflies, a lucky penny Sil had found in the road, and a snippet of Little Earl's hair taken when he was sound asleep in his cradle.

They had walked these country roads in dust and mud first beside their mothers, then later by themselves. Trips to Mrs. Beecham who made quilts were especially fun. They would watch in awe as the elderly lady, assisted by her two daughters, worked at the intricate frame, designing quilts famous for beauty and durability even though the swatches of material had come from worn-out clothing.

Both started their monthly flow during their twelfth summer. After an initial excitement of becoming women, the chore of washing soiled old rags made them understand why their mothers referred to this part of being female as 'the curse'. Occasionally, they stayed overnight at each others' homes. No sleeping occurred, only endless talk about which girls of their acquaintance had got pimples; how Norma Jean Radley would soon be considered 'loose' if she continued to thrust her bosom at so many fellows; and would Sidney Langford ever raise his head and look a girl in the eye. In such a quiet community, their respective parents wondered how two young girls could have so much to talk about.

They were traveling down Smithers Glen. It was too narrow to be called a valley. Even though these were only the foothills of the Appalachians the grades were nearly straight up, dropping down to tiny gullies where the inevitable creek collected the run-off from rain and snow. The gravel and clay road snaked back and forth through Bull Run Creek, which today, was only a trace of what it could become during a fierce summer thunderstorm. Then it became a raging monster that often rose in the middle of the night and carried people and belongings away before they could climb to safety. After a few hours of destruction the water once again became a placid stream that receded within its banks and slid without turmoil on its journey to the Ohio River.

In one of the wider spots the Conroy house loomed in the twilight. The little frame house was built high up on the red clay bank. It clung to the hillside like a small wooden box dwarfed by the steep, rocky grade behind it. The rough brick chimney that hung rather sullenly to one end of the dwelling looked like a hastily constructed afterthought. A motley group of chickens, whose colorings gave evidence to mixed breeding, pecked through the sparse grass for the few table scraps Mrs. Conroy threw out after every meal. It was always a contest between the pigs and chickens as to who got the choice morsels. A yellow tomcat curled around himself at the top step. His split ear, shortened tail, and tattered coat made one wonder if he'd recently tangled with a groundhog. The porch, which looked like it was on stilts, provided shelter for the two household dogs. 'Coon dogs were chained to trees further away from the house so as not to lose their hunting instincts from too much coddling.

    Sil gave Melia a brief hug, waved to Mrs. Conroy then began the ascent to her home located at the top of the ridge. While it was never said aloud, most considered this to be the best location for the hill people. The homes seemed to be bigger – probably because the view was unobstructed by trees and there was more space for a proper foundation. Except for river valleys such as the Ohio, the biggest meadows to be found in West Virginia were on top of a ridge rather than in the bottomlands. This meant homes could have porches, and even a second floor where bedrooms were separated from the downstairs parlor and kitchen. While everyone scrabbled to eke out a living in this terrain, the added land available on the ridges left room for swings and banisters, giving the occupants a feeling of luxury.

    Sil's home was a long rectangular clapboard structure with a porch that ran the entire length of the front view. The second floor ceilings were slanted, making for a cozy feeling that was especially comforting during the cold winter months. At each end of the house there was a large chimney with a hearth both upstairs and down. The roof was slate in various shades of gray. The date '1875' was worked into a pattern across the top. Since most of the roofs were tin, this decorated slate gave Ruth Lockhart much joy. Plants, not unlike those at the hotel, hung from hooks attached to the ceiling of the front porch. A swing to the left of the front door was Ruth's favorite place to string beans and shell peas. On the other side was a sturdy rocking chair where Abner Lockhart could usually be found after a hard day in the fields. During the evenings in summer, when farm work was especially demanding, he often fell asleep while the latest litter of kittens played about his feet.

Sil's parents, along with her two older brothers David and Daniel, farmed the fertile fields that comprised most of their land. The Lockharts had lived on this place for generations. It was a part of their heritage, much like their tendency to be tall.

Sil had been taught from infancy to be thankful for all God's blessings and never failed to thank Him for her good fortune at being born into such a loving family and secure house. Tonight she was especially grateful and took the opportunity to ask the Almighty to make it possible for her to attend West Virginia University and become a teacher like her mother. Work as a cook's helper was something she intended to do only once.

She was a couple of inches shorter than Melia, stockily built, and strong as most boys her age. Her hair was dark brown and straight – a fact she lamented often when she looked at the soft waves that adorned Melia's head. Large gray eyes, well spaced below a broad brow, perused the world thoughtfully. Arched brows and a generous mouth completed a countenance that, while not necessarily beautiful, was pleasing to look upon.

Only rarely did a fellow approach her with any comment that might be construed as an interest other than friendship. This was of little consequence to Sil since her goals did not include romantic notions of being rescued from the hills of West Virginia by a 'knight in shining armor'.

Kay Meredith

CHAPTER THREE

On their third day of work, Melia was shaking out the sheets from one of the fancier suites in her care. This particular room offered a view out the back of the hotel, overlooking the stables and tennis courts. Rowdy voices and raucous laughter drifted into the air, disturbing the morning serenity. She stopped for a moment to have a look. Below her was one of the handsomest young men she'd ever seen. Even in the catalogs her mother kept for use in the outhouse there was not such a face and body.

He was the center of attention in a group of young people who were obviously the offspring of the married guests at the hotel. She watched the age-old game of chasing and seducing carried out with little attempt to make it look innocent.

"Wyatt!" A golden-haired girl dressed in an expensive tennis outfit assembled her tall, slim body in a provocative manner around one of the oak trees that lined the courts. "Will you be at the party Saturday night?"

Wyatt Mathieson dropped his racquet with a clatter and struck a pose of contrived alarm. "Is there a party somewhere this Saturday, Neal? Did someone forget to tell me about it?"

Neal threw up his hands in confusion. "I heard something about it. Might want to check it out. I also understand there will be a band of local renown." The whole group dissolved into more hilarity, displaying a greater glee than Wyatt's attempt at humor deserved.

"I'll be there then, Ellie. But only if you and your friends wear strapless gowns. Then I can live with the hope that at least one will fall down!"

While the boys slapped their thighs in anticipation the girls reddened at this last comment, feigning modesty none really felt. Then, with the untroubled thoughts and carefree antics afforded the young and wealthy, they made plans to bathe and change into jodhpurs and boots. The privacy of riding trails provided a place where goings-on parents might disapprove of could be enjoyed.

Melia looked wistfully at these young people who had little to do but plan for their next outrageous venture. On her way to work that morning, she and Sil had passed several places where wine bottles and cigarette butts gave evidence to regular and boisterous partying. Yesterday when they were on their way home, whispers and giggles drifted in breathless expectation from a secluded spot under a huge oak tree. The two girls had skirted the area quietly, leaving the lovers with their privacy. The following morning they'd picked up a hotel blanket left in one of the favorite mossy depressions. Mrs. Mac was incensed when she saw the grass stains that would take much scrubbing to remove.

Working at the posh hotel had not brought Melia the joy she'd expected it would. Instead, everyday when she gazed at the expensive clothes hanging in the wardrobes, she was beset by a feeling of hopelessness. At first she'd promised herself that one day she, too, would be so adorned. In a short time, however, she faced the bleak fact that one was born into such a life. No one from her impoverished background would ever be allowed into this elite group of people. Accepting this fact had been difficult to swallow.

These people were accustomed to luxuries Melia had never known about until she'd started work at the resort. The one thing that impressed her the most was bathrooms inside the house. They were beyond belief. Not only was everything washed away automatically but the rolled bathroom tissue, paper made specifically for indoor plumbing, was soft – unlike the hard, slick pages from magazines used in the outdoor toilet at her home.

They moved and spoke differently than folks around Boreland Spring. She listened to them pronounce their words. The accent she'd heard since she was old enough to talk began to sound uneducated to her. She recalled making a trip to Parkersburg with Sil and her family. It had been hard for her to understand the clipped and proper words of the sales ladies there. It was like they were speaking another language altogether. Melia wondered how it was possible to grow up living so close, yet talking another way from each other. Privately she began to imitate the way Wyatt and his friends spoke. She took greater care with her personal appearance, making sure her dresses were clean and ironed as smooth as the old hot iron could manage.

"Melia!" It was the shrill voice of Cricket Mathews. "I'm waitin' for them soiled linens." Cricket was hurrying down the hall. Her leather shoes with steel insets in the heels clacked like a broken typewriter.

Melia ran into the hall, reaching Cricket before more harsh words were aimed her way. Just yesterday, she'd forgotten to replace the bottom sheet on one of the children's beds. Cricket had apologized to the stiff-lipped mother then dressed Melia down good and proper.

"Here they are, Mrs. Mathews." She could barely drag the huge basket of dirty bedclothes down the hall.

"You need to get faster, Melia. There's too many rooms and not enough help. We'll be here 'til midnight at this rate."

"Yes M'aam."

The two of them carried the basket overflowing with laundry down the stairs and all the way to the washhouse behind the hotel. It was hot and steamy. Edith and Mayjean Carruthers, the two old sisters who'd spent most of their lives bending over washtubs and scrub boards, took the new load without comment. Their faces were dripping with sweat and their eyes held the flat look of a draft horse pulling a hay wagon. Melia was shamed by her earlier attitude of envy toward the upper class and thanked God she didn't have to work as a laundress.

Melia dreaded a summer that promised sore muscles and little time for her own diversion.. She was fast becoming disheartened at the prospect of going back to school in the fall without having her own vacation.

When the last bed was made, fresh flowers placed in vases, and the hallway swept, Melia sat on one of the back steps waiting for Sil. Her hair framed her face and neck in sweaty tendrils. Her long legs were stretched out in front of her, relieving sore calf muscles. She rested on her elbows, looking into the distance with nothing on her mind other than to get home to her mother's cooking and soft voice.

"Why so pensive?"

Melia jumped from her melancholy and looked into the eyes of Wyatt Mathieson, the young man she'd admired from the upstairs window. "I'm not pensive," she answered with annoyance. "I'm tired. Ready to go home." At the end of an exhausting day this spoiled son of the owner had little appeal for her. Casanova himself could not have evoked a teasing response.

"You're too pretty to be doing the bidding of others. You should be the one receiving attention." His words were smooth, spoken in the same tone he used with the guests. Her frown softened and her eyes became friendlier. "Do you know how to play tennis?" His manner was one of pleasant indifference.

"No," she answered, irritated that he assumed her situation permitted such a frivolous pastime.

"Maybe on Sunday, before the next crowd arrives, I could teach you. It's great fun and easy to learn."

The screen door behind Melia opened with a scrape and a loud sigh from Sil's chest broke the spell. "What a day. I'll be glad when this summer is over." Only then did she notice Wyatt. She stood still, unaffected by the presence of this sought-after college boy. Sil had never been impressed by people who had too much money and very little common sense. Today she was especially peevish. Her deep gray eyes stared squarely at Wyatt, refusing to lower her gaze until some sort of explanation was offered.

Wyatt was flummoxed by the offhand manner in which he was being treated by one of the hired help. Her determined stance was not something he wanted to deal with at the moment.

"Well, gotta go. Talk to you later." He hurried off, waving over his shoulder as he went.

"What did he want?" Sil asked.

"Wants to teach me how to play tennis," Melia replied. She got slowly to her feet, preparing for the walk home.

"Hope you refused."

"Didn't have the chance. You came along and rescued me from the need to answer."

"Pay no attention to his fancy words. He compliments all the pretty girls that way.

"People like us are just someone for young men like Wyatt to trifle with during summer vacation."

"For pete's sake. He meant nothing. Doubt if I'll see him for the rest of the month. Now, let's just get on home."

"Sorry. It's just that you'd believe anything one of those dandies spouts."

"I'm not gullible and I know my place in the scheme of things." Melia rarely allowed her feelings to be so apparent. "Right now a game of any kind would be a welcome relief."

They walked in strained silence, only lightening up when it came time to say 'goodbye'. Melia felt guilty about her cross words.

"I didn't mean to sound belligerent. It's just that I'm tired of a sore body, of taking orders that never cease and rarely please, and crabby mothers who want someone else to raise their children."

"I know," Sil replied. "I never want to see a potato again. My hands are raw."

The two girls hugged each other, all previous bad feelings forgotten. Melia dragged her tired feet into the tiny Conroy house and Sil plodded to the top of Horseneck Ridge.

"Eugene workin' out alright on them deliveries?" Vernon asked Will that question at least once a month.

"Yep. He don't say much and takes orders well."

"That's progress then. In the beginnin' you said he got scared a lot."

"Not any more. He just watches the moon til I need him to help with the crates."

"You're good fer him, Will. Mebbe one day he'll be comfortable with other people, too."

They finished repairing the still and walked back to the house. Eugene was swinging Wilma high in the old tire that was suspended by a heavy rope from the oak tree in the yard.

"Ready fer next Wednesday?" Will gave Eugene a friendly shove on his shoulder.

"Yep. Wish it weren't so late at night though. That's when we're supposed to sleep."

"Not fer us delivery men. We do it at night so we don't get in the way of guests who want to be in the springhouse during the day. Don't want to make 'em mad, do we?"

"Nope. You always say they're the ones who pay our bills. Better not get 'em riled up." He shook his head slowly, studying the space in front of him.

"You wanna do the talkin' when we make the deals?"

Eugene looked at Will like he was eating a raw fish. "Hell, no." He blushed bright red, unused to swearing and proud he'd done it.

"Let me know when you do."

"Why would you want someone as dumb as me do the talkin', Will?"

"You're not dumb, Eugene. Whoever says so is the dumb one. You learned to write, didn't you?"

"Only my name."

"That's about all I ever write. You can add and subtract, too."

"Only if there ain't many numbers."

"Good grief, Eugene, we don't take in enough money to need big numbers."

"You mean I don't need to know more'n I do now to get along."

"Nope."

"Shit, Will. Mebbe one day I'll be as smart as you." He was feeling proud enough to swear.

Will reckoned that was a good sign.

CHAPTER FOUR

It took only a week for the girls to fall into the pattern of the summer: monotonous chores that a dummy could do followed by exhausted evenings and not enough sleep. Wyatt waved to Melia if he saw her in his vicinity but didn't ask her to play tennis again. Sometimes she sneaked a look out the window to watch the wealthy parents cheer for their offspring during tennis games, horseback races, and bow and arrow target practice. Wyatt was the center of everything -- yelling, laughing, winning, and getting closer to the pretty girls than protocol allowed. Melia hurried off to clean the bathroom.

"Why would anyone want to get close to a girl who smells like laundry soap and dirty commodes?" she whispered while she scrubbed a chamber pot. "No wonder none of us ever gets out of boring Boreland Springs." She threw the sponge into the bucket so hard it splashed water all over the tile floor. Hardest to clean was the cast iron tub with complicated brass fittings. It was wide, deep, and difficult to reach for even Melia's long arms. The molded feet held it off the floor just far enough to catch the dust and close enough to make it hard to get under with a mop.

She wiped the sweat that was dripping off her nose, stowed her cleaning utensils, and answered Cricket's call for help with the dirty laundry. She threw a look over her shoulder to make sure the brass was shining and the tub had no spots. On her way down the hall it was impossible not to hear the joyous noise of a tennis game, Wyatt's voice the loudest of all.

Melia kept out of his line of vision for the remainder of the week. She was so adept at eluding him that by Thursday her mind was on what to wear for Sunday church and not how good Wyatt looked in summer shirts. Without him knowing, she'd seen him look for her in the usual places where she worked. It felt good to make one of the privileged learn that he didn't make the world turn around. She smiled at the thought.

"Have you talked to Wyatt this week?"

"No. Have you?"

Sil laughed. Melia joined in. It was the best walk home they'd had for weeks.

On Friday evening, while Melia waited on the back stoop for Sil to come from the kitchen, she was once again approached by Wyatt.

"Are we on for Sunday afternoon?"

Melia covered her surprise with a yawn. "What time?"

"Three o'clock?"

"I'll try to make it, but if I'm not there, go on with whatever you normally do on a Sunday afternoon." She got up and went into the kitchen, not wanting Sil to walk into the conversation again. Like I've got a big schedule, she thought gloomily. She made no mention of the appointment to Sil.

A twinge of guilt settled in Melia's chest when she told her mother she was going to see Lila Compton for the afternoon. The words of the old hymn 'Yield Not to Temptation' haunted her as she followed the path to the tennis courts adjacent to the hotel. It had been hard for her to look her mother in the eye when she'd told the lie. I'm not doing anything wrong, she mused, except that Mama wouldn't approve of me mingling with one of the Mathiesons.

Wyatt leaned on the fence, racquets in hand, and watched Melia come toward him. God, she's beautiful, he thought. Inexperienced too, I'll bet. Probably take a while for her to get comfortable with me.

"Glad you could make it."

"So am I. Just remember, I've never played this game before. It'll be tedious for you to teach me."

"Never."

He was a patient and sensitive instructor. When he had to put his arms around her to demonstrate how to hold the racquet, he was careful not to press her in any personal way. He smelled so good – and his clothes were spotless. Not soiled or torn like most of her friends.

Before long she was enthralled with the game. She caught on fast. He marveled at her strength and endurance, even though her footwear was clumsy and her feed sack skirt restricted her movement. Melia would be a vision in sackcloth, he thought. There was an elegance about her that transcended wealth and position. He couldn't take his eyes off her long legs that never seemed to tire. Or her arms that showed a budding bosom when she reached high to return a serve. He wanted the lesson to go on until nightfall.

Too soon for Wyatt she looked at the sun, stopped mid-stride and ended their rendezvous. "I've got to go. Thank you for the lesson. Tennis is a game I could get to like real quick." Rivulets of perspiration ran down the cleft between her breasts.

"Maybe we can do this again sometime. You learn fast."

"Don't want to get hung up on something I can't afford. It's best to leave it at this." She handed him the racquet and wiped her sweaty face with her sleeve. "Good-bye."

"Wait! I'll walk partway with you."

"You needn't do that. I know the way quite well."

"I want to."

"It's up to you. But I warn you the deer flies are beastly this time of day."

"No matter. I've been bitten before."

They walked slowly. Melia felt the heat from his shoulders. She tried to put more space between them, to make it clear she was not overjoyed at his attentions just because he was a Mathieson. A sideways glance revealed a bright young man trying to be friendly. *I'm making more of this than it is*, she thought. *I'm just an afternoon tennis partner, not someone he thinks of as special.*

"What are you studying in college?" she asked companionably.

"Business and hotel management. Hopefully I can run the resort as successfully as my father one day . . .maybe improve it."

Her eyes widened. "How so? The resort is full throughout the vacation season with guests from everywhere."

The conversation became animated and easy as Wyatt spoke of adding more rooms, offering excursions to places of interest in the area, and possibly rebuilding the large underground basement into a private club for gambling.

Melia stopped in her tracks losing her balance in the loose gravel. He took hold of her arm to steady her. "Isn't that illegal?" she sputtered.

"Maybe not by the time I'm in charge." He laughed. "Don't get so upset. I was only thinking out loud."

They parted company at the fence that was the boundary of Mathieson land. Melia walked the rest of the way in a trance, hugging to herself the enormous pleasure she'd had for such a short time. For an instant in her life she'd allowed herself the luxury of pretending she was one of 'them'. It had been glorious.

"How were Lila and her family?"

"What?" Melia hadn't realized her mother was in the yard as she walked through the gate. "Oh fine. Just fine."

"Nice family, the Comptons'."

"Yes." 'Yielding is sin. . .yielding is sin. . .sin. . .sin.' The words of the old hymn pelted the inside of her head until it was splitting. I'll never do it again, she promised, feeling nauseous. Kneeling beside her bed that night she asked the Almighty for His forgiveness.

The promise was short-lived. The Sunday afternoon tennis sessions became a regular rendezvous for Wyatt and Melia. It took all of her imagination to come up with different explanations to her mother concerning her Sunday outings. Fear of discovery made her edgy and racked with guilt.

Chance encounters in the grape arbor crept into the schedule. They seemed to know intuitively when they might pass together through this shadowed passageway. It gave them a feeling that they were fated to meet – arranged by an unseen force they couldn't deny.

Melia was caught in a tangle that would not turn her loose, with no power to change what she believed to be her descent into Hell. All her life she'd listened to Preacher Knox harangue about 'feet of clay' that dragged humankind into degradation. She reckoned that was happening to her now. Her remorse took much of the fun away from the time she spent with Wyatt, yet the unholy trysts went on.

Wyatt had no feelings of guilt nor was he a patient young man. He wanted a girl to be so smitten with him that by the second encounter they could be into heavy petting. Melia was having none of that. She hadn't allowed even the slightest explorative touch. Normally he would have dropped her and gone on to an easier conquest. However, she held a fascination for him that he couldn't resist.

One afternoon in the grape arbor he tried a different approach. His face was crestfallen, his voice plaintive. "I only want to get to know you better, Melia."

He held her close to his chest, ignoring her slight pull to get away. He smiled and rubbed noses with her. Her breath gave a little catch and she relaxed. He slipped his hands under her waistband and touched her bare skin. She felt like silk.

"Don't Wyatt. This isn't right."

"What's wrong about it? It feels good." He grinned into her shocked face then swayed with her like they were dancing. Her body moved with his and her mouth opened slightly. They were so close she could see beads of sweat on his upper lip.

"Melia!" The summons was shrill and demanding.

They came apart like a tree struck by lightening.

"I'll be right there, Mayjean." Melia straightened her clothes, caught her breath, and ran into the laundry.

"Dammit!" It took several minutes for Wyatt to gather up his wits then he stomped to his room and changed into riding clothes.

The following Sunday they played tennis again. Afterward he invited her to sit with him under a big oak far from the mossy glen that by now was littered with the debris of promiscuous teenagers.

"Let's sit awhile."

"Not long. Mama will be looking for me."

"Summer will be over soon and I'll be going back to Morgantown. Will you miss me?"

"I don't know you well enough to miss you. . . .I'll miss playing tennis though."

Wyatt was dumbfounded. No girl had ever treated him with such offhandedness. Melia became a quarry he was determined to win.

"I'd like to think I mean more to you than someone to play tennis with."

"You've got more girlfriends than a dog's got fleas, Wyatt." She chuckled deep in her throat. "You're one of the luckiest guys I know. A different girl for every evening of the week." Her eyes dared him to deny her statement.

"You've hurt me to the core, Melia Conroy. It's my job to entertain the guests. I spend these Sunday afternoons with you because you're the woman I really want to be with."

She laughed. "How many girls have you told that to?"

He fumbled with his ring finger. "Here's proof of how I feel." He handed her his high school class ring. "Put this on a ribbon and wear it around your neck if you like. To let everyone know you're taken." He pressed the ring into her palm.

Her eyes were full of amazement. She was flabbergasted.

His arm circled her waist and pulled her toward him. Wyatt knew the ways of these country girls -- Melia would never allow anyone to see his ring. It would cause too many tongues to warn her about the danger of getting too close with a man of his social standing. Furthermore, her parents would forbid her to ever see him again.

The ring was her undoing.

The feelings she'd stifled during these pleasurable games took over her heart and put her at the mercy of first love. She looked at her hand with his ring laying in it, making her palm look small. He tilted her chin so she could see the sincerity in his eyes. Before she could stop it, his mouth came close and kissed her lightly on the lips. Her arms crept shyly around his neck and she kissed him back. The admonitions of Preacher Knox paled beside her growing desire to understand what men were like. She closed her ears to the Ten Commandments as she unbuttoned his shirt while he unfastened her blouse. Her movements followed his as the strains of 'Yield Not To Temptation' faded into the distance. It felt natural for their skin to touch, for movement against one another to stimulate feelings she didn't understand. He smoothed the hair from her forehead. This simple movement made her feel treasured.

Everything became a blur – out of focus. Melia felt like she was someone else. Not the everyday country bumpkin who cooked, scrubbed, and milked cows. She felt desirable – like Cinderella. He eased her onto the soft ground. Sun shadows played through the canopy of leaves like colorful jewels she might place around her neck. Her ecstasy was briefly interrupted by a sharp pain that brought a small groan. He covered her mouth with his own, surprised she was a virgin. She basked in his tenderness and knew for certain this was love. She inhaled the musky smell of earth and listened to Wyatt's masculine sounds. Time meant nothing. She stretched like a cat in summer sun.

"Where's your other shoe?"

His words startled her. She raised her head then covered her breasts with her petticoat, suddenly embarrassed. Wyatt was already brushing his shoulders off and picking up his trousers. Her right shoe was gone – he was frowning. *Where in God's name is it?* She got up on her knees and scrabbled around the spot where they'd made love. *Love? How can it be love if we have to hurry to cover up the evidence and get ourselves dressed and back on the path?*

She found it behind an exposed root, partially buried in the moss. Hair kept falling in her face and her skin itched from shredded leaves and black mud clinging to her sweaty body. *I'll never be able to get this filth from under my fingernails,* she murmured as she pulled her shoe from the muck. Wyatt was leaning against a tree trunk, smoking a cigarette. *How can he be so indifferent,* she wondered? He exhaled a chest full of smoke and stared up at the sky.

Fury welled in her stomach and up into her throat. *He's completely over it – satisfied – like nothing deep touched him.* Tears hit her lids. She squeezed them back, refusing to let him know how hurt she was. Melia gritted her teeth, stood up, calmly recovered her shirt and panties, and went behind the tree to get dressed. It was a clumsy effort – she stumbled on the uneven ground then caught herself on the rough tree bark. Her nose detected a faint, unfamiliar odor: musky, cloying, and somehow unclean. Belief in romantic love was fast disappearing as she tried to dislodge twigs from her hair and brush the dirt from her blouse. Wyatt had finished his cigarette and was looking at her impatiently.

"I can make the rest of the repairs on the way home," she said, as ready as he was to leave. Neither of them spoke and great care was taken not to look at each other while Melia tried to smooth her wrinkled skirt as they walked. He didn't even hold her hand.

The parting was short – a mumbled 'goodbye', a quick embrace that fumbled more than it comforted -- then they went their separate ways. The path home had never seemed so far, yet the little house appeared long before she wanted to face her family. Her eyes were red from crying. She wiped her nose and dried her blotchy face with a soggy handkerchief. How had she allowed her virginity to be stolen away so easily? She'd always figured that only her husband would claim that right. Wyatt had said nothing about marriage.

A night of contemplation however allowed Melia to forget her disenchantment and revel in the feeling of being loved by someone as charming as Wyatt. It was like a cocoon that protected her from a harsh and disapproving world – a soft place she refused to look beyond. He never mentioned a wedding so she concentrated instead on his declarations of love. In the ensuing weeks, shyness and indecision no longer plagued her. Each time they laid under the oak tree she gave herself wholly to his lovemaking.

Fate, however, can be a silent partner that plays havoc with the plans of men. In his excitement of the 'hunt', Wyatt had not taken into account his own fallibility. In his determination to capture Melia, he'd become entranced with her – perhaps as much as she was with him. When they were apart she was constantly in his thoughts. He wondered what it would be like to live with her for the rest of his life. What would his parents say if he told them he wanted to marry a local girl. He closed his mind to the furor such a statement would bring.

"Happy?" he asked her one day.

"More than I ever thought possible."

Toward the end of July when Sil came down the familiar path, her response to Melia's friendly greeting was guarded. She looked past Melia's shoulder as though there might be someone behind them. Melia turned to see what Sil was staring at. There was nothing that should have taken Sil's attention away from their normal enthusiastic morning 'hello'.

"What's wrong?" Melia's eyes clouded with concern.

"Nothing." Sil turned in the direction of the hotel. Melia reached for her arm. Sil pulled away.

"There is something wrong. Is your mother sick? Has something bad happened at home? Why are you so quiet?"

"Don't act innocent, Melia. You're the one who should be explaining what the game is."

"What are you talking about?"

"Yesterday at church your Mama asked my Mama how you and I were doing at collecting the wildflowers to dry for fall arrangements to sell at the Grange. Mama had no idea what she was talking about. Neither do I. How about an explanation."

Melia stopped in her tracks. She reddened from neck to forehead. "What did you say?"

"I mumbled something about storing them in the barn." Sil gave Melia a rough pull on her arm. "What's going on? I'll not take another step until you tell me the truth." Her eyes shot sparks of fury into the frightened face of her best friend.

Melia's face drooped. "I'll tell you on the way."

While they plodded toward the hotel Melia told Sil how she'd gotten involved with Wyatt. "I'm so ashamed. I don't know what to do."

"I'd think it wouldn't be too hard to figure that one out. Stay away from him, for God's sake."

"I wish I could, but I love him. He says he loves me. Look. He gave me his ring to wear around my neck." She pulled out the ring that had been strung on a ribbon and concealed under her dress.

"Wyatt loves no one but himself. I've seen him leading other young girls down under the trees. He plays on their pride during the week just like he does to you on Sunday." Her words were harsh. Cruel.

Melia tried to explain his actions away. "It's his job to entertain the guests. That's the only reason he spends so much time with them."

Sil shook her head. "I don't believe that for a minute."

They walked on in silence. As they began the steep climb to the hotel, Melia spoke again. "He isn't like you think, Sil. If you'd just get to know him, you'd understand."

"I'm telling you he's not the sort of man who will ever be true to any one woman."

They parted at the hotel and went about their respective duties. It was not an amiable leave-taking. For the first time in their lives a barrier had been thrown between them. A degree of separation began to erode the companionship they'd shared all their lives. Their conversation became awkward, about inconsequential matters that had occurred during their workday.

Sil was angry and hurt. It was beyond bearing for her lifelong friend to desert her for a summer fling with a spoiled rich boy. During the day she thought of nothing else. Mrs. Mac had to remind her more than once to tend to her job and quit daydreaming. The resentment wouldn't go away. It gnawed at her constantly. She couldn't look Melia in the eye without revealing her rage. They walked home together, yet apart, each furious that the other was unwilling to accept the situation as it was; both determined not to show how much they cared. As the days wore on the tension mounted.

Finally, Melia could hold her thoughts no longer. "Will you at least let me explain?"

"What's to explain? You lied to your family and me, and you're wasting yourself on a worthless boy who'll forget you as soon as he goes back to school. Worse than that, you're willing to discard our lifelong friendship for this fling." She turned her defiant eyes full-force on Melia. "So, like I said – what's to explain?"

"It's not a fling. He loves me. I admit he's spoiled and I apologize for misleading you."

"Mislead! You lied. Big difference. And you wouldn't be apologizing if you hadn't been found out. What would your mother th. . ."

"Stop! You make me sound like an awful sinner. I'm having fun in a summer where there hasn't been much of that around. Wyatt will leave soon for Morgantown – I accept that."

"You *don't* accept it – you only say that to get me to shut up. Well, I'll be quiet and leave you to your own downfall."

"You do that, Sil. You're so stubborn and think you're always right. So self-righteous that you begrudge everyone else a little pleasure."

"We'll see just how much *pleasure* it is at the end of the summer."

The Conroy house was in front of them. Neither wanted to leave the discussion where it was. There were still too many points to be made on both sides.

"Are you coming by for me in the morning or should I go ahead without you?"

"I'm coming by like always. I'm not in the habit of abandoning friends like some people I know." Sil knew her words were immature but she figured Melia had it coming. She turned on her heel, flipped her hair fiercely, and headed off.

"That's not fair," Melia began, but Sil's departing stride didn't miss a beat.

A night of sleep didn't improve either girl's disposition, but at least they walked in quiet disagreement. Not touching. No comment on the beautiful day. Or plans for the weekend. When evening came they were too tired to argue. At Melia's house they muttered a 'see you in the morning' and left each other to spend another uncomfortable night in thought.

Saturday arrived sunny and with a slight breeze. Mother Nature was evidently unaware of any conflict on Bull Run Road. When the girls separated to their various duties at the resort, Sil couldn't resist a parting shot. "I suppose you're going to have another tennis lesson tomorrow." Her voice was sarcastic. "Didn't think it took that long to learn such an easy game."

"It's not an easy game. You should try it sometime." Melia walked quickly upstairs before Sil could reply.

Sil fumed at Melia's lack of guilt. *Doesn't she know how wrong she is? I think I'll just go home without her.* When Melia came to the kitchen that evening Mrs. Mac informed her that Sil had left about ten minutes earlier.

By Monday both girls had gotten all the hostility out of their systems. They walked quietly, commenting about the weather and wondering would there be any interesting new guests for the coming week. It wasn't their old friendship but no spiteful words crossed between them.

Sil covered her hurt by taking a more active part in church, helping her mother in the kitchen, and offering to milk Bessie when her father looked tired. Rev. Knox was exceedingly happy for her assistance and wondered what had brought on such new interest in home and community.

As exasperating as it was, Melia couldn't erase Sil's proclamations and predictions from her mind. The warning that lay in Sil's words troubled her every time she and Wyatt made love. She was furious that Sil had the power to taint her involvement with him. A tiny particle of doubt had invaded the sincerity of Wyatt's words.

One morning while she was making up beds, she glanced out the window into the tennis court. Wyatt was sitting with a beautiful girl whose dark hair and long slim legs complimented her ready smile. They were very close, faces nearly touching, laughing at some private joke. Jealousy hit Melia in the belly with a vengeance. No amount of repeating Wyatt's words that he truly cared for her, that it was his job to 'entertain the guests', made the scene she'd just witnessed palatable. Suddenly she felt foolish. She'd believed Wyatt because he said the words she wanted to hear and implied there was a future for them together. I've been so stupid, she thought. Sil's right. I'm just another one of his conquests.

She avoided him in the following days, making sure her duties took her well away from any place where he might find her. Each evening, she waited inside the kitchen for Sil to finish work so that they could walk home together, albeit it a strained and awkward effort. It galled Melia to admit that she'd not lost any of her attachment for Wyatt. She felt like an old quilt put away for a newer, less used one. When he finally cornered her in the grape arbor as she was hauling the laundry down, she made excuses why she couldn't meet him on Sunday.

Wyatt was confused. Not by Melia, but at how much he missed her. He knew she'd watched him flirt – that was because he wanted her to be jealous enough to accept him under any circumstances. None of the others made him feel as good as she did. They were more interested in the flirting than the loving. For them, too, he was just a summer fling. Didn't she realize that? Have I made her so mad that she'll never come back, he wondered?

Nothing was going his way. Vince Palmetto was threatening to go to his father regarding the gambling debt. Certain that Sil had a hand in Melia's attitude he headed for the kitchen to confront her. He met Millard Hart on the way. Wyatt's eyes gleamed like a feral cat.

"Tell Will I want him to meet me Tuesday, not Wednesday, this week."

"Yessir," Millard mumbled.

"It's important. Don't forget, hear!"

"I won't."

Wyatt forgot about Sil and started planning what he'd say to Will on Tuesday.

CHAPTER FIVE

The shot ruptured the evening like lightening splitting the skies in a savage summer storm. The blast was followed by an eerie silence as if to emphasize the fact that the terrible noise bore a message of evil.

Every guest in the elaborate ballroom froze in place. Unfinished comments hung in the air like tiny soap bubbles ready to burst. The orchestra stopped mid-measure as if cut down by the conductor's baton. Silence roared through the room stunning the revelers with its weight. For several seconds no one dared to move.

Before a word was spoken, John Mathieson took off at a dead run. He had a good idea where the noise had come from. It was imperative for him to get there first to learn what had caused it.

The sound of John's body hurtling out the door and down the drive brought the roomful of guests to pandemonium. Servants and patrons alike rushed to the front portico, fighting to get through the double glass doors. In flimsy shoes and long gowns the women stumbled and a few fell, trying to keep up with the men who raced down the long pathway and over the suspended bridge to the springhouse. Those who got to the meadow first heard the unmistakable rumble of a Model T rushing off with as much speed as was possible in a lumbering truck over winding terrain. The identity of the driver was lost in the shadows that came and went as clouds scudded across the full moon. Few even noticed, focused as they were on what had occurred in the springhouse.

John Mathieson didn't have to see the driver. He'd heard that engine every Wednesday night for the last seven years. He wondered vaguely why Will and Eugene had made a delivery on Tuesday.

The scene that awaited him inside the springhouse went beyond any sight he'd ever imagined -- even in war. He stood in the doorway, locked between the pristine meadow outside and the ungodly gore illuminated by the flickering gaslights. It occurred to John that he was viewing something from the underworld -- and if he went no further it would all remain as a dream.

Blood, mixed with pieces of Wyatt's body, was splattered over the floor and walls of the stone building. It had dripped into the springs, giving the water an unearthly red hue as it slid into the drain that carried the excess back into the earth. Wyatt's Colt 45 lay just inside the door. It was a gift John had gotten him the previous Christmas.

Footsteps scrabbling through gravel brought him to action. He grabbed the gun and checked the chamber. One bullet was missing. With a move so swift that he wasn't aware he'd actually done it, he stuffed the weapon into the side pocket of his suit jacket just as his younger son Clay ran through the door. Clay slid to a stop, his fist in his mouth to stop the scream that tried to come out of his chest.

John heard his wife, Roberta, about to enter the room. He blocked her way.

"Clay, get your mother back up to the hotel. Take her to her room. Have Martha give her some laudanum. Now!"

Clay was more than happy to leave. It had taken more self-control than he thought he had to keep from vomiting on the spot. The gruesome mess he'd viewed in that brief moment had made his eyes water. At sixteen, the most blood he'd ever seen was when he went deer hunting every fall.

Forcing his mother back up the hill, away from the son that she knew must be dead or dying, took more strength than he could muster. Martha pushed while Clay pulled. Both tried to stay clear of her flailing arms and sharp fingernails. Roberta's gown, an off-the-shoulder white satin with sequined bodice and long fringes that swayed around the form-fitting skirt, hung in a torn caricature of what it once was.

Someone handed John a blanket to wrap the body in. Ironically the one part of Wyatt that remained as it had been in life was his angelic face -- the delicate blond eyebrows, the mass of curly hair, the finely chiseled cheek and jawbones. Only his beautiful blue eyes, which now stared without expression, had lost their luster. John closed the lids and tried to wipe away some of the bloodstains.

John's friends carried Wyatt to his room upstairs in the family suite where he was laid out on the big oak bed he'd slept on since he'd outgrown his crib. Josh Wilkerson, the grounds keeper, rang up Barclay's Funeral Home in St. Marys requesting them to send a hearse. With as brief an explanation as possible he made arrangements for the body to be removed the following morning to be prepared for burial as soon as possible.

When all the guests had been herded back to their rooms and assured that their own safety was not at risk, the staff was permitted to leave. Sil noticed Melia standing alone and forlorn beside the kitchen door as though waiting for Sil to finish her work. Her eyes were dazed and tear streaks marred her pretty face. She must have fallen in her headlong flight down the hill for her knees were scraped and bloody. She seemed unaware of what was going on around her.

Sil watched her for a few minutes. Then Melia seemed to crumble on the spot, taking hold of the banister and easing herself to a sitting position. Sil ran to her and put her arms around her.

"Cry on my shoulder Melia. I'll cry with you." She held Melia like she would a baby, cradling her head and rocking back and forth to soothe her.

Several minutes passed beforeMelia raised her swollen face. "You're so good, Sil. After the way I've treated you."

"There've been times I could've been nicer to you." She clasped Melia's face in her palms. "I know you must be heartbroken, but can you walk now? We both need to get home for some rest. It's been a night few people ever live through."

Melia nodded and accepted Sil's hand of support.

It was slow going. Melia's feet dragged and she leaned heavily on Sil. Sil reckoned the sorrow that wracked Melia was normal. After all, she'd truly believed Wyatt loved her and Sil suspected that in the end Melia believed he would forsake his family obligations and marry her. The night that had begun as a beautiful, star-studded spectacle had become menacing. Foreboding marched with their measured steps. Sil's head was pounding -- Melia's melancholy was frightening her. Why doesn't she speak, Sil wondered? She tried to coax Melia into a better mind-set with conversation.

"I don't know what to say or do to make you feel better." She wiped Melia's tearstained face with the hem of her own skirt.

"Just being with you helps." Melia snuffled softly for a while. "I've missed you these past weeks Sil. You're more important than anyone to me."

"You're important to me too. . . . We've both been silly. I'm sorry I said all those things about Wyatt. We'll help each other get through this."

Melia nodded.

Sil hummed 'God Will Take Care Of You' as they trudged the bumpy way home. After a few verses Melia joined in, her voice nearly a whisper. It was a hymn that had always comforted them when a pet died or a flood had ruined the crops. Melia's shoulders gradually relaxed so that by the time the Conroy house was in sight, Melia's sobbing had abated. As they approached the gate to her yard, however, a cloak of sadness once more settled over her.

Sil tried to offer some words of hope. "Remember what Preacher Knox says when we're discouraged. 'This too shall pass'."

Melia faced her best friend with eyes full of fear and shame. "No it won't, Sil. I'm pregnant."

Will held tight to the steering wheel of the old Ford as it bumped over the ruts and chugged through the shallow creeks where the road had no bridge. His shoulder throbbed. Blood had soaked through his shirt and a damp spot darkened the upholstery where he'd leaned into it for support. He prayed the thin right front tire would hold and that water wouldn't flood the engine as he sloshed through the creek. When he thought he couldn't move the stiff steering wheel in one more turn the murky shape of the Hart home came into view.

Vernon Hart was standing in the shadows holding a muted gas lantern. He'd always known of the danger their life held and he'd had a bad feeling about this night. In the years the Harts had done business with John Mathieson, the deliveries had always been made on Wednesday. So he wasn't surprised when the truck swerved into their property with Will shot and Eugene in a state of semi-awareness. He supported Will into the house. Eugene trudged behind them, his feet dragging a line in the dirt like the trail of two big night crawlers.

In a voice threaded with pain and with as few words as possible, Will explained to his father what had happened. Eleanor Hart hurried into the kitchen and gasped at the sight of him. After her momentary loss of composure she got directly to work.

She put a sling around Will's shoulder to keep it as steady as possible whenever he moved. Then she led Eugene to his bed. He was mumbling to himself about Wyatt, guns, and how his head ached. Eleanor washed his dirt-streaked face with a soft wet cloth. She crooned to him like she always did when he was upset. When finally the sound of regular breathing let her know he would soon be off in a dreamless sleep, she got up quietly and returned to care for Will's wound.

The bleeding had slowed to a trickle, giving her the opportunity to have a thorough look. The shot had made a clean hole through the outside portion of his shoulder just below the collarbone. It would be easy to clean. She packed it with a muslin rag that had been soaked with alcohol and hydrogen peroxide. Will gritted his teeth and quietly bore the burning that numbed his shoulder. Eleanor prayed there would be no serious infection so that healing could be accomplished with home remedies. Calling out a doctor for such a wound immediately following a shooting at the hotel could do nothing but cause trouble. When Will could tolerate the pain, he and his father stowed the weapons in the well, then took the truck to the creek and washed all signs of blood away. Vernon talked quietly to his son.

"Ma will have to bind your shoulder up pretty tight, so's you can mingle as usual amongst the neighbors. You'll have to attend the funeral. You up to that?"

Will grunted.

"Might be some authorities nosin' around lookin' for someone who's injured. Thank God it was your arm. . .easier to cover up than a shot in the leg."

"Yeah, Pa. But John Mathieson knows who did this. He'd recognize the truck. He'll be plannin' his revenge."

"That's why you've got to offer your sympathy just like all the other folks. More'n one of our neighbors would've noticed those Wednesday night meetings at the springhouse. Some of the men probably even had suspicions about what was goin' on. But nobody knows for sure who was makin' the deliveries and they'd only be guessin' what the encounters were about anyhow." He took a deep breath. "Besides, everybody who's been to Satterfield's lately knows Vince Palmetto had threatened him, makin' him a possible suspect. We've got to make it look like we're as bamboozled as everyone else about such a terrible happenin'."

It was more sentences than Vernon had strung together in a long time. Nonetheless, he wasn't finished. "John just *thinks* he recognized our truck. All them Fords sound alike. Nobody will deny that."

They walked into the kitchen where Eleanor waited with coffee. The two sat down wearily, thankful for a chance to rest.

"It don't matter what the others think, Pa. John knows. Sooner or later Eugene and me might have to get scarce."

"Maybe. First we'll try to figure out what John's got up his sleeve." Vernon spoke slowly, forming a plan as he went. "If he's bent on revenge, Millard's bound to get wind of it from someone up at the hotel."

Eleanor looked at her husband through the steam that swirled from her coffee. "We'll need a reason why if the boys have to leave."

"Let's wait 'til we know for sure what's goin' on in John's head."

"You're right. No sense jumpin' into somethin' before we know if it's necessary." She took a swig of the strong coffee and swirled it around her mouth. "It don't take long to make up a story. Hasty disappearances around here are normal for whatever the occasion might be: pregnancy, revenuers, bill collectors -- whatever. Shouldn't be too hard to come up with an ailin' relative, or some such."

Vernon nodded. "This'll cause a commotion for awhile but before long butcherin', cannin', and cuttin' the last hay crop will have everyone too busy to think about who killed Wyatt Mathieson. Besides, they wouldn't say nothin' if they did have a good idea."

"After that Thanksgivin' and Christmas will be on their minds," Will added. He kneaded his sore knuckles thoughtfully. "If it does come to that, how will you convince Eugene to leave, Ma?"

"Don't know yet. I'll have to pray and think hard on that one."

Vernon let out a great sigh. "For the time bein' we sit tight and listen carefully. We won't make a drastic move unless we have to. Now, let's get to bed. I'm so fagged out that I'm seein' two of everything. We're gonna need ever bit o' wit we can scare up to keep our heads above water durin' the comin' months."

Next morning the people of Boreland Springs could talk of nothing but the awful calamity. On every dilapidated porch that day old women sat snapping beans, sorting peas, and peeling peaches accompanied by a steady stream of questions: Who did it? Why? Evelyn Barnsby sniffed haughtily. "Always did think them Mathiesons was too high-falutin'. Mark my words, when all's said and done they'll find a woman at the bottom of all this."

"Don't go spewin' that around, Ma," her daughter Darline warned. "We don't need the Mathiesons to hear such gossip comin' from us. Besides, Preacher Knox says it's sinful to gossip." The old lady sniffed again and went on with her work.

Throughout the valleys and ridges, barn chores were tardy and breakfasts got cold. Reverend Knox was on his knees asking God how to handle this tragedy that had befallen one of his flock. No one would go unscathed. He foresaw the possibility of loss of work for the hill folks. The resort might even close if the Mathiesons were too bereaved to face living so close to the spot where Wyatt had been killed.

Up at the hotel, Harvey Bledsoe, a stable hand, was spreading sawdust over the bloody footprints that traced the path where Wyatt's body had been carried. He couldn't believe the blood he was concealing belonged to a young man he'd seen at the tennis court just yesterday. It took countless trips with a large wheelbarrow to cover the ragged red smears that tracked out of the springs, up the graveled pathway, and onto the Persian carpet in the foyer. Rosemary Foley was scrubbing at the grotesque fingerprints that had dried on the stained glass windows of the brass-framed door at the front entry.

Mrs. Mac was beside herself trying to run the kitchen where all the workers were sobbing quietly. When the meal of steaming ham, fried potatoes, hot bread, and assorted fruits was finally carried into the sunlit dining room, few guests had arrived. Those who were there wore strained faces and sat in silence. Very little food was eaten and in half the normal time they were finished and had placed the linen napkins beside their plates.

In the east wing Cricket Mathews had been advised by nearly all the guests that they would be leaving just as soon as the hotel could provide transportation to St. Marys. The sound of trunks being hastily packed and dragged to the vestibule was the only noise that broke the morning air. Probably for the best, she thought. Who could remain here after what has happened? She directed Melia to take the laundry down, pretending not to notice the girl's solemn expression. "We'll need to have everything ready for next week," she said. "By then things will be going on as usual, the sooner the better as far as I'm concerned." Melia stared at Cricket's bustling backside and wondered how anyone could think about 'usual'.

In the Mathieson apartments John waited for the police and the hearse to arrive. He sat on a hard wooden chair beside his son and fingered the steel barrel of the gun he'd given Wyatt for Christmas. The pearl handle did nothing to warm the coldness of this weapon that had given a young man the feeling of power he didn't really have.

CHAPTER SIX

Brian Paige, the detective in charge of homicides for the small St. Marys police force, arrived Wednesday at daybreak to begin investigating the famous springhouse. He'd moved down from Pittsburgh to get an idea what less sophisticated police forces had to deal with. Since his arrival he'd heard about the renowned Boreland Springs Resort but had never had the money to spend any time there. Today it looked more like a place where hogs had been slaughtered. He shook his head and tried to decide where to begin.

His mind was buzzing from all the questions he'd asked of the bewildered hotel staff and guests. The only thing any of them could remember was their own confusion and horror at what had happened. No one had seen or heard anything that might give a clue to the cause. Even Mr. Mathieson had been vague when asked if his son had any enemies and had he seen anyone leaving right after the shot was fired? Brian couldn't understand such an attitude. Most fathers who'd just lost a son in such a horrendous manner would be spouting the name of every acquaintance or incident he could think of. It was not unusual in cases such as these for innocent friends to be accused.

Brian took a deep breath. Even in Pittsburgh this would be considered a grisly crime scene as well as a confusing one. Shotguns, a favorite weapon of small game hunting, made a loud explosion and created a bloody mess that murderers wanted to avoid. Bootleggers normally used a shotgun during a chase when aiming from a moving vehicle, utilizing this cumbersome weapon only in emergencies. When confronting a troublesome interloper up close they preferred a rifle or handgun. To Brian's knowledge Mr. Mathieson had never been suspected of offering his guests moonshine.

Why had the killer used a shotgun? Brian had been sickened by the many pieces of Wyatt's body that remained in the springhouse – barely visible and too small for the embalmer to use. He was at a loss as to what to do when he found part of a finger in one corner. Should he give it to the parents? In the end, the caretaker had agreed to give it to the funeral home.

John Mathieson watched Brian inspect the crime scene for whatever clues were to be found amid such devastation. John's face was grim and he was reluctant to talk. Most of the time he stood in front of the shed just outside the springhouse. When Brian had a question, John merely nodded yes or no, offering no insight into the reason why such a ghastly thing should happen to a family esteemed by all in the community. After about three hours of the repugnant work Brian wiped the sweat from his brow and looked at John.

"That's about it, Mr. Mathieson. Can't take fingerprints since we don't have the equipment. Wouldn't matter anyway. Every guest in the hotel probably walked through here last night leaning on walls and doorways, leaving their own prints in the process. That means there's also not one clear footprint that can be identified as any different from the others." He stopped for a moment then asked the important question again. "Did you notice anyone leaving this area when you ran down the hill?"

"As I said before, my eyes were completely focused on the springs. There wasn't time to look about for strangers." His words were angry, causing Brian to hesitate about probing further. Men as important as Mr. Mathieson made even detectives defer to their moods.

"Well then, I'll gather up my equipment and get back to the station to make my report." He bent to pick up his black case that contained all the instruments he used to assess and record an area where a crime had been committed.

"What will you say?"

"That the place where the body was laying was too contaminated by the hands and feet of hotel guests to make proper conclusions. The body was so destroyed that only the direction of the discharge could be ascertained. It appears that Wyatt was shot by someone coming through the door whereupon he turned and ran back into the springhouse. It's hard to understand why he ran into a structure that had no other door of escape. . . .must have been blocked by his attacker."

He swiped his grimy forehead with a dirty handkerchief. "My boss will plan an investigation to try to find out who shot your son. Even with such a compromised crime scene it will be necessary to seek out the motive. Doesn't appear to be a robbery. His friends and your staff must be questioned as to what may have precipitated such an act of brutality."

John nodded then walked with labored steps up the hill to the hotel.

Brian gathered and cleaned his equipment. "Bootleggers don't make this much mess when they kill," he whispered as he studied the bloody scene again.

The mid-afternoon sun was beating a path through the heavy foliage into the meadow where Brian had toiled most of the day. His head was pounding and his muscles ached from the uncommon work he'd forced his body to perform. He stood up and leaned into the doorjamb. The dirty handkerchief he pulled out of his back pocket smelt of blood, but it was all he had to wipe his itchy neck. He stretched his shoulders to work the kinks out. For a few moments he let his body relax.

Then he saw it. A spent cartridge from a small handgun lay in a crack just inside the doorway entrance to the springs. At first he thought it was an illusion caused by salty sweat running into his eyes. He looked again. Then stooped low to make sure his eyes weren't playing tricks on him. They weren't. He tucked the shell in his pocket. Bullet's probably lodged in the wall, he thought, energized by such a find.

Even in daytime light inside the springhouse was dim at best – hopeless in the far corners. Brian put his nose close to the wall and traced every piece of stone around the doorway. His fingers probed every hole and crevice. "The owner of the gun that made this shot must have found the bullet and dug it out before leaving," he muttered. "Must've been two assailants." Then the late afternoon sun sent a kindly ray in his direction. An errant splice of light slanted through the doorway, highlighting the imbedded bullet Brian was searching for.

He pulled out his Swiss Army knife and selected the blade that would do the job of extracting the bullet without damaging it. It was one of those tasks that looked easier than what it was. In the end, he had to use a hammer and chisel to reach around and under the projectile in order to finally pry it from the stone wall.

The sound of heavy footsteps brought him upright. The large body of John Mathieson was hurrying toward him.

"You still here?"

"Yes sir. I just found this bullet – from a small handgun. Thought it might help us figure out who shot this. Could be a clue as to who and why your son was killed."

"I ain't interested in playin' host to a bunch of lawmen comin' out here to find out who shot Wyatt. He's dead and that's that. Doesn't matter how many did it or why. He's still dead."

Brian was so dumfounded by John's attitude that he simply nodded his head and packed his equipment into the truck. I'll see what my boss has to say about this, he thought.

John watched the policeman leave. "I'll handle my own investigation," he muttered.

Brian got back to St. Marys as fast as he could. "Pete, I investigated that crime scene out at the hotel." He handed Pete the cartridge and bullet. "There were two guns involved: a shotgun and a handgun. Found the cartridge and bullet for the handgun. If we could find the gun, we might know who the second shooter was. But Mr. Mathieson ordered me off the place, said he wouldn't tolerate any more searchin' on his property. . . .can we get a subpoena and go out there to search?"

Pete looked at his young assistant through the smoke that curled from his newly lit cigarette. "You don't know much about mountain folk do you?

Brian shook his head.

"Best know the people you're dealin' with before you go in expectin' them to put forward who they think may have committed a crime." He knocked the ashes off the cigarette and took a drag. "Mountaineers never rat on one of their own even if they think they know who's guilty." He exhaled the smoke from his nose in one big sigh.

"Well, how do you. . ."

Pete waved his hand to forestall the question. "When a mountain man is killed by anyone, even if it's another mountain man, retribution comes quick and in the dark of the night. No policemen involved." He leaned back and blew more smoke. "When a mountain man is suspected of killing someone outside his class, the suspect melts back into the community and lips are sealed as tight as a cat's ass."

"But. . ."

"And they'll use the subpoena to wipe their butts right after they run you off their property with their own twelve-gauge. You can bet your right arm that the Boreland Springs folks who work at the resort will have sullen eyes and blank memories when it comes to who they think did it."

"Then how. . ."

"For all practical purposes this case is as solved as it ever will be."

"Then what's our job if not to bring killers to justice?"

"We work on cases here in town and the close vicinity. We could spend all our time and the city's money and still never find out who killed Wyatt Mathieson."

Brian's shoulders fell. This would never happen in Pittsburgh, he thought bitterly. He wanted to go back to that icon of justice but he'd married a local girl and she wasn't about to leave her beloved mountains!

Kay Meredith

CHAPTER SEVEN

Roberta's forehead dripped with sweat. The ceiling fans did little to relieve her from the brutal heat and confining black mourning dress. Had it only been yesterday when she'd lost her favorite son? She needed more time to get used to the idea of his death before she had to pick out his casket. Her head drooped nearly to her chest. *If I live to be a hundred I can never accept his being gone,* she thought. *Why does it all have to be done so quickly? Why wouldn't John help me with this horrid chore?* She couldn't bear the thought that somewhere in this building Wyatt's mutilated body lay waiting to be placed in whichever casket she chose today.

"Do you see anything you like, Mrs. Mathieson?"

She dabbed at her moist face. "Show me the loveliest coffin you have, Mr. Wilson. I must decide before I collapse of the heat."

The attendant, Luke Wilson, had hovered just behind her right shoulder as she prowled through the small selection that Barclay's Funeral Home had to offer. She was distracted: her fingers touching here, lifting there, and sometimes just standing in front of one with unseeing eyes. He hurried to pull a chair out for her. "Sit down Mrs. Mathieson. Take some time to catch your breath before we continue."

"There's not time to rest. Show me the best you have."

The only time she'd ever seen caskets was when the deceased was already in place and the viewing was in progress. Her mother had passed away five years earlier and by the time she'd arrived in Philadelphia for the funeral, her older sisters had already made the selection and decided what clothes she would be buried in. Roberta was sad there would be no time for them to travel so far to stand beside her in this, the worst time of her life. John had said he couldn't abide a long period before the interment. He wanted it over as quickly as possible. Roberta couldn't understand why. She'd wanted Wyatt to remain at their home for a day or so, where she could sit beside him and think on all the years they'd been together. But no, it had to be done now! Sometimes she really resented her husband.

"This is the finest we have on such short notice," Luke was saying.

The inside was lined with violet colored velvet. *It will be a lovely* contrast to Wyatt's golden hair, she thought idly, as though she were picking an outfit he might wear to one of his university functions. The frame was polished mahogany with brass fittings, enclosed in an ornamental steel vault.

"This vault will last a hundred years," Luke said as he thumped on the solid structure. "Won't collapse and allow the earth to sink in on the body."

Her mind nearly snapped at the thought. "That will do just fine, Luke. Add whatever accessories are needed to make it look right." She turned and hurried toward the office. "Tell me the cost and I'll write the check now. Any extras you can bill me." Her words stumbled as did her feet. He ran to support her.

"Yes, Mrs. Mathieson. Sit down right here." He guided her to the straight-backed chair in front of the desk. Within fifteen minutes Roberta was on her way home, selection made and bills for the service paid. It takes so little time to arrange for the entombment of my son and sentence me to a life of sorrow, she mused. The road bumped and twisted under the silver-spoked wheels of the shiny black Dodge they'd bought last year. She didn't notice.

On Friday, the day of Wyatt's funeral, Roberta wandered slowly through his room. One wall was covered with photos that chronicled his life from the time he'd been born to the day she and John had left him in Morgantown to start his education. His first dog. His first pony. He and John holding up the fish they'd caught when Wyatt was five.

Her favorite was one taken when he was about eighteen months old and she was holding him in her lap on the veranda. She was three months pregnant with Clay, so both her sons were with her, in a manner of speaking. She'd not known John was photographing her. Her fair hair lay in tendrils around her face that shone with every mother's love. She took the picture off the wall and held it to her heart. She planned to put it beside her bed so she could look at it whenever she wanted.

On Wyatt's marble dressing table was the ornate gift box that held the Colt 45 he treasured so much. It had been his first handgun. She approached it with a wistful smile. Guns, she thought with revulsion. Why must they be so important to men? She was surprised to see that the gun was not in its place of honor. The carved depression where it should have lain was empty. I must ask

John about that later, she mused, and returned to her own room to dress for the ceremony that was due to start within two hours.

Will wasn't looking forward to attending the funeral. He winced as his mother tightened the bandage that would steady his arm against the movement and shoving which always occurred at a public gathering. Funerals were notorious for grieving mourners who paid little attention where they walked or who they bumped into. He'd never liked attending these solemn exhibitions of man's sorrow. However, be it close family, a distant relative, or slight acquaintance, Eleanor Hart insisted that her family pay respect to those who had passed away. She reckoned the sight of someone familiar lieing stone cold dead in a wooden coffin would reaffirm the need to follow God's rules. Otherwise, as Preacher Knox so loudly pointed out, the fires of Hell awaited all sinners when it came their time to spend eternity in a rotting box. Furthermore, as it would be proven today, no one could depend on enjoying a long life of transgression, followed by a rebirth of faith just before dying. Sometimes one died without having a chance to repent.

He grimaced as she pulled the bandage tight. "Don't make them faces, Will. You'll have to suck the pain into your stomach. Don't show your feelins' to nobody."

Will nodded, holding his breath while she finished.

August in the hills was always humid and uncomfortable. Not even in the deepest parts of the mountains could one find respite from the clammy clothes and voracious insects that tortured the mourners on this Friday. The steps from Bull Run Road up to the churchyard were steep. Many of the older folks had to rest every now and then. A large green canopy sheltered the grave and protected the family and close friends from the hot afternoon sun. The fringe that dropped down to provide yet more shade was frayed and the white piping had long since gone to gray. The Mathiesons likely took no notice.

Powder and rouge slid down puffy faces, soiling the dresses of women who would rather be canning than attending the burial of Wyatt Mathieson. Their husbands were ill-at-ease as well, wondering if the upper class had a different ceremony for their departed than that of humble folk.

Paper fans with the most familiar psalms printed on both sides whizzed back and forth in front of weathered faces, providing some relief from the heat. They were constructed of lightweight cardboard. Many years of use had left them crumpled and torn. Some of the handles were barely hanging on. Nevertheless, it was what one did at funerals. Fanning and wiping the noses of toddlers kept their minds off viewing a friend in that final expression of death.

At times like this they could not escape the fact that man is a puny part of the universe with no ability to change the events God has in mind. How else could the death of one so young be explained? Not for an instant did they blame anyone or any circumstance. It was the way of life, and that was that. God's will. They went no further for a practical explanation of who lived and who died.

Undoubtedly, there would be secret discussions as to who and why the crime was committed. Nonetheless, no one wanted to interfere with an act that was obviously God's will. They would leave the job of bringing the killer to justice to the investigators. Interference from the locals could only cause more grief. After the burial the community would put on bland faces and disappear into their religious beliefs.

All fans ceased moving as the Mathiesons filed into their place to stand beside the coffin. A slight breeze ruffled the awning. Roberta leaned heavily into her husband's side for support. He held onto her and offered a handkerchief to replace the sodden one clutched in her hand. Reverend Knox took his place at the head of the casket and motioned for the family to sit.

As the sermon droned on, Roberta's mind wandered through Wyatt's childhood like a thief stealing treasures from hidden places. He'd been bright and active from the time he'd taken his first step until the very last day of his life. She glanced at her younger son Clay and supposed he, too, was remembering the times they'd shared together. She recalled the Sunday when the two had disappeared to the swimming hole while still dressed in their Sunday-best suits. She'd been frantic, yelling and searching until she heard their squeals of joy. When she'd looked at their radiant faces as they splashed water toward one another, the ruined clothes were forgotten.

How she would miss his beautiful smile, those mischievous eyes, and his way of hugging her shoulders when he wanted a favor. She intended to leave his room as it was. The quilt that had been made from all his favorite clothes would be a colorful reminder of the stages of his life: the flannel plaids he wore during fall; the swatch of tweed from the coat he bought in New York City when he was thirteen; the fuzzy pieces cut from all his childhood coverlets. His first pair of rubber boots would remain atop the bookcase that held his favorite books. All of the report cards he'd ever gotten from school were stored in the desk by the window. He'd not been keen about studies, she recalled, always managing to fall in the middle of class standings. It would be a place for her to go when she needed to see his things and smell his scent.

John Mathieson had no feelings about God, or life, or the hereafter. He was filled with hate. He wanted the pathetic words of a minister who'd never experienced the loss of a child to cease. He wished the day to be over and done with. It wasn't Wyatt in that pretentious box. It was what was left of the container for a spirit that John would miss every day for the remainder of his life. Nothing from the Bible could change that. Not the promise of seeing his child again at Judgment Day – what person in his right mind believed in that tripe anyhow? Nor the hope that Wyatt was now in a better place. Who the hell made that story up? He'll be buried under six feet of dirt in a tight container that will hold him while he decays until there's nothing left but bones and teeth. How could that be better than the life of sunshine and promise Wyatt had had just a few days ago? Don't talk religious platitudes to me, Reverend Knox, he thought grimly. Vengeance will be my saving grace, sooner or later. His fists clenched into tight balls that, when released at the end of the ceremony, left his palms red with fingernail marks.

The Harts clung to the edges of the gathering where they went through the motions required at a burial. The youngest had dropped a bouquet of wild roses at the foot of the grave while Eleanor held Roberta close to her breast and told her how sorry she was that such a thing had happened. John looked the other way. Vernon and Will stood back, making sure Eugene remained quietly between them.

Melia stood quietly with her family, none of whom could understand the depth of her grief. True, he'd been an engaging member of the community and hope for the hotel's future, but after all, he wasn't family. Yet she'd stayed in her little room, inconsolable for hours on end. On the few occasions when she joined the others for meals, or walked to the outhouse, her eyes were swollen from crying.

Today she looked over those who'd come to pay their respects. Among them were all the Sunday school teachers she'd ever had. As she'd gotten older Melia had learned that these teachers quite often had a checkered past. They'd sowed their wild oats, often bringing disgrace to their families, then found salvation through prayer. Once redeemed, they were expected to steer other youngsters away from a similar path of misbehavior. It was ingrained in the mindset of poor southern Protestants that doing such penance would absolve them of any offenses previously committed against God's word.

Consequently, parents whose first child had been born shortly after the wedding could hold their heads up. Likewise, the errant son who'd spent some time in jail for petty theft was accepted back into the bosom of his family and put to work on the farm. The husband who'd been abusive when he drank too much, was forgiven by his wife and children when he brought his paycheck home, passing by Satterfields on his way. Melia reckoned these were the people who made the best teachers. Who better to preach against sin than those who'd experienced it first hand and overcome the Devil through salvation and perseverance?

How can they do that, she wondered? I'll never be able to look anyone straight in the eye again, she thought, as she passed Wyatt's coffin. Her eyes were closed. She couldn't bring herself to look at him, knowing her unborn baby would never know its father. *I feel so dirty and ashamed. Teaching Sunday school is the last thing I'd think of doing after the mortification of getting pregnant out of wedlock.*

'Out of wedlock'. It was a term she'd heard all her life. When she'd finally understood what it meant Melia had tossed her head gaily, reckoning it was a condition she'd never have to face. *How wrong I was,* she sobbed inwardly.

On Sunday, the Lord's day, sunlight edged around the muslin curtains that covered the wavy panes of the window in Melia's little bedroom. Soon the noises of a farming household would resound through the little house. Chores had to be finished early so as not to miss church. The boys were yelling at one another as to who took whose shirt. Mr. Conroy asked that words be spoken in quieter tones in respect for the Sabbath. Maxine warned them not to spill their milk all over. She didn't have time to clean up after them and still dress herself properly for the morning service.

Melia dragged her weary body out of bed. She clutched the flannel cover to her chest and hurried to the porch pump to draw water for a sponge bath. The cold water brought a shiver that went all the way to her soul. When she thought the outhouse would be free of the many male Conroys she made her way out the path that was fringed with clover and sour grass.

Maxine watched Melia walk the path to the outhouse. Maybe I can talk her into going to church with the rest of us, she mused. It'd be good for her. Work all that misery out of her heart and give her a good start for the week. After about ten minutes Melia plodded back into the house.

"Could you fry the bacon while I tend to the eggs?" Maxine hoped that putting a normal face on might coax Melia back into her regular routine.

"Yes, mama. Just as soon as I dress." She went to her bedroom, pulled her best gingham over her head then returned to help in the kitchen. Without warning the smell of the meat frying made her gag. It took her by surprise. It hadn't happened before. Twice more when the urge to vomit nearly overcame her, she swallowed hard and made herself busy with tasks as far away from her mother as possible.

Maxine had borne four children and suffered two miscarriages. She knew what morning sickness looked like. Even when the sufferer tried hard to cover it up. The cold hand of terror grabbed her chest and settled there like a garden crow in early morning. It can't be, she prayed silently. Maxine watched Melia push her food around her plate without actually eating. How had it happened? Who was the father? Then she shook her head slightly, clearing away the ridiculous thought. Vernon and the boys wolfed down their food, oblivious to the quandary that was taking place under their noses.

That afternoon Reverend Knox remarked to his wife how the normally talkative Maxine and Melia Conroy had had very little to say that Sunday in church.

Melia walked down Bull Run Road in the direction of the intersection of Horseneck Ridge Road. Puffs of dust rose and swirled around her legs from each heavy footstep. She'd had to get out of the house, away from her mother's worried eyes. She doubted if there would ever be another week in her life that lasted so long. Preacher Knox was always saying that God wouldn't give a person more problems than he or she could bear up to. She doubted that too. In a week, no, less than a week, she'd learned she was pregnant -- then Wyatt was murdered. And I'm only sixteen, she whispered into the evening shadows. How could God think I could handle all that?

The peaceful valley echoed with the toneless hum of locusts as they shed their old skins for new. How lucky they are, she thought. Able to start another season in a brand new set of clothes. I wish I could do that.

She was enclosed in the comforting sounds of oil wells as the black gold was pumped out of the ground to be stored in huge tanks nearby. It would then be shipped by barge to Cincinnati or Pittsburgh. Melia didn't know what happened to it then. All she knew about oil was that the pumping of it was like a heartbeat that let a person know there were some things that never changed. She'd heard it from the time she was born and couldn't imagine a time when the pumps would stop.

Like a broken promise, life *had* changed for her. Tomorrow she would go to work as usual. Her time at the resort would soon be over. This fall there would be no school for her. She would miss the smell of books, blackboards, chalk, and the happy sounds of classmates as they began another year of education that might make their lives a bit easier than their parents. She wondered vaguely how long it would be before her stomach would begin to enlarge.

She'd have to tell her parents, except for who the father was. Arrangements would have to be made. Would they expect her to have the baby? Without a father? How had other girls in this predicament known what to do? Did they run away? Did their family make them leave long enough to have the baby then come back to teach Sunday School? Where was she to find the answers to all these questions? Where was God now?

Melia had known some girls who'd gone away. Her mother had explained they'd be back in a few months. At the age of twelve she had figured out what was really going on regardless of the reason put forth by the family. She and Sil had talked about the terrible plight of these acquaintances. They wondered how it felt to be pregnant. Who were the fathers of these children? Why couldn't they just get married? Now *she* would be leaving. Where would her parents take her? Parkersburg? St. Marys? The only house she'd slept in besides her own was Sil's and that didn't really count. She felt like she was twelve again and lost in the woods.

Maybe I won't have to go, she thought. What if I fall down and lose the baby? Formerly a wicked thought like that would have sent Melia into a flood of guilt. With the realization that she was the one who would be living through her own downfall, she had little care what God might think of her blasphemous soul.

The strains of 'Onward Christian Soldiers' wafted toward her in the dimming twilight. She'd forgotten. It was Sunday evening prayer service at the little Boreland Springs United Brethren Church. All the young folks would be there, maybe even Sil. It was their favorite time since there was no sermon, only singing and reading bible verses. She turned quickly and headed for home. Melia couldn't face her friends knowing they would soon be speculating about her departure, making unpleasant guesses concerning the reason.

Kay Meredith

CHAPTER EIGHT

On Monday newcomers to the resort would never have believed such a devastating tragedy had happened just a few days earlier at Boreland Springs Hotel. Early that morning John Mathieson met with all his employees and informed them that no mention was to be made to guests about what had occurred the previous week. All evidence of the shooting had been eradicated: the springhouse had been washed down with lye and the stone floor was painted black to obliterate the bloodstains.

It had to be handled this way he'd gone on to explain. Guests had paid lots of money to be entertained, not dragged into the heartbreak of people they didn't know. If one sign of gloom came to light, he promised to dismiss the offending staff member immediately. Everyone was to act like they always did, encouraging guests to take part in every activity and directing them to places where the beautiful landscape of the area could be enjoyed.

Only Melia was depressed, discouraged, and uncomfortable. Knowing she would need all the money she could earn made it possible for her to paste a happy expression on her face and get to work in an efficient manner. It surprised her that by mid-morning the hectic schedule of getting new guests settled in took all of her attention. She bustled from room to room, dusting, cleaning under beds, and replenishing fresh flowers in the crystal vases in every room. Without help from Cricket she collected the soiled laundry and dragged it out to the shed. Already the guests were growing fond of the friendly upstairs maid called 'Melia'. She'd been given several generous tips for the good service she lavished on them. There were times when she actually forgot about her dilemma.

Admonishing his workers to forget the past and return to their regular routine was the best strategy John could have come up with. It pushed the horror of the previous week to the backs of their minds and allowed them to begin the process of getting back to normal. Since Wyatt had had very little contact with the servants they didn't miss his presence like they would one of their own. By the end of the day the resort looked and sounded like it always had. The new guests commented on the expert service, excellent food, and elegant accommodations. Several mentioned to John and Roberta that they'd heard about the high quality of the moonshine served at the resort and looked forward to sampling it for themselves. Roberta clenched her jaw and found another chore she needed to see to.

After dinner, during the usual mingling on the veranda, the Mathiesons performed their hospitality by instinct. Their faces were highlighted by wide smiles and effusive conversation. If Roberta was seen to swipe at her eyes now and then it was put down to a wayward gnat. Clay made engaging remarks to attractive young daughters who didn't notice the pain in his eyes. John laughed uproariously with the men when they told jokes he'd heard many times. It worked. The dancing was wild and the drinking made a healthy profit that night. When the three Mathiesons finally fell into their respective beds, their exhausted bodies got the first full night of sleep since Wyatt's death.

The following morning Melia and Sil walked to work together enclosed in another awkward silence. Since Melia had disclosed her pregnancy to Sil neither had known how to proceed from there. Sil wondered should she encourage Melia to talk about it? Melia supposed Sil might be ashamed of having her as a friend. They'd always talked to each other about their deepest secrets. Now there were limits to what could be spoken about. Each waited for the other to begin.

Sil broke the stillness. "How're you feeling?"

"Alright, I guess." Melia's words were spoken without emotion, as though she was answering a question that concerned someone else.

"What are you going to do?"

"Dunno. Thought I'd go to Wheeling at the end of the month. Should have saved enough for the fare by then. "

"That's the craziest thing you've ever said in your life, Melia. Parkersburg is the biggest town you've ever been to and we were with my family then. Wheeling's big. And you don't know a soul there." She hesitated, angry at Melia's thoughtless scheme. "Have you no thought for your family? They'd wonder why you were gone. Maybe think you'd been kidnapped and killed." Melia was unable to get a word in edgewise. "What do you have in mind once you get there? Look for Santa Claus and stay at the North Pole til the whole thing's over?"

"I didn't really mean it."

"Why did you say it then? This is no time for jokes. You need to tell your mother so we can make some sort of plan."

"I think Mama knows. She looks at me funny and doesn't ask me to fry anything."

"When will you tell her?"

"One thing I won't tell is who the father is. . . .and don't try to change my mind on that. They can plead all they want but no one is to know. They'll be so ashamed. Won't be able to hold their heads up in church." They were beginning to climb the hill to the hotel. "I really do wish I could go away by myself and not get them involved. I just don't know how I can go through with it."

"I won't tell who the father is but you'll have to face the pregnancy like the others before you. It won't go away just because you want it to." Sil scowled at Melia. "Don't say anything about me being 'lofty', as you call it. Right now you could use a sane word or two. You've got to eat the stale bread whether you like it or not. While I'm not saying 'I told you so', you have to face the results of what you've done."

Melia puffed up as if to object to Sil's harsh words. Sil waved an arm at her. "Forget about getting mad and be honest. You've got yourself in a mess and you're the only one who can get yourself out. Don't blame me or anyone else."

Melia's chest deflated. Sil was right. Snippets from another old hymn clouded her mind: 'Rescuing the perishing, . . .snatch them from sin.' Would they never stop? Why must I constantly be reminded of how wicked I am? Sometimes she wished she'd never gone to church.

"Maybe I'll tell her on Friday."

Preparations were being made on Wednesday for the dance that night. John had made a deal with another of the local bootleggers to start delivering moonshine. He'd told Cyrus Willoughby that the Harts were too busy now what with all the orders they had from St. Marys and Parkersburg. Cyrus had raised his brows slightly but agreed to be the supplier.

Melia was heading back to the hotel from hauling dirty laundry to the shed. As she passed the grape arbor loud whispering caught her attention. While she was not one to eavesdrop, the voices were angry and sounded familiar. She stopped, breathing lightly so as not to be discovered. She slid behind the hedge that outlined the tennis courts and peered through the tightly knit branches. It was John and Roberta Mathieson. Whatever disagreement had brought them out of the hotel, away from staff and guests, was serious enough to have them shouting at one another in whispers, if that was possible.

"You'll not change my mind, Roberta. I intend to get even with those two if it's the last thing I do on this earth." His voice was hoarse.

"You have no proof of your suspicions, John. God will punish you taking action against people who may be innocent."

"Who was He punishing when He allowed Wyatt to be killed? He was just a boy, Roberta, barely begun to live."

"It's that sinful moonshine -- been nothing but trouble from the start. I'm positive that had something to do with it." Roberta struggled to keep her voice low. "I said from the beginning it wasn't necessary to serve illegal beverages. Our guests would be satisfied with good wine and liquor from Europe."

"And I've tried to convince you that they expect the taste of mountain moonshine. All the best places offer it as you well know. You heard what the customers said the other night – how much they like it. We've got to continue that service if we're to keep our clientele."

"Maybe so, but having Will and Eugene killed won't make up for Wyatt. How can you be sure that's who it was anyway? They normally delivered on Wednesday, and the vehicle was gone by the time we got to the springhouse." She paused, wanting him to feel her uncertainty.

"Didn't have to see 'em. I could pick their truck out blindfolded in a field full of Fords just by the sound of the engine. I just don't know why they were there on Tuesday."

He was immovable. He towered over her, legs braced, daring her to disagree.

She gathered herself as tall as she could. He was surprised at her boldness. "Well you can be sure whoever you hire for such a job will blackmail us or turn us in to the authorities. Then where will we be?"

"I don't intend to *hire* anyone." His words forced their way through his clenched jaw. "Come hunting season, there's no telling where a stray bullet ends up. When I've got my sights on a big buck, anyone in the way will suffer."

She gasped, stepped back then glanced around to make certain they were alone. "You're mad! We'll all be at risk. Do you think another shooting under such circumstances would not bring suspicion to us? I realize no one says it out loud, but underneath the shirt of every person, policeman or not, lies the knowledge of who deals in moonshine."

"There'll be no proof." His words froze her with his contempt. "Just like there's no evidence in the springhouse to prove the Harts killed Wyatt. You can 'turn the other cheek' if you want, but as far as I'm concerned 'an eye for an eye' is what I'm going on."

"For all your anger, John, I can't believe you'd take the life of another human being." Her eyes were accusing – burning with disbelief.

He spun on his heel and marched out into the pasture. She watched him go, knowing there was nothing she could do to alter the revenge he had in mind. Her shoulders slumped. She turned slowly and walked back toward the hotel, fastening a thin smile on her face and waving to happy guests as she went.

Melia stood still for perhaps five minutes. Over and over in her mind she relived the scene she'd just watched. She looked again at the empty space so recently inhabited by a couple in their deepest sorrow and at odds with each other as to how to right the wrong done to them. She shook her head. Did she hear right? Did John Mathieson admit to dealing in moonshine? Did he intend to 'accidentally' shoot Will during the fall hunting season? She rehashed the argument once again in her head. The answer was the same: sometime in the coming fall, Will would be dead from a shot supposedly aimed at a buck. John would make certain it looked like an accident by being part of a group of friends, anyone of whom might be the shooter. They would unwittingly provide the shield behind which he would hide his guilt. She hurried back upstairs.

    The following day Melia rushed through her daily chores in order to leave work early. Cricket was happy that the girl had finally learned to work fast and didn't object to her leaving ahead of the normal time – just this once. Melia ran to the kitchen and informed Sil about the slight change in schedule. Sil's eyebrows arched.

    Melia was already on her way. "It's for a good purpose, Sil. We'll talk about it later." She threw the words over her shoulder and prayed Sil would forget to ask.

    Maxine looked up from her ironing when she heard the screen door open and slam shut. "Why are you home so early?"

    "I was fast with my chores and Cricket said I could leave early as long as I didn't make a habit of it." She folded the clothes her mother had ironed and put them in piles according to the wearer. "Thought I'd ride Patches up to the Harts to visit little Imogene. . .maybe take her some sassafras for tea. She was coughing last week."

    Melia's voice was full of enthusiasm. She'd been more normal lately than Maxine would have expected. For the flicker of an instant Maxine thought she might be mistaken about Melia being pregnant. Then she remembered all the times Melia was nauseous and knew she hoped in vain. She wondered when her daughter planned to tell her. Nonetheless, Melia's eager demeanor was a welcome departure from her attitude of late. Maxine decided to go along with the visit.

    "Take these lima beans along. I've more than we can eat and they have so many mouths to feed."

    Melia nodded and took the sack her mother handed her. "I'll be back before dark."

    She felt no guilt at this slight stretching of the truth. She was going to the Harts for a good reason. Revealing John Mathieson's plan to shoot Will Hart would only worry Maxine. *Ma would tell me to mind my own business,* Melia thought, as she saddled Patches. *But one shooting in Boreland Springs is enough. If I can stop another, I will.*

Just after dipping down into the meadow where the Hart clan lived she was accosted by three of the youngest of the lot. Melia slipped off Patches and was soon engulfed in three sets of arms welcoming her. Eleanor came out on the porch wiping her hands on her apron as she came. She took the beans gladly.

"Those are a welcome sight! My vines are straggly this year. Should've planted more to feed this gang." She grasped Melia's shoulder with her free hand. "And sassafras! You must have heard Imogene cough. Come in before those scalawags drag you into the dust."

Melia smelled a ham baking in the wood-burning oven. String beans seasoned with a ham hock bubbled on top and a platter of sliced tomatoes was already set on the table. Everyone ate heartily during the summer months, gaining weight and strength for winter when food was scarce. She swallowed hard to keep from gagging. I hope this nausea goes away one of these days, she thought miserably.

She talked with Eleanor and her three youngest for about an hour, trying to make her visit appear normal. The scuffle of heavy feet, accompanied by remarks about the heat and lack of rain announced the arrival of the rest of the family. Will was the last to walk in the door. His eyebrows arched when he saw Melia sitting comfortably at their table. She didn't visit them very often.

"Stay to supper with us," Vernon said, extending the highest form of hospitality a mountain man could offer. "Since you come so seldom, the least we can do is offer you some good vittles. You're lookin' a little peaked."

"Thank you Mr. Hart, but I've just come to bring Imogene some sassafras for her cough. I must get back home and help Mama with supper."

Imogene ran and hugged Melia around the waist. "Come again soon. Please?"

"Absolutely," she answered with a laugh.

"Will, help Melia with her horse. See that she's safely on her way."

Will nodded. "Let's get you started before your brothers come lookin'."

Melia followed him out the door and down the path to where Patches was tethered. The evening sounds had already started. Between the frogs, locusts, and hoot owls, there was little room for words.

"Its good when you come. The little ones love to play with you. The rest of us are always too busy for fun."

"Will, there's something I must tell you."

"Let's walk down toward the road. I'll help you mount at the mailbox."

She told him everything she'd heard when the Mathiesons had argued in the grape arbor. Will studied the pink-streaked sky and listened. At one point his jaw clenched hard enough to display the bones in his face. When she was finished he looked her squarely in the face. "Why are you tellin' me this?"

"Because even if you did have a part in Wyatt's death, and I'm not saying you did, I know it was an accident. I've heard he owed money at Satterfield's as well as some man up in Wheeling by the name of Vince. There were plenty of people after his hide. You and Eugene shouldn't suffer on his account."

"How do you know all this?"

"It's hard to escape all the gossip when you're working with adults whose pleasure comes from knowing private things about the well-to-do. The first day I was there we were told that no one was to be in the vicinity of the springhouse on Wednesday nights. Doesn't take much to figure that's when the moonshine got delivered. She never mentioned which one of the bootleggers supplied the stuff, though."

Will exhaled carefully. "I'm beholden to you, Melia. Took a lot of courage for you to risk your job comin' here. Did anyone see you ride in?" She shook her head.

"Good." Relief smoothed the worn look he'd had since the funeral. Knowing John's strategy gave Will the information he needed to make plans of his own.

He helped her up and watched her begin the descent to the valley. Will was three years older than Melia and ran in different circles than she and her friend Sil. He doubted if he'd spoken ten words to her before today. He didn't understand why she'd made such an effort on his behalf, but he wasn't one to examine a free can of fishing worms.

When the younger Harts had gone to bed, Eleanor, Vernon, and Will sat at the knife-scarred table and talked.

"Seems John Mathieson will be aimin' his deer gun at me durin' huntin' season. Melia overheard him and his wife fightin' about it. Missus Mathieson thinks he's wrong but John won't change his mind."

They sat in a silence as heavy as a morning fog. Each had hoped nothing would come of their worries; that reason would overtake John's fury; that he'd realize revenge would bring them all down. That was not to be.

Vernon stood up quickly nearly overturning his chair and began to pace back and forth. "Could Melia have misunderstood what she heard?"

"She's not one to upset easily. If she says she heard 'em arguin' then she did."

Eleanor spoke up. "We can't ignore this any longer, Vernon. It's time we made plans."

Worry lines framed Vernon's nearly black eyes. He didn't want his sons to leave. They knew nothing of a world away from Boreland Springs. Moonshining was how they'd made their living for nearly ten years. Good money too! Kept safe in a heavy metal box under his bed. Other than himself, Eleanor and Will were the only ones who knew where it was.

How would he manage the stills without their help? Distilling corn into liquor demanded the strength of his two oldest sons. Cousins, uncles, and other close relatives had their own stills to mind.

What about Eugene? Vernon was certain the boy could not be persuaded to leave his home. They'd had enough trouble just getting him into Waverly for a new pair of overalls.

"Vernon?" Eleanor tugged at his elbow.

He jumped at the sound then forced the words from his mouth. "You're right. It's time to put the plan together." He sat back down at the head of the table. Will and Eleanor listened as though it was the word of God Himself.

"Huntin' season is a few weeks off. Gives us time to buy another old truck. We'll keep it here in the back of the shed til we need it. Toward the end of September word will get 'round that my sister's husband has died up near Cleveland and that you and Eugene have gone to get her settled."

"What about questions?" Will's voice was thready – worried.

Eleanor shrugged her shoulders. "If anybody's fool enough to ask we'll give them fuzzy answers that lets them know they heard something but doesn't give 'em enough information to do anything with." When Vernon nodded, she continued. "Same as keepin' bootleggin' close to our skin, Will. Nobody 'round here gives a straight answer when it comes to tellin' about family business."

Will was amazed at the cunning of his parents. "How will you convince Eugene to go?"

"Won't be easy. I'll start puttin' the idea in his head tomorrow," she replied with a sigh.

They decided a return date would not be announced. Once across the Ohio River they would travel north, re-cross at Wheeling then head on up to Weirton or Pittsburgh. It wouldn't be hard to find work at one of the steel plants thereabouts and disguise themselves under steel hats and grime.

Melia felt good about what she'd just done – probably saved the lives of Eugene and Will. It made up, in part, for the terrible guilt she carried with her about the lies she'd lived this summer. The gaslights of her home twinkled through the trees. Her heart filled with real pain when she realized this sight would soon be only a memory.

Her home was her anchor to the hills, the oil wells, church, family, and friends. It didn't matter that the house was plain. Poor by most standards, she reckoned, nevertheless it was a home full of love. Where poverty had been beaten back by skillful use of the natural world around them. Nothing went unused. Curtains were made of feed sacks; rock gardens sprouted wild flowers, garden greens, and herbs; tree trunks were whitewashed; old tires were spliced so they ruffled and served as planters. There was a small patch planted in popcorn so that at Christmas it would be popped and strung on strings and used as tree garlands.

Christmas! Last year she'd crocheted a doily set for her mother's armchair, and mittens for her father and brothers. It had made her feel good to present them all with gifts she'd made herself. A breeze with a hint of chill brushed her shoulders. She shivered, and thought about snow and sledding parties with huge bonfires. Where corrugated tin with no steering mechanism was used for sleds. More than once a load of sledders would land in the creek making it necessary to run for home and dry clothes.

What will Thanksgiving and Christmas be like this year, she wondered? Her eyes filled with tears. She blinked them back – didn't want any sign of crying to be evident when she got inside. She couldn't shake the sorrow. It crept into her soul and lay there like clabbered milk. Her life was changed forever. She had no idea what the future held for her. Once she and Sil had been sure they'd finish high school and maybe college, get a good job, – meet a nice fellow, get married, and have a family – visit their parents on Sundays – and wander into a comfortable old age like their parents before them. Neither girl wanted excitement or surprises – only dependability. The fear of not knowing how her life would turn out now frightened her so much that she dreaded the coming of each new day. Regardless of what Sil says, I really do wish I could die. She unsaddled and fed Patches then walked up the dusty path and into the house.

Kay Meredith

CHAPTER NINE

The following morning Melia helped her mother feed the family before they went out to work. Silas and the two older boys, Harold and Troy, had begun the last of the harvesting. The hay would be scythed then stacked to dry before hauling it into the shed barn for winter storage. This was always a ticklish time of year. Heavy rain on a field of mown hay usually meant the crop was lost since it would probably mold before it dried.

Little Earl was pulling the last of the tomatoes off the vines, even the green ones that would be dipped in flour and fried. This was a dish he especially liked if the fat was hot enough to get the outside crisp while leaving the inside tender. After that he would pull and sort the string beans. They would be shelled because while the skins were tough, the beans themselves were quite tasty and good for soups seasoned with bacon. When all usable vegetables had been removed from the garden it would be plowed under, ready for next year.

Maxine and Melia were busy setting up the washtub and scrub board on the back porch. It was Saturday – the day when all the clothes that had been dirtied from a week of work in the fields would be washed. Melia had taken the day off in order to help her mother. It would take most of the day with one scrubbing while the other rinsed and hung them out to dry. By nightfall their bodies would be aching and tired all over. It would be a long time before the Conroys could afford hot and cold running water and one of those new-fangled wringers. A hand-pump in the kitchen was the most modern appliance they had.

"I've got something important to tell you, Mama." Melia continued to rinse and wring as she spoke.

Maxine stopped scrubbing. "Let's sit down then. It's about time for lunch anyhow."

Melia nodded.

Maxine sliced tomatoes and cucumbers and put them beside yesterday's bread and freshly churned butter. "What was it you wanted to talk about?"

Melia's face reddened. Her skin got hot and she thought she might be sick. "I'm going to have a baby." She laid her head on the table and wept.

Now that the words had finally been spoken Maxine was unsure what to do. Should she punish her daughter's sinful act with cold indifference? Should Melia receive a 'hell-fire and damnation' lecture like those shouted by sweaty, arm-throwing evangelists at all the revivals she'd ever attended? If the truth were to be told, Melia was not the first of her family to fall prey to pleasures of the flesh. Maxine's younger sister had produced her first child only seven months after the wedding.

Maxine remembered how angry she'd been when Trilia had made her announcement. The whole family paid dearly. They were embarrassed beyond belief – no matter that 'early pregnancies' happened more often than one wanted to admit. Her brothers had demanded to know who the father was and promised to go with shotguns in hand unless a wedding was planned forthwith. That hadn't been necessary and when Trilia's blue-eyed baby arrived, everyone forgot whether or not the child was early or on time. Why couldn't that happen with Melia?

"Who's the father?" Maxine's voice was cold, demonstrating the anger, no – fury, that such a loss of principles demanded. She feared it might be one of the Wilkerson boys who were noted for poor morals and little care when it came to owning up to responsibility.

"Doesn't matter," Melia whispered.

"Who?"

"I said it doesn't matter, Mama. I don't intend to marry him."

"You what! Of course you'll get married. I'll not have a daughter of mine bringing up a child without its father. It would be called a bastard. I couldn't bear it."

"You won't have to. I'll go to the Sisters of Hope in Wheeling so the baby can be adopted."

"You'll do no such thing! Not see our grandchild -- your father would die of sorrow, and your brothers will find out who the father is and make him marry you." She paced the floor and her hands tore at her apron. She adjusted her hair then looked out the window. Melia had never seen her mother in such a state. It was frightening.

"The boys are not to be told. You, Papa, Sil, and her parents are the only ones to know why I'm leaving. If you don't allow me to do this, I'll run away, I promise. There will be no wedding. There will be no embarrassment. I intend to stay away longer than it takes to have a baby so there won't be any talk."

"How did it happen?"

"The way it usually does. I thought I was in love and allowed it to happen."

"Are you sure?"

Melia blew her nose into the hankie and nodded. "I've missed one month and get sick every time I try to eat, especially anything greasy. Aren't those the symptoms?"

" Yes." Maxine sounded tired – defeated. She sat down opposite Melia. She faced her daughter with angry and confused eyes. Her shoulders slumped into her chest. Melia was showing an obstinacy Maxine had never seen before. The sound of masculine voices coming in for the noon meal stopped the discussion.

"We'll talk about this tomorrow."

For Maxine, the day and night was interminable. She mulled over all the meetings she'd attended of the Women's Christian Temperance Union where a subject often discussed was what to do with pregnant daughters who, for one reason or another, could not marry the father of their child. The most reasonable solution had always been to send the girls to the nuns. Now she must make plans for Melia to follow that path. Taking her to a local doctor with a dirty facility and no scruples was out of the question!

Maxine felt like a huge stone had been laid on her heart. The thought of never being able to see her first grandchild, always wondering what had happened to the child, was almost more than she could bear. She was furious with Melia for putting her in this position. Why wouldn't she reveal the father's identity? Had she no thought of the pain she was inflicting on her parents? How had Melia forgotten the teachings and warnings that had been a constant part of her upbringing? She thought of all the young men who lived in the area and none fit the picture of someone Melia would be attracted to, nor had any young man come calling. Maybe Melia would have changed her mind by morning.

Her hopes were dashed when once again a stubborn Melia insisted there would be no wedding.

"Why are you so pigheaded? Why won't you get married like everybody else?"

"Because I can't, Mama. I refuse to marry someone I don't love."

"What's love got to do with it when you're in such a pickle?"

Melia turned away in stony silence.

Maxine was at the end of her rope. Arguing was getting them nowhere and calm guidance was needed now. She loved Melia with all her heart and would not send her away in a cloud of ill feeling that had caused Doreen McAllister's daughter to leave and never return. Doreen still tried in vain to learn what had happened to Stella.

"So be it, Melia. We need our wits about us to get through this."

Melia looked at her mother and was ashamed. She doesn't deserve to be treated this way, she thought. The church songs that had battered her conscience all summer faded into the past. Her time of debt paying had arrived. "I'll do whatever you think best. Will Pa think I'm bad?"

"No. You're still the same girl you were yesterday. The only difference is that you've got a problem we need to work on. The boys don't need to be brought into this. Your Pa and I will discuss it with you tonight while they are at prayer meeting."

Melia nodded. It was easier to finish the rest of the day. Knowing she wasn't alone gave her faith that the future might not be as bleak as it had seemed. The nausea even lessened.

That evening Melia sat down with her parents. She sobbed inwardly at the sadness in her father's face. His words were gentle but hesitant, belying his inability to understand how his precious daughter had allowed this to happen.

He cleared his throat self-consciously and began to explain the plan he and Maxine had come up with. Melia looked at the floor and tried to absorb the monumental changes the entire Conroy family would have to make. She could not bring herself to look at either parent. Once again she was overcome by remorse. Her brothers would be told she'd gone away to accounting school (which is what Maxine and Silas planned to tell them) while listening to snide remarks made by neighbors who didn't believe the story. Silas and Maxine would have to face the community with smooth faces until another piece of gossip replaced theirs. Melia's emotions changed like the swing in the big oak tree out back – going back and forth from elation to desolation. Try as she would there was no way she could force herself to remain steady.

"So we'll write to the convent," he was saying. Melia's head came up. "Askin' how soon they might have room for you. Then I'll drive you into Waverly where you can take the train to Wheeling." Melia's eyes looked like a frightened deer. Silas shook his head. "There's no need to worry. Your mother says you'll be met by someone from the convent as soon as you get off the train who will take you directly to the nuns."

Maxine took over and explained that Melia would spend the entire time there working at tasks appropriate for whatever stage of pregnancy she was in. She'd heard other mothers whose daughters had gone to the convent say they were happy to be away from home and in a pleasant environment during such an embarrassing dilemma. Her steady voice had a calming effect. "You'll have lessons in English and math, to prepare you for a job once the birth and adoption has occurred. Just like if you finished high school." She hoped Melia would feel better knowing that her education would continue.

Melia sat very still, eyes glued to the wall, staring at the picture of Christ hanging on the cross. It was weathered and cracked and had hung over the kitchen table for as long as she could remember. The sightless eyes seared into her wicked soul. She recalled all the revivals she'd attended over the years -- sometimes at the little valley church, and at others in a tent put up in a meadow near Waverly. She'd sung with the choir and exulted in the fiery words of the evangelist. She'd been ready to give her life to Jesus, maybe be a missionary in China.

When the sinners repented at the foot of the cross, Melia had been amazed at the wailing and gyrating coming from friends only a little older than herself. What must they have done to make them plead desperately with their Savior for forgiveness? Now she understood. It had never occurred to her that falling into the clutches of the Devil could be done with such ease. It had all seemed so innocent. The enormity of her folly engulfed her like a burlap sack.

The words of her parents planning her life for the next several months, maybe years, sounded muffled. As if her ears were full of cotton. The meaning, however, was clear. Within the next few weeks she would leave her home, travel to a far off place, and live among strangers. How would she be able to stay away for so long? She'd never seen a nun before. She only knew they were different from other women. Would they treat her like a sinner? What would it be like in a convent? Would the other girls be nice? Was having a baby painful?

Melia stifled the urge to cover her face and run into the woods until all the bad things went away. The days when her mother could comfort her with the assurance that everything would be all right were long in the past. She was a grown-up now. That's what being pregnant meant. Her parents were doing the best they could to preserve what pride she had left.

She remembered when Letha Mae Radcliff's folks had taken her to a doctor in Parkersburg. He was supposed to 'take care of the situation' and promised Letha would be up and around within a couple of days. She'd bled to death the night she came home.

CHAPTER TEN

"You know you're my right hand man, don't you?" Eugene nodded and watched Will's face for what he'd say next. They were sitting on a bench under one of the big oak trees. Vernon had built it years ago so Eleanor could string beans and husk corn while she watched the boys build forts with fallen tree limbs and the girls pretended to mother their rag dolls. There had always been an assortment of dogs of all sizes running in and out, disrupting the games. The laughter of then floated through the branches like ghosts.

Will swallowed hard. "Pa's asked me to take a job up toward Wheeling. Told him I wouldn't go if you didn't."

"What's Wheeling?"

"A town like Waverly, only bigger. We could make lots more money so we could buy that new truck we've been wantin'."

"New truck? Oh boy. What color would it be?"

"Don't know. You could pick it out if you want."

Eugene's face was wreathed in a big smile. "Boy oh boy oh boy. When can we do that, Will?"

"Soon as we get that job up north and save our money."

"Will Ma and Pa come too?"

"They have to stay here to care for the farm and the little ones. You and I are the oldest and smartest. We have to go."

Eugene's smile faded. His shoulders slumped into his chest. "Don't know if'n I could leave then. Who'd fix our food and mend our socks?"

"We would. There are places where they sell all kinds of things to eat. Cakes, candy, hot bread. We wouldn't have to work in the garden either. No firewood to chop or hay to stack."

"I don't mind stackin' hay, Will." Eugene scooted to the far end of the bench. He stared at his feet like he always did when confusion made it hard for him to understand.

"We'd be down close to the river where all the steamboats are. Even the ones that play calliopes and have stage shows." Will filled his voice with false enthusiasm.

"You mean like the ones we watch float past Waverly when Pa takes us to Cleggs to buy boots?"

"Yep."

"Would we be able to get on one?"

"Yep."

Eugene's brow smoothed. "When does Pa want us to go?"

"Soon."

John stormed about the study, swearing and kicking furniture out of his way. Roberta could smell smoke from the detestable cigarettes he'd started smoking after Wyatt's death. There had also been the smell of alcohol on his breath more than usual.

She pushed the door ajar and stuck her head in. "For god's sake. Keep your voice down before you scare all the guests away. What's wrong now?"

He'd been increasingly difficult to live with. At times Roberta feared John was losing his mind, or at least all objectivity regarding the death of Wyatt. Even Clay was beginning to question his father's ability to manage the hotel he'd run successfully for so long.

He turned on her as she walked toward him. "They're gone," he shouted. "Two weeks ago! No one told me. I overheard it from the kitchen help."

"Who's gone?" Roberta's voice was quiet, trying to cajole him into lowering his voice.

"Who the hell do you think, Roberta? Will and Eugene Hart. Went up toward Cleveland to help a widowed aunt, so Vernon says. That's a cock and bull story if ever I heard one."

"What does it matter to us? We've got a business to run."

"Don't come at me with that. The hotel is making more money than ever before. That ad agency I hired in New York has got us booked solid for next summer. People who would normally be going to the Poconos."

Roberta whispered. "You've done a superb job of increasing the business, John. It means we've got to build more facilities for all those people. Why spend time worrying about what the Harts are doing?"

"I won't be satisfied until they've paid for their crime. That will never change."

"You're putting us all at risk with this unreasonable revenge you live for." She picked up several volumes of books strewn about the floor and replaced them on the shelf. He'd even overturned his desk chair. She struggled to set it upright. He didn't offer to help.

"They'll come back. That half-witted Eugene won't be able to stay away long. And I'll be waiting."

Roberta had never heard her husband speak so viciously toward Eugene. "This will bring you nothing but grief, mark my word."

"I'm already grieving. A little more won't make any difference." He strode out of the room, slamming the door behind him.

Roberta shook her head sadly. He'd become someone she didn't know. She had no idea how to go about restoring the man she'd married. The one who had smiled more than he frowned; who hugged his family without embarrassment; who gave generously to those less fortunate; the one who loved his sons, especially Wyatt, more than life itself.

When Wyatt died, John felt that his life was also over. In his place was a man filled with so much hostility that it clouded any vision of the blessings that remained. Roberta feared what would happen to all of them. Never before had she faced catastrophe alone. John had always been beside her. A gnawing hole in the pit of her stomach told her that from now on she would have to manage with Clay at her side. But he was barely sixteen.

Kay Meredith

Affair at Boreland Springs

CHAPTER ELEVEN

Weirton, West Virginia

"Sure miss Ma." Eugene's voice was quieter than usual. His head drooped and his arms hung slack at his sides. "It's so little here."

They'd rented two rooms with a shared bath overlooking the main thoroughfare in the town of Weirton. The walls were painted light green with stains in several places where the ceiling had leaked. Two steel framed beds with a side table between took up most of one room. The other contained a threadbare sofa with a tarnished lamp beside it. The yellowed shade had a scorched spot where a hot light bulb had touched. On the opposite wall Will had stacked their trunks of clothes. He'd had a rough time coaxing Eugene to go to an inside bathroom where he sometimes had to wait for strangers to finish. The sight of the water swirling out of sight had frightened him.

There was a washroom for all the boarders on the first floor, toward the back of the boarding house. One evening a week, everyone was entitled to fill one of the communal tubs with hot water and soak for twenty minutes. For an extra fifty cents you could have two baths each week.

"We won't be here forever, Eugene." Will spoke with more enthusiasm than he felt. He too missed their home and the neighbors they'd grown up with.

"Why'd we have to come?"

"Remember what we talked about? We're earnin' money so's we can buy that new truck. You're gonna pick it out."

Eugene straightened up. "I saw one down at that corner lot, Will. A shiny red one. Could we look at it?"

"Got to drive this old rusty one til we save some more money. Then we'll have a look."

Will was thankful that Eugene recalled nothing of the horrendous night when Wyatt had been shot. It was like a page torn from a book and thrown into the wind -- a blessed lapse in his brain that enabled him to believe they were in Wheeling trying to earn money to buy a truck.

"How long will that take? Halloween comes up pretty soon. I always like to dress up for that. Would we have enough money to go back then, Will?"

"Don't think so, Eugene. Takes awhile to make enough to buy a truck."

"What about Thanksgivin' or Christmas? Will we miss them too?" His voice quivered. He was close to crying.

"We'll see, Eugene. We'll see."

Will knew they wouldn't be able to go back for a long time. The problem was that one day in Eugene's head was like weeks in a normal person's world. Soon it would feel to him that he'd been away from home for years. I've got to find a way to get him interested in living here, Will thought with discouragement. Otherwise he'll go into one of those melancholy phases where he won't eat or speak. That had happened when Eugene's old dog Jade had died. Only their mother, and a new puppy, had brought him out of the stupor.

"Wait til you see where we're goin' to work. Lots of fellows just like us work there. Makin' plenty of money. So we can save it up and take a trip home."

Eugene's eyes brightened. "I'd like to buy some purty flowers and take 'em to Ma when we go. Will we drive the new truck, Will?"

"Maybe." Will heaved a big sigh, relieved that for the moment at least Eugene had returned to his easy-going attitude.

Melia's departure from Boreland Springs was much harder than for Will and Eugene. Not only was she heartsick, she was physically ill as well and thankful that Sil's mother had allowed her to ride to Wheeling with her. Otherwise she was certain death would have claimed her by now. Sil bathed Melia's brow to ease the heat and nausea she had suffered on the trip to the convent. It had started as soon as they'd climbed into the wagon and bounced their way into Waverly to catch the train north.

Maxine and Silas were glad they had included Sil's parents into the plan. It was good to have friends who gave them support and love. The Conroys knew they could depend on the Lockharts to maintain their silence.

"Take good care of her, Sil." Silas's voice had been gruff, trying to cover the sadness that threatened to overcome him.

"I will." Sil hadn't known what else to say. It was an awkward situation where the less said the better.

He watched the train, hat in hand, until it disappeared from sight. Then he turned with a heavy tread and dragged himself back to the wagon. All the way home, he wept for innocence that was lost so young, never to be known again. It was the first time he'd cried since his Ma had died when he was eleven.

The rocking motion of the train hadn't improved Melia's condition. She'd continued to vomit until there was nothing left but dry heaves. Sil feared she might lose the baby. Perhaps that would that be a blessing. That way the problem would be over before Melia's stomach began to swell. She could return to school and the community would be none the wiser. Yes, Sil thought, that just might be the best thing that could happen. As she cleaned Melia's face again, she mouthed a prayer asking God to forgive her for such blasphemy.

"We'll be there soon, Melia. Just hold on a little longer." Melia nodded feebly.

The shabby old taxi rumbled through the narrow, pitted streets of Wheeling. It was a river town where coal and steel were loaded on barges and shipped down the Ohio to Cincinnati and from there to New Orleans. There was little that was attractive about this trade town with its rough-talking dockworkers and dust encrusted coal handlers. Smoky and hilly, it clung tenaciously to the banks of the Ohio River like cold grease.

For all its ugliness, however, much money traded hands here. Those on the receiving end of the profits built lavish homes further back in the hills where manicured lawns and third-floor ballrooms gave the 'well-to-dos' a feeling of breeding and noble ancestry. It was easy to conceal a less than pristine background under a heavy layer of money and acquired accents.

The cab wheezed to a stop in front of an ornate iron gate. It was flanked by a high stone wall, which formed the perimeter of the convent property. "Here we are," the driver announced and turned in the direction of Sil, who seemed to be the one in charge. "That'll be a fifty cents." His long horse-like face, perched on a scrawny neck, displayed a bored expression that dismayed both girls. He made no move to help them unload their suitcases. Sil frowned at such lack of good manners and began dragging their luggage out of the trunk. No sooner had she slammed the lid down than the old vehicle moved off, leaving a trail of black fumes in its wake.

Melia's steps were labored as she followed behind Sil. She was valiantly trying to carry one of the smaller cases.

"Put that down. You're sick enough already. I'll make several trips." Sil was huffing but determined not to let it show. She pulled at the gate handle but it wouldn't budge. "How do you get into this place anyway? It's locked."

"Try ringing that buzzer there," Melia said, pointing to the black button on one side of the gate.

Sil pushed the button hard, hoping to make a loud noise in the gray brick building where many of the windows were shuttered. She was mad at being treated as if they didn't matter. Like they were ne'er-do-wells who should expect to be kept waiting! First the cab driver and now this daunting place that's supposed to be an institution of God.

"Wait here while I bring the rest of the stuff. If we're lucky someone will come out that door so we don't have to camp here in the street."

Melia smiled in spite of herself. Sil was so funny when she got mad. She sat down on the biggest trunk and watched Sil wrestle with the rest of the bags and cases. How I love her, she thought. I'll miss her so much. Please God don't let her forget me.

The big front door of the convent opened with a clatter and one of the tiniest women Sil had ever seen emerged. The flowing black habit and cumbersome headgear had trouble keeping up with her as she skimmed down the brick walk to let them in.

"Now wouldn't you just know it. We've been looking for you all morning and when you finally get here we're all in prayer. Have you been waiting here long?" She pulled a huge key from within the voluminous gown and unlocked the gate. "Did the cabby help you with your bags?"

"Actually he..."

"If it was Harold I'll wager he just took his money and left. The man has no sense of duty." She reminded Melia of her mother's fireplace broom that was just as fast and equally efficient.

"You're right, he didn't..."

"Too bad it wasn't Neil. He would have walked right up here, rung the bell, and carried all this stuff into the foyer. Good man that Neil." She grabbed two of the lighter ones and started back up the walk. "Did your journey take a long time?"

"Yes, first we..."

"Course if you came from hilly country those roads always take time."

"Yes..."

"And all of West Virginia is hilly!" Her whole body bubbled with laughter as she strode ahead. Melia reckoned the little nun didn't expect answers to her rapier-like questions.

Sil arrived at the gate with the last trunk. Sweat dripped off her nose and she was out of breath. "Who's that?"

"One of the nuns, I think."

"I can see that. What's her name?"

"Don't know. She hasn't said."

"I'm Sister Angela," the tiny figure yelled over her shoulder. "Come along now with those bags."

They hustled after her since the diminutive nun exuded the aura of a very large field commander. The heavy wooden double doors opened into a large circular vestibule with a slate floor. Sunrays pierced the glass transom that capped the door and reflected the colorful hues of the beautiful slabs. Melia hadn't realized this common stone could be so captivating.

The walls were paneled in dark stained oak rimmed with gaslight sconces about nine feet high. An elaborate chandelier dropped from the middle of a cathedral ceiling that was painted with biblical scenes of monumental battles between good and evil. A tall, muscular angel, clad in silver armor, wielded a heavy sword above the head of the Devil who had fallen to one knee and looked with terror into the fate that would soon befall him. Melia was spellbound at the sight.

Sil pulled her none too gently by the elbow. "Hurry up! We're getting behind and I don't think Sister Angela will like that."

Three corridors branched off this foyer. Sister Angela turned right and bustled down a poorly lit hallway with doors on either side. Melia and Sil struggled to catch up with her. She stopped at the last door, pulled out her large ring of keys, selected the correct one, and unlocked it. It was a plain room with a small cot against one side, a straight-backed chair in one corner, and a washbasin atop a marble-topped table in another. A writing desk and armoire finished out the furnishings. One tiny window gave a view into a garden where flowers, herbs, and vegetables grew side by side. It was mostly brown now – just like Melia felt.

"There's a bathroom at each end of the hall. Room for two or three at once and everyone's expected to clean up after themselves. Morning prayers are 6 a.m. and breakfast at 7. After that Melia, Sister Ambrosia will confer with you as to the daily schedule and what duties you'll be expected to perform."

Sil cleared her throat. "Sister..."

"Oh, that's right. I'll have a rollaway brought in for you tonight -- Sil is it?" Sil nodded.

Melia's small voice broke in. "What should we..."

"Forgive me, Melia. I'm running a mile behind myself today. Another girl coming tonight. Yes, you want to know what to do for the remainder of today. Move your things in. Have a look around. Evening meal is 6 pm and vespers are at 8." She turned to go.

"Is there any place that's off limits while we look around?" Sil talked fast, determined to finish at least one sentence before Sister Angela disappeared.

"Not on this floor."

"Am I to..." Once again Melia was too slow.

"Everything will be explained tomorrow, Melia. There are forms to be filled out and you'll be assigned a big sister. You should spend today with Sil. She'll want to know what the convent looks like and it's not likely she'll be able to come again."

"I want to return when it's time for Melia's baby to be born, Sister Angela. You will let me know won't you? My family agrees I should come." Her words rushed out like logs rolling down a hill.

"Of course you can. Before you leave tomorrow, give me your address and I shall make sure you're notified in plenty of time." Before more questions could be launched she was gone in a swirl of black gown.

They spent the afternoon wandering through the convent, commenting on the impressive establishment -- avoiding talk about the future. Each wondered whether this would be the end of their closeness. If so, would there ever be another soul to whom they could divulge their deepest secrets; enjoy a sunset that peeked through brilliant fall foliage from the top of Horseneck Ridge; another 'someone' who wore feed sack dresses without shame. A friend you could depend on. A kindred spirit who knew you were worthwhile no matter what you'd done.

They worried that the precious bond between them might be lost in the complexities of getting older and adding new responsibilities to their lives. Why couldn't childhood friendships, the strongest they could imagine, continue throughout adulthood? They wanted to live in the hills like their families had always done – safe from outside influences. When this was over maybe things would be the same as before. Deep in their hearts, however, both doubted it.

After inspecting the wing where Melia's room was and wondering how modesty could be preserved in the communal bathrooms, they arrived back in the foyer. They followed the corridor that faced the entrance. It led to a small chapel. Never before had they felt such a holy presence. At home there were no stained glass windows where outside light was diffused through multihued scenes of mangers, baby Christ, a holy halo around the Madonna's head, and shepherds tending their flocks.

Sun filtered through wavy panes at Boreland Springs United Brethren Church, brutally displaying pock marked pews that leaned unsteadily for want of a nail or two. The old upright piano, suffering from years of pounding and no regular tuning, led the congregation in hymns sung with gusto but lacking in harmony. Toddlers crawled between adult's legs, playing in the dust underneath and disturbing the sermon with gurgles and squeals. Melia and Sil couldn't imagine such irreverence in this setting.

Here was a solemnity unknown to them, exuding a feeling of ritual that must be executed correctly so as not to insult the Almighty. The air was heavy – still – with an intensity that made them hesitate to approach the kneeling bench. They stood like statues for several minutes looking above the sanctuary at a carving of Christ hanging on the cross. It was life-size, giving them the feeling they were witnessing the actual crucifixion. Rather than a comfort, the sight only made both girls more desolate as they faced the coming months alone in their separate miseries.

"Let's go down the other hallway, Melia. It might be more cheerful."

Melia nodded and gladly led the way.

Sil was right. This corridor led to a dining hall brightened by many windows and tables with dried flower arrangements. Linen tablecloths reinforced the feeling of formality and manners. Melia hoped she could learn proper etiquette from the 'big sister' Sister Angela had mentioned.

The following morning would remain in Melia's memory as one of the saddest of her life. She clung to Sil like a sick child to its mother. They were waiting for the cab that would take Sil to the train station. Sister Angela stood discreetly behind the gate watching the sorrowful farewell. She was uncharacteristically quiet and her cheerful face was furrowed with worry wrinkles. She'd seen so many of these goodbyes and knew that life would never be the same for these young women again. Their time together now was precious. No one should interfere.

Sister Angela knew that from this time forward Melia's actions would be tempered by the torment of what it means to give up a part of one's life. Not something like a dress or doll, but a living being that had come from her own body and carried her family's ancestry. Someone who might later feel sadness, and possibly anger, toward a mother who had not cared enough to keep an innocent baby. Regardless of other children she might have, Sister Angela knew Melia would always wonder where this child was; if the adoptive parents were loving to a child abandoned by its mother; and whether a proper education had been possible. She had counseled many women who were never able to banish these destructive thoughts, allowing their lives to be tainted for the remainder of their years.

Sil's heart was already filled with guilt for leaving her friend in such frightening circumstances. It was like losing a sister. No, even worse. Lifelong friends are often much closer than sisters. What was it like to live with nuns, she wondered. Could Melia come home right after the birth or does it take weeks to recover from such an ordeal? Would she be treated with respect? Would she be made to feel beyond redemption – someone unfit for happiness in the future? Was there a library with books other than religious to read? Please God, she prayed, don't let her die.

Affair at Boreland Springs

Too soon the sound of an ailing engine announced the arrival of the cab. Oh dear, Sister Angela thought, it's Harold. Wish it were Neil. He'd have Sil feeling better by the time they reach the station.

Sil carried her suitcase down the walk and stuffed it and herself into the cluttered backseat of the rickety vehicle. Harold pulled away in a cloud of smelly exhaust. Melia waved frantically, hoping Sil could see her through the smoke. Then Sil rolled the window down and stuck her head out. "Write to me every week. I'll see you in April!" She blew a kiss just as the cab disappeared down the hill toward town.

Melia's favorite place in the convent was the vestibule. When she wasn't attending to her assigned chores she loved to sit on the soft cushions of the bench hidden in the shadows and stare at the slate floor.

"It's God's special stone,'" her grandmother had told her from the time she was old enough to sit and listen. "Tells the story of life. Its gnarly and layered swirls of color come from the beginnin' of time," she'd said.

"See there, Melia. That streak of red could be the blood of Christ." Melia had stiffened at the thought of blood. "And them there," Granny McBride had pointed to delicate curls of yellow. "Them's probably the last of the dandelions some year afore time began."

Melia had been fascinated with all the shades of green, blue, silver, brown, and black, and the way they drifted around one another without a noticeable pattern. "Them's the colors of the sky and water and soil," Granny explained. "It's all there in front of your eyes," she'd continued. "God's story right here in this piece of rock." She'd rubbed her fingers carefully over the rough surface of a slate tabletop while Melia looked on in awe. "You know don't you, child, that slate was part of this earth long afore even Christ was born?"

Melia shook her head solemnly. "How's slate like life, Gran?"

"Well, sturdy as it looks, them layers peel off and blow away with the wind if'n somethin' hard hits it. It's frail thataway. Like feelins' people have that can be hurt real easy."

"Like when Eli Boone hit little Ellen when she dropped a basketful of eggs – and she ran away from home and drowned in the creek?" Melia's eyes had been big as saucers.

"Yep."

They both had mulled this over for a while.

"Is that all there is about slate?" Melia' eyes had saddened thinking about little Ellen Doone.

"No. Slate's strong too. If'n you lay a slab down on a level spot to clean your feet on afore you come in the kitchen, or make a table out of it with a strong-built oak frame, it'll last long as steel. It's soft and tough all at the same time."

Melia had stared hard into her grandmother's brilliant blue eyes. "And that's what life's like, Gran?"

"Yep," she'd answered. "Soft and tough all at the same time."

Granny McBride died the following winter. Melia knew for sure that her world in Heaven was not paved with gold, but rather a street made of her beloved slate.

On this dusky afternoon Melia thought about the layers of her life – and how they would gradually peel off as time trod through her destiny. She'd been a happy young girl just a few months ago. That layer was gone – replaced by a swirl of sad smoky gray, stretching ahead of her into a future of unknown challenges. What would come then? More gray? Could there possibly be some blue and gold in the scheme of her life? Or would her years drag on in shades of brown and black?

Melia saw her grandmother's face smiling back from the enchanting floor. "Slate never stays the same for very long, Melia. It's a livin' stone – one that up and surprises you bad and good. No tellin' what the next patch might look like."

She couldn't take her eyes off the slate. Beside a sliver of black might be brilliant gold or rich green. Granny was right. Nothing stays black forever. Maybe next year there'll be a scrap of silver for me.

CHAPTER TWELVE

The chill of December would soon be upon her. During the past week Melia had felt her baby begin to kick. She was frightened the first time it happened, thinking something had gone wrong inside her. Sister Angela had assured her this was normal and that it would increase in strength in the coming months. Every time the tiny movements occurred she was overwhelmed with love and sorrow: love for the little person growing inside her and sadness because the child would never know its blood family. It made her realize the depth of her mistake – because that's how she thought of it – *her* mistake. She couldn't blame God, Wyatt, her family, the church, or Sil. She alone had made the decision to sleep with a man who was not her husband – and she was well aware of the possible consequences. Most disheartening of all was that she'd dragged so many others into her disgrace.

She looked through her frosted window down into the wilted garden that had disappeared under a layer of wet snow that had crept up on them during the night. From behind the convent walls she could hear shrieks of joy from children clad in mittens, boots, and snowsuits, sledding off the top of Maple Street on their Red Flyers. She knew that mothers would be helping their little ones negotiate the lesser hills and in someone's house would be a kettle of hot cider to warm cold bodies for another go.

The slick snow had put Wheeling into slow motion until the dangerous footing melted. The holidays were just a sniff away. Streets had been decorated with pine garlands and bright lights, concealing the grime for a while under a blanket of white that reflected the colorful lights. None but the most jaded of people could resist the Christmas season. Officers of the Salvation Army stood on every corner with their bright suits and cheerful bells, cajoling as many coins as possible from a population that had little extra to give. But give, they did. If only a penny.

As Melia's abdomen enlarged, her thoughts were always of home. This place, while pleasant, would never be more than a bad dream. She lived for news from Boreland Springs. She'd memorized the letter Sil had sent in October.

Kay Meredith

Dear Melia,

Well we had the Annual Homecoming last week and you'll never guess what. Myrtle Baumgartner announced she's marrying Jase Higgins. Remember him? He moved away two years ago – had a bad case of face pimples. Came back couple of months ago and looks a lot better. The Carruthers' sisters are being courted by the Smith twins. Can you believe people that old still want to get married? Hilda Meeks is pregnant again – we're all hoping she doesn't have another miscarriage. Oops, not a good subject for someone who's about to give birth. Sorry. Will write later. Mom's yelling – needs help in the kitchen.

Love, Sil

She clutched the letter to her breast and could feel the crisp wind that wasn't really cold. She closed her eyes and saw the hillsides in their colorful fall leaves. Rich yellows of the oaks, bright red of the maples mixed with subtle browns and reds of all the other trees, highlighted by vibrant green pines.

It was the time everyone who'd ever lived in the area tried to come back for a day or so to renew friendships. There would be strings of pine garlands forming a bright canopy over tables of food brought by the many former and present residents of Boreland Springs. The thought of pumpkin and mincemeat pies seasoned with cinnamon and allspice made her mouth water; or fresh pork with moist portions of sage dressing -- that was the favorite, with venison and beef not far behind. Vegetables of every combination would arrive in serving dishes stored in cupboards for just these occasions. Melia knew her mother would have taken one of her famous apple cobblers and succotash seasoned with ham hocks. These sumptuous celebrations often made it necessary for the families to eat sparsely at home, but they didn't mind. This was when they forgot their hardships and laid down tables of food fit for a king.

Her mother's letter told her all about the annual Thanksgiving Box Supper.

Dearest Melia,

We missed you at the Box Supper but you'll be here next year, I know. Homer Leach tried to get Bill Riggs to buy one of Regina Willis's fried chicken boxes, but no deal. Bill was saving his money for Tilly Janes's box. I think Regina's food would have tasted better, but she doesn't look as good serving it as Tilly does.

The funniest thing though was watching Sil's embarrassment when Jeb Wilkerson bought her box for five dollars! Everyone wondered where he got that much money. Anyhow, it will certainly help the fund to buy second-hand clothing for some of our less fortunate folks.

Your Pa and I pray for you every night and hope that your morning sickness is over.

Love, Ma

Melia had smiled, knowing how embarrassed Sil would have been sitting beside one of the fellows none of the other girls wanted.

Melia looked down at the letter she'd received yesterday from Sil. It was impossible for her to read it without tears coming to her eyes.

Dear Melia,

I'd like to make you laugh and tell you all about the fun we're having getting ready for Christmas, but it would be lie. We all miss you terribly – me especially. The men have brought in the tree for the front of the church. The younguns are practicing their verses to recite on Christmas Eve and Madeline Foley is rehearsing 'Oh Little Town of Bethlehem'. I still don't know how Frieda Morgan can look down into that old manger with the Jesus doll for the entire evening. I doubt if the Madonna herself would have that much balance.

Ma is gathering up the hard candy and walnuts and putting them in little paper bags for the children. We're all wondering if the Mathiesons will add the oranges like they always do. Most of us don't think they'll feel like celebrating much this year.

I hope you're not in too much discomfort. It'll all be over soon.

Love, Sil

Surely this is my punishment, Melia thought, to be away from my home through the most meaningful time of the year. Nothing can be harder than this. She brushed a tear from her cheek so that her 'big sister' Sharon Dulaney wouldn't notice her red eyes.

Sil sat forlornly on her bed. With Melia gone, she felt like she'd lost one of her arms. There wasn't another girl in the whole community who understood her like Melia did. Most of the others were so busy trying to attract a boyfriend that they'd think it silly to still be saving childhood treasures in an old tree trunk. On this night she was writing another letter to Melia. She knew Melia must be lonely too, probably worse than she was. Should I make it sound like everything is normal here? Or would it better to tell her how much I still miss her? She chewed the end of her pencil, thinking. Either way she'll be sad, I think.

She was huddled by the window in her bedroom under the eaves. One of her mother's Afghans was thrown over her shoulders to keep the cold air that seeped around the sill from giving her a chill. She sighed and stared at the moon. It was one of those winter moons that looked like someone had rubbed its edges with a dusting cloth, making its round shape muted, unclear. Like our lives, she thought.

Nothing has a definite border anymore. Some things are clear -- like Melia having a baby. That will happen no matter what. But then what? I'll be with her when that happens but then I'll come home and go back to school and eventually to college. Sil knew that hope of Melia finishing high school, much less college, was only a pipedream. Did she, Sil, want to be true to her friend and forego an education as well? Wasn't that what best friends did? The answer was 'no' and that tore at her soul. Remaining in Boreland Springs instead of going on to college would break her heart and spirit. On the other hand, deserting Melia went against all the pledges they'd made to each other – it made her feel like a traitor. So many blurred edges, she thought, just like the moon.

She shivered and pulled the afghan closer. She told Melia the truth – that she was missed sorely by everyone (most of all by her) and that the Christmas program hymns would all be off key since Melia was the only one in the church who could carry a tune.

Weirton, WV

"I can't stay here no more, Will. Gotta go home. . ." Eugene was pacing about the room, beads of sweat on his forehead and upper lip. "Tain't right – not bein' with Ma and Pa on Christmas."

The past few days had been a nightmare for Will as he tried to make Eugene forget that Christmas was only a few days away. But carolers strolled from house to house singing the old familiar songs, store windows displayed an abundance of gift possibilities, Christmas trees were everywhere, adorned with every kind of ornament possible, reminding all that Christ's birth was soon to be celebrated. Eugene was beside himself wanting to be home sleeping in his own bed and decorating a tree with his own kith and kin. He'd become upset in ways Will had never seen before.

After a hard day of work, Eugene would often lay motionless on his bed, refusing to go to the dining room for an evening meal. At other times when they were walking down Main Street he would clamor for every goody within sight: caramel apples on a stick, spiced cider, hot-cross buns, or rich fudge from Woolworths.

Will was at his wit's end. "Eugene, we've not got that new truck yet. Thought you wanted to ride. . ."

"No! I want to go home now." Eugene turned toward Will with a fury in his eyes that was frightening. Will wasn't sure but what the boy might actually attack him. He's not a boy anymore, Will thought. He's a man – with the strength of an ox..

"Alright Eugene, we will." Will filled his voice with enthusiasm he didn't feel. "Get some things packed and we'll leave tomorrow after we've told the boss we'll be gone for few days."

Eugene jumped up and down like a child – laughing and running to Will, enclosing him in a hug that would have crushed a lesser man. "Can I buy some posies for Ma? One of them big red flowers we seen down at Garber's flower place?"

"Yep. We'll take some water in a mason jar so's it don't get dry on the way home."

Eugene pulled his battered cardboard box out from under his bed and put some socks in it. "Should I take a shirt?"

"I'd take three or four if I was you. So Ma don't have to wash while we're there."

Will heaved a great sigh: relieved that Eugene was back to normal and worried at how they could sneak into Boreland Springs without John Mathieson's knowledge.

A couple of nights later, Will maneuvered the second-hand farm truck into the shed beside the Hart home. He smiled sadly at how similar it was to all the times he'd sneaked the Hart's panel truck in beside the springhouse at the resort – with only moonlight to illuminate the way.

CHAPTER THIRTEEN

April 1925, Wheeling

    The pain went beyond anything Melia had ever imagined. She seemed to be possessed by a demon that was pulling her guts away from the insides of her body in an effort to get out. There was nowhere she could run, nothing she could say, to escape her penance for the sins she'd committed. During her months at the convent there had been lectures by the nuns explaining what happened when a woman had a baby. They'd said that while labor could be painful, when the birth was eminent ether would be administered to make the final birthing pains barely noticeable.

    The problem was that Melia had been in labor for almost twenty hours and still the baby would not come. Her voice was hoarse from groaning each time a contraction occurred. In the beginning she'd tried to be as quiet as possible so as not to bring attention to herself. But as the hours dragged on, her will was beaten down by the never-ending spasms that got closer together. The nurses urged her to bear down hard to help the process along, but all that did was exhaust her to the point where she was limp as a rag doll between pains. She lay on the hard bed, dwarfed by the huge belly that tried in vain to shed itself of the tiny being within.

    Sil sat in a corner and wondered how such pain could be borne. She'd heard the doctor say the dilemma was because Melia wouldn't dilate. She didn't know what that meant and no one could take the time to explain it to her. She only knew the baby wanted to come but couldn't pass down the birth canal.

    Doctor Tyson shook his head as he watched Melia deteriorate with every minute of the struggle. "I'll give her a small amount of laudanum so she can get some rest. Watch her carefully and call me immediately if she begins to dilate. I'll be at the Wilson home." He snapped his bag shut and hurried out into the humid spring day. Sister Marie nodded. A frown wrinkled her brow. She knew the doctor was at the end of his ability to help. Mother and child were in the hands of God now.

    The nuns bustled about, giving Melia cool water to sip and applying damp cloths to her face. They walked around Sil as if she wasn't there, able to maintain a steadiness in their movements that indicated they'd been through this sort of crisis before. The hours crawled by like heavy mud.

Sometime in the late evening Melia roused from the effects of the laudanum. Her hand reached feebly for Sil who sat dozing beside her bed. "The pains are coming back but it feels different somehow. . .like the baby is lower in my stomach."

Sil didn't wait for further explanation. She ran to find Sister Marie. "Come quick. Melia's. . ."

Sister Marie headed for Melia's bed before the sentence was finished with Sister Angela close behind. Sister Angela held the covers back while Sister Marie made a quick examination. It took only a few seconds for Sister Marie to come to a decision. "Ring up Doctor Tyson. Tell him the baby is about to crown."

In an instant the room was busy with nuns working like a well-oiled machine: bringing clean cloths, hot water, metal pans, and instruments that made Sil wonder if they were planning to cut the infant out of Melia's body! She stood unnoticed in the corner and watched with horror at the scene before her. They rolled Melia over so a rubber sheet could be placed under her, then pulled her knees up and spread her wide in position for the actual birth. Melia's screams reverberated through the little room, out into the hall, and down to the foyer.

It was all Sister Marie could do to keep the frantic girl from falling off the bed. "I hope the doctor gets here soon. We could certainly use that ether."

"For such a stubborn beginning this wee bairn seems to be in a hurry now." Sister Maureen's quaint Irish accent was comforting.

Sil looked at the door, willing Doctor Tyson to walk through. The sight of Melia, finally too exhausted to moan, made her wonder if she ever wanted to put herself through such an ordeal. Melia's ashen face looked as if she was near death or perhaps had already passed on. Her beautiful hair was tangled beyond rescue – Sil wondered idly if it might have to be cut. That would be such a shame.

The door burst open and Doctor Tyson rushed in, took one look, and announced there was no time for ether. The baby had to be delivered immediately. Holding the baby's head until the ether took effect could jeopardize the infant's health. The doctor and nuns attending Melia crowded closer together. Sil stretched her neck trying to see what was happening. It looked like things were coming to a conclusion. She bowed her head and prayed both mother and child would survive.

Sil would remember, for the rest of her life, the two sounds that announced the birth of Charity Conroy. First was Melia's unholy scream that seemed to come from the bowels of Hell, followed by the first cries of the infant finally released from the confines of Melia's belly. After that everything became a blur for Sil. She collapsed into the chair beside the window. As if in a dream she watched Sister Maureen take the baby to be cleaned while Sisters Marie and Angela tended to Melia. I've not been much help to Melia, Sil thought morosely. I might as well be on the moon for all the good I've been.

Late that afternoon Sil sat beside Melia and coaxed her to eat the broth and bread on her tray. She had tried, with little success, to comb the tangles out of Melia's hair. Melia was listless, wanted nothing to eat, and had little to say.

"Please Melia. You've got to eat to get your strength back."

"I'd have died without you here. I'm sorry for being dull. There's so little to be happy about."

"Yes there is! You're alive and so is the baby. What else do you want?"

Sil's practicality brought a wistful smile to Melia's face. "I wish none of this had ever happened."

"Well, it did, Melia. Quit feeling sorry for yourself. We have to go on from here."

The door opened and Sister Marie brought in a squalling baby girl. "What a voice. Here, let's get her nursing before our eardrums are broken."

Unlike many adoption foundations that never allowed the mother to see her baby, the nuns were adamant that the infant should get the mother's first milk, so important for the child's health. This was painful for many mothers who then found it nearly impossible to give up their newborn. Cruel as it seemed, it was a rule of the convent put in place for the good of the child and not to be changed.

Sil watched as Melia accepted the red-faced, squirming bundle of baby girl vociferously declaring her hunger. She choked back her tears as Melia tenderly pushed back the baby blanket so she could get a better look, then smiled with the radiance only a new mother has. "Isn't she beautiful?" Melia beckoned for Sil to come closer. "I've decided to name her Charity." She looked up at Sister Marie. "How do I get her to nurse?"

"She probably won't yet – takes a few times of trying before your milk comes in. She'll get a supplement until that happens." Sister Marie positioned Melia's arms so she could get Charity to feel the nipple on her little lips. "You need to keep showing her the nipple so that when your milk does come in she'll be ready to latch on."

Sil was aghast. *Why has Melia named this baby? Has she forgotten that soon the adoptive parents will arrive to claim the child? All this bonding will only make it harder. Why do they have to put the baby in her arms, only to take her away forever within a few days?* She masked her concerns by sitting beside Melia and offering a finger for the tiny infant to feel. Maternal feelings flooded through her body, making her want to shield Melia from the sorrow that lay ahead of her. *I couldn't give this child away and I'm only a friend. How can she do this? How can her family ask her to do this?*

Melia was engrossed with the wonder of her first baby – examining the perfection of such a tiny little person. Charity already had a cap of bright chestnut hair – it looked like it would be curly – just like Melia's. Her eyes were corn-flower blue – like Wyatt's. She nuzzled the little face that was searching for nourishment. Finding none, Charity screwed her face into a red knob and howled at the top of her voice. Melia looked up at Sister Marie, concern written on her face.

"I'll take her back to the nursery now for a bottle. We'll try again later." Melia's eyes filled. "Not to worry," Sister Marie assured her. "This is normal. Usually by the third try the baby is able to suck." She wrapped the little bundle back up and left, cooing and snuggling to soothe the agitated baby.

Melia could contain the tears no longer. They spilled out all over her face and onto her gown. She covered her face trying to hide her anguish from Sil, but there was no end to the weeping. Sil hugged her tight, trying to absorb some of Melia's pain. Melia's shoulders would not stop shaking and soon Sil's blouse was wet from all the crying.

Sil couldn't say how long they sat this way but she knew there was nothing to do but let Melia cry until she was too tired to continue. Sister Maureen peeked into the room once but neither girl noticed. She tiptoed away, knowing such a private moment between the two friends should not be interrupted by strangers.

Finally the heart-wrenching sobs slowed to sniffles and hiccups. Melia's body lay hot and heavy on Sil's shoulder. In time she pushed away and accepted the hankie Sil handed her. Normally Sil would have offered advice and reason, but today she had nothing to say. What words could alleviate the sorrow Melia had ahead of her? Sil had swallowed her own tears in order to be able to comfort Melia what little she could. Melia lowered herself into the pillow. She looks so pale, Sil thought. It's like facing the loss of her daughter has taken all the blood from her body, leaving her colorless and weak – without hope.

It frightened Sil to think Melia might be giving up. "Don't quit fighting Melia. With time this will dim. The Lord will. . ."

"God has forgotten me, Sil. . .can't say I blame him. Truly I want to die. I mean this sincerely. Giving up my baby is more than I can bear." Her voice was flat, without hysterics. "And I'd like to do it before they take her from me and give her to the new parents."

"Don't say that Melia. You'll live through this like all the others have. I'll help you, I promise."

A tiny smile played around Melia's mouth. "I know you would if you could. But you've your own life to live. You can't be helping me through mine."

"Then reach down and find that backbone you've always had. I'm telling you there's a future for both of us to share."

"Go to bed, Sil. You've a long trip tomorrow. You'll need to be rested."

Sil turned and left the room, defeated in strength and spirit. Next morning she stopped in to say 'goodbye' but Melia was sleeping soundly. She placed a small box beside Melia's bed then hurried out to the waiting taxi.

Inside the box was a little necklace with a heart pendant that opened up where two tiny photographs could be placed. The note was simple: "This is for

Charity to keep with her for luck. I hope the new parents will allow it. I've stayed with you through a terrible time. I'll be there for you always. You must be there for me. Love, Sil."

"The greatest gift of my life is the friendship of Sil," Melia whispered and tucked the little box in her purse beside the bed.

Melia didn't die. A week after Charity was born Sister Marie told her the adoptive parents would come for the baby the next day. Melia held tightly to Sil's note. It gave her courage to keep calm. She handed the necklace to Sister Marie. "I know they will change her name but would you ask them to keep this necklace for her? They can tell her it was *their* gift to her when she was born if they want. I'd just like to know it goes with her always."

Sister Marie had grown to love Melia during her stay at the convent. She'd become adept at her studies, particularly in accounting, and she was always pleasant regardless of how poorly she felt. But it wouldn't be right to give her false hope. "I'll pass your message on to them but it is their decision whether or not to accept the necklace."

"Thank you, Sister Marie. I know it goes against the rules and I appreciate your help." She turned into her pillow and cried silently.

Giving up Charity hurt more than a dozen days of labor. More than leaving home. Melia would gladly have suffered the rest of her life if she had her daughter by her side. She cried until there were no tears left – grief so intense that it felt like a hot stone had settled in her chest, reminding her constantly how dearly her irresponsible actions had cost. Nightly she knelt beside her bed and asked God for forgiveness. "Surely my punishment is complete. I've given up my child, my home, and my self-respect. I only ask for wisdom to guide me in the years ahead."

The sadness only deepened. Not a moment of the day passed without her thinking of Charity – her perfect little body, bright blue eyes, and cap of curly chestnut colored hair. Charity hungrily sucked Melia's nipple while her hands kneaded the breast much like a kitten. Afterward she slept soundly in her mother's arms while Melia crooned the lullaby Maxine had sung to her. Melia studied every part of her baby, committing to memory her fair skin, rosy cheeks, chubby legs, and tiny toes. She pretended these days would never end -- that she'd continue mothering Charity throughout her days.

One week after Charity's birth, the adoptive parents arrived for their child. Sister Angela stayed with Melia throughout the morning. She'd done this many times, yet the task never got easier. She explained to Melia that the parents were lovely people, financially well-off and staunch members of their local Baptist church. She could not reveal personal details of the couple – only general facts that would reassure the mother as her baby was taken away. When finally Melia fell into an exhausted sleep, Sister Angela left quietly, saddened beyond reason and wondering how a woman could survive such a loss. She reckoned that while the life of a nun included many hardships, nothing could compare to the heartbreak of a mother giving up a child for adoption.

The week after Charity was taken away, Sister Marie called Melia into the formal office. She felt she was at the will of so many unfamiliar forces: the nuns, adoptive parents who took one's child away; rules of society that shunned unwed mothers; and the harsh retribution for going against the laws of God.

It was only after she sat down that Melia noticed another woman sitting near Sister Marie's desk. Maybe they've brought Charity back, she thought. For a moment her heart sang. I'll keep her this time no matter what God and the community thinks. We'll move away and I'll say my husband died.

". . .so I told her about you."

Melia realized the two women were looking at her strangely. "I apologize Sister Marie. I missed what you said."

"This is Cecile Thompson. She's the manager of Tidball's Department Store down on Main Street. One of their accountants has had to move to Ohio to care for her ailing mother. She's come today to see if one of our girls might be interested in the position. You were my first choice."

Melia turned slowly and looked into the eyes of Cecile Thompson. Her mouth was thin and her nose had a slight hump, but her gray eyes were large and without meanness. Her suit was expensive mauve linen with a pristine, white silk blouse that ruffled down the front. Her hair, which was black with a bit of gray showing at the temples, was cut short and curled over her ears like a cap. Melia's staring caused her to pat at her hair in case something was out of place. The action brought Melia to her senses.

She looked at Sister Marie. "Do you think I'm qualified to do the job properly?"

"Yes. You're the best with numbers we've ever had here."

Melia looked back at Cecile. With the speed of a lightning bolt an answer of sorts had been presented to her. "I hadn't thought to stay in Wheeling but I'd try my best to be a good employee for you."

Cecile smiled broadly. "With such a recommendation I feel Tidball's will be fortunate to have you with us." She strode forward and reached out to shake hands. Melia clasped her hand self-consciously – it was the first time in her life anyone had ever treated her in such a grown-up way. "We've arranged for you to come next week. That gives me time to find you a room and set up a small amount of your first wages to get you started." She turned to Sister Marie. "I shall keep in touch."

Sister Marie nodded. Cecile turned on her heel smartly and walked out the door. Melia looked from one to the other in amazement. In the space of minutes she'd decided not to go home to her family and had accepted a job in a department store doing something she'd never done before. How would she explain it to them? Would they think she no longer loved them? Would they understand that this was a path that could help her feel better about herself again? She would not be subjected to embarrassment by returning to Boreland Springs nine months after she'd left; she could begin earning her own way in the world and send something home as well. Maybe she could work hard enough to overcome the mantle of sorrow that had settled over her shoulders like a heavy winter quilt.

Dear Ma,

When I thought I'd die from the pain of losing my baby, God has sent just a little light to help me carry on. I've been offered, and have accepted, a position in the accounting department of Tidball's, a fashionable store here in Wheeling. Sister Marie and my new boss, Cecile Thompson, have made arrangements for a small apartment that will suit my wages. I'm so grateful for the opportunity to begin to gain a little self-respect. However, I know I'll be unhappy for the rest of my life. I wish God, in His wisdom, would take me now, in my sleep, so I don't have to spend the rest of my life wondering where my little girl is.

I apologize for all the distress I've brought on you and Pa. There's nothing I can ever say to make it right. It's probably better for me to stay away, at least for a few years. You're the best parents a body could have – and I broke your trust. Please forgive me.

Love, Melia

Maxine clenched her jaw to stifle the tears as she read Melia's letter. This will break her father's heart, she whispered. Still, she was proud of her daughter. It took great courage for a girl never before away from home, sheltered by her family and farm community, to decide to stay in a city where the air must be stale and a body would be living right on top of someone else. Her own sorrow at never seeing her first grandchild had caused an ache in her chest that wouldn't go away. It must be much worse for Melia, she thought. I must be strong for her.

Dearest Melia,

Don't talk like that! You'll live through this, even though it'll take a long time to bury the sorrow deep enough so that it doesn't ruin your every day. I'm so proud of you – to get hired at a fancy department store. Making your own money. Pa will sulk for awhile, but he'll get over it when I tell him you'll come home to visit when you can. You will do that, won't you? I couldn't bear it if you didn't come see us.

The train can't be too expensive and we can pick you up in Waverly. Please say you will. As soon as possible. We all miss you and are proud of you at the same time. I'll send some of my fudge that you like – then maybe you'll feel a little bit of home."

Love, Ma

Next morning when she was stirring the fudge, Maxine got lost in wondering what Wheeling looked like. Were there lots of big stores and would Melia be living at one of those boarding houses where everybody ate in the same place at the same time? I hope there are other girls her age there, she mused. Otherwise it could be lonely in a big city.

The furthest away Maxine normally ever went was Waverly. It took a real special reason and lots of planning to make a trip as far away as St. Marys or Parkersburg. By the time Silas and the boys came in from work she had covered up her sadness and enthusiastically told the rest of the family how smart and thoughtful Melia was. She said Melia had promised to write every week and would be sending home half of what she earned. So they talked themselves into being happy that Melia would be working at a real job in a big city.

Sil cried all night when she read Melia's letter telling her the news. She'd waited so long for her to come home. Now it seemed she didn't plan to return at all. Weekly letters weren't the same as talking face to face. "We'll drift apart, I just know it!" Sil thumped her pillow angrily. Once she had vented her fury she took pen to paper and answered the hated letter.

Dear Melia,

Besides being even sadder than usual when I got your news, I'm so proud of you. You've way more courage than I. I know you'll be the best employee they have at Tidball's. Secretly, I hope you don't meet another friend you like as well as me – now it's not a secret, is it?

Nothing special happening here. Please come home to visit as soon as you can. I miss you so much.

Love, Sil

CHAPTER FOURTEEN

"This work ain't fun, Will. I feel like a chicken Ma's scalded and plucked. When can we leave?" Eugene was panting. "I thought Ma was gonna come up."

"She is. Soon as she can." With that, Will strode off to the toilet to end further questions.

Will's patience with Eugene was as thin as the shirt he was wearing. It had taken every ounce of perseverance, along with his mother's persuasion, to coax Eugene to return to Weirton after their visit at Christmastime. Years of concealing illegal stills and midnight deliveries of moonshine had made it possible for the family to keep their arrival secret from the community during wintertime. However, the possibility that Eugene might slip away and visit the Wilkersons or Moores would have been disastrous. Someone had remained with him constantly, conjuring up reasons why it was necessary for him to stay on the Hart property. Imogene and Wilma kept him busy playing pick-up sticks or jacks; Millard showed him the pet raccoon; Vernon and Will took him into the woods to inspect the stills. He was particularly happy about being included in discussions about the business of bootlegging. He felt important, smarter. There were times when he actually felt brave.

His nerve had ended, however, when the time to return to Weirton got closer. One late afternoon Eleanor invited Eugene to sit with her on the sofa in front of the fire. Spending time with his mother without the others around was what Eugene loved more than anything. She was so gentle and always made him feel the same as everybody else.

"Sure am glad you came for Christmas, Eugene," she'd said. "We miss your face at dinner table and church."

"I don't want to go. . ."

She seemed not to notice he'd started to answer. "You've made our lives so much better by sendin' money to buy shoes and food." She stretched her legs toward the fire to warm her feet. "Never thought I'd have sons smart enough to work in a city. Can't wait to see that new red truck."

"Them furnaces are so hot. . ."

She turned and clasped his rough hands in hers. "We're so beholden to you for your sacrifice. Every night you and Will are specially mentioned in our prayers." She saw the look of confusion on his face and cried inwardly at this sweet-tempered soul who had no idea how he would be treated if the law ever caught up with him and Will. "Once you and Will get back and settled in again, maybe I could come up there for a visit."

"Would you Ma? I could show you where we work. You could meet Tyrone – he's from Sistersville. Sometimes he gives me licorice. Then we could go. . ."

Like quicksilver Eugene had forgotten his desire to stay home and was ready to leave so his mother could come for her visit. "Will said we're goin' back tomorrow night. When will you be comin' up?"

"In June. After plantin' and before first cuttin' of hay. How's that sound?"

"Fine. I've got to go tell Will."

She'd watched him hurry away, sadness and anger scribbled in the frown on her face. "Damn that Wyatt. Why'd he have to cause such a mess?" She twisted around to make sure no one had heard her swear.

Eugene's new feeling of worth, along with his excitement over his mother's visit, kept him at work through May. But hot weather, coupled with shoveling coal into the enormous smelting furnaces, had brought him once again to the point of quitting. In the beginning he'd been fascinated by the flames that burned hot enough to melt iron into liquid. As time went on, it was like feeding a great dragon whose appetite could never be satisfied and that meant the job would never be finished.

They were going down to take their weekly bath, so exhausted neither felt like saying a word. Eugene started in again about the only thing he thought about these days.

"Can't take it any longer, Will. My body's burning up inside to out. You'll have to find another job closer home for us to buy the truck and send money home."

Will opened his mouth, but Eugene interrupted. He'd gained a certain amount of confidence since they'd been in Weirton. Working hard, getting paid, being accepted by the others who labored in the unbearable heat, let him know he had an opinion too. He'd done a good job without Will being at his side all the time. Some of the other men bragged about how strong he was – not many could keep up with him when it came to working for long periods without taking a breather for water.

"Don't like all them others waitin' for me to shit. Cookin' don't taste as good as Ma's. Things is too close here. Hardly room to breathe."

"Have you forgotten? Ma said she was comin' up to see us."

Eugene's head shot up. "Did we get the letter?"

"Nope, but I'm expectin' it any day now. Wouldn't want to leave just when Ma's wantin' to see Weirton, would we?"

"S'pose not. But if she don't write soon let's just go on home and save her a trip."

Will was not on speaking terms with God – he believed a man made his own way with his brain and body. That night, however, he fumbled around with a prayer asking for a letter from Ma. Sneaking home in summer would be too dangerous. Days were long then and the hills full of farmers planting, picking, and repairing fences, not to mention the bootleggers who would be relocating their stills. John Mathieson would get wind of their arrival within hours. What the hell am I doin', he thought, askin' help from a God who's busy with important people. He's got no time for the likes of us.

The first Wednesday in June, Will and Eugene dragged their filthy bodies into the boarding house wondering if they'd have the strength to wash up before supper. Hilda, in charge of the front desk, looked up when she heard the door open.

"Will! Here's a letter. Came yesterday but didn't see you fellas since I was busy helpin' out in the kitchen. Becky's off sick." She pulled the letter out of a cubicle behind her and waved it in his direction. "Hope it's not bad news. Letters and phone calls usually mean trouble."

Will wished she'd just give it to him so he could get on up to his room and read it. But he took a minute or two to be neighborly. Never paid to talk short to someone friendly.

"Is it from Ma?" Eugene was jumping up and down wishing Will could get it open faster.

Will nodded.

"What's it say? Is she comin'? When?"

"Yep. She'll be here Saturday." He tousled Eugene's sweaty head in his own thankfulness that Ma would be here in three days. She'd make everything right.

He looked once more at the piece of paper written in his mother's familiar scrawl with a message he'd prayed for. Then he stared out the smoky window into the busy street below, filled with folks as poor as he and Eugene, scurrying hither and thither in their quest to provide for their families. Maybe God does have time for people like us, he mused thoughtfully.

Eleanor put on her new cotton print dress, tightened the garters that held her heavy hose in place and shut the blood off to the rest of her legs, and forced her feet into the uncomfortable black lace-up shoes. She checked her face in the old mirror that had cracked down the middle when one of the kids had knocked it off the bureau, to make sure her hair was in place and her nose wasn't shiny. Then she fitted her little straw hat on and fastened it secure with a long hatpin. If she were just going to church the pin wouldn't be needed, but a long trip meant jostling and she didn't want to look untidy when she met her boys at the train station in Weirton.

Vernon had insisted on buying the dress over at Cleggs in Waverly – he didn't want his wife to look destitute. So he'd taken enough cash out of the metal box hidden under the house to buy the new clothes and the train ticket. He was troubled about her going so far away. She'd never traveled further than Wood and Pleasants counties – neither had he for that matter. He doubted if she'd been to Parkersburg or St. Marys more than ten times during their marriage – and she'd never spent a night away from Boreland Springs.

It was one thing for Will and Eugene to run all over hell's half acre, but women, especially mothers, should stay close to home. What would he do if she got lost? Or was attacked? She was handsome for all her forty years. He'd heard about the terrible things that could happen to women alone. But he knew she had to go. Eugene and Will would have to stay away for a long time. Mrs. Mac had whispered to Eleanor that she'd overheard an awful row between John and Roberta. John had been infuriated when he'd found out Eugene and Will had snuck in for Christmas and left before he'd had a chance to aim his deer rifle at them. He'd promised Roberta that would never happen again if he had to set up camp in the woods overlooking the Hart house.

Vernon knew that wouldn't happen since John spent every waking hour increasing the capacity of his resort. More rooms had been built, more people hired, and John stalked the grounds constantly making sure no one shirked their duties. The hotel satisfied their clientele so well that reservations were being made a year in advance. Mrs. Mac had said she'd heard John instructing Clay to chum-up to the younger employees and listen to who was coming and going in the community, especially around holidays.

On Saturday morning, with a sliver of moon still showing in the cloudless pre-dawn sky, Vernon helped Eleanor up into the wagon and they started off for the early train in Waverly. Few words were spoken. Both worried about such a deviation from their normal behavior but neither wanted to voice their fear to the other. They pulled into the little village of Waverly that was just a afterthought on the banks of the Ohio – a place where short stops were made by steamboats and trains to pick up a few passengers and drop off supplies for the country folk who came to Cleggs to buy provisions they couldn't provide for themselves.

They were fifteen minutes early so they prowled through the old general store while they waited. Vernon picked up some licorice to add to the sassafras Eleanor had bundled up for Eugene. Eleanor bought six big work hankies since Will's letters had told how dirty they got everyday shoveling coal into the huge furnaces. She stared at the little rubber boots that reminded her how fast her children had grown. She'd always had to fasten Eugene's since the closings were too complicated for him to figure out. She'd never minded. He was one of God's special children. She picked up a needle and thread in case there was mending to be done.

Vernon came toward her with a package wrapped in heavy white paper and tied with a string. "Take this cheese. It'll last til you get there." She nodded.

The whistle sounded shrill, unfriendly. The time of departure was upon them. Wordlessly they gathered their purchases and got Eleanor plus her small suitcase to the boarding area. They briefly clasped each other, embarrassed at making such an intimate act in public. Eleanor stepped into the passenger car and found a seat on the left side of the aisle so she could wave goodbye to Vernon. He followed the train's departure with his eyes until only the smell of coal smoke indicated it had ever been there.

She'd never been on a train before. The smoothness with which it covered the ground surprised her – so unlike riding in a wagon that knocked one's innards about at every bump in its path. At first the swaying motion was a bit unnerving, causing her to glance sideways to see if other passengers looked apprehensive. Also, it was loud – deafening when compared with the calm countryside she came from. The thing belched and coughed like a sick cow and smelt as bad as the mineral water wealthy folks paid so much to drink. Furthermore, as far as Eleanor was concerned, the inside of the coach needed a good cleaning. The seats were stained and the floor was layered with dried clay dragged in by farmers' boots.

By the time the conductor announced that St. Marys was the next stop, she was relaxed and confident the trip to Weirton would be made safely. The landscape slid by to the music of the engine and click-click as the big machine wheels crossed each section of track. She dozed, hypnotized by the sight of the Ohio as it rolled on its muddy way to the Mississippi. On her right, after about a quarter mile of bottomland, the steep foothills began their arduous voyage into the interior of the Appalachians.

She sat back and enjoyed a peace she hadn't had time for since she'd gotten married twenty-three years ago when she was barely sixteen. As the miles drifted by her eyes closed and her mind opened up. Twenty-three years! It sounded so long ago yet they had sped by so fast she felt she'd missed a lot of what had actually happened. Raising six children plus helping Vernon on the farm made it necessary to get two hours worth of work out of one. There had been time to enjoy Will: his first teeth; first birthday; and all the other 'firsts' a child has. But when Eugene was born four years later followed by four more in close succession, there was barely time to breathe much less keep track of 'firsts'.

The boys wore out shoes and pants so fast that the usual hand-me-down system never had a chance to work. Knees and elbows poked through before there was money to replace them and mending did very little to prolong the life of trousers that were constantly being worn. During winter months when bare feet made them sick, Eleanor put their rubber boots over top to keep their feet dry. Will had become a surrogate parent to Eugene in those years when it took all her strength to keep track of the others who were into everything.

The girls were easier since they spent more time inside learning the jobs they would need when they were married – although at the time Eleanor needed them for the help they gave to her. They had contests to see who could snap the most beans or shell peas the fastest. She never had to rescue them from climbing too high or pick them out of the creek while still holding onto a water snake like she did the boys. Both she and Vernon were so tired at the end of every day that after Millard was born, neither had the strength to consider producing another child. The marriage had developed into a relationship of mutual respect and care. Before marriage she'd heard this talked about by older women but never believed it would happen to her. She wondered now if there would ever be a time in the future when making love would be tempting.

Yet nothing had been as worrying as this past year. What with Eugene and Will needing to stay away for fear of John Mathieson, she doubted if their lives would ever be right again. How long could this go on? This trip she was making would mollify Eugene for the time being, but she couldn't afford to do this more than once a year. She could tell by his letters that Will was lonely too. It wasn't right – having a family broke up this way. Even in this half-sleep she sweated with the futility of it. She and Vernon had discussed every possible way to solve the problem, but there was nothing to be done except to keep the boys away until they could see a difference in John's attitude. So far, though, his hatred was so fierce that he refused to stay within sight of any of the Harts.

The train slowed and the conductor came through yelling that the next stop was Weirton. Eleanor fussed at her hair much as she could without a mirror and straightened her hose. She wanted to look her best for her boys.

Eugene had been dressed since before sun-up. He kept pacing the floor, clomping around in his heavy work boots until Will's patience was close to breaking.

"It's only six o-clock, Eugene. Ma doesn't get here til eleven. What are you goin' to do for that long?"

"Can't we go down early, buy the flowers, and have a cup of coffee?"

"Flower shop ain't open this early. I'm wore out and you're makin' too much noise for me to sleep." Will turned over in the cramped cot and covered his head with the pillow.

Eugene sat down so hard on the settee that it sounded like one of the supports cracked. Will sat up fast. "Ma has to sleep on that, Eugene! If you break it she won't be able to stay." He knew it wasn't fair to say something that would frighten Eugene but he'd literally come to the end of his tether. "Sit on you own cot and have a look at that picture book we got at Woolworth's. The one that shows the furnaces where we work and the boats that go up and down the river. Ma will want to know all about that."

A huge sigh exploded from Eugene's chest. "Alright." He picked up the magazine put out by the local merchants and started thumbing through the layout that advertised the many businesses located in Weirton. Within minutes, as Will expected, Eugene was engrossed in the photos that showed the streets of Weirton full of people going to work, children at play, and women shopping. In the end, Will had to remind him it was time to get Ma. They picked up the old truck from the storage building that charged them $10 a month to park and were at the station long before the train arrived. Eugene heard the whistle and saw the smoke before Will did.

"She's here!" He jumped up and down like a child.

Will took him by the arm and guided him to one of the benches that lined the boarding area. "Let's sit here and wait til we see her get off."

Eleanor saw her boys as the train glided smoothly into the station. She'd gotten used to the feeling of coming to a complete stop where each car bumped into the one in front of it. She wiped some of the grime off the window so she could study them better. Eugene has thinned down some and Will's more muscled, she thought. They look healthy and their clothes are clean she further noted. Her arms ached to hold them close again.

Will watched his mother step off the train. He'd never noticed before how straight and tall she was. She moved with the grace of a cat stalking a bird. Her bearing caught the attention of others who couldn't take their eyes off this modestly dressed woman whose perfect posture and milk-white skin made them think she might be a princess disguised as a charwoman.

Eugene jumped off the bench and ran toward her, his normally shy demeanor vanished at his happiness at seeing his mother. He nearly knocked her off her feet with his enthusiasm. Will took her arm and her suitcase and kissed her on the cheek. The months of loneliness and homesickness only heightened their need to hold onto each other. Eleanor was overcome again by the dilemma that kept them apart. The only thing worse would be for them to return to Boreland Springs and be shot by John Mathieson.

They drove out of the station in the old vehicle that rattled and threatened to stop at any time. "One of these days we're gonna buy that new shiny one," Eugene reassured her. "Let's take her to Maude's Home Cooked Restaurant, Will. I could use a bite too."

Will laughed and they drove down Main Street to their favorite place to eat on special occasions. Eleanor enjoyed having someone ask her what she wanted and then bring it to her. It was roast beef with mashed potatoes, gravy and green beans on the side. Normal food that somehow tasted better when she didn't have to fix it herself.

After a short time to recuperate and have a look at the sparse rooms where the boys lived, Eugene and Will took her by the arm for a walk around Weirton. Suddenly, a place that had made them long for their home in the country, now gave them pleasure to show to their mother. To Eleanor's amazement, Eugene talked constantly.

"Look there, Ma. See them furnaces blowin' smoke out? That's where we work." Eugene was the proudest Eleanor had ever seen him. "I work longer without drinkin' water than anyone else." He pulled her forward so they could peer through the wire mesh fence that formed the perimeter of Weirton Steel Works. The huge furnaces that jutted from the roof of the foundry, along with the maze of structures that seemed to be built with little sense to a pattern, took Eleanor's breath away.

There were so many things to look at: streetcars clanging loudly as they delivered housewives and businessmen to their destinations; steamboats towing barges up and down the Ohio loaded with products needed on both ends of the line; workers wearing steel helmets and carrying lunch boxes, hurrying to work. She hadn't realized there was a place where farmers were not the main part of the community. So much confusion, noise and smoke. She wondered how anyone ever got used to it. Her eyes watered from the noxious air full of soot that filtered back to ground after being spewed from the smokestacks.

Yelling back and forth was apparently an accepted way of communication. Sometimes the voices were upset – at other times friendly. At home no one would think of being so loud when talking to another person, whether they'd annoyed you or not. Eleanor shook her head at it all. The fact that Eugene seemed at home in all this disorder shocked her. He'd never been able to put up with anything out of the ordinary without hiding in his secret spot in the woods close to where the distilling took place. Many a time either she or Will would go and coax him back to the house. It would usually be two or three hours before he would stop trembling.

She studied his enthusiasm and realized Eugene was now able to function in a more complicated setting than ever before. Even though it took all of Will's persuasiveness to keep him there, it was an advance in Eugene's development she'd never thought possible.

"What an excitin' place to live. Makin' so much money and havin' the other men look up to you. You must look forward to every day."

Eugene's eyes flashed with pride for an instant, then his eyelids drooped. "Only two or three of 'em say that, Ma. And I miss bein' home."

"Lots of men don't even have two others who think they're special. You must be so proud."

"Yeah, but. . ."

"Sendin' all that money back helps me feed and dress the others so much better. They all want to work in a town like this when they get old enough to leave home. Richard and Imogene are already talkin' about bein' like you and Will, livin' in a city where it doesn't flood and the stores are right on the streets, handy and all."

"Leave home. You mean the rest don't 'tend to grow on up in Boreland Springs?"

"They might not go so far away as Weirton. St. Marys or Parkersburg wouldn't be bad. Wilma and Millard are too young to think of leavin'."

Eugene relaxed. "Maybe me and Will could work there, too."

"Right now there's not many jobs available. They don't have the big factories like Weirton. Where you can make such good money and meet so many people."

Eugene's face fell.

"So until there's more places for work at home, I'll come visit now and then. All this experience you're gettin' here will make you and Will top choice when that time comes."

Eleanor had used up all the ideas she had to coax Eugene to remain where he was without giving Will so much grief. She didn't know for a fact that jobs were scarce in Parkersburg – or that Imogene really wanted to live anywhere else. She just knew it was too soon for the two of them to return – and right now it looked like it would be a long time before it would be safe for them to live anywhere near Boreland Springs.

She spent three days with them and even enjoyed a good part of it. The muddy smell of the river and acrid smoke from the steel mills was laced with bakery aromas of sticky buns and fresh baked bread. She looked with awe into windows where ready-made loaves of bread could be bought for a dime – a pittance when one considered how hard it was to travel to Waverly for flour and yeast, then chop wood for her old stove at home just to bake enough bread for a day. They bought some bread and sweets for her to take home on the train. It was cheaper than at Cleggs General Store and the selection was much greater. She was impressed that the money Will and Eugene made allowed them to save half and live off the rest. She chuckled when they showed her the big metal box at the bottom of their trunk where the money was kept.

"Don't trust them banks, Ma." Will explained that most of the men put their wages in a bank and got a little book that was called a checkbook. "They write amounts on those slips of paper to pay for things instead of carrying cash around in their pockets," he explained.. "Me and Eugene would rather keep our money the way Pa does – close to hand. We take out what we need each day and leave the rest safe in the trunk." He was whispering since they were walking down a crowded street and you never know who might be listening. "I don't trust a place that takes your money and gives you pieces of paper that pretend to be cash. We'll just keep on doin' it like Pa taught us."

"I'll tell Pa. He'll be so proud that you don't let strangers handle your hard-earned wages."

Too soon it was time for her to leave. Eugene's eyes got that scared look she dreaded. She put on a big smile and spoke with gusto. "I've had a grand time! I'll bet it's pretty around here in fall – gettin' ready for Thanksgiving and Christmas. Could you come meet me at the station sometime around the middle of October?" She reckoned she'd find the money somewhere for a second trip.

Will nodded with so much enthusiasm his black hair splayed down over his forehead. "Come anytime, Ma. When you're here we get a feel for home that knocks the loneliness back for a time."

She hugged him close. "One day it'll be back like it was," she whispered in his ear. "I just know it. But for now we've got to be patient."

She turned to Eugene. "Maybe you could find me a pretty pot that I could plant my begonias in. Then I could bring them in out of the winter cold so's they'd be ready to grow early in the spring."

The tears that had puddled in his eyes vanished. "There's a place they call a 'flowerist' down by where the trucks are sold. I'll go there and have it by October."

"Could we go back to the bakery, too?"

He nodded joyfully, happy he could do things for his mother that no one else could.

They helped her onto the train. She kissed them both on their foreheads. When Eugene looked like he might sniffle, Will took his arm and suggested they watch as the train pulled out of the station. "We'll stop at the florist on the way back and look at some pots Ma might like."

Eleanor's return trip went smoothly. There were not so many passengers as when she'd traveled up to Weirton. No one sat beside her. Exhausted at the effort of facing new surroundings and using all her tact to coax Eugene to stay where he was, she drifted off into a deep sleep that precluded any dreams of what had happened in the past or what might come in the future.

Vernon had been waiting for nearly an hour. He'd not wanted her to arrive without him being there to meet her. On the way home she explained all that had gone on: that both men (for she now considered Eugene a man) had adjusted to a loud, smoky place and in many ways actually enjoyed the hullabaloo; that Eugene acted more normal than she'd ever known; and while at times he reverted to his fear and loneliness, it was easier to talk him back into a confident attitude. She would tell him later that she'd promised to return in October.

Eleanor was back into her normal work routine the following day, like an old horse in his harness. Richard was planting alfalfa, Imogene and Wilma were tying up the tomato plants, and Millard was dropping onion bulbs.

They were low on all the ingredients to produce moonshine, so Vernon had gone off early in the morning. It was a tedious job since buying in bulk would be suspicious and bring government men sniffing around like hounds after a wounded buck. It would take all day to collect the barley for the malt, corn meal, sugar, and yeast – each from at least three different locations. Most times he didn't get back until well after dark. Some of the coils needed replacing on the still but he'd do that another day.

She leaned over the porch banister and threw the breakfast scraps to the waiting dogs and cats. Looking around the quiet countryside she decided that while the city offered excitement and modern conveniences, life in the hills where she'd grown up calmed her soul and lifted her spirits. She breathed the soft smells of summer deep into her lungs: newly plowed ground; wood burning from someone heating water to wash clothes; the heavy odor of honeysuckle that climbed the banks into the trees above. She had only to make one sweep of her head to see forests of redbud, dogwood, and wild crabapples. Their two cows and two workhorses grazed contentedly nearby. Shrill squawks of agitated squirrels grated the ears while the distinctive voices of whippoorwills and bob-whites obliterated the sounds of more ordinary birds. Close to the well a red headed woodpecker invaded the bark of a chestnut tree in search of the worms within.

No noxious fumes here – or loud dockworkers taking the Lord's name in vain. Only peace. The sounds of forest animals; the dependable oil wells that worked day and night pulling precious liquid from the ground; bees in hives hidden in hollow tree trunks, busy making honey which would be harvested and used to sweeten corn mush and pies.

She wanted to walk and savor this freedom – to reaffirm her commitment to the land and all the labor that living in the country entailed. She'd gladly wash their laundry by hand, do their baking in a wood-burning oven, and make quilts out of worn out clothes. She wanted to smell the sassafras and see how the wild berries were coming along.

Eleanor gave a cursory look at the breakfast dishes, grabbed her gloves, and headed for the blueberry bushes that grew at the edge of their property on the far side of the oak trees. She always walked carefully in the underbrush, not wanting to disturb the creatures that lived there. Her soft moccasins protected her feet and were not so harsh as to destroy a nest of wild turkey eggs.

She passed the still on her way. Soon the dead leaves and dried mud would have to be cleaned away from the apparatus that provided their livelihood. Vernon had told her it would have to be relocated soon since the path was becoming worn enough to attract attention of the wrong people.

The blueberry bushes grew close to the fence that was the boundary of the Hart's land. There must have been twenty or so growing willy-nilly outside of the shade of the oak trees. She hunkered down, careful to put her gloves on since these low growing bushes were a favorite place for blacksnakes to hide. No one killed blacksnakes since they were useful around the farm, being non-poisonous and stalkers of mice that could riddle a corncrib.

The berries were healthy, smooth-skinned and on the way to becoming plump enough to harvest. Her mouth watered at the thought of blueberry pies spiced with rhubarb. A dog barked in the distance reminding her of chores waiting in her kitchen. Reluctantly she stood and turned toward home.

A stick snapped somewhere ahead of her. She stood stock-still and listened. Another sound – this time like a hatchet chopping at a tree. No doubt about it. There was an intruder in the vicinity of the still. She knelt down, hiding behind the heavy underbrush, and crept forward. The sound of chopping became louder. Obviously the interloper did not expect anyone to be around.

Her knees were cramped and her hair lay in a mass of knots from twigs and branches that pulled at her as she made her laborious way forward. When she was close enough to hear heavy breathing and whispered curses, she dared to part the leaves and identify the trespasser.

She looked up to see John Mathieson holding a deer rifle equipped with a scope that enabled him to stalk prey from a long distance. From this vantage point, he was aiming directly into the yard of the Hart's home!

Kay Meredith

CHAPTER FIFTEEN

Fall was one of the most beautiful times in the mountains. Even Wheeling looked and smelled better than usual. Melia woke up feeling better than she had in months. The sorrow of giving up Charity would be a part of her for the rest of her life – like a heart or kidneys. It was the atonement God had exacted for her recklessness and she didn't begrudge Him this penance. Nonetheless, she was thankful that her diligent study in the convent had enabled her to get a good job far away from accusing comments and sideways glances. Only one other girl had secured a suitable situation – the others she had known returned home to face the degradation of having gotten pregnant 'out of wedlock'.

At seventeen, Melia was one of the youngest members of the staff at Tidball's Department store. Her position as an assistant in the Accounting Department allowed her to learn the science of marketing by studying the monthly reports. The company publication listed which sections lost money due to over-ordering and which sections were profitable because the managers were better at judging the buying public.

She'd asked Cecile why some buyers were better than others and how could managers of poor performing sections keep their jobs. Cecile had pointed out that these decisions had to be made at least one season ahead of when they were needed and sometimes it was difficult to know what would be saleable in the next season.

"How do they try to figure that out?"

"By studying current financial conditions, reading magazines from the New York fashion houses, and looking at the pictures in those publications. Then our buyers eliminate the garments that are too sophisticated for this area and order what suits the lifestyle of our citizens here. Additionally, about 50% of our sales are done in the bargain basement, so we must always remember to get the best deals for those customers as well."

"Can I look at those magazines?"

"Of course. You'll find them in the women's lounge. We get new ones every month."

Cecile's eyes had filled with amusement as she talked to Melia. She remembered when she, too, was young and eager to make her mark as a businesswoman. It had paid off. She was Purchasing Manager for the entire store, the first woman to hold this position.. While she'd not married and produced a family she never lacked for escorts to every special event Wheeling had to offer.

"Does one have to graduate from college to advance to such a level?" Melia had asked.

"Not necessarily. The best way is to become an assistant to one of the buyers. This offers the chance to understudy the methods of evaluating current and future trends. In fact, that's how most of our buyers have advanced."

"I'd like to do that."

"I'll keep that in mind when the next opportunity comes up." Cecile had hurried off to settle a sales price in Lingerie.

Melia worked harder than all the others to make up for her youth and inexperience. Within weeks she'd made friends and was included in office activities such as baby showers, birthdays, and retirement parties. The other women adored her and the unmarried men tried unsuccessfully to take her to dinner.

She was never prouder than when she picked up her paycheck. When payday fell on Friday, she was careful to keep the precious check hidden until Monday during lunchtime when she would take it to the bank, get it cashed, and buy a money order for the half she sent home. Every time she mailed that money home she felt like she'd taken a small step at making up for her sinful act that had brought so much heartbreak and embarrassment to her family.

On Monday she and Alicia Mead, who worked in Linens, went to the bank together.

"Don't you have a checking or savings account?" Alicia asked as she watched Melia go through the process of cashing her check, buying a money order, then pocketing the rest.

"No," Melia answered. "What's the advantage of that?"

"Savings accounts increase in value due to interest accrued and the checking account means you don't have to go around carrying lots of cash with you."

"You mean the money that goes into the savings account makes more money the longer it stays there?"

"Yes. Not a lot but every little bit counts."

"Sure does," Melia answered. "Tomorrow I'll come back and get that started."

Melia, in the following weeks, put as much of her half as possible into the savings account and still have enough left for her living expenses. More and more, she began to feel she was as worthy as everybody else.

Eleanor had to wait until early October before she could get away from the farm for a second visit with Will and Eugene. She wiped at the smoky train window but most of the grime was on the outside. She slept all the way, exhausted from canning and butchering. The conductor's shout pulled her from her slumber.

Weirton looked like a hobo down on his luck. Bare trees exposed the ugliness of industrial trash, piles of sooty coal, and stacks of lumber that looked more like sodden cardboard than something intended for use in construction. She was glad she'd brought her old wool coat and galoshes to fend off the chill. Mist from the Ohio River combined with dust from the furnaces had coated the entire city in a sticky brown shroud. A chilly wind drove the cold through the heaviest garments.

One glance at Will and Eugene dispelled her gloom. There they were -- Eugene carrying a bouquet of mums and Will waving his handkerchief to get her attention. Their smiles were so big that all she saw were two mouths stretching from ear to ear.

The disagreeable weather kept them inside making plans for the boys to come home for Christmas. When Eugene was occupied with a catalog Eleanor had brought him from Cleggs she took Will aside and told him about seeing John Mathieson spying on the Hart home.

Will was furious. "I'd like to put a bullet through his black heart."

"Don't talk like that," she whispered, looking toward Eugene to make sure he hadn't heard Will's outburst. "It means that more care than ever must be taken not to let anyone know you've come home," she said. "We'll go to the evening church service for Christmas as usual and watch the younguns say their pieces. You can keep Eugene busy trimming the tree with popcorn garlands."

Will nodded. "I can't believe he's still after us."

"It's only been little over a year. It'll take longer than that for him to forget. Fact is, I don't know if he'll ever give up."

"What'll we do if it's like this for years?"

"Pa and I've talked our tongues nearly out but haven't come up with anything. At least for now, Eugene seems to be settling in here and the two of you are makin' good money."

"Yep, we're doin' that alright. Last I looked there's nearly enough money to buy that truck but don't see no need to spend it on something we don't use much. The old rattletrap does just fine. It'll get us home for Christmas."

During her visit she again complimented Eugene on how much his money had helped her at home – she said she'd bought shoes for Imogene, Wilma, and Millard, with enough left over for high-buckle boots. She promised to fix his favorite pork roast with mashed potatoes and red-eye gravy. He clapped his hands like a child.

"Will it be long before we can come?"

"No," she answered and hugged him as tight as she could.

Two days later Eleanor boarded the train and headed back home. "Well, Lord," she mumbled, "if ridin' up and down the Ohio is to be my lot in life, at least the goin' is smooth."

In November Melia accepted Alicia's invitation to attend the First Methodist Church of Wheeling. She tried to refuse, but Alicia would not be deterred. She thought it would be a good way for Melia to make friends. Melia finally agreed just to get her new friend to stop the incessant talking. After the first couple of times in the big brick structure she began to feel comfortable with God again. The old hymns and responsive readings soothed her. Joining others who asked for forgiveness reminded her that all humans are imperfect.

Attending the mid-week prayer meetings and Sunday morning church services brought her back to the rhythm of life she'd grown up with. It didn't soften her anguish of wondering where Charity was, but it provided her a haven where she could begin to accept her loss with grace.

More comforting than she'd thought possible was her regular correspondence to her home. It made her feel closer – and that maybe constantly writing the letters would preserve a place for her in Boreland Springs in the future.

Dear Ma,

You'll be glad to know I've started back to church. At first it was awkward but the young people are fun, the older members friendly, and the preacher is more realistic than Preacher. Knox. Makes me feel like there are probably more sinners than saints in this world. Still doesn't take away my longing to see my baby, but at least I feel God will accept my plea for forgiveness.

Miss you all. Love, Melia

Dear Sil,

Told Ma I've started back to church – I knew that would make her and Pa feel good. Actually, I'm beginning to give thanks for the blessing I have and try to put my losses to the back of my mind. Most girls in my situation don't have a good job or friends who don't judge me by my mistakes. I'm proud of sending money home and also to making progress in my job. Guess you'll be happy that I'm not so sad anymore.

Still miss you and home. Your letters are among the best blessing of all.

Love, Melia

P.S. Remember your promise to never reveal the father – then tear this letter up. I must know that secret is safe.

Dear Melia,

You've always had the quality to overcome hardships. There will come a time when you'll appreciate the strength you've gained from not letting this mess get you down. Your 'blessings' have come from your own perseverance. Never forget that.

Things are boring here. Usual fall work, not much time for play. Miss you so much.

Your secret will always be safe with me.

Love, Sil

As Christmas got closer, Sil couldn't keep her eagerness in hand. Her footsteps were fast and heavy everywhere she went. She made such a racket in the process of getting her bedroom ready for Melia's visit that Ruth ran to the bottom of the stairs thinking something had fallen.

"What on earth's gotten into you?" her mother yelled at the uproar in Sil's bedroom.

"Getting ready for Melia. She'll be here in less than a week. I can't wait." This was followed by more noise until Ruth thought the light fixture might fall off the wall.

"Do your jumping outside then, before you come through the ceiling."

"I just want everything to be ready. I know she'll spend a night or two with me."

"Sounds more like you're breaking the bed," Ruth replied with a chuckle.

Melia's heart was light as the snowflakes that had begun to fall. Boarding the train to return to Boreland Springs was so different from her desperate journey a little over a year ago. Then, she'd thought the world was ruined forever. During those long months she'd learned that life truly was like the layers of slate, with changes constantly appearing which made things look different from day to day. The dark swirl that was the loss of Charity lay further away from the happiness she felt today. It would always be a part of the pattern of her life but lighter hues were beginning to emerge. She would always be thankful to Granny McBride for her wisdom.

The landscape slid from the industrial area surrounding Wheeling to the rural setting of the counties to the south. The houses were farther apart and the snow, free from wet sidewalks and heavy traffic, stuck to the trees and fields. The late afternoon sun had little warming power, however, allowing cold winter wind to sneak through the window.

Melia pulled her new scarf closer around her neck. It had been the one extravagance she'd allowed herself. The remainder of the money she'd allotted for Christmas had gone to gifts for her family: a leather wallet for Pa; flannel shirts for Harold and Troy, a book by Robert Louis Stevenson for Little Earl; and soft leather gloves for her mother to wear to church. She'd gotten a monogrammed linen handkerchief for Sil – something probably too coarse to use but would be a nice accessory at college. The presents had taken every cent she'd earned for the whole month of December, but next year she intended to put even more money in her savings account.

The train jolted to a stop. The conductor yelled 'Waverly', and suddenly she felt like a stranger. How would the people behave toward her? Having been gone so long, would she be considered an outsider undeserving of familiar talk and a square look in the eyes? Would a lifetime of living here be overshadowed by a year's absence? If she wanted to be dealt with on a familiar basis they would expect her to answer their questions. What should she say: that she'd gone to school or she'd left because she was pregnant? She realized that both were correct. She decided to give the first answer and leave out the second – at least that was half of the truth. With the decision made, she picked up her suitcase and climbed down the steps of the train.

"Melia!" Sil ran toward her, her straight hair flying behind like a dark banner.

They met in a collision of shrieks, hugs, and stumbling to remain upright. Both talked at once, emphasizing their words with elaborate waving of arms. Abner, Sil's father who had driven the wagon in the icy conditions, shook his head and grinned as he watched the reunion. The two were oblivious to the stares and smiles of other passengers who may have envied the bond that only childhood friendship brings about.

Conversation was non-stop and loud all the way back to Boreland Springs. Sil wanted to know what fashionable young women were wearing, had Melia made any new friends, and wasn't it grand to be independent? Melia asked how Sil was faring in algebra, did she mind living with relatives while finishing her senior year, and did she know the exact date of her graduation? When the brightly lit windows of the Conroy house shimmered in the distance, Abner tried to get a word in edgewise.

"We're about there." His words were lost in a bombardment of plans for the coming days.

"I'll come down for you tomorrow afternoon, Melia. Ma and the boys are anxious to see you. You're considered a woman of the world now so everyone wants to know what that looks and sounds like."

Melia shoved on Sil's shoulder like she used to do. "No different than ever. Just a little further along in finding a way not to be a servant to the wealthy."

"That's the spirit." Sil shouted as she helped drag the suitcase to the door, thinking how much happier this was than the last time she'd carried Melia's trunks.

The door opened to mayhem. Maxine hugged her and announced she was thin; Silas commented that he thought she looked healthy; Harold and Troy wanted to know how much money she made; and Little Earl stood quietly by, waiting his turn. She answered their questions as fast as she could then turned to Little Earl. "You've gotten so tall! We can't call you 'little' anymore. From now on it's just 'Earl'."

His face reddened from neck to forehead. Earl had never loved his sister as much as tonight. Maybe now everyone else would look at him as an intelligent person rather than the youngest and smallest of the Conroys. "I'll be ten soon. Am I tall as other ten-year-olds you've seen in Wheeling?"

"Taller," she answered and hugged him so hard he got even redder.

"Missus Lockhart says I'm reading books normally assigned to eighth-graders."

"You didn't tell me that, Earl," Maxine exclaimed. "I'm so proud of you. When did she say this?"

She hadn't called him 'little'. And all because of Melia. "Last week," he answered tentatively, then boldly continued. "My arithmetic is at seventh-grade level."

Suddenly all eyes were focused on Earl. Nonplussed at the attention he normally got only when he was sick, he didn't know what to say.

"I knew you were the smart one in this family." Melia's voice was full of pride. "I may have to return the Christmas present I brought for you and get something more difficult."

All three brothers lost any shyness at seeing their sister after such a long time. Demands to see their gifts rocked the rafters of the little house. Melia shook her head so hard she fell onto the old sofa in a heap with the housedog, Clementine, landing in her lap shortly after. Maxine threw her hands in the air in mock despair and Silas warned them not to throw too many hard knocks at the aged furniture.

The evening was filled with reminiscing where words from all speakers, including Earl, spilt on top of the other. Sometimes it was hard to tell who was talking about what. Melia told Troy and Harold that Wheeling was a busy city with young men comprising the largest portion of the work force. She assured Earl that the public library was so big that even schoolteachers used it as a place to find information. Maxine and Silas were happy when she informed them she was a member of the First Methodist Church and had made many friends there.

Maxine brought her up-to-date on the happenings in Boreland Springs: that Doris Knox, the preacher's daughter, was stepping out with Pete Brady, the oldest son of a family who'd just moved into the area. Talk was that the reverend was not happy about Doris forming such an attachment to a stranger. Melia laughed hard when informed that the Carruthers' sisters had retired from the hotel after inheriting the family farm from their parents, and that it had taken an offer of more money and modern equipment to coax Betty Lou Meeks and Ida Mae Smith to replace them. She was surprised to learn that Mr. Mathieson had greatly enlarged the resort and that advertising in New York City kept the rooms full during the entire warm season and a few even came in October. He'd had to get workers from St. Marys to come in to get all the added work done.

Finally even the talkative Harold began to yawn.

"It's time we all got to bed," Maxine announced and woke Earl from a sound sleep in front of the fireplace. No one objected and Silas was heading toward the bed before anyone could change his, or her, mind.

Maxine helped Melia bank the fire. "It's good to see you happy, Melia. God has answered our prayers in helping you overcome this predicament."

"I don't feel like I've overcome anything, Ma. My heart never stops aching for my child. I feel like a hypocrite for pretending I really did leave to get an education. There are times I think I'm a worse sinner than before I let my baby go." She spoke slowly, carefully choosing every word.

"Preacher Knox always says the Lord works in mysterious ways and won't give us more than we can bear. This is His way of forgiving you."

"I cannot forgive myself. God has nothing to do with it. I'll go to my grave wondering what kind of life my child has lived."

"Don't talk like that, Melia." Worry flashed in Maxine's eyes. "In time you'll realize we did the best possible thing for all concerned."

The frantic tone in Maxine's voice stopped Melia from forcing her mother to think about a situation that, in her mind, had already been solved. "I know, Ma. Let's forget about the past for now and enjoy being back together again."

Maxine nodded. It was an episode best left alone forever as far as she was concerned. The Conroys were truly blessed that Melia's pregnancy came and went with the community none the wiser. Her good fortune at being hired as an accountant had satisfied everyone that Melia had, in fact, gone away to school – and not to bear an illegitimate child. Who else but God could make such a plan happen?

Back in her familiar bed with moonlight filtering through the wavy pane Melia prayed that someday it would be possible to forgive herself. She knew a happy future depended on putting this terrible sin behind her.

Melia, in the following days found herself engulfed in a deluge of greetings, sledding parties, and renewing old friendships. It didn't matter if some curious looks were cast her way or pointed questions asked about where she'd been the past year. She deflected them easily, secure that those who really mattered didn't care what she'd been doing – they were just glad she was back. The holiday raced along as fast as a winter storm. Soon mothers and daughter were asking Melia what was in fashion -- even though none of them could afford such clothes even if Cleggs did have them in stock – which they didn't. Maxine watched it quietly. I'll get no more sidewise remarks at the WCTU meetings, she breathed with relief.

One night, under a clear cold sky and full moon, Howdie Meeks hitched his team up to the logging sled and as many as could, climbed on for the ride. Melia found herself sitting beside Imogene and Wilma Hart. She held onto them tightly so they didn't get jostled off into the deep snow. They hugged her grandly and said how glad they were to see her.

"How are all your brothers?" she asked, curious as to what had happened after she'd told her tale to Will.

"Fine," they giggled. "Richard has pimples and Millard got his first gun this fall."

They made no mention of Will and Eugene. Melia didn't ask.

It was the afternoon of Melia's last day at home. She and Sil had finished a big meal with the Lockharts after which they planned to walk to the Conroy house on Bull Run Road. They intended to follow the familiar trail through Boreland Springs Resort on down to the Conroy house. Sil would spend the night and go with Melia to the train station in the early morning.

With every step through the woods on the Mathieson property, memories flooded Melia's brain. Sil kept her silence, not knowing what to say. Covered under a heavy layer of snow, the spot where Wyatt and Melia had first made love was still recognizable. She hesitated then knelt under the tree that had shaded them. Sil tried to pull her away. Melia shook her head. "I need to remember," she whispered. "Maybe sitting here, recalling the lies he told me and the shame I felt then, the guilt will be washed from my soul."

Her eyes misted and in the frosty air Wyatt's beautiful face swam through her consciousness. She called back the feel of his hands on her cheeks and their moist skin when their hearts and bodies merged for an instant in Time. Although he was fickle and self-centered, Melia knew that in his flawed way, Wyatt loved her. Somewhere in this world there is a beautiful child – the result of that love. She didn't fool herself into believing he would have married her. She wouldn't have asked. One thing she knew for certain: he had cared for no one else as much as he'd cared for her.

She stood up and drew herself tall and straight. "I'm ready to go now, Sil."

Throughout the week before Christmas John Mathieson was obsessed with hunting down Will and Eugene. "I know they're here," he ranted loudly since there were no customers to hear him. "I've been out every night spying on that miserable cabin they live in. Haven't even seen them going to the outhouse. Surely they don't piss and shit all the time in the slop jar."

"Stop such language, John. Your mouth has gotten filthier by the year."

"Don't play high-and-mighty with me, Roberta. You should be happy I'm willing to revenge the death of our Wyatt." He picked up his rifle and strode out.

She stared at his retreating back with eyes as cold as the icicles that hung from the roof. All respect she'd had for her husband had vanished since he'd begun this relentless quest to exact revenge on Will and Eugene. Roberta no longer cared what would happen to John if he actually accomplished his deadly plan – her concern lay with the fate of Will and Eugene. At times she wanted to apologize to the Harts' for John's behavior but she knew that would only fuel his determination. Twice she'd almost gone to Eleanor at the WCTU meeting to advise her that her sons must stay wherever they were until John abandoned this hatred. In the end, she did neither. If he knew her feelings he'd turn against her completely and maybe even ask for a divorce. Then what would she do?

Eleanor and Vernon waved until the taillights of the old truck disappeared into the midnight of the forest. Will, Vernon, and Eugene had spent the afternoon hidden in the shed, fitting the old truck with heavy chains that would get them out of the hills and into Waverly. The farewells had been hushed since sound carries well on a cold windless night. Richard and Imogene had been lookouts to make sure John Mathieson wasn't lurking somewhere in the shadows with his rifle. It was an unlikely time for them to leave – just before midnight on December 24^h. Vernon had reckoned John would expect them to leave after Christmas Day.

Their visit was tainted by John and his buddies who had hunted in the woods near the Hart farm. Vernon, Maxine, and the younger ones had pretended not to notice and the family routine went on as normal. There was no sign that Will and Eugene were anywhere about. At church, Eleanor and the children spoke friendly to Roberta and the younger Hart children took part in the annual Christmas program. Tonight was the final charade – the safe escape of Will and Eugene until next year when another visit would be done in the same clandestine manner. Eleanor had promised two visits to Weirton in spring and fall. Eugene had reluctantly agreed after a serious talk from Vernon in which he emphasized the need for the money they sent home. Vernon was thankful it never occurred to Eugene to ask where all the moonshine money went.

Eleanor's shoulders slumped as she walked beside Vernon into the darkened house. They needed no light to let them know where every article they owned was placed. She could feel Vernon's misery in his rigid shoulders. Both wondered when the need to hide their two oldest children would be over. No need to talk about it. They'd done that for more than a year and found no answer. More talk would only make them feel worse.

Tomorrow the hardships of a farm family trying to survive an Appalachian winter would hit them all in the face like the frost that stiffened their faces now. Every chore was harder: heating water to wash clothes; enduring frozen hands when hanging the laundry out where it would freeze before it dried; milking a cow that held her milk at the assault of cold fingers; feeding livestock in the face of a bone-chilling wind, then chopping ice out of their water troughs; rationing food so it would last until the roads into Waverly were passable.

Eleanor hoped Will and Eugene's hand-me-down boots and overalls would fit Richard. He would be Vernon's main help since Millard was only ten and spindly for his age. The girls would be expected to help with light outside chores such as gathering eggs, feeding the chickens and the outside dogs, and collecting bundles of small twigs for kindling to start the fires in the cook stove and fireplace.

Every year it got harder for Vernon to hike over the rough ground, constantly moving the distilling apparatus. His shoulders hurt after being pulled through spring plowing. Bending over to plant tomatoes, potatoes, beans, peas, and pumpkins left him with a permanent ache in his back. He had little strength left in fall when it was time to cut and stack hay then slaughter hogs. He wondered how he'd make it through another winter. Other men his age had their sons to take over. With Will and Eugene being gone and the others too young, he saw no relief in sight.

They lay down in the bed they'd shared for twenty-two years, too tired to do more than pull the quilts around their cold shoulders and get as much rest as possible before sun-up.

CHAPTER SIXTEEN

The let down after the holidays hit Sil harder than the rest of the family. At least that's how it felt. She envied Melia's exciting career in Wheeling. She renounced the envy, however, when she remembered the reason why Melia had gone to Wheeling in the first place. Sil was in her last year at Williamstown High School. Each Sunday afternoon she traveled from Boreland Springs to the Clancy's, relatives who lived in Williamstown. After school on Friday she returned to her family. It was a schedule that made her tired, melancholy, and out-of-sorts.

Her relations, considered well-to-do by most standards, often made her feel like a burden. She was shy, her clothes were not stylish, her manners lacked refinement, and making new friends came slowly. Her two cousins, Ethel and Edna, snickered behind her back when they thought she wasn't listening. One day they'll wish they'd treated me better, she vowed.

She concentrated on her studies, determined to be ready for college. Teachers, as well as other students, took note of her dedication to make good grades. It wasn't long before her classmates were asking for her help. At first she was fearful of making mistakes and was quick to proclaim her difficulty with math. Eventually, she agreed to tutor Sally Matheny in English Literature if Sally was willing to help her with algebra. Before long the entire class traded off strengths and weaknesses for the good of all. They accepted her as if she was a 'town person'.

"Can you come to my party Saturday after next?" Sally asked.

"I'll have to get permission with the Clancy's to stay the weekend."

"If they don't agree, plan to stay with me."

"I couldn't. . ."

"No excuses accepted," answered the irrepressible Sally. "You're a part of the gang."

Mr. And Mrs. Clancy agreed and Sil packed her best wool skirt the following week.

"Surely you're not going to wear that old thing to the Mathenys, are you?" Ethel asked in a querulous voice.

"Yes."

"Won't you be embarrassed?"

"No."

"You should be."

"I believe they've seen my clothes enough to know I'm not a fashion-plate, Ethel. Odd as it might seem, they may have invited me because I'm good fun."

"Are you being sarcastic?"

"No."

Ethel flounced out of the room without a backward look. Sil watched her departure with a big grin on her face. Probably jealous since she didn't get invited, she muttered to herself.

Sil became part of a large circle of friends that included much laughter and hard work.. She finally began to feel like a part of her graduating class. She knew, however, it was only for the present – that after graduation, they would all go their own way. If some went to West Virginia University as she planned to do, they would travel in more exclusive sets. There would never be a kinship so close as the one she shared with Melia.

As the months progressed toward the end, Sil experienced a pang of fear as she thought of giving up the school she'd attended for the past three years. She was comfortable here. Getting acquainted at a big university was not something she looked forward to. The future was full of uncertainty. Did she have the intelligence and training to attend college? What would she do if she failed?

It was the last assembly of the year and the school was gathering in the auditorium for the presentation of sports and scholastic awards. Sil had no expectations of any such honor, giving her support instead to Sally, who was breathlessly waiting for the High Score in Algebra.

"Honestly, Sally. You have so many fingers crossed, you look deformed." Sally laughed nervously at Sil's comment.

To nobody's surprise Biff Rector was the best football player; Betty Ralston was the top Home Economics student, and sure enough, Sally won the coveted Algebra prize.

"And the most popular student in the senior class is!!!" Principal Cline hesitated until he had the entire audience holding their breath. "Pricilla Lockhart."

The whole senior class stood, clapping loudly while Sally Matheny pulled Sil to her feet and shoved her toward the podium. They laughed uproariously at her bright red face and stammer as she accepted the little round medal. Finally the hilarity abated and Principal Cline got on to more serious business.

"Through the past year," he said, "Mrs. Baylor has kept track of the senior class grades, so as to determine who will be the Valedictorian and Salutatorian for this year." The auditorium was hushed. "First, as to the Salutatorian." He looked up, perusing the spectators as if he'd just realized they were there. "That would be Sally Matheny!"

Sil elbowed her friend in the ribs, encouraging her to move. The normally unflappable Sally was only capable of mouthing a breathless 'can't believe this'. Sil hugged Sally so hard when she returned to her seat that someone had to grab the beautifully framed certificate before it fell to the floor. Pandemonium subsided and all faces waited to see who was the best student of the senior class.

"The Valedictorian of the 1926 graduating class is Priscilla Lockhart – a young lady who is not only popular but smart as well."

The walls shook. Hats were thrown in the air, and an embarrassed Sil walked again to accept an award. On her way she winked at Ethel Clancy.

Melia sat with Sil's family in the auditorium of Williamstown High School. The graduating class of 1926 sat solemnly behind the school principal who would soon to deliver the Commencement address, offering congratulations and advice to the young folks soon to be turned loose on the world. She looked into Sil's shining face, sitting between Lyle Lindamood and Stacie Morgan.

She was so proud of Sil. Of the two of us, Melia thought, she's the one who will make our original dream come true. Melia had long since stopped castigating herself for the path her own life had taken. Today though, just for a few minutes, she experienced a feeling of being left behind when she saw some of her classmates waiting to receive their diplomas. A few of them were eager to get on to college while the rest hoped a high school diploma would help get them into an occupation off the farm. College would never have been a possibility for her anyway, what with three brothers still at home and barely enough money coming into the house for that.

It wasn't too bad, really, when she considered the good job she had in a position that was exciting and provided her with a slightly bigger view of the world. Except for the heartbreak of losing Charity, the whole mess had turned out better than she'd ever thought it would. Enough of that, she reprimanded herself. It's past time for self-pity. Today is Sil's day.

She glanced to her right and out of the corner of her eye she could see Abner and Ruth, people who were like second parents to her. They sat so straight and proud. Ruth dabbed at her eyes now and then. Abner had the biggest smile Melia had ever seen. Further back with the other young men were David and Daniel, who were as close as her very own brothers. How she loved them all and was happy they included her in such a special occasion.

Principal Cline went on about the promise of youth and how it was up to these young folks graduating today to make the world a better place to live. That they must go forward and make a positive influence on mankind since they were the leaders of the future. Melia remembered when her own goals were this lofty.

Since Sil was the Valedictorian, she was required to give a speech to the graduates and their families. Melia knew she'd rewritten it at least six times and was still afraid she'd forgotten something. She came to the lectern with cautious steps. Melia smiled, knowing Sil had a fear of stumbling. Her first words could barely be heard. Everybody strained forward to hear what she was saying. By the time she'd thanked everyone for the privilege of a fine education; assured all faculty and friends how much they would be missed; and given her opinion that there would not be a failure in the entire Class of 1926, her voice could have been heard out on the playground. She covered all her points in about twelve minutes, after which the room resounded with loud applause. Probably because it was so short, she thought as she nodded her appreciation of their enthusiasm and resumed her seat.

It was a long drive home that day, up Waverly Road that ran parallel to the river, then on up to Horse Neck. Conversation and plans were non-stop for Sil's entry into West Virginia University in September. Everybody had an opinion. Ruth thought she should take warm clothes; Abner said she'd need two pairs of sensible shoes and one pair of boots; and the boys thought she should major in agriculture rather than teaching.

"What about you, Melia?" Sil asked. "You might as well put your two cents in."

"I think it's time we withdraw the lucky rabbit's foot from the tree and put it in your trunk for good luck."

David and Daniel howled. "She's probably gonna need that more than the boots!"

Kay Meredith

CHAPTER SEVENTEEN

September 1926, Morgantown, WV

Priscilla Lockhart was one of what seemed like thousands of students who had arrived at West Virginia University the previous week. Like most of the others, Sil was homesick, tired, confused, and not sure whether she could get along with her roommate. Even with a map it was difficult for newcomers to find the proper building since the entire school was nestled in a maze of mountains and lakes. During Orientation the freshmen were warned about infamous Cheat Lake, a body of water whose calm surface belied the treacherous undertows that had claimed many lives.

Female students were warned of the dire consequences of missing curfew, which was ten o-clock Sunday through Thursday and midnight on Friday and Saturday. This was strictly enforced by Housemothers who were either spinsters or widows. Students showing signs of inebriation were quickly reported to the Dean of Women's Affairs. Punishments for this unladylike behavior were posted on all bulletin boards and ranged from losing one's library privileges to being expelled.

Sil was thankful she'd been taught proper table manners at home. Many girls broke the rule of passing dishes directly across the table rather than passing to the left until it made its way round the table. Others had trouble eating with the right hand while the left lay in one's lap. They were expected to dress for evening meals in what Sil considered 'Sunday clothes', leaving her frocks from Cleggs slightly wanting.

None of the male students were restricted by these rules. It seemed as if the faculty reckoned if the women were under close watch, the men couldn't get into much mischief. They came and went as they pleased, threw wild parties, and drank all they wanted. Local girls took the place of college women who had to leave these goings-on just when the fun was beginning.

Sil's roommate, Rachel Biddle, was sorely disappointed in this state of affairs. When Sil had asked which degree she was interested in, "Honey, I'm here for my MRS" was the glib answer.

Sil was horrified. The idea of attending college for the express purpose of acquiring a husband was beyond her comprehension. It took away some of the shine of getting a higher education if there were those who attended such a school with no plan of preparing for a career of their own.

When Rachel inquired as to her field of interest, Sil mumbled something about becoming a schoolteacher. "You'll be wonderful," Rachel said loudly. "If I'd have had a teacher with your integrity when I was young, I'm sure my grades and ethics would have been better."

From that moment Sil knew she and Rachel would get along fine. Few people had such honesty as to admit that a lack of attention to early education and character building had corrupted her scruples.

Rachel pushed every rule to the limit, arriving one minute before the dorm doors were locked and disguising her liquor-laden breath with Listerine. To Rachel's dubious credit, she could hold her booze, whether it was expensive imported brands or local moonshine. She was never one of those who spent time in the communal lavatories throwing up after a rowdy party.

Sil envied Rachel's lack of inhibitions – how wonderful it would be to wear without guilt, gowns that revealed more than they covered. Or make the most outrageous comments without fear of God's reprisal. And every woman in their dorm wanted one of her glass cigarette holders that made even a plain girl look sophisticated.

Rachel was not totally self-absorbed. She was a wild young woman who wanted lots of other souls to party with. For this reason she was more than willing to lend clothes, give advice on proper use of cosmetics, and provide sympathy and counsel to any girl who'd been 'stood up'. Her father was a big-time lawyer in Charleston, the capital of West Virginia, and much of the abrasiveness that comes from such an environment had rubbed off on his daughter.

"You don't have to look so mousy, Sil. You've a great figure. Wish I had a bosom like that." Sil blushed. "You can wear one of my dresses when 'rushing' starts next week. I'll do your hair and makeup too, if you want."

Sil looked at the low-cut, red-sequined dress with longing. She'd only seen gowns like this in the Montgomery Ward catalog and had never expected to wear one.

"Come on. Don't be dull. Say 'yes'."

Sil's face flashed with indecision. Rachel grabbed the chance.

"Come here. Look how beautiful you can be." She pulled Sil to the full-length mirror and stood her up straight. "Here's what you can do with your hair until you have it cut in the cap style that's in fashion now." She took Sil's long dark hair and piled it on top of her head, making it look like a nest of curls. Then Rachel dropped the makeshift coiffure and picked up the gown. She held it in front of Sil. "It'll fit you perfectly. You'll look like a queen of the Nile." She studied intently. "Might have to let that bust out a bit so you don't fall out of it."

Sil hesitated. "I'm not sure. . ."

"You'll be fine. We'll go together. Just do everything I do."

Nevertheless, Sil intended to wear a light shawl over her shoulders to retain a small amount of modesty.

When Sil and Rachel walked into the elegantly appointed house, the officers of the sorority nodded discreetly in approval. They were the kind of girls sororities wanted to receive into their influence – especially the tall one with the flaming red hair. She carried her flamboyant costume with grace, a characteristic sought after by associations known for supporting the 'modern' woman. The risqué dress of the quiet dark-haired girl seemed at odds on one whose solemn personality was not disguised by the low-cut red gown and upswept hairdo. However, seriousness was also a character needed to make a well-rounded club, therefore Sil was high on the list of new inductees.

Sil spent a week following Rachel from house to house, fielding questions about where she came from, what did her father do, and was her mother a member of the Ladies Auxiliary? She felt like a piece of meat being inspected for freshness. The borrowed dresses itched, she constantly stumbled in the high-heeled shoes Rachel insisted she wear, and the smoke from cigarettes made her eyes water. Conversation was not interesting and the charters of these organizations seemed to be an introduction into the clubwomen they would become after graduation. In her opinion, sororities had very little to offer when compared with the time and money they demanded from the member.

Sil was disillusioned by the attitudes of most of these girls. She doubted if one of them would ever put to use the education they would spend at least four years earning. Sororities were expensive, therefore most members came from affluent homes -- and they'd brought their arrogance with them. Eyebrows raised in disapproval when Sil mentioned that her father was a farmer and that she wanted to become a schoolteacher like her mother. Her name slid lower on the suitability list.

On Monday the bids were sent out, placed with the proper degree of fanfare in the mail slots of all the girls who'd trekked through a week of 'rushing'. Much shouting and crying could be heard in every dormitory on campus. Sil was appalled at how devastated some were when the sorority of their choice had not sent them a bid. How could any social club mean so much in an institution of learning? She opened her mailbox and found three bids. They were invitations for parties to welcome new members into the fold. Accepting one of these expensive summons would mean four years of conforming to uncomfortable clothes, pompous mind-sets, smoky rooms, and little preparation for a career other than that as the wife of a wealthy man.

"What bids did you get?" It was Rachel running toward her waving a handful of envelopes in the air.

Sil quickly shoved her envelopes into a nearby trashcan. "None. Can you believe it, Rachel? Guess they didn't like my hair."

"Don't worry. We have another chance next semester. By then, I'll convince whichever club I choose to accept you."

"I'll survive without a sorority, Rach. Come on, let's go have a hot chocolate."

They walked together toward the dorm, Rachel jabbering about how she'd get Sil into a club if she had to get her father to pull some strings. Sil was relieved that she wouldn't have to cut her hair in the cap style that was so fashionable now.

She didn't fit in anywhere, it seemed. The place was too big, everyone else seemed better prepared for college-level studies, and there were too many people. How could anyone find answers to questions posed to professors whose attention had to be divided between so many other students needing attention as well? Sil was accustomed to small classes where the teacher had plenty of time to explain concepts that were hard to understand. She especially needed help with mathematics -- but so did everyone else.

Dear Melia,

I hate it here. I can't make friends with all these people – I'm too shy to even speak to the person sitting next to me at dinner. Many girls, my roommate included, are only looking for a husband.

Could you find me a job in Wheeling? Otherwise, I might have to return to Boreland Springs and marry someone familiar, either a farmer or bootlegger. Don't know if I can face the shame of failure though – Ma and Pa are so proud of me going off to get a college education.

I'm probably too argumentative to suit any of the fellows back home anyways. I could use some advice about now.

Love, Sil

Dear Sil,

What a shame you're as cowardly as I was. When I said I couldn't bear the shame and embarrassment of my predicament, you reminded me that, like those who've gone before, I had to face the future with courage. You made me realize I was luckier than most in the situation. That regardless of the challenges I must never stop overcoming the obstacles in front of me.

Sounds like you're on the verge of quitting! How can you possibly think of such a thing when you forced me to go on? Here's my advice: 'Reach down for that backbone you've always had!' Remember saying that to me? It plucked me out of my self-pity and helped me walk into my future without allowing sorrow to defeat me

It's about time you do the same! I'm reluctant to say my misery was worse than yours, but there it is. Don't let yourself be derailed because you're having trouble making the straight A's you did at home where you were coddled and encouraged. That can't compare with having an illegitimate baby and allowing it to be adopted by strangers.

You're intelligent and determined. What more do you need?

I'll see you at Christmas and know I'll be congratulating you on making the Dean's List. Otherwise, which one of the 'familiar farmers or bootleggers' have you got your sights on?

All my love, Melia

P.S. Can't believe I'm beginning to sound as high-minded as you.

At first Sil was furious – what kind of advice was that? After reading the last sentence a second time she doubled over laughing. Rachel ran in wondering what was so funny.

"Nothing much. Just some crazy advice I got from my 'sorority sister' in Wheeling."

"Is there a sorority in Wheeling?"

"A very small one I joined when I was two."

Rachel shook her head, checked her makeup, and hurried off to meet the latest boyfriend. Sil sat down at her desk.

Dear Melia,

Thank you for your sensitive counsel. Since my entire wardrobe was bought for the purpose of going to college; I'd have to milk cows and carry firewood if I returned home; and I'm too healthy to die, I've decided to forge boldly into my future with as much flair as I can manage with hair and skirts that are unfashionably long. Can't wait to see you at Christmas!

Love, Sil

CHAPTER EIGHTEEN

January 1927

The holidays came and went much the same as they had for the past three years. Will and Eugene had once again made their winter trip to Boreland Springs under the dark of night; Sil had just barely made the Dean's List due to a 'C' in math; Melia had gotten a raise in her salary; the business of bootlegging was more profitable than ever; and John Mathieson was biding his time.

In Morgantown Sil had signed up for tutoring classes in math. It was a free service offered by the university and conducted by graduate students. Her sessions were scheduled on Tuesday and Thursday evenings at 7 p.m. Rachel couldn't understand anyone being so obsessed with getting a 'B' when a 'C' was perfectly acceptable – even a 'D' now and then could be tolerated. The girls, so opposite in their outlook, had become good friends. Both admitted they would miss each other when Rachel went to live in the sorority house at the beginning of her sophomore year. Rachel assured Sil that was only temporary since women accepted after their freshman year were allowed to move right into the sorority house – and Rachel was determined that Sil would become a member of her sorority.

Sil hurried down the endless steps and ran across the campus lawn to the library. She was late. Dinner had taken forever. Sticking to the precise rules of Emily Post's etiquette made it tough to be on time for evening commitments. She wanted to make a positive impression and arriving after the bell was not a good beginning.

Just as the late bell jangled she shoved through the heavy door and slid into a chair at one of the tables in the back of the room. Every head turned in her direction. Her hair, damp from the January mist, along with her heaving chest at having run across campus and through the library, caused the student to her right to go to another table.

"Probably a member of the girls softball team," the instructor muttered with a sour expression.

His name was Christopher Nelson and he was in his first year of graduate school. Serious and with very little money, he'd paid his way through the first four years by working in the dining room. He was majoring in Agricultural Engineering.

"Just a fancy name for 'farmer'," his father had said when he'd left the family farm near Clarksburg. "Only education you need is what you've gotten all these years workin' here."

"There are more scientific ways of doing things now, Pa. Technologies concerning land rotation, health practices that keep down loss of livestock, and fertilizer that produces bigger crops are just a few of the new methods to make a better living off the land."

"Hogwash! Farmin's been done for generations without all them new-fangled ideas. You'll just be spendin' time and money for things you already know."

"Maybe, but I've got a job in the men's cafeteria to pay most of my expenses. The rest will come from what I've saved from selling the cattle you've let me raise."

Edmond Nelson reddened. "Don't come tryin' to borrow money from me when you've spent all yours learnin' stuff you don't need to know."

Christopher had loaded his meager supplies into the farm wagon and his father drove him to the bus station. They shook hands and Christopher said he'd be home for Christmas. "Yer Ma will be glad to hear that." They parted on uncertain terms. The ensuing years had continued in this manner: Edmond treated his son offhandedly, making light of his intense need to study while his mother supported his spirit, encouraging him not to let go of his dreams. Every month he received a money order from her for the amount she'd brought in from selling eggs.

She lived to see him graduate. Edmond was goaded into making the trip in their old Model T so Elizabeth Nelson could be there to watch her son receive his diploma and be applauded for being in the top ten percent of his class. The following month Christopher rode home on the bus to attend her funeral. After struggling with her health long enough to see her son educated, she finally succumbed to tuberculosis. He doubted if anything could ever sadden him so much again. He rarely went home after that, preferring to remain in Morgantown working through the summers to earn money for the coming semester.

Now he was into the last stretch and tired of spoiled students trying to slide through on barely average grades. He especially resented the ones who didn't even have the courtesy to arrive to class on time.

"Your name?" His voice was unfriendly.

"Priscilla Lockhart." She hoped the heat in her face was not visible.

"Do not make a habit of being tardy Miss Lockhart. It takes valuable time away from the others who are serious about improving their math grades."

"Yes, Mr. Nelson."

At the end of class Sil waited patiently beside Mr. Nelson's desk until he finally raised his head. "What do you want?"

"To apologize for being late. I ran as fast. . ."

"Don't make it worse with excuses, Miss Lockhart. I can't abide treating education as though it were a bauble to be plucked at will. Some have to work very hard for the privilege of being at this fine university." He turned his attention back to correcting papers. Sil swallowed hard. He looked at her again. "Is there something else?" His voice had a condescending tone.

"No sir," she replied.

He watched her walk away, back stiff and hair swinging like a pendulum in time with her hurried steps. He shrugged his shoulders and got back to work.

"What on earth is wrong with you?" Rachel asked when Sil stomped into the room and threw her books on the bed.

"Mr. Nelson. He's the instructor for those of us in remedial math. I barely made it in under the bell and he thinks I'm spoiled and unappreciative."

"Why does his opinion matter?"

"With his attitude toward me I doubt if he gives me any help – and I need it desperately."

"Is there no one else?"

"I checked. He's the only one this semester."

"Then grin and bear it, girl. A semester isn't that long."

". . .and quit that frowning. It makes wrinkles."

Sil laughed and hugged Rachel. "You're right as usual, Rach. Anyway, I can always copy the notes of whoever sits beside me."

Wheeling always looked best in spring and summer. Lush trees and abundant flowers concealed the dinginess that lurked after a winter of potholes and mud. Ladies tried on the new summer fashions, young girls looked for the scantiest swimsuits, and mothers shopped for their babies who'd outgrown the past year's clothes. Tidball's had hired more help to keep up with the rush.

"It's a wonderful opportunity, Amelia. You'll be in charge of purchasing lingerie which doesn't take nearly so much insight as street wear." Cecile paced nervously back and forth behind her desk, knocking the ashes off her cigarette from time to time. She saw the uncertainty in Melia's eyes. "Tilly will be here to help you until she's in her seventh month. . . .and of course I'm available before then in the event she's plagued with morning sickness."

Melia sat quietly, her hands clasped in her lap.

"Amelia, this is not a position where you will endanger the financial security of Tidball's if some of your choices don't sell right away. What's so complicated about underwear? It'll sell sooner or later."

"It's different from keeping accounts and reading the monthly reports, Miss Thompson. I'd be afraid. . ."

"For God's sake. Just purchase what *you* like to wear for the younger women and what your *mother* would wear for the mature women. You'll have lots of supervision to guide you." Cecile exhaled thoughtfully. Smoke curled around her face like a halo, at odds with her intense devotion to worldly goods. "It would be a mistake to turn this chance down. Once an employee does that, the company rarely offers again." She turned to face Melia. "It's your decision."

Consequences of previous hesitancy shot through Melia's memory like thunder. She stood up and shook Cecil's hand. "I accept, Miss Thompson. Advancing in the company is what I've hoped for from the beginning and I intend to make you proud of me."

Dear Sil,

 Just got a promotion – in charge of buying for the lingerie department. Good increase in pay. My savings account is looking better and better. Tell me what kind of underwear you like so I know what's 'in' with the young crowd. Ask your mother what she likes so I know what the older women wear. Sure would help. Maybe I won't buy too many wrong things.
 I know you're doing better in math because that's just how you are.

Love, Melia

Dear Melia,

 I knew you'd be successful because that's just how you are. I'm so proud of you. Am enclosing pictures from catalogs that my roommate, Rachel, gets. It shows everything any female, regardless of age, would want.
 I'm struggling with math but managed to pull a 'B' at mid-term. My instructor wastes very little time on me since he's decided I'm frivolous and unappreciative of my education. Will tell you more about this toward the end of summer when I'll be home for a couple of weeks.
 That brings me to another announcement. I'll be staying here for summer classes – I want to finish in three years if possible. Will also take a job working on Saturdays at the drug store to pay for incidentals. At Christmas I overheard Mom and Dad planning to get a loan for my tuition so must do as much as possible to earn my own way. Will probably go home for a week or so during August.

Love, Sil

Kay Meredith

Dear Sil,

So sorry to hear that you'll have to work through the summer. I'll plan to come home for a vacation during August so we can visit eye to eye. Let me know the exact dates once you've made up your mind.
Meanwhile, we're getting pretty good at writing letters.

Love, Melia

Math had not gotten to the point where it was easy for Sil. Thank goodness my other classes are relatively easy, she thought, as she stumbled through another difficult assignment.

"Come on Sil. You need a break from all that studying. A bunch of us are having a swimming party and wiener roast at Cheat Lake this Saturday."

"Can't Rach. My grades are more important than a party right now. I'm trying to pass math so I don't have to do the remedial thing again."

"Please."

"It would be fun, I know. But finances are difficult at home. I'm going to spend the summer here taking classes that will get me to graduation in three years instead of four. Overheard my folks talking at Christmastime about getting a loan to keep me here. I can't afford another 'C'."

"If you join us I'll introduce you to fellows who come from wealthy families and are looking for a serious young woman who also happens to be beautiful. That's what they all want when it comes time to marry."

Sil shook her head. "Can't put my hopes on something as unreliable as your certainty that my 'beauty' can attract a man with enough money to take care of me. Those guys always get a new wife when they're forty anyway. Thanks anyway though."

It was midnight the following Saturday when Morgantown was awakened by the sound of screeching sirens and vehicles careening through the narrow streets. Sil lurched out of bed.

"Rach. Wake up. Something must be on fire!" She switched on the light and started grabbing clothes. "Rachel, get up!" Hearing nothing Sil went to shake her. Rachel's bed was empty.

The dorm was filled with the noise of feet running through the hallways. Voices were shouting, asking what was going on. Sil joined the melee. They ran to the balconies and watched as lights turned on in all the buildings. An ambulance rushed by. "It's headed out toward Cheat Lake," someone said. Fear clutched Sil's stomach. Please God, she prayed, don't let it be Rachel.

By morning the news had spread like wildfire through the town. A group of students having a wild party out at Cheat Lake had gotten drunk. One of the girls displaying her expertise at dancing the 'charleston', had lost her balance, fallen off the pier, and had not been seen since. Dragging operations had started at first light. The name of the missing student was being withheld until her parents could be located.

Sil knew who that student was. Rachel, one of the kindest, albeit rowdy, persons she'd ever known, drifted somewhere beneath the calm surface of Cheat Lake. It was beyond belief that one so beautiful and vivacious was gone. With all her material comfort she was always ready to help anyone who wanted to look or feel better. Sil had always thought of her as an exotic bird that flew higher and farther than anyone else.

When her body was found on Monday, her parents were already there to make arrangements to take her home for burial. Sil was glad. She couldn't bear looking at beautiful Rachel laying white and still in a coffin. She wanted to remember her as she'd last seen her: laughing uproariously, dressed in green sequins, running off with a bottle of Tom Collins clutched in her hand, to her friends and the bonfire.

On the following Sunday morning, while most of the student body was either sleeping or attending church, Sil went to the library. It was the only place of privacy on campus. She found a quiet corner on the second floor and sat down. She laid her head on the desk and wept silently. Only her shaking shoulders were evidence to the depth of her sorrow.

She didn't hear the steps behind her. "Can I help?"

The question went unanswered. A light touch to her shoulder stopped the sobbing. She hastily wiped her face with the hankie she'd brought along. When she finally looked up, it was the concerned face of Christopher Nelson looking down at her.

"Excuse me. I know this isn't the place to grieve but I thought there'd be no one here."

"Normally there isn't. I had to do some research for class tomorrow. That's why I'm here." He sat beside her. "Why are you so sad?"

"It was my roommate who drowned. I can't stay there anymore -- it's so lonely." She didn't care if it was the difficult Mr. Nelson. At least it was someone, and Sil really needed to be close to a living person right now who might be willing to sit and not ask questions.

Her heartfelt sobs were at odds with the self-absorbed girl he'd thought she was. He didn't know what to say so he just sat close enough to touch her arm. It was a long time before the crying ceased.

She blew her nose and pushed her chair back. "Thank you for staying with me. I'm ready to go back now."

"I'll walk with you."

"What about your research?"

"I can do that later. It's not such a big deal."

They walked wordlessly through the library and out onto the campus. It had just been mowed leaving the air filled with the wonderful smell of newly-cut grass. Sun sparkled off windows and dew-covered flowers. There was no evidence that the university had lost a student and Sil had lost a friend. They walked beside a game of croquet and further to the right a softball game had attracted a big crowd of spectators. No one seemed to care that Rachel was dead. They've forgotten so quickly, she mused. "It isn't fair," she whispered. "They should be too sad to play."

"Don't blame them, Priscilla. They didn't know your roommate."

"Some of them did." Suddenly she needed to be home – to see her family and know that that part of her world was still intact. She started to sniffle again.

"Let's sit under the tree over there," he said.

She let him guide her to a shady spot under an oak tree. When once again she was quiet, he walked with her to the dorm and wouldn't leave until she promised to have a quiet dinner with him.

"Isn't that against the rules?"

"We'll do some work on remedial math. Sometimes rules have to be stretched when circumstances demand it."

Sil was flabbergasted that the proper Mr. Nelson was willing to 'stretch the rules'. For a moment Rachel's death slid to the back of her mind.

The only restaurant open on Sunday evening was a little place that specialized in a 'meat and potatoes' menu. The booths were oilcloth and the waitress was tired. Christopher wished she wasn't chewing gum while she took their order. *I doubt if Priscilla even notices*, he mused.

"Do you want to talk about it?"

She shook her head and picked at the mashed potatoes and gravy.

"Will you be able to perform properly in your classes with so much sadness draining you?"

She wasn't surprised that his main focus was her studies. He knew better than most how badly she needed good grades. "I have no choice. My folks' budget is stretched to the limit so I've decided to attend summer school. I'd like to finish in three years so they don't have to take out a loan to pay for all this." She didn't feel like talking, especially when it came to explaining embarrassing family problems. But he'd been so helpful -- he was entitled to know why she was so driven.

"Is there any way I can be of help?" He remembered his own melancholy when his mother passed away and how easily it affected one's ability to concentrate.

"You've been more than generous." She realized what a thoughtful thing he'd done for someone he didn't respect very much. "I apologize for my lack of manners. I've dwelt in my own grief and not thanked you for being so kind to me."

He shook his head. "No trouble at all. I know what it's like to lose a loved one." She'd regained some of her color and her voice was brighter. "Would you like to walk back now?"

She nodded.

The tension drained from her body as she walked beside him. Her steps were long and supple. How ironic that he'd been the one Fate had chosen to pull her out of her quagmire so she could get back on firm footing again.

"Goodnight Priscilla. Please try to get some rest. You'll need strength for the program you've set out for yourself."

"I will. Thank you again. You have no idea what a help you've been to me."

They shook hands. He turned back toward the library. She lifted her chin and strode forward to where she and Rachel had lived.

Throughout the summer they passed each other as they rushed through their hectic schedules. While Christopher's friendly 'hello' made Sil feel good about his more positive impression of her, she hoped it would not be necessary to take remedial math again. He noticed she'd lost some weight and hoped it was due to the running she did to get where she needed on time as opposed to anxiety over how quickly life can change.

CHAPTER NINETEEN

"Can we take Ma on the ferry over to Ohio and back?"

"That's a good idea, Eugene. I think she'd like that."

"Than can we take her to the park?"

Will smiled. "We'll have her so wore out she'll be too tired to come back in the fall."

Eugene looked up, his eyes full of concern. "Don't wanna' do that, Will. Maybe we should just stay here in the rooms."

"I was kiddin'. She'll love seein' things and eatin' where somebody else does the cookin' then sets it in front of her."

It was June and Eleanor had been more than ready for a visit with her 'boys'. The trips to Weirton had become something she looked forward to. One day when Imogene and Wilma were older she wanted to bring them along. The city no longer frightened her. Between trips she kept a list of items to purchase that were not available at Cleggs. Vernon was more than happy to pull out enough money for these little luxuries. Between the moonshine money and what the boys sent home, his stash had become large enough to require a second metal box.

It was fun for Will and Eugene as well. It made them proud to take her to places they thought she'd like, such as the library and museum. She no longer had to coax Eugene to stay. He'd grown into his new environment and liked being the same as the other men – almost. He'd never be exactly like most of the men but he'd met others who were very much like him – souls who fell into the 'below average' category but were still able to make a living and form relationships.

"Eugene's confidence is almost worth your leavin' home," Eleanor said to Will while Eugene was taking his weekly shower. "I've prayed since he was born that God would see His way clear to help him fit in better. It took all this mess to bring it about. He certainly does work in mysterious ways."

"One day I hope we'll be able to come home and hold our heads up. I'm lonesome for old friends and quiet hills. It don't seem right for one old man to keep us away. But the web's too tangled to get the law in on it."

"He can't live forever. All that hate he's holdin' in is bound to bring him to grief sooner or later."

"I wish it'd be sooner." Will sighed and helped his mother pack her things for her return to Boreland Springs tomorrow.

Eleanor pretended not to hear the blasphemous comment.

Summer came and went at Boreland Springs. Sometimes it was hard to believe time passed so quickly when it seemed to take so long to get all the work done.

It was Wednesday morning and already hot. Vernon looked over the hayfield that he should have mowed two days ago. Fall rains will start soon, he thought. I've got to get it down today so it can dry before it gets wet. Then it'll be ready to be stacked by Saturday or Sunday. He looked toward the shed where Maude stood placidly munching her alfalfa. He should harness her up and get busy – before the humidity made the heat even more unbearable. The barn looked so far away. He forced his feet toward the work that waited for him. The back door slammed and Richard and Millard came out, hitching up their overalls and brushing hair out of sleepy eyes. Vernon was thankful for their help.

They worked all day – mowing hay and repairing the still. Eleanor and the girls carried water to relieve the thirsty workers. Millard, fairly young for such hard work, needed more rest periods than Richard, who at fourteen was nearly full grown. By twilight everyone sat down at the supper table -- too tired to do other than eat what was passed to them. The entire field was mowed and lay like a silk blanket in the dying afternoon sun. Vernon planned to go up and double-check the distillery apparatus before he went to bed.

"If the weather holds up we should be able to stack that hay by the weekend," he said when he came back in the house after dark.

Millard and Richard nodded unenthusiastically. By the time all the hay work was done, they knew it would be time to prepare for fall slaughtering. In addition, the stills had to be minded daily. Orders had increased.

"Sure could use Will and Eugene," Millard said wistfully.

The next two days were spent working on the stills and loading the truck with moonshine to be delivered Monday night to Satterfields. Saturday

Affair at Boreland Springs

and Sunday was spent stacking hay. We got it done, Vernon thought. Might be able to rest a couple of days before I have to plow the garden under. He could smell Eleanor's strong coffee. He followed the aroma toward the kitchen. At the back steps his feet felt like lead. He couldn't lift them. Eleanor heard him grunt followed by a crash into the handrail. She dropped the coffeepot and ran.

Will fought though the fragments of sleep, trying to get to the incessant pounding on their door. It got louder. Someone was yelling. He pulled the sheet around his naked body and stumbled out of bed. He struggled to get the crooked door open.

"This telegram came for you in the middle of the night. Says it's urgent." Cornelia handed Will the envelope then hurried back down the steps to the front desk.

Will dropped the sheet and tore it open. He'd never received a telegram before. His fingers fumbled and his heart was beating so fast he could almost hear it. The words stunned him. 'Pa had heart attack. . . .Come soon as you can. Ma.'

Few words were spoken as Will forced as much speed as possible out of the old truck that had been worn out when they bought it. Sure could use that new one we talked about buying, he thought, but said nothing so as not to alarm Eugene. He'd simply told his brother that their Pa had a chest problem and Ma needed them home to help with chores. Eugene had been elated, saying he'd wanted to go home anyway.

John Mathieson stopped in his tracks when he heard the soft voices. Whispers made him suspicious. He backed behind the bushes. It was two of the gardeners from down on Bull Run Road – he couldn't remember their names. But he'd never forget what they said.

"Did you hear 'bout Vernon Hart?"

"Yep. Heart attack. Hope Will and Eugene make it home before he dies."

"Is it that bad?"

"Heart attacks is always bad."

John was flooded with a feeling that vindication was near at hand. It had been such a long time coming that he hardly knew what to do with the sensations running through his mind and body. He felt like a mountain lion ready to take down its prey. His thoughts ran forward faster than he could keep up with them. He forced himself to breathe slower so he could make plans.

Deer season starts on the first of October. I'll call Harvey and the gang now, he mumbled. They're always ready to try out their newest weapons. We'll plan several expeditions. There will be many shots and undoubtedly many misses. Sooner or later, Will Hart will be at the business end of one of my bullets.

Sounds like Vernon isn't long for this world either he laughed inwardly. That'll leave Eleanor with a brood of kids to bring up without a husband or older son. Maybe there is a God after all, John thought. I'll be the first one on the Courthouse steps when their land goes under the gavel for non-payment of taxes. He slipped out of his hiding place and quietly walked into the hotel.

He was in no hurry. He knew Will and Eugene wouldn't be leaving their Pa's side and upon his death they would remain to be the breadwinners for the rest of the family. His steps were lighter -- his breathing easier. An enormous weight had lifted from his chest.

Vernon slept lightly, never really waking up nor falling into a deep sleep. He was aware of voices, sounds, and smells around him but had no energy to see what it was all about. He swallowed the food he was fed him with no knowledge of what it was. He had no strength to help Eleanor and the girls when they raised him to use the bedpan. They asked questions that he understood but had no power to answer. Somewhere deep in his mind he hoped they were getting along without him. He'd done his best. Someone else will have to carry on, he thought, surprised that there was no guilt attached to the admission.

New voices filtered through the fog he lived in. Familiar. Loved. Not often heard anymore. He squinted his eyes, hoping that would help his hearing.

"Will he live?"

It was Will. Why was he here? He should be in Weirton with Eugene. If John Mathieson gets wind of this they're dead for sure. He tried to sit up but only his fingers fluttered slightly. He tried to talk but not even a whisper came out of his tired mouth. He tried to open his eyes but they remained closed, like windows painted shut.

"What's wrong with Pa?"

That was Eugene. Even in his dazed condition Vernon could hear the fear in Eugene's voice. Whatever the answer was it was given so quietly that there was no sound. I must be nearly in my grave Vernon thought. Ought not leave before I've had a chance to say 'goodbye'. But no amount of determination would raise his head or open his mouth. He tried to remember how old he was. The number didn't come to mind but he reckoned he was too young to die. What's happened to me, he wondered? He got lost in his mind trying to recall what was the last thing he'd done.

He wanted to yell at these folks, his family. Tell them he wasn't a fool – that he could hear every word they said if they spoke loudly enough. Don't treat me as if I'm already gone. Can't they see when I try to open my eyes that I'm conscious? That I'm just too tired to talk?

Will sat carefully on the side of Vernon's bed and took his father's thin hand in his own callused one. He'd never considered life without his parents. He knew death eventually claimed everyone, but the Hart family was known for longevity. He'd expected his parents would be around until he was old enough to go on without them. He wasn't ready yet. It was too soon. Millard wasn't even twelve and Wilma barely thirteen. They needed their father.

He forced himself to look at the man lying beside him, engulfed by the quilts that kept him warm. It was hard to believe this was the same man who worked tirelessly day in and day out plowing, mowing, bootlegging, logging, repairing, or building. Will couldn't recall his father ever being too sick to work.

Will looked into the face of his father and saw a man who had simply worn his body out. Proof that health and strength didn't last forever – that if neglected or overworked, the human body collapsed. Just like trucks, horses, and cows. Tears slid reluctantly down his face. He put his father's hand over his own strong heart as if to infuse Vernon with the will to live. I'll never leave you here again if you'll just live, he promised silently. I'll do all the work. You can sit on the porch and rock. Just don't leave me now. He was praying and it made him feel better.

There was a slight tremor in the frail hand. "Ma. Pa just squeezed my hand."

Eleanor came and smoothed Vernon's forehead. She bent over close and noticed a flicker of his eyelids. "Vernon, can you hear me?" She thought he nodded slightly.

Her head lifted and her whispers resounded throughout the room. "Your Pa needs nourishment. Bring some warm milk and soft bread."

Footsteps scurried throughout the house returning with chest grease; clean shirts, and more quilts. Within an hour Eleanor had stewed vegetables with chicken meat then strained it into a gruel Vernon could sip. "Richard, ride into Waverly and get Doctor Johnson. Tell him we need him as soon as he can get here."

Will vowed to buy one of those crank-up phones like they had at the boarding house so all this riding back and forth would not be necessary.

Every night Eleanor listened to all her children pray to God for the health of their father. While they were doing eveything the doctor ordered such as food, and rest, it was still up to the Almighty whether Vernon lived or died.

They were so busy that the days went by without anyone remembering what part of the week or month they were in. Will took charge. It was like putting on an old shoe he'd worn a long time ago – and it still fit. He assigned the girls to do the house chores leaving Eleanor time to care for Vernon. When it looked like Millard was left out, Will said he needed an assistant and Millard was just the one for the job.

With the money they'd made at the steel mill it was possible to get out of the bootlegging business. Eleanor was elated at this turn of events. Richard and Eugene destroyed the site where the distilling process had taken place. At last we can use the vegetable truck for what it was originally bought for, Will thought with relief.

The years he'd spent in Weirton melted away like ice in a warm rain. Only a healthy amount of cash under the house attested to the fact that working for Weirton Steel had not been in vain. The first thing I intend to do, he vowed is start buying some devices to make our work easier.

It took them all about a day to figure out how to operate the telephone. Then it was hard to keep them off it. The only saving grace was that not too many of their neighbors had one yet. When Will hauled in the washtub with the wringer attached Eleanor couldn't wait to try it out. He'd also brought collapsible racks to dry clothes inside during the wintertime.

"Are we spending all our money?" she asked.

"Why have money under the floor when it could be makin' our work easier and our lives longer?" In reality the expenditures had been small when compared to what they'd brought home to add to the moonshine money already there.

She hesitated.

"Ma, three years of us sendin' wages home added to all that moonshine money puts us in good shape. Instead of workin' on that damned still, I can concentrate on growin' vegetables like we used to. One day I'd like to start up a vegetable market in St. Marys or Waverly."

"What about John Mathieson?"

"Damn him to Hell"

Eleanor shook her head at such blasphemy. "Don't talk like that."

"I mean it, Ma. First chance I get I'm headin' up to the resort for a talk. If he won't talk then I intend to threaten him like he's done to us for the past years. He's not the only one who can go huntin' with a rifle that ain't too accurate."

"I can't listen to this."

"If Mr. Mathieson is willin' to be reasonable, then so will I. Otherwise, he can get sight of me stalkin' his place like he does to us. It'll be interestin' what he does about that."

In the days that followed, however, Will was so busy running the farm that Eleanor was hopeful he'd forgotten about his threats against John Mathieson.

It was the first Saturday in October and John was expecting his hunting buddies to arrive in about thirty minutes. He was in the shed, the usual cigarette hanging out of his mouth, removed only when he had to cough. He was cleaning his rifle. He wanted nothing to mar his aim. If Will didn't come into his scope today, then maybe tomorrow, or the day after that. Eventually it would happen.

Harvey Willis's new Ford truck chugged up the hill throwing gravel in its wake. The vehicle was filled with men, dogs, and guns. The noise coming from all this should have scared game away for miles. John shouldered his weapon, threw his cigarette over his shoulder, coughed hard, spit phlegm, then went out to meet them.

"Let's drive as far as Horse Neck Ridge," he said as he climbed in beside Red Hodges who was sitting in the back seat. "Saves time and legs," he laughed. "That's where I saw a big buck just the other day."

"Sounds good to me, John. You know the best places around here."

They stopped the truck in a curve in the road and got out.

"Isn't that the Hart place over there?" Harvey asked. "Heard Vernon had a heart attack a few weeks ago. . .helluva a mess what with all those kids to take care of."

Dan Bates nodded sympathetically.

The dogs were in hand, rifles shouldered, ammunition checked. All talk ceased as the serious business of hunting began.

Red stopped, stuck his nose in the air, and sniffed loudly. "I smell smoke."

The three men studied the horizon. A thin curl of smoke rose above the tree line.

Even as they watched the spiral became bigger and darker. "Looks like something's on fire over toward Boreland Ridge," Harvey mumbled.

The sight of smoke rising from a distant hill eclipsed all thoughts of hunting. They ran like the buck they were stalking, repacking weapons and herding the dogs back into the truck. It had been a fall with little rain, and fighting fire in a dry forest was left to the whims of wind and a creek big enough to stop the flames from spreading. Fire trucks in distant towns were slow and offered no help for outlying areas. The truck roared back down Horse

Neck to Bull Run Road where dense clouds of smoke announced what they all feared. The Boreland Springs Hotel was on fire!

"You got water on hand, John?"

"Only what's in the hotel reservoir."

It seemed to take forever before they got to the driveway that led up to the resort. Rolls of smoke undulated like a black serpent over the big structure. It burned their eyes and lungs. John forgot everything except that he must get to Wyatt's room before the entire building was destroyed. The loss of his business or remaining family never crossed his mind.

The truck stopped and the occupants threw themselves into the melee. Only Roberta, Clay, and a few grounds workers were there since it was the off-season. They were trying to get the horses out of the barn and pull the hay away from sparks that flew from the flaming building. The men who had left less than an hour earlier for a day of hunting found themselves fighting a losing battle with fire. They took their places beside Roberta and Clay in an effort to save what was possible. Except for John. He leapt from the vehicle and ran directly into the burning hotel.

"John!" Roberta screamed. "Don't go in there. You'll burn to death!"

He ignored her, kicked through the entry doors, and ran up the already crumbling stairway toward Wyatt's room. Flames fed by heavy curtains, delicate table linens, and polished oak wainscoting, galloped through the rooms like runaway horses.

He crawled down the hallway on his hands and knees, trying to stay under the blanket of smoke that filled his chest and burnt his face. John felt like he was on fire from inside. His lungs were raw – he could taste blood in his throat. I can't stop now, he thought. Just a little longer. Wyatt wouldn't want his gun to go up in smoke – he loved it so much. Fire licked into the ceiling, destroying rafters and banisters. The sound of beams collapsing urged him on. With a tremendous crash, the stairwell buckled behind him. Where am I? The smoke and his ebbing consciousness had him confused.

He pushed the next door he came to open and pulled himself inside. He felt the claw foot of Wyatt's bed and knew he was almost there. His jacket was on fire, his hands were raw, his hair singed. He didn't notice. All he wanted was Wyatt's gun. With his last ounce of strength John stood up, clutched the box to his chest, and threw himself out the window.

Roberta fainted when she saw his body hurling through the air. Clay tried to get under his father to soften his fall but he was too far away. It was too late anyway. John Mathieson took his last breath when he propelled himself through the window that cut through his jugular vein.

PART TWO

CHAPTER TWENTY

Sirens of every fire vehicle in both Wood and Pleasants counties could be heard screaming through the winding roads that led to Boreland Springs. Brian Paige was right behind them. By the time they arrived, all that could be saved were stables, tennis courts, and the carriage house. Only the large acreage of manicured lawn surrounding the resort saved the adjoining forests from extending the fire to a greater calamity than it was. Firemen spent their time hosing down the smoldering ruins and spraying water on buildings close by to prevent a resurgence of the fire that had taken the wooden structure to the ground in little over an hour.

Roberta had been taken to the carriage house where she had regained consciousness. Cricket Mathews and Mrs. Mac washed her sooty face and hands, reassuring her constantly that Clay was unhurt. Between them they wondered how she could survive this catastrophe less than three years after losing Wyatt.

No one had yet taken the time to recover John Mathieson's body from the smoldering muddle. Brian Paige got to him first. It didn't seem right to leave the man face down in the filth. He struggled to roll John's heavy body onto its back. Brian had never seen so much blood. It was impossible to determine what had actually caused his death, the fire or loss of blood. Doesn't matter, he thought. Either way, he's dead.

John's arms were criss-crossed over his chest, clutching a box. Brian knew what it contained before he opened it. I'd bet my best Sunday suit this is the gun that shot the bullet I've got stashed in my desk, he mused as he turned it over in his hand. 'Wyatt Mathieson' was written in beautiful script on one side of the inlaid silver handle.

With this little weapon, Brian pieced together how he thought that entire scene had played out that night. An argument must have occurred between Wyatt and whoever shot the twelve-gauge, probably a dispute over moonshine. Wyatt shot first and was then killed by the other person, or persons. "Course I can't prove any of this since it's just my theory," he whispered, "but I'll lay odds there was someone at the funeral hidin' some sort of wound back then. Wonder why John refused to cooperate and show me the gun then. Too bad the whole damned community was struck with 'lockjaw' when asked who they thought might be responsible." He shook his head disgustedly. "Pete's right. We'll never know who shot that twelve-gauge. His identity will be buried up in the Bull Run Cemetery this week along with the rest of John's secrets." He put the case in his jacket and carried it to his car.

Next morning he handed it over to Pete Jones, his superior officer. "Here's more evidence on that unsolved Wyatt Mathieson killing in the unlikely event anyone might want to have another look into the case." Brian couldn't conceal the dislike he had for this mountaineer mentality that stood in the way of justice. Pete snuffed his cigarette out on a jar lid and eyed the fancy box that held the gun in question.

"It's got Wyatt's name on it," Brian said and lit up his own smoke.

Pete nodded. "Might as well give it to Mrs. Mathieson to do with as she pleases. She'd probably like to keep it with his other things."

Roberta and Clay had spent the night at the St. Marys Inn. When offered laudanum, Roberta had declined. "No. I need all my wits about me now. This is one misery I intend to go through without the benefit of a drug-induced stupor."

Clay was dumbfounded. He'd thought she would decline into melancholia like when Wyatt had been killed. Instead, she was up early, knocking on his door saying they had to get a move on. She had much to attend to and needed his help. Her eyes were clear, her step lively, and she wore a dark gray dress rather than traditional black.

On this trip to the funeral parlor it took very little time to pick out the casket, select the suit John would be buried in, and arrange for flowers. Clay could barely keep up with her. Next she went to the telegraph office and wired her sisters in Philadelphia what had happened, not to worry about coming, and she would be in touch. Roberta was attending to business so fast that Clay had had no time to believe his father was actually gone. When they finally sat down to lunch at the inn's dining room, he studied his soup thoughtfully. She looked at him sharply.

"Clay, you and I have suffered enough in these miserable mountains. As soon as all our paperwork is completed here, we will move to Philadelphia

Affair at Boreland Springs

where we have family who love us." She hoped this would take away the lost look in his eyes. "This afternoon I have an appointment with our lawyer who can tell us what's left after we pay the balance of all the past improvements. At least John had the good sense to buy a life insurance policy that was considerable. . . .one of the few reasonable things he's done since Wyatt's death."

Clay's eyes clouded. "I appreciate your thoughtfulness, Mother. But this is where I was born. I don't want to leave and be with family I don't know – or try to make new friends in a strange place." He coughed nervously. "I've thought all night. With your permission I'd like to sell off the one hundred acres that borders the Hart's land. That still leaves three hundred acres. I want to be a farmer."

Roberta interrupted. "You don't know what you're saying. Where would you live? Who'd help you? You can't do all the work by yourself." She took a deep breath. "I say we sell all four hundred acres and you can have that money to buy decent farmland in Pennsylvania."

Clay was shaking his head before she'd finished. "This is where I want to be. I'll fix up the carriage house and live there. Don't need lots of room for just one person. With the money from the sale I can hire the men who've helped us all these years in the resort."

Roberta was speechless. She and John had come into West Virginia and bought the old Boreland Springs Resort so they could develop it into a world-class mineral springs spa. They had come from well-to-do circumstances in Philadelphia as a young couple and wanted to increase the family fortune more. They were cultured. Sophisticated. How could one of their sons want to be a farmer?

She looked into his bright blue eyes – so much like Wyatt. No. That wasn't true. There was an innocence and honesty that had never been a part of Wyatt. She could admit it now. Finally. In the years since he'd been killed, Roberta had realized that Wyatt's less than sterling character was due to John's constant attention and permissiveness -- he'd left his younger son to the care of Roberta. Clay was all she had now. How could she go away and leave him? On the other hand, how could she stay and confront the memories that nearly drove her out of her mind? She covered her face with her hands, fighting to maintain her composure.

"Mother, please. I'll come to Philadelphia to see you now and then. You'll visit here when you feel comfortable. It's not like we won't ever see each other again."

"I know, but. . ."

"I'm nineteen, Mother. Old enough to know what I want to do with my life. Like you and Father did. Having a resort or going into any other business that means living in a city is not what I want. Please try to understand."

Wyatt never tried to make me understand what he wanted, Roberta thought. He just *told* me what he was going to do – like his father did. How I love this child who would rather communicate than dominate. She covered his hands with her own. "I'm proud of you, Clay. Your plan is sound. I'm behind you one hundred percent. Let's go see Mr. Mays."

Clay caught his breath, grabbed their coats, and followed his mother as she hurried out to complete her agenda for the day. The meeting with the attorney who had handled all the Mathieson affairs since they'd bought the resort shortly after the turn of the century went pretty much the way Roberta had figured. She was left with enough cash to live comfortably, though not extravagantly. The land and remaining buildings of the resort would be deeded to Clay. Both left the office feeling that matters were under control and the future shined brighter for both of them. While they were filled with sorrow over his death, John had become someone they didn't know. His hatred had invaded everything and everyone around him.

They left the office of Handler and Mays with pensive faces. The only remaining occasion to endure would be in two days when John would be buried beside Wyatt.

Three years after the death of Wyatt, the community of Boreland Springs attended the funeral of his father. It was not a ceremony that evoked the same degree of sadness. John had become a harsh and unfriendly man who had not endeared himself to his neighbors during this time. He'd not been cut down before he'd had a chance to live as his son had, and he'd brought death upon himself by running into a burning building for no obvious reason.

The hill people came – not because of John but because of their respect for Roberta and Clay. They brought casseroles and offers of a place to stay until they could get resettled. When Clay announced that his mother would be leaving, they were sad but not surprised. She'd lost too much at Boreland Springs to continue to live there. She'd always been good to her employees and the community as a whole: making certain food was delivered to a family down on their luck; buying shoes for children who went barefoot too late in the fall; sending quilts to the poorest among them.

Clay, too, was well thought of – mature and reasonable for his age. They'd all looked forward to the day when he would be their boss. Now that was not to be. Even though it meant many would have to go looking for lower paying jobs or return to farm their own land, they knew it was the end of a lavish lifestyle for Roberta and Clay as well. They held no grudge that the glory that had been Boreland Springs lay in ashes at the top of the hill.

Roberta was grateful for their sympathy and care. She hugged and cried with them as one does with friends who've known each other for many years.

The Harts did not attend the funeral. They reckoned Roberta didn't need to be looking at a family rumored to be part of the reason it had all come to this final overwhelming end. Eleanor sent a side of ham with the Conroys, along with a note of condolence.

When Sil and Melia got the news from their respective parents, both at first refused to believe it. Surely it must be a cruel joke. Neither could imagine coming home to a place where the famous hotel no longer existed.

Kay Meredith

CHAPTER TWENTY-ONE

Eugene ran into the house, out of breath and fear in his eyes. While he'd never understood why, he knew they'd not been friends with the Mathiesons for some time. And Clay Mathieson was coming up the lane in the old farm truck.

"Ma, come quick. Clay's outside."

"What?"

By that time, Will had walked out of the shed and ambled over to where Clay had stopped his vehicle. It wasn't in much better condition than the rickety truck he and Eugene had driven back from Weirton.

"What brings you over here, Clay?"

"Wondered if you'd be interested in buyin' some of that land of mine that backs up to yours."

Will swallowed his answer for the time being. He studied the expression in Clay's eyes, looking for the same slyness that had always been a part of Wyatt. While nothing had ever been said, it was commonly accepted that the reason the Hart boys had been absent for the past three years was because John Mathieson had a death wish on both of them. Upon their return after Vernon's heart attack the community had lived with fingers crossed, wondering what the next calamity would be. With John's death they breathed easier and reckoned Will and Eugene no longer had to look over their shoulders.

"I know you're probably surprised -- but I don't need four hundred acres and I figured you'd be stayin' on to help your Pa and might want more land."

Clay shuddered inwardly at Will's stare that was filled with distrust and anger. He couldn't blame him really. But everyone had suffered, hadn't they? When it didn't look like Will was going to answer, Clay cleared his throat. "Well, I'll be goin' then. Just thought I'd ask you first." He turned to leave.

"What's this about, Clay? You know the stories and that Eugene and I had to leave our home since your Pa intended to shoot one or both of us since he figured we killed Wyatt. Our Pa had to work without us here to help – probably caused his heart attack."

"I know. And the whole mess lost me my father as well." He stared into the valley where Bull Run whispered through the community of Boreland Springs. "The fire was a blessing actually. You're back where you belong and my mother and I aren't living with a man who'd become so riddled with hate that his family and business were pushed to the background."

Will chewed a dry sassafras twig and watched Clay's young face shaded with defeat at not being able to brush away the past with another funeral. He's got grit, I'll give him that, Will thought. If Wyatt had had Clay's sense and John had been able to live beyond the tragedy, maybe both would be alive today and the hotel would still be standing

"I just want to farm and be happy among the people I've grown up with. But I don't need the whole acreage."

"What're you askin' for it?"

"Ten dollars an acre."

"I'll talk it over with Pa and let you know."

"Then he's better?"

"Yep. Still weak and won't ever be able to work like he used to but it looks like he'll live."

"Thank God. Maybe the dyin' will stop now."

Will thought he saw a tear on Clay's cheek.

"Try to get it for seven-fifty an acre. Bargainin' is part of makin' a deal, Will. See how that sets with him." Vernon's voice was stronger than it had been since he'd gotten sick.

"How about seven-fifty, Clay?" Will narrowed his eyes, studying how Clay reacted when it came down to business.

"Nope, but I'd take eight."

"You got a deal."

They shook hands and set a date for the transaction to take place in the lawyer's office.

When Eugene learned that part of the money they'd made up in Weirton had bought a big slice of Mathieson land, his chest puffed so big he popped a button.

"Land's better'n a shiny red truck anytime."

Kay Meredith

CHAPTER TWENTY-TWO

By Christmas of 1928, life for the folks of Boreland Springs had become as unreliable as the weather they'd grown up with. The mysterious shooting of Wyatt Mathieson, followed by Melia Conroy and the two oldest Hart boys leaving, then John Mathieson dying in a fire apparently of his own making three years later, had the community wondering what they'd done to bring so much trouble down on their shoulders.

The hotel had been the source of employment for the local population, providing money to buy warm clothes to make it through cold winters or lumber for siding to stop the wind that blew through cracks of cheaply built houses. Had their belief in God not been so steadfast, most would have stopped going to church altogether.

They all needed a soft spell. A time to forget losses, deaths, and what was going to happen to them next -- an occasion to laugh together, eat a lot, and try to be optimistic. December was a good time for that since there were no crops to tend. The week before Christmas everyone, including several visitors, congregated at the Boreland Springs Grange for a party.

They talked with humor about the many changes their little community had undergone since Wyatt Mathieson's death in 1924. Even the eldest among them couldn't remember a time when so many drastic incidents had disturbed their little world in such a short time. Calamities of such monumental proportions usually happened over a decade or more, supplying fodder for discussion for a whole generation. In less than four years they'd garnered enough turmoil to discuss for longer than anyone wanted to think about.

The chairs lined in a double row along the walls were full with more being dragged in from the porch. No one wanted to miss any gossip so it seemed like they'd all arrived at once. Elbows poked stomachs, heavy boots stepped on toes, and the smells of farm life permeated the moist air in the small structure. No one complained. In one end Harley Bailey and his two brothers, Earl and Farley, were tuning up their fiddles. Talk was fast since everyone wanted to learn all they could before the dancing started. In the opposite corner, hot cider and beer was available, doled out to the appropriate age groups under the strict supervision of Dora Williams. No moonshine was apparent since this was just the sort of gathering where one could expect the government men to come snooping.

No area was more enthusiastic than the corner where the Conroys, Harts, and Lockharts were holding court.

"You mean Clay Mathieson sold land to Will Hart?" Sil's eyes were big as early persimmons.

Maxine nodded. "Roberta comes back from Philadelphia to see him once in awhile. She's really proud of his farmin' sense – never thought that'd happen."

Ruth Lockhart smiled. "It's good to see Will and Eugene back too. . .I think that's what saved Vernon's life."

"They'll be needed since they've got two hundred acres to work now," Melia chimed in.

"Why don't you come home to stay, Melia?" Abner Lockhart didn't usually ask such a personal question but he knew how much Silas missed his daughter. They'd talked about it over at Cleggs.

"Maybe I'll come home when Sil's finished school, Mr. Lockhart. I really love my job and hope to bring some of my marketing ideas back to Cleggs. I'll have saved up more money by then as well."

Much scuffling and laughter ensued and more chairs were added when the Hart family arrived. Even Will had cleaned up and made an appearance. He walked beside his father, discreetly supporting Vernon by an elbow. Eugene talked as readily as the next; Richard was out at the bonfire with the other young men; Imogene was making eyes at Virgil Meeks while Wilma and Millard clung close to their parents. It wasn't long before the fiddles were tuned to satisfaction and a wild square dance put an end to all conversation.

Will sat by the pot-bellied stove tamping the pipe he'd taken up since Eleanor had never approved of cigarette smoking around the house – more so now since a smoldering cigarette butt was said to be the cause of the Boreland Hotel fire. For the first time since he'd been back he allowed himself to take a deep breath and look around at his surroundings. They all take their homes for granted, he thought, remembering the years of loneliness in Weirton and the furtive visits home. He smiled when Eugene got up the nerve to ask Regina

Sinclair to be his partner. That would never have happened before their years in Weirton, he mused. Guess it was worth it.

The rustle of a taffeta skirt to his left brought his head around.

"I'm glad you're back again," Melia said. "It wasn't right you had to leave your home. I don't even feel sorry for John Mathieson anymore."

"It wasn't all bad. Eugene got a lot better and we made enough money to make our lives easier once we got back."

He slugged down the rest of his beer. She looked at it hard then turned her attention to his face with raised eyebrows. He smiled and bent close. "No moonshine for me anymore." They both laughed, sharing their personal secret.

"Why don't you come back? I never understood why you stayed away in the first place. No one was aimin' a deer rifle at your heart."

Worry furrowed Melia's brow. Will was surprised. He thought she'd think his remark funny. His face reddened and he looked at the floor. "Didn't mean to pry."

"Don't be embarrassed, Will. We all have our reasons to leave. Once I left there just never seemed a good time to come back. Ma asks me all the time why I don't. Maybe when Sil's back I will."

"Don't you miss your home?"

"Yes, but it makes me feel good to send them half my salary to make their lives easier. We don't have good land to farm nor do we have enough of it. It barely produces enough for us let alone anything to sell. Harold and Troy are on the hunt for a wife and will be striking out on their own soon. Earl wants to go to college so bad that I'd like to have enough saved to at least get him started."

"I know how it feels to want the best for your family. . . . Do you think the oldest child in the family feels responsible for that?" He'd never really looked at her before. While she was the prettiest woman he'd ever seen, and he'd seen a lot, it was her sensibility that kept him riveted.

"Probably." Her face broke out into a big grin. "Come on. They're playing a slow dance. Let's get in on some of this fun."

He led her into the group of slower dancers while the rowdy ones took a rest.

"I think it was Stephen Foster's song that advised that one should 'gather ye rosebuds while ye may'."

He shook his head and laughed. "That don't fall into my songbook. But I do know 'You are my sunshine'."

At the end of the evening every soul left with stiff legs, sore backs, and happiness in their hearts. They would be more than ready for the religious celebration of Christ's birth planned for Christmas morning.

On the way home Sil and Melia sat together in the back of the wagon Abner was driving. They swung their legs off the tailgate and stared into the star filled sky like when they were children. Sil pointed out the Little Dipper. Melia looked through a skiff of clouds for the Big Dipper.

"Eugene's learned to talk more." Sil said quietly.

Melia nodded. "And you've stepped down a few rungs from you soapbox." They both laughed at that.

"We've both figured out how to earn a living without being servants," Sil continued.

"Will has learned to laugh," Melia whispered, nearly touching Sil's cheek. "It's about time. He's such an attractive man but never had much to do with the rest of us. . . maybe he has his reasons," she added thoughtfully.

They were quiet for a time, reflecting on the reasons anybody does anything, and why those reasons were best kept to oneself.

Finally Sil let out a long sigh. "Next year I graduate. Hope there'll be a need for a teacher at Pumpkin Knob."

"There will be. Mrs. Clemmons has wanted to retire for a long time. I'll come home then and try to hook up with Cleggs. Do you think he'll be willing to listen to a young woman with modern ideas?"

They both giggled, reckoning it would take a deal of talking for Sid Clegg to agree to Melia's city hats and feminine ladies underwear.

"Did you ever get the gist of math?"

"Barely. I think I can handle first through eighth grades, though." More giggling.

"Did you ever see that Mr. . . .what was his name, again? The one who treated you so badly in remedial math."

"Christopher Nelson. Actually, he turned out to be nice. . .helped me when Rachel drowned. I never had to take his class again. That might've had something to do with it."

"That had to be so difficult."

"It was. . . so sad for such a spirited person to die so young." Remarking about the loss of a vibrant young person no longer bothered Melia. She's getting better, Sil thought.

Their shoulders rubbed together as the wagon rumbled through the muddy ruts. Both girls were silent, each lost in her memories. Savoring the feel of the country roads they'd followed all their lives. Much had happened. Changes that had altered the original plans they'd had for themselves. The comfort of being back in the cocoon of home lulled them into a half-sleep. . .hoping the tempests were over for awhile.

Kay Meredith

CHAPTER TWENTY-THREE

The spring of 1929 blew into the hills of West Virginia with its usual bluster of intermittent snow showers followed by brilliant sunshine.

"Amelia! These sale items are poorly presented." The shrill voice of Cecile Thompson floated across the second floor of Tidball's and brought Melia on the run. Cecile was always a case of nerves during sales weeks. She lived in fear that competing stores such as Larson's would get the edge and outdo them. All confidence she'd ever had in Melia seemed to fly with the spring winds. To be honest, none of her assistants were immune from the high-strung chain-smoking supervisor.

At times like this Melia thought she might as well resign early and get on back to Waverly and her own plans. She'd done well since that first promotion. The following season Incidentals and Accessories had been added to her responsibilities in the Lingerie Department, bringing with it a substantial increase in salary. Her department had always been in the top three when it came to revenue for the company.

"What is it Miss Thompson?" The nervous tirades no longer bothered her like the first time she'd been subjected to one.

"The sizes are mixed up and the folding is sloppy."

"I'll see to it immediately."

I'll hang in for the rest of the year, she thought, as she made the corrections Cecile had pointed out. By that time Sil will be home and my savings account will be fatter. She glanced up when she heard Cecile attack Garnet Linger over in Linens.

Sil sat in the front row of the audience watching the graduates of 1929 receive their diplomas. How she wished she were one of them. Her requirements for her teaching certification would be completed at the end of the fall semester. She'd come on this day to watch Christopher Nelson accept his Master's Degree in Agricultural Engineering. It was still hard for her to think of him as a farmer and an engineer.

Through the last two years they had become good friends. While their schedules were full they usually found time for a quick visit once a week. They had discovered there were many qualities they had in common: seriousness, dedication to education, and a desire to be good at their chosen careers. They were not frivolous people but they weren't without humor either. They were simply devoted to making a good mark in their chosen professions. Sil knew Christopher wanted to work for the Farm Extension Service set up by the government and implemented by offices in every agricultural county in the United States. He'd had several offers but she didn't know which one he'd accepted. He had mentioned that an area where improved farming methods were needed was his first interest.

She would miss his cheerfulness when he strode with long steps across campus to say 'hello'. Since Rachel's death she'd never gotten close to another classmate. Not because she didn't want to but because she was always running from class to class in her determination to finish her schooling early.

When Christopher walked tall and confident to accept his degree Sil felt she must be the proudest person there. He'd never mentioned having brothers or sisters and she knew his mother had died. He'd never had much to say about his father.

The campus was filled with proud families milling about, most in awe of having a college graduate in their family. Sil ran to Christopher, arms outstretched, to give him the hug of his life.

"Here now. I'm still just a farmer. Only difference is I've got a piece of paper that puts it in writing."

"I hope all the time you've spent here will be worth it," a gruff voice from behind them said.

"Pa! I didn't know you were coming. You didn't answer the invitation so I figured you were too busy."

"Reckoned I could just show up. Figured I'd go back after the qualification was safely in your hand."

Suddenly Christopher remembered Sil standing beside him. "Pa, want you to meet a good friend of mine – Sil Lockhart. She graduates at the end of year. Wants to be a teacher. Did the same thing I did -- worked year 'round so she could finish early."

"I'm pleased to meet you, Mr. Nelson." She stretched her hand forward.

He took her hand in a quick handshake. She studied the taciturn face, weathered skin, sinewy muscles, and enlarged knuckles that he massaged unconsciously. A man whose eyes glinted steel and his unyielding stance indicated someone who rarely took anyone's advice except his own. Yet, when he looked at his son an almost indistinguishable softening occurred. It only lasted for an instant before the gnarled and irascible mountaineer returned. Sil could tell that he felt awkward with women.

"My father's a farmer."

There was a slight turning of the head. "Cattle or crops."

"Some of both. We don't have enough land to raise crops to sell, so Pa and the boys keep a few beef cattle and raise as much hay as the best meadow can handle."

"Hogs?"

"Just enough for the family. None to sell."

"Fruit?"

"A few apple trees and lots of blueberries, blackberries, and raspberries."

". . . . .then of course the vegetable garden. I'd like to have a penny for every jar of corn, beans, and tomatoes I've helped Ma put up."

Did she see a hint of acceptance in those gray eyes? Probably not.

"I'll leave you with your Pa now, Chris. Got to go get ready for summer school."

They shook hands and he pulled her close. "Sorry about the third degree."

"Don't be," she whispered back. "Wish my college tests were so easy to answer."

They wished each other luck and success. She told Mr. Nelson she'd enjoyed meeting him. He nodded in response. She took that to mean he didn't dislike her too much.

By next morning the graduation receded into the back regions of her mind as she prepared to face a class of eighth graders. She enjoyed her practice teaching sessions when an experienced teacher stood beside her. Teenagers intimidated her – they were unpredictable, rambunctious, and not always completely honest. First through third grades were her favorite. However, she could be called upon to teach anything from reading to astronomy – a subject she'd enjoyed much more than math.

Eugene had forgotten how hot it could be working in the hay fields at home.

"This is harder than workin' in the steel mills, Will." The sun beat down on Eugene's neck that was blistered and sore.

"Yep. But at least it's at home." Will stood up and wiped his sweaty hair out of his eyes.

"Even moonshinin's easier. Most of that work's done at night or in the shade."

"Yep. But we quit that."

They were pulling stumps out of a piece of the land purchased from Clay. It was a meadow covering about four acres and had grown over with scrub pine. Will and Eugene were hauling the trees to the middle of the field where Richard and Millard were pushing them into some sort of stack. What couldn't be used for firewood would later be burned.

"It'll be a top hay field when we're done," Richard pointed out. "Since we ain't bootleggin' anymore we'd best do more plantin'."

"That slope on the far side will be good for vegetables." Will was shading his eyes with his hand. "Ought to be plenty extra to sell after we've got what we need."

"Can we get new lettering on the truck, Will?" Millard asked.

"Maybe."

At the end of the day the four Hart brothers joined the rest of the family for supper. Vernon said grace, thanking God for being together and looking into a bright future.

"And thank you God for saving our Vernon," Eleanor added emphatically.

There was no more talk until empty stomachs were full. Even then little was said since no one had the strength to say much after a hard day in the field.

"When will them stumps be out, Will?" Vernon was anxious to get it plowed and planted.

"Soon Pa. We're workin' fast as we can. Maybe by next week."

"Seems like we're always runnin' to catch up," Vernon answered.

"We'll try to work faster." Will sighed knowing they were pushing themselves to the limit already.

Richard, Eugene, and Millard groaned and dragged their sunburnt bodies toward the outhouse, which had been enlarged to hold two big cauldrons for taking baths. Except for Eugene, no one would come right out and say it, but they all reckoned that while bootleggin' might be dangerous, it was a damn sight easier to do!

"I'm nearly finished." Sil was humming 'I'll be comin' 'round the mountain'. "When I go home for Christmas, I'll be a full-fledged teacher. I can't wait."

The nearer the time came for her to finish, it seemed the work got easier. Maybe it's because I can see the end now, she thought. Back in 1926 this time seemed so far off that it was more like an impossible dream. Now, even math is easy. She smiled at the thought. Christopher would be pleased. Her schedule had been so busy that he hadn't crossed her thoughts in months. Today, nearing her own graduation, she wondered what had happened to him – where he was working and was he happy. They hadn't agreed to keep in touch, knowing that was an improbable promise to keep.

"I just can't wait to be called Miss Lockhart," she said aloud. She dreamed of her own classroom, her own blackboard and pointer, and students to assign to do the erasing.

"It's all done, Pa." Will spoke slowly and quietly as if the effort had taken away his ability to talk. "Clearin', plantin', harvestin', slaughterin', plus the sellin'."

"Don't forget the cannin'," Imogene reminded him.

"Sales good?"

"Yep. Coulda' sold more if we'd have had it."

"Next year might want to plant more."

Will nodded. The other three Hart boys hung their heads.

"Better get started on choppin' firewood. It'll be November before you know it and feels like winter's comin' early this year."

Even Will couldn't stifle a groan. Eleanor shot a hard look their way and they all straightened up, knowing this was the best year they'd ever had, especially without moonshine to peddle.

On October 1st, Melia gave notice that she would be leaving at the end of the month. She'd made the decision during the fall sales. Cecile's demands on her department heads had gotten unreasonable. No one could possibly make a twenty percent increase in sales regardless of how prosperous the country was. Cecile was obsessed with Larson's Department Store and a new Sears Roebuck she'd heard was coming into town soon.

"I don't understand why you're leaving, Amelia. You've been promoted regularly and your salary is more than most women make."

"I know, but it's time for me to go home now. I'm homesick. I appreciate all you've done for me. But my mind is made up." She'd decided not to get into a discussion with her boss as to the real reason she'd resigned. I was going to leave at Christmas anyway, she thought. Might as well let her think I'm simply not motivated.

"You will be missed. You've done a good job. I'll hold this resignation letter for awhile in case you change your mind."

Her friends were sorry to hear the news. She would miss them too. They planned a farewell party on Halloween weekend. "It will be so much fun, Melia," Alicia bubbled. "We'll have a costume party and make it part 'goodbye' and part Halloween. That way, it won't seem so bad you're leaving."

They were gathered in the ladies lounge. The overstuffed chairs were dimpled from years of use; the air was stagnant with cigarette smoke – that was the sheik thing for daring young ladies nowadays. A habit Melia abhorred. Makes your breath smell bad and your teeth yellow, she'd thought when she saw so many ashtrays laying about the place. Today she didn't care. Soon she'd be back where there was enough space to get away from cigarette smoke.

Melia woke up early on the Thursday the 29th. She'd closed out the last of her work on Monday and Cecile had said she might as well go ahead and

Affair at Boreland Springs

make preparations to go home. Should have gotten this done yesterday, she thought as she gathered up her bank statements. Too much to do what with rechecking lists to leave with the girl who was taking her place plus sorting out what she'd take home and what would be put in the charity box at church. She intended to stop at the bank and withdraw all the money from her savings and checking accounts. I can pack on Friday, go to my party on Saturday, and take the train home on Sunday, she mused. It'll be so good to see Boreland Springs again.

She bundled up in her camelhair coat against the breeze that came rolling off the river then grabbed her hat with one hand as the wind became stronger. Seemed like there was more traffic than usual – and more irate drivers. The pedestrians were edgy as well, shouting obscene remarks toward the rude drivers. It will be good to get away from all this, she thought. I was never meant to be a city girl.

She turned the corner and found herself at the back of a riotous crowd brandishing fists at something, or someone, she couldn't see. Many were holding papers in their hands. They shoved, swore, and threatened. Melia was confused.

"What's wrong?" she asked the man beside her. "I'm just trying to get to the bank and it's on this street."

He looked at her like she was speaking a foreign language. "Where've you been, lady? We're all tryin' to get to the bank. But the doors are locked and the police won't let anybody close."

"Why are the doors locked? It's nearly noon."

"Because of the stock market crash! Don't you listen to the radio? There's no money in the bank to cover their customer's accounts."

Melia had no idea what the stock market was – or did – and why it had anything to do with her savings account. She tried to push to the front of the line – the man had to be wrong. She was shoved back with such force she nearly fell. "Stay in line, lady," a burly dockworker muttered. "You're no better than the rest of us."

"But I just want to withdraw my savings."

"Wouldn't we all. If them policemen weren't there on the steps we might be able to storm the doors and get our money."

"Will you just tell me what happened to the bank's money?"

He gave her the same incredulous look the first man had. "Go ask your boss. Maybe he can explain."

There was no way she could press through the mass of enraged people. She turned around and darted between vehicles and people to get back to Tidball's. There it was as chaotic as outside. She ran to the ladies lounge. Alicia and some of the others sat crying, mindless of who saw them and too distracted to light up their cigarettes. "What's happened?" she screamed. "Will somebody tell me please?"

Cecil explained what the stock market was and why the country was bankrupt when it crashed. "It would take longer than I have to tell you how it happened. All you need to know is that what money anyone had in a bank is gone. There are probably a lot of 'paper millionaires' between New York and San Francisco who are as confused as you. Some have already thrown themselves out windows in New York so they don't have to face the consequences of their imprudent and illegal actions."

Melia was numb. All these years she'd put half of her wages into the savings account – and now it was all gone! Was that what they were saying? How could such a thing happen? Cecile had had no answer – just that it had. Wasn't that like robbery – to spend somebody's money without their knowledge? She didn't understand the stock market and now it seemed, she didn't know about banks either. She'd noticed terms such as 'interest' and 'monthly service charge', but had no idea what those words meant or how that was linked to some kind of market in New York City where people were throwing themselves out of windows.

Cecile had said the whole country was affected. Did that mean banks all over the United States were closed – or just in Wheeling? All the money I have to my name is from my last paycheck.. She nearly choked. Thank God I cashed it before the bank closed last week. I hope it's enough to buy a train ticket home.

Home. At least she had one. And in a place so primitive that people hid their money in mattresses, dry wells, under floors – anyplace they thought no one would look. They'd never trusted banks. It hadn't made sense to them to take cash money and give it to a stranger in a bank who then gave you pieces of paper in return. I'm such a fool, she thought, to let Alicia talk me into using a bank. Why did I forget what I'd been taught?

Melia shoved herself back into the pandemonium, scrabbling through yelling, infuriated people to her little apartment. She didn't care how rude she was. Like a whirlwind she tore through the two small rooms, throwing clothes suitable for home into her trunk and discarding ones that wouldn't fit in. Won't be using this curling iron, she thought, and tossed it into the wastebasket. It went against the grain to get rid of useable items as she continued weeding out what to keep and what to pitch. "I doubt if the frantic people out in the streets of Wheeling are going to want my radio and toaster either."

In thirty minutes she'd forced the locks closed on her two suitcases and phoned for a taxi. After an hour of waiting beside the curb, the cab drove up with a disgruntled driver at the wheel.

"Like pushin' your way through a field of locusts," he muttered. "Takes three times as long to get anywhere."

She nodded but said nothing – the commotion and uncertainty had unnerved her to the point of tears. The train station was relatively quiet. Evidently no one wanted to leave the vicinity of the bank in case the doors were re-opened. After purchasing the ticket she looked around for a phone booth. There were two in line ahead of her. She chewed her fingernails, something she'd not done since childhood, until it was her turn.

A bored voice asked what number she was calling. "The Silas Conroy residence in the Waverly exchange, please." The operator cracked her gum. "Hold, please." Doesn't she know the world is crumbling, Melia thought, listening to the lines crackling as the call went through. After what seemed an eternity, she heard her mother's tentative voice on the other end.

"Hello?"

"Ma? It's me. Melia."

"Who?"

"Melia!" She shouted.

"Yes?"

"I'll be home tonight. Can Pa come with the wagon?"

"You're comin' home?"

"Yes. Can Pa meet. . ."

"Yes. Is something wrong?"

"I'll tell you when I get there."

"Alright." The phone clicked off.

The rhythmic sound of wheels sliding smoothly over the tracks did not soothe her as they had in the past. Her mother's words indicated they hadn't heard the news. Even if they had, a stock market crash in New York City would mean nothing to them. They had no understanding of stock markets and banks. They had cashed Melia's money orders and placed the money, along with their own savings, in a metal box stored in the shed. It was a World War I ammunition container that her uncle had brought home from the war. They had no money in a bank, did not know what a stock market was, and had no idea how its crash could affect someone in Boreland Springs.

They barely recognized her when she entered the house late that night. Maxine could see she'd been crying and her brothers were surprised at her loss for words. When she finally got it across to them that her half of what she'd saved for the past few years was gone, they hugged her and tried to make her feel like it didn't matter.

Her explanation to them was no more enlightening than it had been to her. In fact, after the third time she'd said the whole country was bankrupt it made them more confused. They asked the same questions: How could it happen? When did it happen? Would her money be returned? The last question sent her into uncontrollable tears. She'd left a city paralyzed by this calamity. She'd seen for herself the closed doors of the bank. Yet ,the world in Boreland Springs was the same as it had always been. Melia felt like she was being tossed between dreams and reality, and she wasn't certain which was which.

"Here now," her father said gently. "No one has died, no one is sick, and no one else owns our home. We grow our own food, make most of our clothes, and have all the money you sent plus what we've been able to save, in the ammo box. From what you say, we're better off than the rest of the country."

Her father's words stopped her right in the middle of a sniffle. He's right, she thought. These hills and valleys have supported us for generations without banks or a stock market, whatever that is. We're the same as we always were. Poor. . .but self-sufficient

By Christmas all of Boreland Springs understood the ramifications of a stock market crash and the depression it brought with it. Suddenly offspring who'd left the hills for more money and less hard labor returned home, glad to have a place to come to, humble though it might be. Newspapers pictured lines of hungry people waiting to be served soup. Their gaunt faces mirrored defeat and humiliation. The people of West Virginia, long separated from the rest of the world by their forbidding mountains, soon became acquainted with the anguish of the rest of their country. Photos of men lined up in front of an employment office; children playing in dirty streets because they'd lost their home; mothers crying because they couldn't feed their families, went beyond what the folks of Wood and Pleasants counties believed possible.

What an irony that primitive Boreland Springs seemed better off than much of the rest of the country. The natural resources around them provided everything they needed: firewood, gas, food, and shelter, none of which was lavish but in these days a home of any kind was a luxury. Furthermore, they had never been burdened by a conscience to obey laws put in place by a government that did not take their circumstances into account. Year-round hunting, cutting timber for homes and warmth, farming unclaimed land, not paying taxes, and filching drip gas for their vehicles was the accepted way of surviving in the mountains. That way of life came in handy now. They wondered why people in other areas needed a stock market and banks. Why couldn't they live as moutaineers did – off the land?

Christmas was a solemn reunion for Sil and Melia. They were thankful their troubles seemed small when compared with an entire country whose financial system had collapsed. Soup kitchens became the norm. Whole families lived wherever they could find shelter.

"Thank God I finished school early," Sil said. "I'd already planned to live at home and teach at Pumpkin Knob. Ma's happy beyond belief!"

"All I came home with was half my wages that Ma put in the ammo box and my experience in selling clothing that no one can afford to buy."

"There you go again. Feeling sorry for yourself." Sil grinned. "Thought you'd learned better than to give me a club like that to hit you with."

Melia cowered in mock fear. "Oh God. I'd forgotten how fierce you can be when you think you know it all. . . .do you?"

"Do I what?"

"Know it all."

"Maybe not everything, but I do know that this little corner of the world has the same amount to spend it always had. With all the young folks coming back home there will be more people needing food and clothing. I also know Mrs. Clegg wants to take it easy – says it's time to retire. Mr. Clegg's been looking for someone to take her place."

"Really?"

"Yep."

"I'll see if Pa can take me there tomorrow. . . .you may not know everything Sil, but you know enough for me."

CHAPTER TWENTY-FOUR

1930, Boreland Springs

The Great Depression made its impact in Boreland Springs when the older offspring returned home after losing their jobs in places such as Cleveland, Akron, Pittsburgh, and any other large city. Some had married and brought back wives and children who had to be cared for. It put a strain on families who hadn't expected these extra bodies who needed beds, clothing, and food. Houses seemed smaller and wore out faster. Tempers flared and the homebodies began to damn the stock market crash that had brought old children back with their new-fangled ideas.

More pews had to be built for the church. Reverend Knox had to plan sermons that were meaningful to the influx of people unaccustomed to living in a rural setting. Children who knew how to cross busy streets and stay out of alleys after dark had to be educated to avoid flooding creeks, walking into a big forest unaccompanied, and to stay away from poison ivy.

Some of the native mothers were scandalized by the lack of manners they felt the city children exhibited. Much time was spent on the importance of God during the meetings of the WCTU. This didn't go over well with the city mothers who felt that Boreland Springs' ideas were antiquated and unnecessary. Whereupon Lucille Wilson said 'fine – go back to the city'. There ensued a heated discussion where angry feminine voices resonated through the valley about the pros and cons of raising children to be independent as opposed to 'being seen and not heard'. Doris Knox called the meeting to order, reminding those in attendance that the WCTU had to do with the Womens Christian Temperance Union, and that perhaps the business of child-rearing should be handled within the family.

She was promptly overruled with proclamations from the local women that the new children had come into Boreland Springs at the generosity of its inhabitants and should be expected to adhere to the rules of the community. On no account would the natives allow their offspring to become besmirched by outlandish city ideas that went against the rules of God!

It all got settled as time went on when everyone over the age of four was assigned chores. Before long all hands had calluses from hoeing, stacking hay, scything weeds, and chopping firewood. Legs got scratched from picking berries and looking for lost livestock. Muscles were sore from harnessing horses, plowing fields, and snaking logs. Skin was red and inflamed from scrubbing clothes that then had to be wrung out by hand and hung out to dry on bushes. There was no question of which policy was best. Everyone had to do his or her share in this place where few modern appliances could be found. City life with its streetcars and store-bought food was irrelevant in the hills where most all needs had to be provided by the dwellers.

Husbands and wives for whom this was a return to home fell back into the furrow with relative ease. For their spouses it meant keeping their opinions to themselves while living in another woman's home and praying for the time they could leave. However, within weeks the offspring of these oddly matched marriages were beginning to fit in like they'd grown up in the hills. They formed friendships with children their own age who were more than happy to teach them how to catch a crawdad or a butterfly; attach a June bug to a string; catch lightening bugs in a bottle, or find honey in a hollow tree.

By March it was apparent to all that the increased mouths to feed made it necessary to find ways to make their land more productive. A problem had already reared its ugly head – lack of rain. Normally, late winter snows and early spring rains had the ground ready for plowing and planting. Not this year – at least not so far. And while there was still time for a reasonable crop yield, folks were afraid the depression was just the first of many catastrophes to come. That's the way it worked according to the Bible, as Reverend Knox was quick to point out. Furthermore, he'd continued, all the tribulations the world was suffering had to do with sinful living. People had to return to God; he expounded in loud predictions and wild gesticulations. Otherwise, a drought could well be the first of many plagues Boreland Spring would suffer. His dire warnings were accompanied by purposeful stares in the direction of church members he thought to be moonshining, one of the worst curses of mankind in his opinion. The city women rolled their eyes and shook their heads at his archaic ideas.

A meeting was planned and on March 5th, the Grange Hall was full of uneasy farmers. Abner Lockhart took charge and explained that he and his boys, David and Daniel, had already looked into the possibilities of increasing their productivity. They'd contacted the West Virginia Extension Services in Parkersburg which had agreed to send out one of its men the following Saturday.

"What about the drought? How can anyone from an office make it rain?" It was Clyde Hendershot, who had a family of eight to feed.

"The drought ain't far along yet, Clyde. This man probably has some ideas about how to prepare for such an event before it's in full swing. Another head, especially an educated one, can't hurt nothin."

Abner watched heads drop and whispers begin. "I'm not sayin' you have to join in with our plan. This is a meetin' where everybody has a say and all ideas are welcome." He looked over the group of farmers, ill-at-ease when asked to share thoughts with other men; even though it was folks they'd grown up with. "How 'bout you Will? You've added more land to tend and must have something to say." Abner stood off to the side, hoping young Will would be willing to support the effort. Even knowing they might come up short when crops were harvested, these farmers were still mountain folk -- stubborn and set in their old ways.

"Me and my brothers will be at your place on Saturday, Abner. From what I've heard this depression is in for the long haul. We need to raise and save as much of our crops as possible. Ought to clear more of our land to farm. We should stack timber from the cleared fields to use as firewood. Takin' advantage of a government agency willin' to help us in other ways seems to be another smart step to take."

"Does that mean we don't have to sign up less'en we want to and won't owe no money either way?" Cliff Bayliss wasn't too good at stringing a sentence together that made much sense, but Abner got the gist of it.

"That's right. Come -- listen. If you don't like his ideas you can do it your own way -- if you want to join in, it doesn't cost anything. Hard to find that kind of a deal these days."

The men nodded their heads then went off to talk among themselves.

On Saturday not a man was missing at Abner Lockhart's barnyard meeting.

"Want you to meet Mr. Nelson," Abner said with a nod in Christopher's direction. "He's here to answer your questions." With that Abner joined the group and waited to see what this young man had to say.

He looked like them: muscled, sun and wind burnt, and obviously edgy at facing so many truculent farmers. I was asked to come here, he thought. Why do they look so negative?

"I'm from over 'round Clarksburg. Brought up on a farm. Went against my Pa's notion and attended college in Morgantown to try to learn how to get a better yield from the land." He scanned the group. Most were rocked back on their heels, arms crossed over their chests, and spitting tobacco to beat the band. "What we do is evaluate the soil and decide which crops would be best for the area in question. When the soil is not so rich, other strategies can be applied such as growing pine trees to be harvested and sold at Christmas in urban areas. . . .or sometimes nutrients can be added to improve the soil." Still no sign that the men understood what he was talking about. "Maybe this would be a good time for any questions you might have." He looked up hopefully.

"Who'd want to pay money for a scrub pine?"

"They wouldn't be scrubs. The agency provides long-needled pine mostly, mixed with a few Frazier firs and Blue Spruce."

"What's that gonna cost?"

"There's no charge as long as we feel the recipient is serious about planting and caring for the seedlings.

"Seedlings! Them take years to get big enough to cut."

"I agree the pine trees are a long-term program. Meanwhile, teaching you how to select and use fertilizer to improve your growing capabilities in better soil is something that can improve productivity this year."

An old man at the edge of the group stuck up his hand. Chris acknowledged him with a nod. "What's a 'nurban, area?"

"And what's a 'sipient'," someone yelled from the back.

In an instant Chris changed his tone from the stilted style of university professors to the language he'd used growing up in rural West Virginia.

"An 'urban' area is just a town or city – where folks can't go out and cut their trees like we can. A 'recipient' is the farmer who is given the trees to plant." He cleared his throat. "I know how you feel. First time I heard those words I thought they were diseases." Laughter rippled cautiously through the crowd. "I'm glad to be where I can talk like my Pa again. . . ." He looked Abner squarely in the eye and shouted. "Now let's talk about this shortage of rain we're noticin."

He'd known that was their primary concern. "Plant your gardens as close to the creeks as possible. That way you don't have to carry buckets of water so far when the wells get low. The creeks might dry up with time but hopefully the gardens will have gotten a good start by then. Look in your cellars for all the canned goods that's collected in years you didn't use it all. Bring anything you can spare to the Grange and we'll distribute it to those who're runnin' short. Same for the hay. Pile up the remains of last year's crop and guard it with care. If this drought continues we'll need every stick of hay we can find." Every man in the crowd was fastened as tight as a wood tick to his words. "See how many ideas of your own you can come up with and we'll share them at the next meeting."

"When's that?" It was Clyde Hendershot again.

"How about in two weeks?"

Every head nodded. With some awkward hand-shaking and downcast eyes, they thanked Chris for coming and said they'd all be at the Grange in two weeks.

Two weeks later the situation had worsened. No rainfall added to lack of humidity and high winds had the little community worried about fires, loss of topsoil, and low crop yield. In a matter of months they'd lost their 'edge' on the depression.

"This won't go on forever," Chris promised. "In the meantime we must ration what we have on hand and try to produce as much as possible from our gardens for as long as the creeks last." For the next hour each farmer reported how much food was stored in smokehouses and cellars. A sizeable amount of extra canned goods was available. It would be kept in the Grange and doled out when necessary.

Abner had a suggestion. "Advise your wives to search every corner of your homes for pieces of material that could be used for quiltin'. Save even the smallest snips. I know from experience that babies arrive durin' depression and drought. They'll need warm clothin', too." Everyone reckoned Ruth had reminded him to mention that.

During the next hour Chris taught them about crop rotation, how to use lime to help enrich the soil, and the need to change cattle from pasture to pasture at regular intervals to allow new grass growth. There was some cocking of heads at talk of leaving fields 'fallow'. Chris explained this meant unplanted or ungrazed for a season to let it rest. They complained there wasn't enough land as it was, let alone to leave fields unused.

Clay Mathieson had a solution for that. He offered one hundred acres, divided up in whatever size parcels were desired, to anyone willing to clear the land in return for eight years of use at no charge to the farmer. After that time there would be an option to buy, lease, or return the land to Clay. Harold and Troy Conroy signed up for twenty-five acres on the spot. The remainder was snapped up in a matter of minutes.

The methods put forth by the extension service concentrated on using what the farmers had on hand. There was no money to buy tractors so horses would continue to provide the main source of power for plowing, pulling stumps, and harvesting. While lime would require an expenditure from the farmer's flat pockets, it was still the least expensive and most effective fertilizer for their region where acidic soil produced low quality crops.

Will suggested that each farmer contribute what he could to a common fund for the purchase of seed and lime so that it could be bought in bulk at a better price. The cost to each man would be pro-rated according to acreage. At the end of harvesting farmers who'd put in more than their share would be reimbursed by those farmers who'd in effect taken a loan in order to purchase supplies at optimal prices. Vernon Hart was put in charge of keeping the records on these accounts.

Eventually Chris spent most of his time working in the Boreland Springs section of the county. He no longer looked like a university graduate with a Master's degree. He was muscled, brown, and swore with the best of them. Land had been cleared, fertilized, seeded, rotated, left fallow and watched over like a newborn baby. Every member of the Boreland Co-op, as they'd called it, wanted to see that their efforts with new-fangled ideas had been worth it.

Nonetheless, each night everyone in the county prayed for rain.

For Sil, the first three months of 1930 had not been easy. Her young charges were not as easy to teach as her 'practice teaching' under an experienced teacher had been. Nor had she been taught at the university how to educate a roomful of students that included children from First to Eighth Grade. She'd grown up with the few students her mother had taught at home -- children who came because they wanted to, not because their parents insisted on it.

Pumpkin Knob School opened in January and Sil attacked her first year of teaching with energy and hope that promptly plummeted to despair. The older ones played tricks on the younger ones and were not averse to putting a frog on her chair as well! There was a constant stream of chatter between youngsters glad to be visiting instead of working at home. At the end of the day she'd spent more time trying to keep them quiet than in giving them an education.

After a month of feeling like she was on a merry-go-round that was getting out of control, she went to her mother. "They're good kids, Ma. I just can't seem to keep their attention. The older ones won't work on an assignment while I spend time with the First and Second graders – they just make a ruckus. While I'm back to settling them down the little ones giggle and trade lunches. Got any suggestions?"

Ruth Lockhart had lots of ideas. Mother and daughter spent the afternoon planning new strategies that would make school educational as well as fun.

Next morning she greeted each one as they came through the door. All whistles, sticks, balls, and glue were collected and placed in a tub to be retrieved at the end of the school day. Every pocket was turned inside out to free any creatures that might be used to cause bedlam. Coats and hats were hung with boots neatly placed on the floor beneath the coat they belonged to. Everyone, even the First graders, had to write their names neatly on their lunches which were then placed on a table behind Sil's desk. In about fifteen minutes these little chores were finished and the students were sitting at their desks.

After leading the class in saying the Pledge of Allegiance, Sil stood in front of them making a big show of looking over the roll call. For the first time since she'd started teaching every eye was on her and not a mouth was talking out of turn. It was one of those moments she wanted to frame and hang on the wall so she could look at it during the times when teaching became tedious and discouraging.

"Roy Ferguson." She scanned the class looking for him. "Are you here?"

"Yes, Miss Lockhart." A tall red-haired fellow with sapphire blue eyes and enough freckles for two people raised his hand.

"Mildred Hudson?"

A girl with curly brown hair, soft gray eyes, and tiny stature raised her hand. "Here," she said. Size-wise she could have been mixed up with the fifth graders but her voice was as firm as any one of their mothers.

"Would the two of you come to the front of the room, please?"

A quick intake of breath by those still in their seats, followed by furtive glances back and forth, indicated that they wondered what kind of trouble Roy and Mildred had got themselves into. They watched with trepidation as the two oldest students in the class walked to teacher's desk. While the two made their ponderous way through the rather untidy rows of desks Sil spoke to the others.

"While I'm talking with Roy and Mildred, I'd like the rest of you to take out your reading assignments and study for awhile."

Much scuffling and turning of pages ensued as no one wanted to be called to the front of the room. Faces were buried between pages while twelve sets of eyes were glued to the scene in front of them.

Sil motioned for Mildred and Roy to sit down beside her. Her voice was confidential, as if she were going to share a secret. The two leaned toward her. "I need help here and you are the two I feel are most qualified for the job." She watched their faces smooth with relief. "You know this is my first year of teaching and frankly sometimes it feels like I'm trying to carry five gallons of water in a two gallon bucket. If you're willing, I'd like to enlist you as assistants. Roy would be captain of all the boys and Mildred would be in charge of the girls. I, of course, will be overseeing and teaching all the time."

"Is this a contest?" Roy asked.

"In a way." His shrewdness surprised her.

"How does it work?" Mildred asked.

"Each of you would be responsible for the manners and tidiness of your 'team'. For instance, talking in class loses a point; late to school, forgetting assignments, crooked desk rows, and so on. More infractions can be added as we go along. At the end of each week, points are tallied and the team with the least points is the winner."

"What's the prize?" Their words were nearly in unison, making all three of them laugh.

"The losing team has to carry your books, let you to the front of the any line, and be especially polite in every way for one week. In the case of a tie I shall bring a big platter of my mother's sugar cookies and the whole school will have an extra long recess."

Roy and Mildred were proud to accept the challenge. The rest of the students were fascinated that such an interesting project could occur in a school. Sil felt that she'd made her first inroad toward communicating with students – thanks to her mother.

In early March Melia got her father to drive her into Waverly. She'd spent the winter and early spring months helping her mother reorganize and clean the house. Truthfully, she was reluctant to leave the farm and put herself in a position where old suspicions might come across familiar faces when they saw her in the little village of Waverly. Sil finally convinced her that all anyone could think of was the drought and depression they were facing. An obscure shooting back in 1924 had long since been forgotten.

Thus, Melia worked up her nerve to step back into community life again. As they approached Cleggs, however, her mouth got dry and she felt uncertainty descend on the words she planned to speak.

"Here we are," Silas said. "I'll look out back to see if he's got any field corn while you talk to Clegg." He wrapped the lines and walked around to the back entrance of the store.

"Thanks, Pa. It won't take long."

She took each step onto the porch with the deliberateness with which one would walk across a swinging bridge. Mr. Clegg was looking through the window to see if it was an elderly person needing help. He opened the door just as she grabbed hold of the knob.

His face brightened. "Hello, Melia. Heard you was home. Need somethin' for yer Ma?"

She cleared her throat. "No, Mr. Clegg. . . ." Her voice failed.

His brows arched like question marks. "Well?"

"I was hoping you might have need for another person." She hurried on when his forehead furrowed with concern. "I'd not expect much in the way of wages," she said.

He nodded vigorously. "I'll say! Ain't much money for anything nowadays. Be lucky to have enough to buy supplies much less pay someone to work fer me." He shook his head, causing particles of dust to fly from his shaggy gray hair. He'd been working in the grain bins. "Can't understand Maggie pickin' this time to retire – when the country's in such a muddle."

He threw his comments about his wife into the air while he brushed off his shoulders and headed to straighten up the meat and cheese that was displayed in the glassed-in cooled counter. It had gotten messed up yesterday and just when he'd started to sort it all out, the barge had stopped to drop off his order of cattle feed.

He sighed and waved his arm in Melia's direction. "I know we're not as bad off as most but that's just because the rest of the country is finally gettin' to be as poor as we've *always* been." Melia followed him to the shoe section of the old store. "And mark my words, it'll get worse here before long." She pulled off her winter coat and laid it across a pickle barrel.

She sneezed when they got to the back part of the building where hay and grain were stored. "Got a cold?"

"No, just some dust in my nose."

"Get sick often?"

"No. Never missed a day in all the years I worked in Wheeling."

"How're you gonna get here and back from your place."

"Pa will drive. That way he's got the use of the Silky during the day. Doesn't take too long. When we can buy another horse, I can drive myself."

He looked up. "Wouldn't count on makin' enough money here to buy a horse." His bushy brows rose in indignation at such a thought.

"When I was away, I sent half my wages home. Might be able to use part of that to buy one."

"What happened to the rest?"

"Had it in the bank. Lost it in the crash." She knew better than to speak in long sentences. Mr. Clegg didn't have time to listen to complicated reasons. It was also his way of finding out how reliable and responsible she was.

"Clyde Jenkins has a mare he wants to sell cheap. Might ask him. She's long in the tooth so he's lookin' fer someone who wants somethin' to pull light loads." He gave her a quick glance. "You look like a light load to me." He guffawed at his joke. Melia smiled. "Heard he wanted ten dollars."

"I'll go see him right away if you think you could use my services here." She chewed her lower lip.

"Offer him five."

He walked to a worn-out cabinet held up by two corners near the window. One drawer was labeled 'Orders to be made' and the other said 'Delivery dates'. He pulled out a sheaf of papers from the lower drawer and ruffled through them. "Looks like we'll be gettin' our next big order in around the first of April. Could you start then?"

She masked her disappointment with a smile. "Of course. That will give me time to get back into the habit of driving a horse again."

She went to the back of the store to get her Pa who'd been checking the prices of rubber boots. "Can't start til April, Pa."

"That's better than nothin'. Meantime, Ma's happy to have you back in the house. She's missed you since you left."

They walked back out to the wagon. "It's good to have you home, Melia."

His heartfelt love, coupled with a difficulty at expressing it, tugged at her heart. "I love you, Pa. Nobody ever had a better home than me."

Even with a stiff March wind Will had worked up a sweat. He'd finished plowing the upper field and was seeding it, hoping there was enough moisture to get a crop started before summer heat killed it completely. He stopped to wipe his dirty face and noticed a dust plume coming down Horse Neck Ridge. Can't be a car, he mumbled. Movin' too slow. Hope no one's behind and wants to pass. At this rate it'll be sunset before that driver gets where he's goin. He fanned his face with his hat and took a swig out of the water jar Eleanor had sent with him. It was Sunday, a day she tried to herd her brood to church. Those that wouldn't go were encouraged not to do any hard work such as planting. But these were new times. A body had to get as much put by as possible while the sun was shining and the land was ready.

Echoes of the depression filtered down to Boreland Springs through borrowed newspapers and hearsay from Jeremiah Pope who had the only radio in the area. When the batteries were low, it was sometimes a week before he could get over to Cleggs to buy new ones. They worried, fretted, and speculated about what awful things could have happened during those days without news. That's what made it so frightening – not knowing what was going on in the outside world. It was the first time Boreland Springs' people had ever cared a lick what happened beyond their borders. But already shipments of cattle feed and lime had begun to dwindle. Mr. Clegg had said he'd been put on 'back order' for clothing as well. The mountain folks had no idea how much worse it would get. Therefore, Eleanor reckoned God would take that into account as to why one of the Harts was working hard on the Sabbath.

Will walked to the edge of the field as the horse and wagon got closer.

"Melia, is that you?" He craned his neck to get a better view through the haze of dust that hung over the vehicle.

"Yes." She chuckled. "I'm practicing."

"For what?"

"April 1st when I start driving into Waverly. Got a job at Cleggs."

"Hope you're plannin' to get started before sunrise. It'll take that long at the speed you drive."

She nearly rolled off the wagon laughing. Will couldn't ever remember hearing her this happy -- of course he'd never been around her much. "You've got a point. I do intend to start early. Why are you seeding today? You're the only one I've seen working hard in the fields on a Sunday."

He leaned on the wagon bed. "Tryin' to get a head start on whatever's ahead of us in this mess. Havin' trouble gettin' lime already."

She looked at him with troubled eyes. "I think it will be terrible – what's ahead of us, I mean. Our only hope will be if we can provide all our needs from the land around us."

"What makes you say that?"

She laid the lines across her lap and studied the horizon. Will's stomach knotted up as he listened to her words describing the chaos, desperation, and fury she'd witnessed the day she'd left Wheeling. Her voice gathered strength as she continued with chilling authority. "The people were prevented from retrieving their money from the bank by armed guards standing in front of locked doors. Like me, most probably had no idea how banks work. They didn't know that when you put money in an account, those funds are reinvested in this stock market which is located in New York."

She stood up. He helped her step down so she was on his level. "My boss tried to explain the complexities of the crash and how it would affect small depositors like me. However, I think understanding the stock market belongs to those who live in New York. In the end the only thing that was understandable to people like me was that the bank no longer had the money we'd deposited there. And regardless of how unfair it was, there was absolutely no way any of us could get our savings back."

"Did you lose much?"

"Half of all my wages which I'd put in a savings account. My friend Alicia said it would accrue interest making it worth more when I withdrew it. Both of us lost all the money we'd deposited in the bank. Thank God I sent half home where it got put in a metal box and buried in the shed."

He shook his head in disbelief.

"At least I had a place to come home to. Those who work and live in towns and cities have no place to go. No land to grow their own food and no money to buy it. Most don't own the houses they live in and without jobs will soon be out on the street. Even folks who live in the middle of the state who've been working for coal and timber companies are having a rough time."

He nodded. "I've seen the pictures in newspapers over at Cleggs. Sometimes old-fashioned ways ain't so wrong. Pa always said don't give your money to a bank. Cash money hidden in a tight, dry place is better'n any brick buildin' where you hand your earnin's over to strangers."

"Wish I'd remembered that."

"At least you only lost half. Think what a good lesson you learned in the process."

She socked him a good one on the arm. "I could have learned that for a lot less money." He grabbed his arm in mock pain.

"I'd better get back to my driving," she said. "When she stands very long her legs get stiff."

"Can't have a stiff-legged horse for the speed you like to travel." He chuckled and helped her back up on the wagon.

"All of us have places where we go slow, Will. I recall how long it took you to get into a dance at the Christmas party. Took all the strength I had to keep you moving."

"You got me there."

It was the end of May and the last day of school. The children would be needed at home for summer work in the fields to prepare for winter. Sil arrived early to set out the cookies she'd brought as a special treat for the class that had turned the corner on their education and given her confidence as a teacher. She jotted her notes in the journal she'd kept since following the advice her mother had given her.

A degree of competition has been good to stimulate their desire to excel in studies if that's what it takes to win a reward. This will prove to be an invaluable lesson as they enter the world of adults, where those with motivation, determination, and innovation achieve success.

They've learned achievement is a goal to aspire to – not something to belittle simply because it involves learning to speak better and solve everyday problems with that education.

Learning to lose has helped them be more compassionate when winning and more humble when on the losing side.

Working as part of a team has taught them to think and perform beyond themselves. To accept a responsibility for the group rather than too much concentration on the self.

By rewarding them with words and demonstrations of encouragement, they have gained a feeling that it's not wrong to need help.

With time the boys were willing to help the girls in mathematical problems while the girls assisted their male counterparts in English assignments.

Toward the end of the semester there were more 'ties' than winners, making it necessary for me to supply cookies. I finally had to start baking these myself since mother had other things to do and mentioned it was my project, not hers!

She looked up as her group of rowdy students ran down the path to school. Many were carrying bouquets of wild flowers while others had brought cookies and candy to add to what 'teacher' had. In orderly fashion, each entered the little building and walked quietly to his or her seat and stood there, waiting to repeat the Pledge of Allegiance. Mildred and Roy came last and straightened desks, smoothed down unruly hair, or picked up a dropped handkerchief. No one wanted the last day of school to be untidy.

Tears burned the backs of Sil's lids as she watched them put their little hands over their hearts and follow as Mildred and Roy led them in the pledge. She would never forget this group – her first class. It would always be more special than any other. They had taught her so much: to encourage imagination rather than stifle high feelings; to discipline in a positive way rather than put the offender in a corner, only making him or her more rebellious; to understand their exuberance by joining in their games at recess; and to let them laugh at *her* mistakes so they'd know even adults aren't perfect. What a relief that had been – not having to pretend she was always right.

She graciously accepted all the gifts they'd brought – even the tiny box turtle that little Elma MacSweeney had found in the creek near her home. Roy gave her a small oak box he'd carved himself, proud that the lid fit perfectly. Mildred brought a muslin handkerchief that she'd edged with her own crochet and embroidered Sil's initials in one corner.

"Class," she said in her best 'teacher' voice. "You are the best group of students I shall ever have. You've proven that young people are smart – only needing a little guidance to eventually become responsible and productive adults." She noticed some of the First graders beginning to squirm. "So now, let's enjoy our refreshments and you have the rest of the day off." A great cheer went up, scaring birds out of nearby oak trees. Soon, however, crumbs dotted the schoolyard and those same birds returned to help clean up the playground.

Sil walked the two miles home, reflecting on her decision to make a career out of teaching. It was the right one, she thought. Working here where I grew up, helping to make my little community a bit better prepared to face the future, is where I want to stay. Her steps fairly flew onto the porch where her mother was shelling peas. "Ma, I love teaching. You've taught me something I could never have become skilled at in school – how to make children want to learn. I love it."

Ruth laughed at Sil's childlike enthusiasm. That's what *she* had enjoyed about teaching. Working with young people seemed to keep the teacher youthful as well. It was impossible to be boring when surrounded by excited and innovative students. "Will you try to obtain a position at a larger school in town?"

"No. I want to use my education to improve our community." Sil's eyes sparkled with thoughts of the future. "Towns are full of loud, foul-smelling vehicles and boisterous, sometimes rude, people. Not for me. I'll take the farm any day."

Sil put her feet up on the porch banister, leaned back, and closed her eyes. The gentle sound of peas dropping into Ma's kettle soon put her to sleep. Ruth's chest filled with gratitude that all of her three children had made the decision to stay at home. She knew that in time they'd marry and move out of the house. That was only natural. But they'd still be close enough to visit and bring the grandbabies every Sunday to visit.

She looked down the lane at the sound of those other two children – now grown men with ambitious ideas and rowdy voices. When you added the voices of Chris and Abner, it sounded like a riot. They'd been out on the back forty deciding whether or not to use it for pasture for beef cattle or clear and plant it. It seemed beef cattle had won out and the discussion was whether it would be Hereford or Angus. The cost would determine which breed it was as well as how many could be purchased.

"It's a long term plan so even if you could only afford two or three cows and one bull, it would be worth it." Chris's voice was full of passion, trying hard to convince the three Lockhart men to go ahead with the project.

"Especially, if another farmer does the same thing and purchases a bull with different bloodlines. You could use each other's bull on the new crop. It would be some time before it would be necessary to buy another. . ."

Sil's feet flew from the banister and she was off the porch in seconds. "Chris! Don't tell me you're the extension man I've heard about for the last several months."

"And you're the 'teacher in the family' these goons are always braggin' about?"

"Yep."

The rest of the Lockharts looked on while Sil and Chris got tangled up in a good-natured hug. He asked who was teaching math.

"Me!" she shouted in mock pride. "How's your Pa?"

"Mean as ever," but his eyes twinkled when he said it.

Abner tired of listening to a conversation that had nothing to do with the hard work he'd done all day. "Don't know about you, Chris, but I'd end the claptrap and come in to supper." He walked onto the porch with plodding feet, gave Ruth a peck on the cheek, and disappeared into the house.

"Yep," Danny agreed. "Ma's cookin' beats Sil's talkin' any day of the week."

While the men washed up, Sil set the table and her mother brought out the meal. In the process she explained to Ruth how she knew Chris as the graduate student who'd conducted the remedial math class she'd attended during her first year in school. "He was especially nice to me when Rachel died." Her eyes took on a faraway look. "I often wonder what she'd be doing now had she lived. . . .probably be on a safari in Africa."

Loud scuffling announced the arrival of four hungry, tired men. After Abner said grace, only the sound of spoons scooping out huge portions of greens beans, mashed potatoes, gravy, beef roast, and corn bread broke the silence of the meal. Once in awhile someone might compliment Ruth on her cooking but for the most part little time was spent on talk.

Sil looked at the young man who had been the proper professor-to-be when she'd known him in Morgantown. That man bore little resemblance to the sunburnt, muscled, rough talking fellow who sat at their table today. He looked more like his weathered father in his faded shirt and dirt-stained trousers. Sun streaks highlighted his head of dark brown hair that was badly in need of a trim. She nearly laughed out loud remembering his high-handed treatment of her that first time they'd met in his remedial math class. How things change she thought, when we enter the real world.

"What are you smirking about, Miss Lockhart?" he asked in his scholastic pronunciation.

"You know full well, Mr. Nelson." She put her hands in her lap and looked him square in the face. "You look and sound like the farmers I've grown up with – not the pompous graduate student who criticized me for *almost* being late to class. I think I deserve an apology." She couldn't stifle the grin that played around the corners of her mouth.

"Ahh, that was a façade demanded by senior faculty. . .I'll think about the apology."

"You do that."

"I'm goin' to smoke my pipe on the front porch. Anyone want to join me?" Abner was tired after a long day of work and not interested in listening to pitter-patter that made no sense to him. Ruth smiled and started cleaning off the table. Sil helped her as the men took Ab's invitation to join him on the porch.

The kitchen clanged with pots, pans, and plates, as they were loaded into the big sink to be washed. "Such a nice young man," Ruth said nonchalantly.

"Don't get any ideas, Ma."

CHAPTER TWENTY-FIVE

By late August, the more irreverent inhabitants of Boreland Springs complained that Hell couldn't be any hotter than it was right now in West Virginia. "Good thing we planted our gardens close to the creeks," Ruth Lockhart remarked as she took her place at the lectern in the Grange hall. "Otherwise none of us would've had anything to can."

Eleanor Hart gave a discouraged shrug. "On top of the ridge we're prayin' the wells don't dry up."

"We need a square dance," Nelda Ferguson remarked. Everyone looked at her like she had two heads.

"When it's so hot and we've so little food to offer?" Celia Chambers said.

"I agree!" Maxine Conroy replied. "Nothin' but hard work in a summer as dry as any I can remember calls for a little fun before fall and winter set in."

"We'll concentrate on dancin' with only a little eatin'," Birdie Leffel suggested.

"Wish I could've put more in that pressure cooker of mine this summer," Frances Forshey mused. "Already got six mouths to feed and another on the way."

The women broke out in back slapping and congratulations at mention of a new baby in their midst. That was always a good omen, even in hard times. After a few minutes Ruth got them back on the track of rationing. Several groans could be heard.

"This'll be a good time for some of us to lose a little weight," Adele Singleton said, pointing at her ample stomach. More than a few agreed to that.

"We can have plenty to drink. That'll make the men happy." Ramona Atkins offered.

"And good fiddlers!" Ida Mae Delancy added.

The Womens Christian Temperance Union had become less like an organization designed to limit the alcohol intake of men and misguided teens and more like a society preparing for seven years of famine. Everyone had had a big laugh earlier in the year when they'd marshaled their forces and used the old parable as a guideline. Lately though, news from all over the country showed they weren't too far off the mark. The depression was worsening; banks continued to close; more people were lining up for food; it was harder to get even the most basic supplies, and the drought showed no sign of letting up. What with all the added mouths to feed, while laughing relieved the tension, lack of water had to be taken seriously.

At this meeting, the project of the WCTU focused on quilting to ensure that no one would be without warmth when winter set in. The tables were laden with every piece of old material they had found in their homes that had no further use than to be cut up and made into quilts. Sil looked up from her scissors. "Thank goodness Melia had the good sense to buy batting from Tidwell's when it was on sale. Otherwise these quilts would be pretty thin." She wanted to make sure everyone remembered who had had the foresight to part with some of her precious money for an obscure product she knew they'd need. "What made you do that?"

"I don't know. Certainly had no idea about any 'crash'. I just figured it was something we use here every year during quilting and wanted to get it at a good price." She smiled. "Just dumb luck, I guess." Her face became thoughtful. "Glad I did it before all the chaos in the streets the day I left. There would've been no chance to buy then."

The older women couldn't imagine what it was like to be caught in such mayhem. "We're glad you got home when you did. We'd been missin' you for some time but didn't mean for it to take such a calamity to bring you back." Eleanor gave Melia a motherly pat on the back as she took her stack of squares to add to the others. "I'm also thankful Sil finished school before all this hit, too. Got our own homegrown teacher who can live at home rent-free and teach our younguns. Dumb luck all the way 'round."

They all nodded at these timely observations. Melia's sudden departure, which normally signaled a 'pregnancy out of wedlock', had lasted for five years, dispelling the whispered rumors about her reason or who might the father be.

"We've been needin' young blood in this decrepit group for some time. They're strong and got good ideas." Clara Pickens was somewhere in her eighties – no one could pin her down to an exact birth year but they always gave her a party on the Fourth of July. She was the best quilter of the bunch and hid her original patterns with the moonshine money she'd gotten from her husband who'd been shot by the revenuers years ago. She was held in great esteem for hiding it well enough so that neither the government men nor her four greedy children could find it.

The meeting ended with August 30th, a Sunday, being set for an afternoon of a few refreshments and lots of dancing and visiting. Melia and Sil were put in charge of making sure there would be enough fiddlers to last into an evening of square dancing.

No one would have believed there was a depression and drought that Sunday in Boreland Springs. Everyone in the community was thankful for a day of not working in the fields. They had looked forward to some drinking, dancing, and resting before starting into harvesting their undersized crops and slaughtering more hogs than usual. It gave them a boost – made them feel like they had more energy than they really did. Eleanor reckoned there might be a few crooked lines of hay mown on Monday as the drinking and dancing got wilder as the evening got longer. To make the night even more perfect, a light rain began to fall. No one would have minded if it had been a deluge.

"I think you've thrown yourself around with every young man here tonight, Sil." Melia laughed as her best friend, panting and sweaty, sat down for a glass of tea. "You were always the one who said you had no interest in the opposite sex. I believe your words were: 'I intend to spend my life making it a better place for mankind', or something to that effect."

"Why do you have to remember all those ridiculous things I said when I was a child?" Sil poked Melia in the ribs good-naturedly. "What happened to *your* ability to have a good time with friends, men and women alike? It's as if our roles have reversed and now you're the practical one while I'm considered frivolous."

Melia's eyes clouded for an instant. She bent closer to Sil's face. "I lost my exuberance five years ago. Sometimes I look like I'm happy and having fun. There are times when I actually feel lighter and ready to play again. But it fades fast and the seriousness takes over again." She circled her glass of tea slowly in the puddle of water that had dripped off its sides.

Sil was flabbergasted. This was the first time since they'd exchanged letters during Sil's first year in college that Melia had said anything about the sorrow that still remained with her. Sil didn't know what to say. They sat silently in the midst of pandemonium, thinking about that time when Charity had come into their lives and was gone before they ever got to know her.

"C'mon Melia. Let's allemande left and right together, what say?" It was Earl Moore who'd always had a crush on her.

Melia gave him her blinding smile. "Too much food in my stomach to chance bouncing around. But Sil's got plenty of energy."

Earl turned to Sil hopefully.

"She can't." It was Chris, and with a determined look in his eye he grabbed her elbow and pulled her toward the first group he could see that needed another pair. "Sil promised me at least three dances tonight and we've got to get started before the fiddlers get tired and go home." He watched the discouraged Earl walk away in disappointment. "Never had the impression you were such a popular partner," he said as they joined the raucous movements of a mountain square dance. "You always seemed devoted to your studies."

"People change. You're not the self-important, stodgy professor I met in the Library every week for a whole deadly semester either. God, I thought that would never end."

He grabbed his chest in mock distress. "You've hurt me to the core, Miss Lockhart. Allow me to continue to improve your opinion of me by taking a drive next Sunday."

"I could probably manage a short one. I've got to have my classroom ready for a roomful of ambitious students on Monday."

"That's right, the kids will be back in school again." He threw her high into the air. "You'd better get your proper schoolmarm demeanor back on by then."

She stepped lightly on his toe, nearly making him trip. "I think it's coming back already."

"You're hopeless."

Sil nodded but before he could pull her into another set she was off to dance with Earl.

"Would you like a glass of tea?" The question was spoken with the tentative voice of one who feels it was an inappropriate request.

Melia looked up into Will's solemn face. It always surprised her that he never expected to be accepted. Didn't he realize how appealing he was, she wondered? Even to her -- who had very little interest in developing a relationship with any man. All desire had been driven from her when Wyatt's faithlessness came to light.

Will's forlorn expression reminded her of the sacrifice he'd suffered as well. The ordeal had sucked much of her happiness and self-belief away as it no doubt had done to him. Only Sil's support and her job at Tidwells had restored a semblance of her confidence. She felt a need to show Will he was a person of significance.

"I was waiting for you to ask, Will. First though, let's work up a big thirst by some allemandes left and right."

Will hardly knew what to do with a positive answer. She was the most beautiful girl in all of Boreland Springs yet she seemed to be oblivious to the fact. But dancing scared him. His feet seemed rooted to the spot.

She looked at him expectantly. "We've danced together before. Remember?"

"That was a slow dance," he answered. "Not much chance of fallin' down or knockin' someone to the floor."

"Then it's time we learned to make our feet move faster." She tugged at his elbow.

He looked down at his big shoes, then at her. His face reddened. He could feel the heat creep up the back of his neck. Even his arms seemed paralyzed.

Melia couldn't help chuckling. "Hard to believe a simple square dance could put such fear in a man known for his fearlessness. C'mon."

He let her guide him into the melee where he was pushed and shoved to his position in the set. No one seemed to notice his clumsiness. They were busy keeping track of their own two feet. Why am I doing this, he wondered at one point when Melia turned him around when he'd gone the wrong direction and ended up in a different group of people. He tried to force his body to relax

-- to be as supple and nonchalant as all the others. The harder he tried the stiffer he became.

All his life Will had kept his movements precise and controlled. Moving too fast could have cost him his life. He'd learned to travel like a cat stalking a bird – frozen in place until another step could be taken. Nothing could be done with abandon. A government agent worked similarly – treading softly, always listening for the crack of a twig or a bush rustling. Even when moonshining was over for him, the habits of stealth remained. I'm too old to change, he thought. Throwing my body about like a string-puppet will never feel right.

Melia saw Will's shirt begin to dampen with sweat. His face was wrinkled with the effort of trying to perform something he'd probably never done, even as a child. Why have I put this hard-working man in such a position, she wondered. What's fun for the rest of this collection of unrestrained people is agony for Will.

"I'm bushed, Will." She beckoned for another couple to take their place. "Let's sit down and rest. City life has left me out of shape."

He let out a great mouthful of the breath he'd been holding. His face unwrinkled and a smile broke through the stiffness that had made his movements so rigid. Before she could change her mind he guided her to a table in the shade.

"Never been a dancer. Even a bad one." His eyes were downcast as though he'd failed at something easy.

"I apologize for getting you into that. Don't know why I did. It's not anything I enjoy either. Too often I join in activities just to be polite."

"I would'a thought dancin' comes natural to you."

She shook her head wistfully. "When I was a kid I was as rambunctious as the rest. But that was a long time ago."

"I don't ever recall dancin', singin', or playin' games as a kid. Everything I ever did produced somethin' we could use. Couldn't understand them men at the resort who hunted and fished for fun. When I went out with a pole or a gun, you can bet I wasn't expected back 'til I was carryin' somethin' Ma could cook."

"I was brought up the same way. Nothing ever got thrown out or put away. It got used until it was no more." She wiped her brow with her hankie.

"Let's walk down by the creek. Might cool us off a bit." He waved to Eugene and the others who'd struck up a game of horseshoes.

She took his hand to make sure she didn't fall down the bank. "Thanks, Will."

"Wish I'd had the chance to learn to speak like you have, Melia. Don't it bother you to listen to us with our country talk?"

"Speaking properly doesn't necessarily mean the speaker is honest and thoughtful. I'll bet those men who crashed the stock market had perfect English. And how many college men with their excellent grammar would you trust?"

Unwittingly, Melia's statement sent them back to that awful summer of 1924 when both of their lives were forever altered by a smooth-talking man home from college.

"That was a thoughtless thing for me to say," she said more to herself than to him. Her brow furrowed in anger. "Will those memories never go away?"

The spell of happiness fled for both of them in the wake of Wyatt's image. Melia was furious at her words that had returned him to their world, giving him more power than he'd ever deserved when he was alive. Will wondered why the subject of Wyatt clouded her eyes with so much sadness and antagonism.

Will cleared his throat. "I see Sil lookin' fer us. Probably ought to go back before she falls off the bank."

Melia's eyes reflected the thoughtfulness Will had shown to her. "Thanks for bringing me down to the creek. It's so restful. I'm sorry for saying something that brought Wyatt to this party."

Will turned and pinned her to him with the fury that shot from his eyes. "Wyatt can never return to this place for real. He's only powerful if we let his pathetic ghost interfere with our thoughts." She'd never expected Will to speak so passionately about anything. "He was a crook. It's time his memory stays buried in that fancy coffin."

"A crook?"

"That's what I said."

"I knew he was cruel and self-centered. I didn't realize he was a criminal."

"Cruel?"

She nodded.

"Melia!" It was Sil. "Party's over. We've got to pay the fiddlers and go home."

Melia took Will's hand and he helped her up the bank. Sil was so flushed with all the dancing she'd done that she didn't notice the subdued expression of the pair approaching her.

The Harts piled into the old truck Will and Eugene had used in Weirton. Will drove slowly so as not to throw anyone off when they went through a pothole. It was a full moon. As the truck climbed to the top of the ridge, festivity continued with the laughter and joking of all the Harts – except Will. He looked up as they neared the top. Silvery beams filtered through the balding trees at the crest. The fury left his chest as it always did when faced with the wild, yet serene, beauty of his birthplace.

The merriment faded to the background and he became immersed in thoughts inside his head. It was not a luxury he'd ever indulged in, believing little could be done to change one's life whether or not it was satisfactory. But he was tired of being the only one in the family who couldn't be happy; or laugh readily, or joke, or sing. He seemed to spend most of his time brooding about things that didn't bother anyone else. The curious eleven-year-old, proud of his family's vegetable business, had disappeared when they had started the bootlegging.

Why had he allowed the moonshining business to shame him so, when more than half the community was engaged in the same practice? Why did the dangerous life of a bootlegger stop him from living the other parts of his life with excitement? Other moonshiners he knew had more fun than anybody else. They were the fellows everyone wanted to be with. Why couldn't he be like that? Especially since all traces of the distillery were gone and he no longer had to be concerned with government agents. Why did he continue to worry about the possibility that he or Eugene might be pegged as the ones with Wyatt the night of the shooting when he knew there was no way that could be proved?

A great guffaw from Eugene reminded Will that his brother Eugene, thought to be twenty-five cents short of a dollar, had survived it all better than *he* had. Eugene had gone from a boy pandered to, cared for, or outright ignored, to a fellow popular as a hunting partner. Will couldn't be sure but he thought Eugene had even enjoyed one or two of the women over at Satterfields. That's one good thing to come out of all this, Will thought sourly.

All this reflection didn't get to the bottom of Will's problem of disappearing into his own personal cave when subjected to a social situation: he was lonely and shy. He longed for his own home and family but didn't know how to go about it. What will I do when the others are out of the house and in their own places? Who will I take care of then?

Sil's mouth didn't stop as they rode home in the old Model T Abner had been able to get second-hand a few years ago. "Did you have fun with Will? Did he hold your hand? Did he kiss you?"

"Stop!" Melia whispered hoarsely. "Nothing like that happened. We just tried to be friendly to each other." She sighed mightily.

"What?" Sil pulled her close.

"Then I said something that brought Wyatt right in the middle of us. Can't believe I did that. From then on even being polite was hard. . ."

"Why do you think of that creep? Hasn't he done enough to ruin you life? When are you going to leave him behind?"

"I have left Wyatt behind, Sil. I just can't forget the consequences of that foolish summer. I have nothing but revulsion for him; even though, as one deceased, he deserves compassion and forgiveness. I'm ashamed I believed him and forgot the values my parents taught me."

"He deserves no compassion and you must get over your shame." Sil hugged her. "What's done is done and nothing can ever change that. Stop punishing yourself and believe Charity is happy and well taken care of. Otherwise, you're lost, Melia. Don't you realize that?"

Melia nodded.

"You deserve a good husband and more children. Don't let Wyatt take that away from you, too."

Sil's words hit Melia in the face like cold rain. It was true. From his grave Wyatt continued to steal away her happiness. *I'm twenty-two. I gave him my virginity. I will not give him the rest of my life as well.*

Christmas was subdued that year. Everyone gave thanks for the harvest, mediocre though it was; for Clay Mathieson's offer that had allowed more Boreland Springs families to have sufficient land to farm; and with the exception of a few elderly complaints, everyone was healthy. August rains had rescued the land from completely blowing away, but it wasn't near enough to make up for a whole year where they only had a sporadic storm now and then.

The rest of the country had not fared any better. Pictures in well-worn newspapers told the story. A situation the Boreland Spring folks had thought would be solved by this time had only gotten worse. They discussed with familiarity places they'd never known about before the stock market crash. Even the youngest of Sil's students could point out Indiana, Iowa, Kansas, and Oklahoma in the school atlas. They were learning why these states were important to their own welfare. Before the crash, coal and timber from West Virginia had been shipped all over the country to generate energy and provide wood for construction. Likewise, produce from the midwestern states had provided food, seed, fertilizer, clothing, and other necessities for most of the United States.

The farmers in Boreland Springs had always grown their own vegetables and grain for livestock. However, they had always counted on buying seed and fertilizer from Clegg sto grow their crops. The day after Christmas, Mr. Clegg explained to Maxine Conroy that soon these valuable goods would not be so readily available -- that the local farmers would have to collect their own seed and find supplies of lime within West Virginia.

"You'll have to settle for cornmeal, Mrs. Conroy."

"And thankful I am to have it. We've grown up on mush, with or without syrup; cornbread; and cornmeal pancakes to mention a few. I reckon there's lots of folk who'd give their eyeteeth to have just one of them dishes."

"S'pose you're right."

She wasn't through counting her blessings. "Potato crop was better than we'd expected this year durin' a drought – there's endless ways to fix 'em. Yep, we've got a lot to be thankful for." She stopped to think. "We can add onions to most any vegetable to make it tastier."

Mr. Clegg helped her out to the wagon, agreeing all the way. He hoped there'd be enough business to keep Melia on. She worked hard and was pleasant to be around.

Kay Meredith

CHAPTER TWENTY-SIX

Summer 1931

"I feel guilty being so happy." Sil tried hard to paste a solemn expression on her face. "With so many homeless people, without jobs and going hungry, it doesn't seem right to experience such a wonderful thing as love." It was Sunday afternoon and they were sitting on the Lockhart front porch.

"I don't think love can be subdued by depressions and dust bowls," Melia chuckled. "Bad luck comes regardless of the timing. Love? You must take it when you have the chance, I think."

Sil cocked her head. "Hadn't thought of it that way. You're right though. There would never have been a good time for Rachel to die, or for us to give up Charity. The world could have been without wars, famine, or stock market crashes, and we'd still have had reasons to cry. I'll rejoice over love and take the happiness while it's here."

Melia nodded. "Yep, 'cause our turn to cry will come again."

"And give us the opportunity to 'develop more character' as Ma always points out."

"Sometimes I think I've had all the 'character-building' I can stand, but I know my opinion has nothing to do with how much more I'll have to endure."

Sil shaded her eyes and studied the knee-high corn her brothers had planted in the top meadow. "Wondering what the next calamity will be sometimes wakes me up during the night. Seems like the older I get, the more I worry about things I'd never even thought of before."

"Wish there was a way to turn off the brain and get a good nights sleep, don't you?"

"Yes. Especially now, when I wonder if getting engaged to Chris is what I want for the rest of my life."

"I'd take it one year at a time if it was me," Melia replied sagely. "Might get more rest that way." She smiled and elbowed Sil's ribs like when they were children. "Besides, it will be awhile before Chris fixes up the old Howard place. You'll have time to change your mind if you decide to."

Melia's optimism gave Sil courage to inquire. "What about you? Have you made up your mind to be happy, get married, have children?"

"I want all that, Sil. But I'm afraid to put myself in such a vulnerable position again."

"Why?"

"Falling in love and losing control of my senses could bring so much heartbreak again."

"You're older now and wouldn't let that happen."

"Doesn't that take away the love part and leave only the practicality of finding a husband to give me a home and family? Would you trade the excitement you feel at the prospect of spending the rest of your life with Chris for a methodical search for someone you're comfortable enough to live with and who, in turn, could put up with your quirks?"

Melia's questions left Sil pensive. She hadn't loved and lost yet. She had no idea what it might feel like to want to try again, knowing a good deal of the romance might be forfeited in the search for security. She felt Melia's hesitation had less to do with losing Charity and more to do with fearing being hurt herself. Fascinated with Melia's openness, she kept her silence and listened.

"I've accepted the fact that Charity's future lies beyond my sphere of influence – that no miracle will ever bring her back to me. Having faith that the Sisters have placed her in a happy home has allowed me to tuck that misery into the back of my mind, pulling it out only when I'm filled with self-pity. That happens less and less now."

"So?"

"So. . .I'm trying to be friendlier to fellows who seem interested."

"And?"

"And it's slow going. Trying to become an appealing woman seems so paltry with the really serious troubles our whole country is facing."

"You're afraid God will punish you for being lighthearted when you should be concerned with the bigger problems of mankind?"

"Probably," Melia smiled. "I can't escape how I've been brought up."

"You think I'm being self-centered then, Melia?"

"No, this is your first love and you're entitled to every happiness it brings you. I disobeyed my religion and have no right to expect such a passion again."

"You can't believe that! This is 1931 – not 1910. Times have changed. We're supposed to be forgiven for our sins and not punished further for an old transgression."

"I'll try to remember that. . . . .now, let's stop talking about me and start planning what we'll serve at the wedding."

"If there's anything to serve," Sil answered with a smirk. "Let's hope we keep on Mother Nature's good side and at least have berries and cornbread available."

"Funny you should mention that. Every night I ask God to forgive my sinfulness and send us some good, heavy rains."

"I'll never understand how we grew up together, went to church every Sunday, yet have such different ideas of God's wrath."

Due to the lack of rain, the leaves were already changing and it was only the beginning of September. Melia was in the back rooms of the store hanging up the winter coats and sorting the boots according to size. Not near enough stock with winter coming on, she mused. Doesn't matter anyway, I guess, since few have the money to buy them. The old front door scraped open causing the small cowbell to ring. She hurried forward wondering who'd come so early on a Wednesday morning. Mondays and Fridays were the days when housewives came in for supplies.

Will Hart was standing in front of the big bulletin board where livestock, furniture, firewood, and sundries were posted for sale. Before the depression, town ladies came out and looked for good buys on antiques. Country folk always made fun of these fancy people willing to pay good money for things they considered worn out. That never happened anymore.

"What're you looking for, Will?"

"A cheap milk cow, young enough to give milk for the family with some left over to make butter."

The board was so full of snips of paper torn from tablets, catalogs, and broken fans, that it was hard to find anything. "I should sort this all out and pin it up neatly so folks can find what they're looking for." Melia stood beside him and started looking through the disorganized and hard-to-read writing on the ragged pieces of paper. It was impossible. Scraps were pinned on top of one another. Some had even fallen on the floor.

"I think it'll be quicker if we take all of them down and start over. I'll sit here at the counter if you have time to pull them off and hand them to me. Then I can put them in piles that match -- surely there are lots of milk cows up there in that mess."

"I've got time. Maybe some lime will come in while we're workin'."

"Hope we're faster than that. Don't expect lime in for awhile."

He shook his head and started pulling the slips of paper off the board and handing them to Melia. "This year I'm savin' seeds from my tomatoes, beans, and peas. Chris lent me a book on how to dry the seeds then plant 'em in a warm place early in the year. Showed how to build a hothouse, they call it – glass is best, but I had to do it with Mason jars. When they get several inches above ground it's time to plant them outside."

Melia stopped her sorting, fascinated by what Will was talking about. It sounded like a plan that might help provide homegrown seedlings no longer available from outside sources. He went on to explain that the vegetable plants they put in the ground every spring had been started in this manner. He reckoned there was no reason he couldn't at least try to do the same.

"What an incredible idea. Are any of the others going to do this?"

"They're waitin' to see how mine turns out, I think," he said dryly as he looked closely at the paper he held in his hand. "Looks like Mr. Watson, down on Worthington Creek, has a cow that might fit my needs and pocketbook."

His comment reminded Melia she was supposed to be categorizing the sales items. The sound of papers being pushed from here to there according to kind whispered in the front section of the silent store. She couldn't stay quiet for long. "But the others must realize how important it is to prepare for a future when we get very little from outside suppliers. Our people must be convinced to save and dry their seeds as you're doing."

"Melia, what they do is. . . ."

"There should be a community hothouse, is that what you called it? Keeping such a project in one center is always more efficient than having lots of little stations. I learned that when I was working for Tidwells."

"Hold on. You're goin' off half-cocked, settin' up work for farmers who ain't even here – I mean 'aren't' here, to speak their mind. We've got enough community activity with the farmers' co-op that demands lots of time from them already. Let it be." The last was spoken more sharply than he'd meant. "Please," he softened his tone. "That way, if it don't work it's just *my* time and money gone to waste."

"Didn't mean to get so excited. It's just that it's such a great way to provide for our own needs; it's a shame the others hang back. However, you have my promise not to try to convince anyone else to join in."

"They'll come 'round when, or if, I can prove it works."

"Mr. Ables, up on Horseneck, has a heifer. You interested in something that young?"

"Might be. Depends on how big she is. Want to go with me to have a look Sunday afternoon?"

"As long as I can pick your brain about this 'hot house' thing?"

"Won't take long to pick *my* brain. I'll meet you at your house right after church. We'll go to Worthington first, then up to Horseneck."

"Ma would really like it if you'd have dinner with us first. Could you come with an empty stomach?"

"I can do that. Always enjoy jawin' with Harold and Troy anyhow."

She watched him through the smoky store window. He climbed into the old truck, put it in gear, and looked around to make sure no dogs or chickens were in his way.

"Best lookin' man in the county," Mr. Clegg announced as he shuffled into the room. "Honest, too. Don't find that often." He opened his heavy-lidded eyes as wide as he could. "Might want to keep that in mind, Missy."

"Are you trying to get rid of me?" she teased.

"Nope. Just tryin' to find you a home before we've got nothin' to sell," he answered with more truth than she wanted to hear.

"I've got a home now, Mr. Clegg. Don't need a man to supply that for me."

"You're lookin' at bein' a spinster then." His voice was tinged with disappointment. "When I was young, couples was married before twenty, especially the women. Otherwise you were considered past your prime – like overripe tomatoes. Don't understand this new generation."

"You sound like Ma."

"Mothers usually know what they're talkin' about."

She shook her head and went to fill up a pail of water to wash the front window.

She's friendlier than she used to be, Will thought, as he bounced his way home in a vehicle that had seen better days. She thinks my plan is incredible. Even Pa never gets that excited about my crazy ideas. 'Course he's busy bein' the 'tally-man' for the Co-op. Don't leave him much time to think about growin' seedlings.

Sunday was a beautiful day. The leaves were tinged with the beginning of autumn colors. Smells of new-mown hay, albeit it a bit stunted, carried on a sluggish breeze lulled Melia into a feeling of contentment. Will hadn't said much. Sometimes she wished he wasn't so shy. It would be fun to get further into that mind that she now knew to be brilliant. As the truck rumbled along, however, she began to appreciate the tranquility that made his intentions achievable – tension or excitement was not necessary for Will to implement a plan.

As the sleepy landscape slid by, she delved into the obstacles she might be faced with during the days and months ahead. Mr. Clegg had hinted about that. She glanced at Will and studied his quiet countenance, wishing she could be so systematic in the face of hardships to come. She wanted to ask him if under the surface he, too, had some misgivings. If being a man gave him an extra strength that women didn't have. She decided to try.

"Are you ever afraid one of your plans will go awry and you'll lose more than you can afford?"

"Sure."

"Where do you get the courage to go ahead?"

"Don't think about it – I just imagine what might happen if I don't try to prevent a problem. If the money and time needed to try to keep it from happenin' is reasonable, I take the chance."

She was dumbfounded by the simplicity of his approach. He glanced at her. She was staring out the window, a sober expression on her face. "When we're faced with so many troubles like now, I divide my efforts into different areas. That way if one don't work, maybe another will. I don't put all my money at risk."

She turned toward him. "The old 'don't put all your eggs in one basket' idea."

He nodded. "Yeah, but don't forget another one: 'Man proposes, God disposes'. All we can do is try and hope for the best."

The road turned rocky, claiming all Will's attention. Melia lapsed again in thought. He made sense. She might be able to apply his approach to her own problems, such as the prospect of losing her job and the need to be a productive member of the Conroy household. She'd been gone so long that the family had distributed her former duties amongst themselves. Many of those chores had lightened. Harold spent most his spare time at Collette Riley's home proving to her and her family he would make her a good husband. He ate lots of meals there, complimenting Collette's mother on her good cooking, and Melia was certain that some of his grubby overalls and shirts got into the Riley laundry as well. If that marriage came about, and Melia was certain it would, the couple planned to renovate an old wagon shed on the land they'd leased from Clay, and move into that.

Between his blacksmithing circuit and helping Harold with the farming, Troy, too, was often out of the house. He wore the same clothes for days on end since sometimes he was shoeing in the far reaches of the county and might sleep overnight. That left only her, Maxine, Silas, and Earl at the dinner table. Even though Melia sometimes missed the boisterousness of the entire family, she didn't miss how much their absence lightened the back-breaking job of washing clothes.

Earl, too, would soon be gone. He continued to study hard and wrote to every government agency Mrs. Lockhart mentioned, trying to find ways of working for his college education. He was sixteen and determined to shed himself of the hardships of farming. He wanted a career that demanded his brain and not his ability to throw a perfect twenty-foot haystack in less than an hour. He was wavering between construction engineering and architecture. "God only knows where he'll find a job in the unlikely event he *does* receive a grant from our bankrupt government," Melia muttered to herself, her words lost in the noise of the engine. "We'll be lucky if the government survives this mess."

"We're here." Melia was so deep in thought that his words startled her. She climbed down and went with him to see Mr. Watson and his cow.

She watched as Will examined the cow for soundness. He gently massaged her bag to make sure there was no hardening; looked at the feet for signs of soreness; evaluated her weight and brightness of eyes that revealed healthy teeth and proper nutrition. She was impressed with his thoroughness.

"She have any trouble calvin'?"

"Nope," Mr. Watson said while in the process of spitting a stream of tobacco from his black-stained mouth. "She don't mind help neither. Plenty of milk for her calf."

"Why's she for sale?"

"Got more cows. Need money for winter supplies afore Clegg runs out of everything."

Will nodded, still looking her over. "Willya' take five?"

"Askin' fifteen."

"She's fine to be sure, but five's all I got. Headin' up to Horseneck to look at a heifer Hayes Ables has."

Watson muttered and circled the cow, looking to see if he could part with such a fine animal for less than he'd planned. Will took Melia's elbow and turned to leave.

"Hold on," he yelled. "It's robbery but I'm in a bind. You can have 'er fer seven-fifty, but you don't get the halter or bell for that."

Will nodded, surprised that his bargaining had worked so well. "Didn't expect to. Be back with the wagon tomorrow. Got a place to load 'er?"

"Yep. Over there." He pointed to a bank that was built up so a wagon could be backed in, making it easy for livestock to be loaded.

They shook hands and Will said he'd bring the money by when he came to pick up the cow. Watson nodded and let loose with another stream of tobacco.

"Hope I can get the heifer for five," he said as they headed up toward Horseneck Ridge.

Melia watched as the same process took place. The asking price was fifteen but Will got it down to five since she'd not be producing milk for another year and then only if the calving went well.

"Even though she comes from good stock, we don't know for sure just how much milk she'll produce or if she'll be a good mother," he'd said.

Hayes was tired of dickering. "Take her for five, Will. You're like a bulldog when it comes to hagglin'. I've got hay to mow!"

"I'll pick 'er up tomorrow."

They shook hands and Hayes went off to hitch his workhorse to the mowing machine.

"How come you're not talkin' much?" He was worried she was bored with all this farm stuff.

"I'm amazed at your expertise, Will. Watching your offhand manner and casual bargaining abilities makes me want to follow you around more and learn how to use your skills to solve some of my problems."

He stopped the truck in front of the Conroy house and turned to face her. "Any time, Melia. You into stackin' hay? I could use an extra hand there."

She hooted in a most unladylike fashion and shoved him into the door. "Take that, you incorrigible clown. . . .I just might take you up on that offer. Lord knows I've done my share of stacking hay while waiting for younger brothers to take over."

He rubbed his left arm pretending to be hurt. "Now that this arm is sprained, you might have to start tomorrow."

She shook her head in mock disbelief, making her heavy curls fly about her face. "Don't wait for me tomorrow," she yelled as she hopped out of the truck and headed up the path. "You've just given me a real incentive to make Cleggs last as long as it can."

"It's still good to know you've got a job in the hayfield when you need it though, isn't it?"

She waved and listened to his laughter as the old vehicle bumped its way up the road heading for home.

CHAPTER TWENTY-SEVEN

Sil and Chris got married on Christmas day. "What a wonderful way to celebrate the birth of Christ," Melia said when Sil asked her to be the maid of honor. "Just what we need to put a good face on such dismal times."

"It's not going to be fancy. Just you, me, Chris, and hopefully Will, standing in front of Preacher Knox and a handful of friends and neighbors. Ma says the WCTU ladies will serve punch, cookies, and sandwiches but there's no money to pay for fiddlers."

"Doesn't matter. You're getting married. Fiddlers aren't going to change how happy you'll be when the two of you go back up to the old Howard place. Chris has worked hard to get it ready."

"He's one in a million, that's for sure. Who'd have ever thought he'd pay attention to me when there were so many prettier girls after him at school?"

Melia held hard to Sil's shoulders and looked her sternly in the eye. "Get this straight. First, they weren't prettier; second, they weren't very smart; and third he's lucky you think he's special."

Unflappable Sil dissolved into tears, hugging Melia with the strength of a lifelong friendship.

"What on earth's the matter?" Melia was bewildered. "You're. . ."

"I'm scared. What if I don't turn out to as pretty – or as witty – or as good a cook, as he expects?"

"What if he turns out to be dull, or sloppy, or smacks his lips when he eats? You know how you hate that."

Sil laughed at Melia's picturesque descriptions.

"The thing is, Sil, I don't think you'll be expected to be perfect right off the bat. He's probably worried too -- wondering if he can live up to your lofty ideals." They both laughed at Sil's old tendency.

Melia put her hands on her hips and shook her head in disgust. "I can't believe it. Here I am, giving you advice concerning something I know nothing about. Why don't you tell me to mind my own business?"

"Because, married or not, you know better than anyone how to get me back on track when something has me a bit off balance."

"You've done that for me too. Guess we'd better always stay close enough to help each other up when the need arises."

"Seems like a smart idea to me." Sil wiped her nose with the hankie Melia handed her.

The 'big day' arrived with a blanket of new snow that glittered like diamonds in the winter sun. What could be more fitting, Sil thought as she pulled on her wool dress. It was plain by wedding standards: pale yellow, which was the nearest to white she had, with long sleeves, high neck, and long skirt. Ma had spent some of her egg money to buy high-top leather boots. 'Warmth is more important than fashion right now,' she'd said. Sil agreed.

Nature had provided them with a pristine day that looked tailor-made for a wedding. However, the wind was sharp as a butcher knife, cutting through the heaviest coats anybody owned. The snow had come early, replenishing itself weekly. This, along with plummeting temperatures, had made it necessary to burn more firewood than normal for this time of year. On the brighter side, some said when it melted it could provide some relief from the drought.

The Lockharts piled into the old Model T – 'Abner's jitney', Ruth called it. Sil's teeth chattered all the way to the church, as much from fear and indecision as the cold. She rubbed her hands together constantly; even though her gloves were lined with wool. Ruth wanted to say something to calm her daughter but knew only time would do that.

The church was cold. Rev. Knox's breath blew in gusts as he spoke the solemn words. The wood stove took its good time heating up and when it did, the room clouded slightly due to the faulty flue that no one had remembered to fix. Some of the older members of the congregation coughed throughout the service.

Will and Melia stood self-consciously beside their friends and were happy when the final 'pronounce you man and wife' came from the bluish lips of the preacher. With all this discomfort, the church was still overflowing with well-wishers. None of her students wanted to miss seeing 'teacher' get her new name and all of Chris's Co-Op farmers were there to support him in his 'hour of need', as they'd called it. Chris wished that his father had been able come but the heavy snow had made that impossible.

The refreshments were finished off and congratulations shouted quickly so everyone could get back to their own homes. Fires had been banked during the ceremony and no one wanted to stay away long enough to let the temperature in their houses get down to freezing.

Ruth dabbed at her eyes as she watched Sil and Chris clamber in his old truck and head up the road toward the Howard House. I'm glad he got authorization to spend all but one day working out of his home, she thought. If they'd had to move to Parkersburg, Sil would have had to give up her teaching at Pumpkin Knob.

"Our first one out of the nest, Ruth." Abner put his arms around her shoulders. "But she's still close enough to run home if he's not good to her." He looked down at her with a twinkle in his eye.

"She'll run him out of the house with an iron skillet if he's not good," Ruth replied. "T'will be him who has to find another bed." He was relieved to see the grin return to the corners of her mouth.

"Wonder when Daniel and David will find wives who'll put up with them."

"Don't count on that, Ab. They're too comfortable at home. It'll take the Madonna herself to make those two ruffians leave hearth and home."

"You're probably right," he replied. They walked to the old car, where the ruffians in question were chomping at the bit to get home to supper.

The coughing, bumping, and sputtering of Chris's ancient Model T allowed the newlyweds to travel without trying to make conversation. Apprehension over the night ahead was written in furrowed brows and downcast eyes. Chris had little practice in the realm of lovemaking. Once, during his first year in college, he'd gone with friends to a local bar where moonshine and girls were available for a price. They'd teased him at his naiveté and passed a hat to gather up enough money for his initiation into the secret world of women. He was too embarrassed to protest so had picked the friendliest girl in the room and gone off to get drunk enough to let her introduce him to what lay under the dress she wore. Against all odds it was a marvelous experience. He'd gone back several times and fancied he was in love with her – until he arrived unannounced one night to find her in bed with one of his buddies. He'd given all his attention to his studies after that, determined never to pay for a woman's attentions again.

The most Sil had ever had to do with love were the few perfunctory embraces she'd permitted Chris when they were out of the way of prying eyes. Doubt if that could be described as 'love' she thought. Those pecks on the lips had not brought about flashes of light the way Rachel had described. Yet, she loved Chris from her inside. Her chest felt like it was full of cotton whenever he was near her. Her mouth dried up and most of the remarks she was able to get out sounded ridiculous. She missed him on days he was out on his projects and wanted to jump into his arms when he came walking down the lane. That had to be love. Why then, am I so frightened, she wondered.

Because you haven't any idea how to bring this thing called 'consummation' about, an inner voice murmured. When the other girls were learning the art of flirting, petting, and often 'going all the way', you were standing on the high ground, convincing yourself all this mating stuff was beneath you. That wasn't all bad, mind you, the voice continued. But it puts you in a bit of a bind right now.

She hadn't realized the car had come to a stop and Chris was looking at her questioningly. She fumbled out from under the blankets Ruth had covered her with and nearly fell out of the door into the snow. Before he could reach her she'd righted herself and was lifting out the meal Ruth had also sent along.

"You go on in and I'll bring this," he said, taking the cumbersome cardboard box in his big hands. "There's some kindling ready if you want to get that started."

Good, something to do, she thought thankfully. I'll get that done and make a run to the outhouse before Chris gets everything in from the car. Taking care of her personal hygiene privately had always been an issue with Sil. Using the chamber pot, or slop jar as her impudent brothers called it, was something she did in the darkest and loneliest part of the night, when a household of snoring assured her no one was about. This tendency had especially caused her problems in the communal atmosphere of college. Her fanatical need to relieve herself in absolute seclusion had caused her abdominal pain, not to mention constipation, more than once. At times she was convinced that living in close quarters with a husband, regardless of how much she might love him, would be impossible. *Love won out,* she thought matter-of-factly, *as evidenced by the marriage I've just agreed to.*

It took awhile to loosen all the clothes she was wearing. By the time she was back inside, Chris had hauled everything in and the fire was showing signs of life. She lit the oil lamps but even the flickering shadows that made the little house seem like a safe cocoon failed to imbue Sil with any sort of confidence or excitement.

"I'll go out and bring in more firewood. Feels like we're going to need it."

"I'll set the table and get a fire going in the cook stove. A basin of warm water would feel good before bed, I think."

He nodded and put on his heavy gloves. *He's as uncomfortable as I am,* she realized. *We'll make a pretty pair.* She couldn't stifle the smile of irony that flushed her face. It was probably the first time in the history of Ruth's famous cooking that the eaters paid little attention to the taste. They chewed slowly, took their time buttering the bread, and Sil insisted everything was put to rights before the meal could be considered over. But no matter how slow they both tried to move, it was finally time to bank the fire and go to bed.

"I'll take care of the fire if you'd like to take your sponge bath," he offered.

She picked up a small pail of the warm water and went to the bedroom at the back of the house. She poured the water into her mother's old washbasin and pitcher. Sil had always loved the set, which was antique white with a pastoral scene painted in silver. It made her heart stop thumping just to look at it. *Ma must have known it would be comforting,* she thought thankfully.

Since Chris had no furniture of his own, Abner and the boys had helped him move Sil's oak bed the day before the wedding. Ruth had sent along heavy quilts made by various family members through the generations and preserved meticulously, it seemed, for eternal use. A rough table Chris had found in the attic had been cleaned and now stood on his side of the bed – an alarm clock standing proudly ready to open each day with a loud clamor.

He'd banked the fires with more precision and time than he'd ever taken in his life. Can't be too careful with these old chimneys, he thought, even though it had been swept thoroughly and tried out less than two weeks ago. He stood looking down at the cauldron of warm water waiting on the stove. He grabbed a washrag and scrubbed his entire body with the intensity of a cat cleaning her kittens.

When he finally entered the bedroom, he was blue with cold and his teeth were on the verge of chattering. He threw convention out the window and jumped under the covers clothed in long underwear from neck to toe. It felt to Sil like a bobcat had just landed in the bed. She sat up abruptly.

"What's wrong?"

"Nothing," he said through clenched teeth. "I'm freezing, that's all."

"Good grief. Even your breath is cold!" She covered him with more quilts.

Like children they tunneled into the warmth under the blankets, forgetting about what was supposed to happen and concentrating on getting warm. He pulled her into his chest. That makes me warmer already, he thought. It was the first time he'd ever actually held her in his arms. Quick embraces that didn't allow much bodily contact didn't count. He was surprised at how lean and muscled she was.

Sil hadn't realized Chris was big enough to completely enclose her within his big body. For the first time in her life she felt almost delicate. She'd always been sturdy and strong and that made her feel less feminine than her girlfriends. She was happy to know that her husband would always make her look more petite. Having performed heavy work all her life, she'd never considered how much more powerful men were than women. Her father and brothers had worked the fields in hot summer wearing thin shirts or none at all on particularly hot days. But she and her mother had been too busy carrying water or cooking meals to pay attention to sinewy muscles and the effortlessness with which they pitched hay into perfect stacks -- or plowed through hard clay for hours on end. Besides, they were family. Who'd take the time to notice what wonderful male specimens they were?

This was the closest she'd ever been to such strength and it was difficult not to become aware of defined chest and arm muscles that pressed through his underwear. Embarrassed at her curiosity she encircled his chest so her hands would rest on his back. There, too, she was confronted with tight skin. Her hands found their way to his face. She skimmed her fingers through his hair, traced a strong jaw line, and felt the rough texture of a day-old beard. This disquieted her more than the raw power of muscles. She forgot about being cold. Her hands had a mind of their own – without her direction they stroked his arched eyebrows, explored the cleft in his chin, and discovered the delicate insides of his ears. He radiated the combined scents of smoke, sweat, and fresh air.

Warmth and sweat soon permeated their intimate cocoon. Eventually, they felt comfortable enough to raise their heads above the quilts into the frosty air of the room. Sil's hair was wrapped around her neck and plastered in her face like a wet towel. Chris was little better, with tendrils of wet locks hanging into his eyes and curling around his ears. They looked at each other and laughed.

"We look like something the hounds wouldn't waste time with," he said.

"What on earth are you wearing?" she asked.

"My long-johns. What've you got on? You've got ruffles around your neck, your arms – do you have them around your feet too?"

"No." She started to untie the ribbon that kept her gown snug around her neck.

"Let me do that." It took a bit of fumbling but finally the drawstring gave way, exposing Sil's neck down to the tops of her breasts. Moonlight illuminated her silky skin giving it an iridescent quality. He longed to run his fingers across her collarbone and under her arms.

She pulled impatiently at the buttons of his underwear – unconcerned when one flew off and disappeared somewhere in the bedclothes. Within minutes, nightgown and long underwear lay in a heap beside the bed.

Chris nestled his head in the soft skin of her neck. His calloused hands circled the silky skin of her breasts then roamed down to her bellybutton and the slight rise of her stomach. He felt her quiver. He was clumsy – he knew that – for he'd had little experience. Nothing could stop his need to know how he would feel inside her. He covered her mouth with his. She opened her lips and let him into her soul. They were so close she could feel the erection that at first surprised her, then alarmed her at the size of this part of his anatomy that would soon become a part of her.

He pulled her into his chest with his hand on the small of her back. She forgot the fear and opened her thighs. Passion obliterated all thought and they were carried on a wave of feeling so intense Sil thought she would break. They soared, breathless, so high in the heavens that the stars were close enough to touch. To the beginning of Time where love began. Excitement swept them through the ages, suspended in the sky, looking down on other mortals whose tale of love paled in comparison to theirs. They were wise. Naïve. A stone's throw away from dying over the ecstasy.

Their descent to earth was gentle – encased in each other's arms -- too exhausted to speak. Words would only have tarnished the experience. It was a jewel to be held in the heart – quietly – privately. They awoke the way they'd fallen asleep, lips and hearts touching. Sun struggled through the frosted windowpanes, giving off a luster like chipped diamonds. It was more than the chill that brought them together again – to travel the peaks and valleys of sensation that had joined them forever just a few hours earlier.

All thoughts of a depression, soup lines, and hardships ahead disappeared with the strength of their commitment. They were certain there was no obstacle too great for them to negotiate as long as they were together.

Two days later the honeymoon was over. The necessity of holding onto the passion had to be sandwiched between Sil's teaching and Chris's meetings with the co-op to discuss how to survive the depression.

It was a disgruntled group of farmers awaiting Chris at the grange building. They were cold, poor, and left out of most government programs.

"Why don't we get any help from Washington?" The question asked over and over.

"Because we live in the best part of the state for farming. The land here is arable enough for us to produce adequate food for our individual needs. That's what the government takes into account – how an area is able to sustain itself. What it doesn't note is how we're affected by the drought plus the return of so many extra mouths to feed." He paused to let this explanation sink into the minds of simple farmers who'd never cared before what the government did or didn't do. The silence became ominous. "Look at it this way," he continued, "we're no poorer than we've ever been. We notice it more because our land isn't producing crops and our families have gotten larger.

"Then why don't we qualify for government relief?"

Chris was exasperated but valiantly held his irritation in check. "The government doesn't have enough money to satisfy the needs of everyone. The worst effected are the first to get assistance. In West Virginia the coal miners and timber men have been left without jobs or homes, *not* us."

"Why?" Cletus Moore's face got redder than usual. "They live in the middle of some of the best timber and coal land in the whole country."

Chris persevered. "These resources were exploited by large outside companies that have closed due to the depression, leaving those workers without a way to earn money. Previously , they had depended on the company stores to provide for their needs. Now they have no jobs and no farms. Government assistance will be primarily for them."

He watched their reaction. It was one of the longest speeches he'd ever given to them. They were typical farmers, taking their time trying to figure out if what he said was true. He went on to explain some of the ways they could protect themselves. "We're doing the right things. Taking care of ourselves by planning ahead to plant what we need, canning vegetables for a long-term shortage, using all our supplies with care, and not throwing anything away. We're lucky to be in a position to fend for ourselves and not rely on the government to provide for our needs."

The air was filled with heavy breathing "Will's even built a sort of hothouse where he can grow vegetable seedlings so we don't need to spend cash we don't have for something we can plant right here."

He wasn't sure how this would go down.

Abner Lockhart looked at Will. "Would you show me how to build one of them things?"

"Glad to, Ab."

Within minutes Will was agreeing to teach all of them how to build a 'sort of hothouse'. He couldn't wait to tell Melia.

Kay Meredith

CHAPTER TWENTY-EIGHT

"Drought and depression will never disappear until we give our lives to God and the works He wants us to perform."

It was 1932 and Reverend Knox was writing another flamboyant sermon he hoped the Almighty would hear. In the shadowy corner behind the pulpit he'd begun to wonder why the troubles had lasted so long. His words were offered up to a God who might reckon there were still moonshiners among them. That's probably where they get the money to pay their property taxes, he thought darkly. "Can't you see, Lord," he whispered. "Alleviate the drought so they can know pious living produces good results -- which I can credit to You from the pulpit." He'd never before tried to bargain with his Maker but anything was worth a try in these times.

God must have been concentrating on another place needing His help, for dry weather continued and the practices that had started in 1930 continued. Well water was used sparingly and where possible, livestock were taken to the creeks for water. When they dried up, the fire trucks from St. Marys and Parkersburg brought relief with loads of water that had been pumped from the Ohio River. It couldn't be used for human consumption – only livestock and gardens. In any case, the river water gave some relief to the already depleted wells.

Melia knew the instant she looked at Mr. Clegg's crestfallen face that this would be her last day. She'd grown to care for the old man whose curmudgeonly manner failed to conceal the soft touch he really was. She knew it was a defeat he had no control over. The country was overwhelmed: banks in crisis; farmers with more crops than buyers; and a government in conflict as to what to do. There were many to blame: President Hoover; members of the Stock Exchange, although none of the common folk knew who these people were; the Democrats and Republicans who couldn't agree on anything, resulting in useless, constantly-changing programs that benefited no one.

Melia read the newspapers and wondered how anyone could bring the United States into balance again. During Hoover's last year the government had ordered crops to be burned, livestock to be slaughtered, and farmers paid not to grow anything. It was an effort to get rid of the surplus in order to increase the value of farm products. The only problem was that no one had any money to spend, surplus or not! It would take a miracle from God himself to get the Republicans voted back into office.

More banks closed. Unemployment increased daily. The country was filled with people living wherever they could get out of the weather: chicken-coops, abandoned barns, or makeshift shelters at the edge of cities and close to soup kitchens. Hopping freight trains was a popular mode of transportation to California where everyone hoped for warmer weather and a chance to work. These displaced people developed their own communities along the tracks, providing hot fires, watered down coffee, and conversation. This exchange of troubles provided sustenance for souls who had been uprooted by circumstances they'd had no part in bringing about.

At least I don't have to leave my home and live in a boxcar, Melia thought. She squared her shoulders and prepared to make it easy for Mr. Clegg to give her the word. "Morning Mr. Clegg. Looks like there aren't enough supplies in the store to open the door."

He coughed self-consciously. "Been meanin' to talk to you 'bout that, Melia. I just don't need another person anymore. Probably start openin' for a few hours in the afternoon for them that's got any money, or barter, for the measly staples I've got on hand."

"I know you've kept me longer than you needed to, Mr. Clegg. I appreciate that. Who would have thought things would stay so bad for this long."

He sighed, relieved she wasn't going to cry. "I can't figure it out. Why did the government burn crops and kill livestock when so many are hungry?"

She nodded sympathetically. "I think it was a senseless effort to make produce more valuable by making it scarce." She sat down on a stool near the pickle barrel. "It's hard for us to understand because we have small farms – only big enough to produce for our own needs. Most of us keep one or two cows for milk and butter, a few hogs and maybe go into partnership with another family for some beef cattle. We've not had to worry about selling farm products out across the land like the big farmers in the Midwest. With the loss of those farmers we're beginning to realize how much we've depended on their shipments of seed and lime."

"Seems to have been a big failure as far as I'm concerned. Everyday I see newspaper pictures of deserted farms and people hungry and livin' off the land. How come that happened if havin' less crops to sell was supposed to bring business back to the farmers?"

"Because many city folk, who normally buy farm products, have lost their jobs. Those who had money in banks lost that too – just like I did. Therefore, not enough people have any cash to buy even small amounts of what the farmers are growing. The big farmers in the midwest need to sell lots of product in order to pay mortgages on land and equipment. And they're suffering a drought worse than ours. They call it a 'dust bowl' and now heavy winds are blowing away all the precious topsoil."

"You've said it in a way I finally understand, Melia. Readin' them newspapers only makes me more confused. Just goes to show how complicated our dim-witted politicians have allowed the situation to become. Maybe the next bunch will do better."

"Everybody's praying for that, I think. Looks like the Democrat, Franklin Roosevelt, will get the chance to try since the Republicans have worn out their welcome in Washington. Most folks think he's the best bet; although for the life of me, I think it will take a miracle from the Almighty."

"Or a flood -- like back in Noah's time when He washed most everyone off the planet and started over again," Mr. Clegg answered with a scowl.

Melia smiled and stood up slowly. "I'd best get on back home unless you've got something you want me to do before I go."

"If you could straighten up this mornin', then I'd be in good stead for awhile. That'd give you a little more change to put in your pocket."

"Glad to. Not much waiting for me at home. Everybody's able to clean up after themselves now." She laughed. "I was the only one who had to come home after the 'crash' and I don't eat much."

"What about your brothers?"

"They'll be getting married one of these days when they can throw up little houses on their pieces of land. Earlier they'd decided to wait until things got better but now they reckon they'll be gray by that time."

Mr. Clegg laughed hard for the first time that day. "Bad times will come and go. Can't let a depression put off important stuff like gettin' married and havin' kids. If it weren't a depression, it'd be somethin' else." He traipsed off to the back to sweep the grain room floor.

She was cleaning up one of the counters and wondering how anyone could take on an obligation like a wife and children when the economic situation looked so bleak. The old screen door screeched open and Will Hart came through looking tired, dusty, and thirsty.

"Mornin' Melia. Busy already I see."

"Wish there was more to be busy about."

"I'm needin' as many sacks of lime as you've got back there. Would that keep you workin' for awhile?"

"Mr. Clegg is out back. Yesterday he said we're down to about twenty sacks of lime and only a few sacks of seed."

"Thank God. I'll take all the seed and half the lime. Could you spare a drink before I start loadin'?"

She hadn't seen him for some time. Caring for all the farm land he'd acquired had kept him in the fields and her own schedule running back and forth to Cleggs had not allowed their paths to cross in some time. He'd lost weight, making his face look more gaunt than usual.

She poured a glass of water and handed it to him. "How's everything going?"

"The way it always does with farmers." He emptied the glass in about three swallows. "Too busy to stop workin' long enough to know whether or not I'm workin' hard enough. How 'bout you?"

"Looks like I'll be taking you up on your offer to stack hay," she answered with a rueful smile. "We've finally run out of customers with cash and don't have much to sell anyway."

He stopped in the process of selecting a pickle from the barrel. "Sorry to hear that but I ain't surprised." He wiped his mouth with the back of his hand. "What will you do?"

"Help Ma at home and be one of the busiest women in the WCTU meetings with quilting, canning, and mending. I'm happy for that though.

Most folks don't even have a home. While none of us are wealthy most of us own our own land so we're not about to be put off it."

He nodded and handed her back the empty glass. "Get yourself some heavy gloves. I start at the crack of dawn, take a mid-mornin' break, eat one of Mom's big meals at noon, then back to the fields." Melia never knew for sure when to take him seriously. "In your case, I'd not expect the same work as I get from the boys and you could quit after lunch. . . .'course I couldn't pay you as much either." He couldn't hide the smile that lifted the corners of his mouth.

She boxed his ears. "You shouldn't tease about such seriousness."

He covered his head with his hands in mock fear. "I needed a funny spot," he said. "They've been few and far between. No one gives me a better chuckle than you."

"I'm glad I'm good for something. Here, have another drink and get back in those fields. You've been out of them long enough."

Her laughter followed him as he walked to the back of the building to see Mr. Clegg.

He heard the slow rumble of the wagon before he looked up from the mowing machine. Has to be Melia, he thought, nobody else drives that slow. He pulled the horse to a stop, wiped his brow with the back of his arm, and waited for the dust to settle. She had her old overalls on, a kerchief around her head to catch the sweat, and a straw bonnet to protect her face from the sun. A thin long-sleeved shirt was snug at the wrists. She stepped down off the wagon in worn-out leather boots that were laced around the bottom of her trousers to keep fleas, grasshoppers, and mosquitoes from going up her legs. He shook his head. At least she's dressed for the job, he thought and clambered off the mower.

"You look like a field hand."

"That's what you said you needed."

"I was kiddin'. Thought you knew that."

"You sounded serious to me so here I am. Looks like I'm the only one who made it here at the 'crack of dawn'."

"Eugene and Richard are down in the lower field rakin'. Millard's runnin' back and forth between us with drinkin' water. I'm tryin' to get this field mowed and raked by tomorrow. Then we can haul the wheat to the gristmill and start stackin' the hay."

"Sounds like you could use another hand, even if it is a woman. What do you want me to do?"

She really means it, he thought. Can't send her home since she went to the trouble of puttin' all them work clothes on. He didn't have time to waste coming up with a ladylike chore – nothing proper about a woman working fields anyway. "It'd help if you and Millard worked together. He's run himself til he's two inches shorter than he was a month ago. It'd be lots faster if you drive him around with the wagon. Could you manage that?"

"Yep. My driving is much better than when you last watched. Aim me in the right direction."

He pointed toward the other side of the stand of trees that formed the border between the two fields. She nodded and got back in the wagon. "Get up there Wig-Wag!" she said with authority.

"Wig-Wag?" he yelled after her.

"That's her name. It's what she looks like from the rear end."

He slapped Moses on the butt and reminisced over the days when selling moonshine brought in more money with a lot less hard labor. In fact, 'shine' was still a commodity in demand. Seemed like folks could always find money for liquor, and the harder the times, the more they needed the stupor it produced. He shook his sweaty head. Yeah, but it was illegal, dangerous, and brought more heartache to Boreland Springs than anyone could ever have imagined.

He mowed the field and pondered what to do with Melia. Maybe she didn't plan to come everyday. What would he do if she did? The work was too hard and he didn't really have money to pay her – the others were family members and didn't require wages. "Damn," he mumbled "I've got myself in a fine mess now."

The next four days were awkward for Will. The rest of the family seemed to enjoy Melia's smiling face every morning. He'd been hard-pressed to assign her a job to fit her capabilities. In the end, she proved very useful by transporting Millard, tools, drinking water, and anything else the field workers needed. She developed a route that rotated from the house, to the lower field, to the upper one, then back to the house. It was an easy task and the men didn't have to take valuable time away from the primary work to make these runs themselves. The entire operation became more efficient. By Friday both fields were mowed, raked, and ready to load on wagons and head for the mill. They were ahead of schedule – and Melia had been a big part of the effort.

Her presence at the dinner table was as normal as cherry pie. He, Will, was the only one at odds with the situation – and he wasn't sure why. One reason was where he'd find the money to pay her. Still, it was more than that. She was a person he'd only known socially, who'd been instrumental in getting him out of harm's way a long time ago, and now was accepted as part of the Hart family circle. As far as he was concerned, she was a stranger -- someone who probably hadn't been to the Hart house more than twenty times in her entire life. While she was fun to be with and he'd enjoyed her company when they'd gone to buy the cows, she was still a visitor. It went against his grain to allow an outside person so close to family business.

On Friday, just after the noon meal, he pulled her aside. His eyes darted from place to place and his words faltered. "I'm not sure what you expected. . . . I mean in the way of wages." He studied his feet intently. "You've been a big help. . . .saved us men lots of runnin' that gave us time to get the hay stacked. . . .helped Ma in the kitchen and all."

"Are you telling me I'm no longer needed?"

He knew better than to let someone go that the rest of the family liked and, within a week's time, had begun to depend on her services. "No," he said quickly. "Ma and Pa. . .I mean all of us rely on you now. You runnin' the delivery circuit. . ."

"That's a great name for it."

"Uh, yeah. Bein' able to keep on workin' without havin' to leave to fetch parts from the shed and all. . .saves us lots of time. . . .we're way ahead of usual thanks to you, Millard, and Wig-Wag."

She nodded.

"Just not sure how much I'd be able to pay. . ."

"What about trading my help for any extra hay or wheat you might have after your own needs are taken care of?"

He was dumbstruck. And speechless.

She went on. "As I said earlier, even with the added land from Clay, it would be helpful to have more wheat to grind for flour. If you could see your way clear. . ."

"Hell. . . .I mean shit, that ain't worth gettin' up for, Melia. Harold and Troy will be harvestin' enough for all your livestock needs."

She wondered why he thought shit was a better swear word than hell.

She touched his arm softly compelling him to look at her. "I'm up early anyway. Ma doesn't need me until the afternoon. I think she's glad I'm out of the house. . . Working with all of you out in the fields makes me feel good. Harold and Troy don't want me hanging around when they're flying through a field – they let me know that in no uncertain terms."

She took a breath. "Here, I get to drive the wagon all over with Millard, who's such a smart boy to be with, and I've always loved your family."

"Tradin' your time for wheat ain't right. Somethin' else has to be worked out."

"Why? I only work in the mornings, and if you think we don't need hay then maybe you'd have some extra apples and pears. We've never had our own fruit trees and Ma has always wanted to can some for winter." Her piercing eyes brought a nod of agreement before he knew it had happened. "It would make me feel like I'm helping bring in something no one else in the family can supply." Her brow furrowed with worry that he might still find it impossible to keep her on.

He shook his head in defeat.

"The work here gives me a lot of comfort, Will," she pled. "Even more than at Cleggs. For the first time since I've come back, with the exception of you, I feel like the people I work with are glad for my contribution. I feel good again."

"Again?"

"Yes. I got good at my work in Wheeling and became an important part of the rest of my department. When I came back home, it's been like Ma and Pa aren't sure what to do with me. Harold and Troy say I slow them down. It doesn't take them long to work our small fields – they're a fast team with no room for a third person. After I left, my chores were taken over by the others. Here, my little 'circuit' seems to help make your farm work happen faster."

"It does.... I didn't mean to make you feel unwelcome."

"It's only natural for you to wonder where I fit in. You're responsible for all the Harts now that your Pa can't be so active. It must be a heavy burden to bear."

"It ain't so bad." He reddened and turned back toward the house.

She tugged his elbow once again. "I appreciate you letting me continue. Of all the people I know, you're one I admire more than most others."

He half-turned and stood looking at her with disbelief scribbled in his solemn face. "Why on earth would you think highly of me?"

"You're loyal to your loved ones. Nothing will ever stop you from making sure they're safe. Sometimes I wish I was a Hart and part of the family you fiercely protect."

"You can't mean that. Your folks would never let anything happen to you."

"I didn't mean that I don't appreciate them. I do. But my brothers will soon have their own families to plan for and protect. Before long my folks will be at an age where I should think of caring for them." She smiled ruefully. "I seem to be an outsider in my own community. The friends I grew up with are married and concerned with how to keep babies from sucking their thumbs, or fighting with their siblings, or wandering down the road further than they should. I'm the oldest unmarried woman in the WCTU and it's hard to talk about putting up preserves for hungry eaters when I don't have a family." She turned her gaze into the horizon and stood quietly.

Will didn't know what to do with all these revelations. He wondered what it must feel like to not have anyone to provide for.

"Damn, Melia. I'd like to have just one day when there wasn't someone to feed, or doctor, or who needed shoes or coats. A time when I didn't have to think two seasons ahead to make sure there'd be enough grain for the livestock, food for the family, and money to buy clothes for the kids." He sighed. "I was just thinkin' how much easier it was when we were bootleggers."

"Don't talk like that, Will. You've done a wonderful job of getting your family self-sufficient without resorting to that shameful practice. Everyone admires you for that."

He looked at her doubtfully. "Sometimes I wish it wasn't so hard. I could use a few of your days without dependents to worry about. I've got a family of seven who need me to keep on workin'."

Melia's face crumpled. She twisted away so Will couldn't see her struggle to hold back her tears. He was shocked, wondering what had caused such a reaction. "What did I say? Why are you upset?"

She shook her head and waved her hand in the air. "Not you, Will. My problem. One day maybe I'll be able to tell you." She sniffled and wiped her nose with the back of her hand.

"No. You'll tell me now." He guided her toward the edge of the woods. His arm was so strong she had no recourse but to go along. He sat her down on a stump then leaned against the trunk of a large oak. "I need to know why you're sad'. You're always tellin' me I'm solemn, hard to get to know, too reclusive, whatever that means. But that's better than holdin' a smilin' face in front of a heart that's cryin'."

She looked at him through a haze of sunrays and tears. He had little education, yet he was so wise. "Remember when you asked me why I stayed away so long?" He nodded. "Most people thought I'd gone off to have a baby."

"Not me," he said. "None of my affair who left and when they came back. My big concern was keepin' Eugene and me out of range of John Mathieson's deer rifle."

"I know you don't take notice of other people's business. . . .that's an admirable trait." Silence lay heavy between them. She sighed. "Do you want to know why I went away?"

"Yep. I'm breakin' my own rule but I need to know why one of my employees is havin' trouble with the world." He hoped his attempt at humor would brighten her mood.

"Well, I *was* pregnant."

Will concealed his surprise behind a bland expression. "Why didn't you marry the father?"

"The father was dead."

"Dead?" This time he was unable to hide the astonishment that shook him to the core. "You mean between the time you got pregnant and when the baby was born, the father died!"

"Yes."

"How?"

"He was shot."

The forest was filled with beehives, squirrels jabbering, birds squawking – comforting sounds of country life. But Will's throat was dry and his breath came in spurts. "My God," he whispered. . . . "It was Wyatt, wasn't it?"

She nodded.

He slid down the tree trunk and rested against it.

"After the baby was born, I stayed on and got a job working at a department store in Wheeling. As time passed it got harder to come home to stay. So I came back to visit, saved my wages, then lost them in the crash. I reckon that was God's punishment for my sin."

"Hogwash. God wouldn't penalize the whole country for your sin. You're givin' yourself more importance than God has time for."

She hadn't thought of it that way. Will was right. The whole world was suffering, not just her. In fact, the people who lived in Wood and Pleasants counties in West Virginia were better off than most since they'd never relied on the outside world to provide what they needed.

She laughed. "You're right, Will. I've been wearing blinders that have been keeping me tied to my own puny troubles."

"Why didn't you keep the baby? Wouldn't be like you'd have been the only woman with a child and without a husband."

"It was too embarrassing for my family – and myself, for that matter. I was too young to think beyond the humiliation. Even the nuns said it was better for fatherless babies to be adopted by well-to-do, loving couples who could provide for the child far better than a young mother on her own could."

"Are you glad you did it?"

She chewed on her lower lip and pondered the answer for several minutes. "I got to hold and nurse her for three days. If I'd have had enough strength of character I would have stopped the adoption and brought her home." Her shoulders drooped. "She was so beautiful. . .a day never goes by that I don't wonder where she is, what she looks like, and is she happy. There's a hole in my heart that never stops aching. . . No, I'm not glad I did it. I'd give anything to have her back to take care of."

Will's brows arched in disbelief. "You lost your child's father the night of Wyatt's death, yet you warned me of John's plan to get even with Eugene and me. Why?"

"I'd given up on Wyatt several weeks earlier when it became apparent Sil was right about him. He was a self-indulgent, spoiled young man who would never have married me."

"Did you tell him about the child?"

"No. He would have denied it. . . .which would have made me feel more foolish than I already did. I only told Sil and my family. They were heartbroken that their innocent girl had gotten so far away from her Christian upbringing. Now, you're the only other one who knows."

"Did you give the baby a name?"

"Yes. . . .I called her Charity." A tear slid down her cheek.

"I have my own dark memories of that night and the evilness of Wyatt," Will said quietly. "He cost us all so much because of his selfishness. Eugene and I spent years in Weirton that could have been lived here."

"Most folks figured somebody would kill Wyatt sooner or later and that he had it coming. We all knew he was trying to bleed every cent he could from wherever he could find it to pay his gambling debts. While nobody knew for sure who killed Wyatt, and I admit there were those who suspected you, others thought it was Vince, and the rest had no opinion. However, it was apparent that John intended to take his revenge on you whether or not you actually did it"

It surprised him to know that part of the community had figured he'd done the shooting, yet they'd kept it from the authorities. He hadn't realized they'd thought enough of him to protect him from the law. In addition, while Melia may have believed he had killed the father of her child, she still warned him of John's foul plans. And she had barely known him then.

Neither spoke for several minutes. They were so quiet that the squirrels again took up their job of burying acorns. The rustle of leaves let them know that a wild turkey was probably nearby. Imogene and Wilma's laughter floated on the breeze.

"How I'd love to be that innocent again," Melia said, turning her glance in the direction of the happy girls.

"Not me. . . . .Eugene is innocent because his mind can't make sense of what happens around him. While there's been times I thought it would be nice to disappear into the fog that claims him when he's confused, I'd rather have a brain that allows me to think and understand."

He studied his rough fingers a minute then looked up again. "What I wish I still had is the wonder Imogene and Wilma have about life. Nothin's happened to make them doubt that their dreams will come true. They don't even know there's a depression goin' on since their lives haven't changed much since it started. They just think it's somethin' the adults are makin' too much of."

Melia looked at him with admiration. Usually, he fumbled with his words like he was sorting through them to pick out the bad ones. Today, there was no hesitation – his thoughts were expressed as surely as he drove his horses or his truck. His opinions were obviously long-standing and firm. When he realized she was looking at him so intently, he was embarrassed at all he'd said. It wasn't like him to allow others to know what he felt like inside. He reddened and looked at the ground – a habit Melia now recognized as normal when he felt he'd overstepped his bounds – or in this case, let an acquaintance inside his mind. She knew he considered everyone, except immediate family, only acquaintances.

Behind the uneducated speech and his lack of self-confidence in the presence of those he deemed 'better' than he, was a mind of incredible breadth and a soul. She felt dwarfed by his insight. His ability to solve everyday problems in a practical and swift manner came from the common sense he'd grown up with.

She was lost for words, yet had to say something that didn't embarrass him further. "I hope there will never be a time, Will Hart, when I can't listen to your good judgment." He shook his head and remained silent. She *had* made him more uncomfortable. "I mean, since the two of us have gone through the same dilemma in a way, you've done a better job of figuring out how to go about leaving it behind." His eyes looked even more confused. God, she thought, I'm only making things worse. She tried again. "Quit looking like I've thanked you too much for Pete's sake. You've put my mind at ease and shown me a way to escape the awful past. Is that too hard for you to take credit for?"

His face relaxed and it looked like he might smile. Before she could do more harm, Melia climbed into the wagon and urged Wig-Wag forward. She turned and waved. "See you at the crack of dawn." He laughed outright and returned the wave.

She barely noticed anything on the way home. Her mind couldn't erase Will's words and the wisdom they offered. She understood now why he kept his thoughts to himself. His lack of education made him feel that none of his opinions could be worthwhile since he was only a farmer. It was a discovery she'd hold in her breast like a precious gift to be protected.

CHAPTER TWENTY-NINE

"There's nothing left in my stomach to throw up, Melia – except guts. Was it this bad for you?"

Melia held Sil's head while she heaved once again into the chamber pot. "Surely you remember holding me when I was in this predicament. Being pregnant isn't easy, and for some it's even worse. We fall into the second category." This brought a slight smile from Sil.

"You look like you've been dragged through a hedge backwards," Melia went on, hoping to take Sil's attention off her nausea. That's asking a bit much, she thought, looking at her friend's flushed face and mouth dripping with saliva. After several minutes without a new bout of vomiting Melia helped Sil back into the chair in front of the window. "You need strength. Can you take some hot tea and hard bread?"

Sil shook her head slowly. "Isn't worth taking the chance of more sickness.. . .surely this can't go on much longer. I'm in my third month."

"Ma says that's the normal length of time for morning sickness."

"Morning!" Sil spoke angrily. "Constant sickness is a better description. It's getting harder and harder to teach. Thank goodness it won't be long til summer vacation."

The front door opened and Chris stuck his head in the door before allowing the rest of his big frame to follow. His face reflected guilt that maybe it was his fault Sil was having so much trouble with this pregnancy. He knelt in front of her and brushed the hair back from her forehead.

"We'll never do this again, I promise. You're so thin I fear you'll not be strong enough to have a baby." His eyes were surrounded by worry wrinkles.

"It's not your fault," Sil said softly. "It's normal to be sick for the first three months. After that it gets better. Don't talk about not having any more. We want a big family and I'll not compromise on that."

"Let's see how we think after this one arrives," he replied tersely.

"I'm feeling better already. Melia, I'll take you up on that hot tea and bread."

While Chris and Sil discussed things married people talk about, Melia fixed the tea and bread. She watched the love flow between them and knew Chris's support would provide the power to get Sil through this difficult ordeal.

She set the tea and bread beside Sil, kissed her on the forehead, gave Chris a pat on the back, then walked out to Wig-Wag who'd been waiting patiently beside a rhododendron bush. On her way down the lane, Melia met Ruth and Abner on their way in. She pulled to the side so the Lockharts could get by in Ab's jitney. Deep lines in their faces indicated their concern.

"How is she?" Ruth's words were tentative – as though she was afraid to know.

"Better I think." No sense making her worry more, Melia thought, and she is better now that Chris is home.

"I've brought chicken broth and a fresh loaf of bread."

"I know they'll appreciate that, Mrs. Lockhart. Chris is with her now."

Abner sighed with relief. "Glad you're here when Chris is working and we can't be with her." His gnarled hands were sweaty on the steering wheel. "I'll be glad when it's over."

So will I, Melia thought as she watched them drive into the yard and clamber out of the old vehicle with stiff and labored steps. She was amazed at how much they had aged. It had crept up without notice. She'd seen the same in her own parents. They were not yet fifty but lives spent farming a difficult land had made them old before their time. She shook her head sadly and gave Wig-Wag her head to find the way home.

The next two weeks were full of activity all over Boreland Springs. 1933 had brought a token amount of rainfall. Fields were being plowed for planting and old hay was removed from sheds and spread out for the cows to munch on until new grass was high enough to turn them out to pasture. Houses emitted dust from every opening as spring cleaning began in earnest. This work had to be done before work in the fields claimed everyone's time.

Chris worked close to home and always had his dilapidated car nearby so he could check in regularly with Sil. The nausea had subsided at the end of the third month just like the old grandmothers had predicted. She'd grown stronger and over his objections had insisted on returning to teach.

It was Monday morning,, and since Millard was still in school, Melia was driving Wig-Wag on the usual circuit to the men working on the Hart farm. She finished replenishing Will's water jug, gave him a biscuit his Ma had sent, and was heading to the lower field where Eugene and Richard were working.

Shouts, loud enough to carry down to Bull Run Road, broke the rhythm of the morning work. For an instant , even the birds stopped their squawking. It came again, this time so piercing that the horses threw their heads up in alarm. Without waiting to see who it was Will tied his lines to the brake and took off in the direction of the voice. Melia turned Wig-Wag around and followed.

"Come quick! Miss Sil's real sick!" It was Roy Ferguson, the oldest student in the school. He'd run so hard that he was struggling to breathe.

Will reached him first and grabbed him just before he fell into the dirt. "Catch your wind and get down to the lower field. That's where Chris is working." The boy was on the run immediately despite his burning lungs.

Will jumped into Sil's wagon. "Give me the lines." In less than a minute he was urging the old mare as fast as she could go while Melia covered her face with a hankie to avoid the dust they churned up.

They pulled into the schoolyard in about eight minutes. Chris was right behind them. Maggie Monroe, a fourth grader, ran out to meet them. "She was writin' on the blackboard," she panted. "Before we knew it, she slumped to the floor. There's blood on her skirt." Chris and Will leapt up the three steps leading into the little building.

Melia came after them and quietly talked to the children. In the twenty minutes it had taken for help to arrive, they had assisted Sil into her chair so she could rest her elbows on the desk. They listened in strained silence as Melia assured them not to worry. It was the first time in her life that she noticed how fearful children became when a beloved adult is sick. She knelt to their level and motioned them to make a circle around her, hugging the smallest ones who came gladly to lay their worry in her lap. "I'll help you put away all your paraphernalia so that everything will be ready when you have class again."

"What's 'paranalia'?" It was Bobby McPherson's question but they all crowded around to hear the answer.

"It's your school supplies. You know, like dictionaries and encyclopedias plus all the pencils and books you have in your desks." Her big words were diverting their attention away from the incident at the front of the room.

"I've never seen a 'cycloped'. Is it an animal?" Clara Monroe asked.

"No, it's a bird," little Stevie Knowles answered. "I heard one in the tree yesterday." He reddened from head to toe when his brother reminded him it was a blue jay he'd heard.

"Will Missus Nelson be alright? Did she bleed because she's bad sick?" Emma Meeks refused to listen further to word meanings and voiced the question all wanted to ask.

"As soon as she gets in her own bed I'm sure she'll feel better." Melia didn't want to make promises that might not come to pass. Her heart was thumping nearly out of her chest and her fingers trembled when she buttoned their little shirts. As she hustled them on home and assured them school would not be closed forever, Chris and Will carried Sil out and placed her in the back seat of Chris's car. Will jumped into the front seat with Chris and they rumbled off trying to avoid as many potholes as possible.

Will hung his head out the window. "Melia, go get Abner and Ruth."

She turned the tired horse around and headed back down the lane. Wig-Wag was able to manage a trot for the last half-mile, bringing up a dust storm that had the Lockharts out on the porch looking to see who was coming.

"Sil's sick. Chris and Will are with her. They need you."

Abner and Ruth ran to the old truck and were off without taking time to grab supplies or phone for Doc Landry. Melia looped her lines and went into the house she knew so well. She cranked the phone up and told Edna Furbee she needed young Doc Landry fast. After several rings Mrs. Landry answered. "Lola!" Melia shouted into the phone. "Sil's bleeding bad. We need your husband as fast as he can get here."

"Where is she?"

"At their house. It's the old Howard place."

"Hold on." Melia heard Lola shouting on her end. "Ken. Get out to the Howard place fast. Sil's in trouble." Sounds of scuffling could be heard in the background then Lola was back on the phone. "He's on his way."

"Thank God," Melia said and hung up the phone.

She hurried through the house grabbing cloths from dresser drawers and under the kitchen sink. She reached high into the cabinet for laudanum then ran back to where Wig-Wag stood patiently.

"One more trip, old girl. You can do it."

The house reverberated with frightened feet when she pulled into the Nelson's yard. Ruth was trying to care for Sil while dodging three big men who kept on the move because standing still was impossible. "You're getting in my way!" Ruth yelled. "Go out in the yard. I'll call you if I need you. . . .there's Melia. Help her in with that load and take care of her horse."

Glad to have an assignment, all three ran toward Melia. Will took over Wig-Wag, Abner grabbed the towels, and Chris guided Melia into the house with such force she nearly stumbled.

"Thank God you're here," Ruth whispered. "It isn't good. I need a pail of warm water."

As the two women washed the blood off Sil, Melia explained that Doc Landry was on his way. "I brought laudanum just in case, but we'll wait 'til he gets here." Ruth nodded.

The rumble of Kenneth Landry's Model A brought a sigh of relief to Ruth and a glimmer of hope to Melia. He entered the bedroom at a run and had his bag open before anyone could say 'hello'.

"Mrs. Lockhart, stay and help me, please." He turned and looked at the others. "If the rest of you could wait outside, I'll let you know just as soon as I know something."

The door closed with a quiet finality that left a feeling of futility to the people left to wonder what was going on in the Nelson bedroom. The men looked to Melia for words of encouragement – she had none. She felt as helpless as they did. There were no words to say, no hope to be given. Minutes ticked away like hours. The men went outside and leaned on the truck. Melia folded the clothes that Sil had left on the couch.

It took nearly an hour for Doc Landry, with Ruth by his side, to retrieve the fetus and afterbirth. Afterward, he cleaned Sil thoroughly with alcohol and carbolic acid. He gave her a small amount of laudanum so she could rest. "She'll be asleep before long." He looked at Ruth with his solemn gray eyes.

"It will be up to you to tell her the baby has been lost. Can you do that?" She nodded.

"Miscarriages can be very traumatic," he explained as he washed his hands and arms with the same antiseptics he'd used on Sil. "She'll need your support and love to keep her from sinking into melancholy. You must assure her she's a healthy young woman, capable of having other children – that is imperative."

Chris had come into the house. He was pacing in the next room. "Ask Chris to come in now."

Chris's big frame overpowered the room. Doc. Landry looked at him sympathetically and knew it was unnecessary to say the baby had not survived. "You'll be as despondent as Sil over this, Chris, but you're the biggest source of strength she has. Try to be patient. Miscarriages play hell with a woman's confidence. She'll be afraid she will never have another child. When she does get pregnant again, she'll worry endlessly over the outcome." He dried his hands on a clean cloth. "Unfortunately, this is not an uncommon occurrence. Both of you must understand that. When she's recovered mentally and physically, hopefully she'll be willing to try again. You can sit beside her now. I want to speak with Melia outside."

The others were waiting, silent and fearful when he opened the bedroom door. It was the part of being a doctor he'd found hard to take. Not being able to save every patient, especially a baby, rankled him to no end; even though he knew this desire was unreasonable. His wife, Lola, was pregnant with their first child. What if such a thing should happen to her? He couldn't bear the thought.

"Melia, will you walk out in the yard with me?" She followed him outside.

"I've told both Chris and Ruth how important it is to remain with Sil and assure her that this will probably never happen to her again. A miscarriage is nature's way of purging the body of a fetus with serious defects, although right now she won't see it that way. . . .You're her best friend. Be with her as much as possible. Let her talk. Ask questions that make her talk. Get her out in the sun. . . exercise and air will be beneficial for her recovery." He guided her back into the house and picked up his bag that Ruth had made ready for him. "Let me know if anything unusual, such as bleeding, occurs."

They nodded in unison. Kenneth started out the door when he noticed Will and Abner standing forlornly together. As if he'd planned it, he motioned the men to follow him back out to the Ford. "Didn't want to let the others hear what I have to say to you." He stood between them to make the discussion private. "Losing a baby is hard on everybody, but it helps if there are at least a couple of close people able to maintain a degree of calm. That's your job. Be the steady influence that guides the others in a way that helps them accept this phenomenon of nature that is normal."

"But I'm not a member of the family," Will said. "I wouldn't want to pry. . ."

"You're a good friend of Chris, right?"

Will nodded.

"Friends are an extended part of any family. . .sometimes as important as blood folks when it comes to a tragedy such as this." He hesitated then looked thoughtfully at Will. "Melia will be seriously affected too. From what I hear they've been as close as sisters from the time they were toddlers. She needs your support just like Sil needs Chris."

Then he looked at Abner. "You're hurting as much as your wife, I know. Men just aren't supposed to allow their grief to show – but it's there just the same. Talk to Chris; then keep Will informed as to how you think the others are doing." Both men nodded and shook hands with the man they'd hoped could save a baby. Kenneth saw no reproach in their eyes – only acceptance of what they considered 'God's will'.

"It's barbaric," he growled when he was out of hearing distance. "To lose so many babies during the first three months."

Kenneth's confidence was always shaken at the loss of a baby. It happened more often than his schooling had prepared him for. There he'd been led to believe that the doctor is a powerful influence against death and disease. Of course, he knew there were situations where it was impossible to prolong life. But to be unable to manage full-term pregnancies. It seemed like a personal failure – leaving him with a feeling of uselessness -- thwarted by forces beyond his control.

He'd tried to alleviate the family's distress by saying this is normal – nature's way of expelling a flawed embryo. Doctor Kenneth Landry wished his logical explanation matched a composure he didn't feel. He drove slowly out of the ageless mountains that concealed the secrets of life and death beneath its tortured terrain.

CHAPTER THIRTY

"Ho, Wig-Wag. Got a lot of thirsty men in this field." Melia slanted a glance at Sil who had dutifully picked up the water jug and headed toward the edge of the field to refill two smaller jars. She looks strong, Melia thought, but she's not right inside yet.

Will and Chris immediately headed for the fresh water. Their energy was depleted from the muggy weather typical of Boreland Springs during a particularly hot summer. Chris was evaluating the quality of the hay for his records with the Extension Service. They wore heavy canvas gloves but had discarded their shirts when the sun beat down on their clammy bodies. The decision left their unprotected skin covered with ugly red scratches from the rough hay stems. This provided ample fuel for the ravenous sweat bees that swarmed during mowing. 'Haying' was a job no farmer looked forward to.

Chris studied his wife under hooded lids, hoping her eyes might sparkle in the old way. Since the loss of their baby in the spring, her endless enthusiasm and optimism had dimmed. Her family had done all the things Dr. Landry had prescribed: she went on daily walks in the sunshine with Melia; her mother constantly reminded her that miscarriages were not unheard of – that future pregnancies should pose no problem; and since she'd always been full of projects, Chris assigned her duties to help the Boreland Springs Co-Op weather the depression which got worse every year. Dr. Landry had cautioned it would take time for her mind to recover but Chris and the others were beginning to think her lackluster attitude would never end.

"You're lookin' mighty fine today, Sil," Will said. Sil's dilemma had brought Will out of his own shell of hiding. She reminded him of a lost puppy afraid to come out from under the bushes. He realized how much he'd enjoyed her cheerful face and enthusiastic conversation during the times he'd watched her at the get-togethers of the community. She'd always been so different from serious Melia. In Sil he'd seen an uninhibited approach to life that he envied. Her inner light had been extinguished and he wanted it back so he could still believe there really was hope at the end of black tunnels.

Moreover, he'd missed Melia's presence in the fields during the weeks when she'd walked with Sil to get her strong again. When Wig-Wag's plodding steps announced Melia's return to her circuit Will was elated. Sil sat beside Melia holding on tight to the wagon sides. That's smart, Will thought at the time, bringing her out to help might take her mind off the loss. He'd watched the two for the last couple of weeks and realized their personalities had switched. Now it was Melia who laughed and talked, trying to get her best friend to bite into life again.

Sil smiled at his greeting but he could see it went no further than the skin on her cheeks. How hard it must be for Chris, Will thought, to lose the woman he married. She may be alive, but she ain't who she was.

It was nearly noon and Melia was taking Sil home before she joined the Harts for the mid-day meal. Silence covered them like tent worms in the peach trees. Finally Melia could stand it no longer. "You're looking much better, Sil. Are you feeling as well as you look?"

"You were never good at coming in the back door, Melia." Sil let out a great sigh. "What you really want to know is when my mind will be as strong as my body, right?"

Melia nodded, annoyed that her ulterior motive was so evident.

"I don't know." She pondered the skyline for several minutes. "Is there a rulebook somewhere that says how long it takes to get over losing a baby? Will that book assure me it'll never happen again? I wonder if Chris feels he married a defective woman."

"I think I can answer those questions."

"Try."

"The length of mourning for a lost child depends on the determination of the mother I think. . . .plus the stamina of best friends who remind the bereaved mother that life goes on and other children will come." The comparison was not lost on Sil who turned toward Melia with a question on her lips. Melia placed a finger on her mouth. "Let me finish. . . . ." Sill sucked her lip impatiently. "No book or person can assure us of what may or may not happen in the future. It's up to us to have the courage to plow right on, knowing the ground will get rocky from time to time. You taught me that, remember?"

"But. . ."

"I'm still not finished." Melia swatted a sweat bee off her arm. "Chris is worried that you might not love him anymore due to all the pain he's caused you."

"That's not true."

"How does he know that? Even I can see you've shut him out of your grief. He's sad too. Don't you realize that? He has to hold his sorrow within while trying to coax you out into the open again. Of the two, I think his cross is the hardest to bear."

"That's not fair."

"Really? Think about it. We all try to show you how much we love and care for your recovery. One of us is with you constantly, yet our devotion isn't enough to help you shake off the sorrow." Sil nodded at Melia's insistent stare. "Your mother and father have each other to share their unhappiness at losing their first grandchild. I talk to Will about how much I worry over you. Who does Chris talk to? Who cares about *his* feelings?"

Melia let that sink in for a few minutes. "He's not about to talk to Will or Abner – men don't do that. In the end, the miscarriage cost him his first child and his wife as well. He's fearful of what the future holds and I wouldn't be surprised if it hasn't affected his work too. That's why I believe he's the one holding the rotten apple here."

She'd timed the lecture perfectly. They were driving up the lane to Sil's house. Melia jumped down and offered her hand to Sil. "I can do this myself," Sil said angrily.

"I'll be on my way then. Don't like to be late for a meal at the Harts."

Sil's accusing eyes followed Melia's carefree departure. She thinks she's so right. She doesn't know what it's like to lose a child. Then she remembered watching the agony Melia suffered after having lived with strangers for most of the nine months it took to give birth to Charity. Of course she knows the devastation of losing a child! How could I have forgotten? Doesn't matter if it's a miscarriage or adoption, the baby is gone. At least I have the consolation of having a small grave where I can pray. Melia must spend the rest of her life wondering what happened to her daughter.

She fell in a heap on the old braided rug her mother had given her and cried until nothing, tears or recrimination, remained. By the time Chris returned it was twilight. He was hot, exhausted, and discouraged.

The aroma of bacon frying brought his head up. Ruth must be here, he thought. Means we'll have a tasty supper. Can't say I'm hungry though. I'd rather go 'coon hunting with the Conroys than face Sil's glum face again. At least I'd get a good shot of 'shine' and listen to the music of hounds baying.

Sil was busy at the stove where he could see potatoes frying in with the bacon and eggs waiting to be added. It was his favorite meal regardless of what time of day he got it. "Where's your mother?" He glanced toward the bedroom. "Didn't see her outside when I came in." He slumped into the old armchair and began unlacing his boots.

"At home I suppose," she answered slightly out of breath. "It's Wednesday. She and Pa are probably getting ready for prayer meeting." She bent over and pulled a pan of biscuits out of the oven.

He stopped mid-lace and studied her. She was wearing one of the dresses she didn't mind soiling – Chris called it her 'housewife' dress. The table was set like Ruth would have done – tablecloth, plates, silverware, and even a small bouquet of dandelions and wild roses in the middle. Sil bustled through the homey kitchen aromas and started placing hot food on the nearby table. He thought she might be humming.

"Wash up before this gets cold Chris," she said as the eggs were dropped into the bacon drippings. "I baked a peach pie for after." My favorite! he thought. He had a whiff of lavender as he walked past her to the sink.

Chris was a cautious man, however, and wasn't about to get his hopes up regardless of how good Sil appeared to be. He was careful not to slurp his coffee (a habit she detested), he talked quietly and about nothing of consequence, made no eye contact, and left it to her to ask any questions.

"Did you meet with the co-op today?" Her words were strung between bites of large portions of the meal.

"Yep."

"What'd you talk about?" She wiped some egg yolk off her chin.

"I showed them the 'Grit'. It's a week late but the news never seems to do anything but get worse." He leaned back for a moment. "It says in the editorial that most of West Virginia is in worse shape than a lot of the rest of the country."

"Why?" She held her knife and fork mid-air and waited for the answer.

He realized then how much information she'd missed during the months when she'd thought of nothing but her sorrow. "Because the folks in the interior of the state, where the mountains are full of coal and timber and unfit for farming, worked for wages for large out-of-state companies. Those companies are shut down now, leaving the natives without jobs and a land where the forests are ruined and deserted coal mines leak tainted water into the rivers."

"My God. When did all that happen?"

"During the twenties, when the land barons were raping mineral rich areas everywhere, enslaving the local workers with their 'company stores'."

"Why didn't it happen here in our little area?"

"The big mineral deposits such as coal and gas, plus the giant forests, are in the middle of the state. Here, most everyone owns their own farm that produces everything the family needs to survive. It's called subsistence farming – a situation where no one gets rich but it's good in the fact that no one depends on someone else for their welfare."

"Who would have ever believed that living here in poor old Boreland Springs would turn out to be lucky?" She laughed and turned her stare toward her husband. She was so proud of him! He used his education to improve the farming practices, he worked as hard in the fields as the farmers themselves, and designed the meetings so that no one's opinion was ignored. She studied his chiseled face, sunburnt skin and hair, and muscled body that could lift a half-grown hog out of a mud slick. The outline of his chest and stomach stretched the thin shirt he wore. He smelled like new-mown hay and fried bacon.

"I'll help you clean this up," he offered.

"I'll do it in the morning. I'm ready for bed – what about you?"

"Where's Sil?" Will asked next morning when Melia drove up alone.

She smiled. "I think she's busy getting ready for the coming school days."

They were unloading the water jug and biscuits. "Where's Chris then?"

Another smile. "Probably hurrying to get to the fields in time."

Chris's rattletrap car made a plume of dust as he brought it to a labored stop beside the field. He jumped out, adjusted his hat and stumbled over his shoelaces that were trailing along the ground. "Melia! What did you say to Sil? She's a new person. I think she may finally be out of the woods."

"Must have made her mad like she did for me once." She flashed another grin then hurried on down to the lower field, leaving Will to stare after both of them.

"What did I miss?" he yelled at the departing wagon. He slapped his dusty hat angrily on his thigh. "Did they all have a meeting and forget to tell me?"

"We've made it though better than most," Chris was saying to the farmers assembled at the co-op on a chilly October morning. "However, according to the news, the general situation has worsened beyond what anyone had expected. And no one's sayin' how much further we'll fall." He watched their faces droop. "Wait!" He raised his hand. "We're still holdin' our own. Drought wasn't as bad this year and we've harvested enough to get us through the winter as long as we don't waste anything." He pulled out a sheaf of papers. "I just got back from a meeting in Charleston. They've come up with some good ideas down there. One we can use outlines a system of bartering."

"Hell, Chris." It was Harold Conroy. "We've always done that."

"I know. But we can make it even more efficient. Instead of doin' it between ourselves, we'll put up a bulletin board here in the grange hall. Anyone havin' somethin' they want to trade writes it down, says what they need in return, and tacks it up so everyone can read it soon as they come in. That way we don't waste time makin' individual visits tryin' to find somethin' that might be right down the road at the next farm."

"Damned if that Extension Service don't come up with some good ideas once in awhile," Vernon said. "Come on boys, let's get busy."

"I could use a month of sleep." Will laid his head back on the couch and closed his eyes, too tired to pull himself to the pump to wash for supper.

"I could eat for a week straight and still be hungry," Eugene added.

"We'd like to have some fun instead of nothin' but work," Imogene and Wilma piped in.

"I'd like a free Saturday night so's I could court Jessie Mae," Richard said. "She's been threatenin' to go out with Jamie Duncan if'n I don't show up purty soon."

"I'd like a week with nobody givin' me orders." Millard's voice was low, figuring no one would listen anyway.

The whole family shut up for a minute and looked at the youngster with the forlorn face. He was the one they all took for granted. He did his job so well they assumed he expected to be ordered about and never given a compliment on what he did. After all, it was only being the errand boy. How important could that be?

"So be it," his mother announced. "As of tomorrow, no one is allowed to tell you to do anything for a week. Don't you think that's fair, Melia?"

"Absolutely. None of the rest of us could have done our jobs very well without Millard's help. I know, because I'm always with him and it's a tedious and thorny chore to listen to all these irritable men who accuse him, and me, of taking too long, or the water's too warm to drink, or any other of a million complaints they come up with."

Millard couldn't 't believe his good fortune. He'd always been like one of the pictures on the wall – something everyone looks at but no one talks to. After all the times he'd dreamed about what he'd say to his difficult family who constantly ordered him about, he was speechless! He looked around in confusion. He wanted to tell Will to quit being so bossy; to say to Eugene he wasn't supposed to take more than his share of biscuits; to mention to Richard that he needed a few minutes to catch his breath sometimes, and tell his Ma sometimes the loads were heavier than he could manage. But his mouth wouldn't say a word! He looked in desperation at Melia, who was next to God in his opinion.

She stood beside him and faced the rest of the Harts'. "Anybody got a problem with me and Millard not taking any orders for a week?"

They all shook their heads.

"Good." She tousled Millard's heavy head of hair. "Sound ok to you?"

He was besotted with her. She'd become his angel of mercy this past year or so. "I'm glad you came to supper, Melia."

"So am I," she answered with a smile. "Now it's time for me to get on home."

"I'll take you." Will handed her one of his heavy coats. "Put this on. It's cold outside."

"You don't need to take me. I can walk it blind in the moonlight," she said with a laugh.

"Said I'd take you home and I will." He aimed her toward the door.

"You're too bossy, Will." There, I finally said it, Millard thought as he turned and hurried out the back door.

Will stopped in his tracks at such mutiny. Vernon shook his head and chuckled.

They rumbled down in the old Model T from Horse Neck toward Bull Run closeted in silence. They never talked much anyway and trying to make conversation over the unmuffled engine made talking a great effort. It wasn't a tense stillness though. Will was counting up in his head how much meat was stored in the smokehouse, how many hay bales they'd have to barter for come spring, and what could he offer in return. Melia was thinking about how happy she was that Sil was well again and Chris had lost all his worry wrinkles. She was also thankful for being part of the Hart family circle. She'd miss their boisterousness during the coming winter months when working the fields would not bring her in close contact with them.

They reached the valley and the chilly night air that hugged close to the creek. She shivered. He pulled her over close to him. "Aren't you glad you didn't walk all this way?" His words held a smile. "Your teeth would be chatterin' by now."

"Ok. You were right. I'm glad you brought me home."

He parked the old car at the road and got out to help her out the other side.

"You don't have to come all the way, Will. I can get up to the house without freezing."

He didn't answer, just went on around and helped her anyway.

"Millard's right. You're bossy." But her voice was friendly.

She took the hand he offered and stood still while he tried to unlatch the gate. It was stuck. It took both his hands to get it undone. She shivered again. He got the gate open then pulled her into his chest. She put her arms around his waist and clung closer.

Thoughts passed between them like wind currents. He rested his cheek on her head. She pressed into the space between his ear and neck. "Once you said you'd like to be a Hart." He felt her nod against his face. "Do you still feel that way?"

"Yes." Her breath whispered past his ear. "More than ever."

"I'm uneducated."

"You're wise."

"Most say I'm too serious."

"You make me smile inside."

"I'd have to finish my cabin."

"I know."

"Might take 'til spring."

"I'll help."

He lifted her face up with his finger under her chin and brushed away her tiny tears. She pushed his long hair off his forehead so she could stare into those fathomless gray eyes. He kissed her with the intensity of one who thought he'd never been meant to love. She returned with a passion she'd believed she'd lost forever. The embrace skipped across her heart and made her think she could fly. It spun around her stomach and into her loins, searing her with the knowledge she was loved like few women ever are. The remnants of Wyatt Mathieson and Boreland Springs Hotel skittered away like dried broom sage in the wind.

Will's cabin was finished the week before Thanksgiving. When the community learned that Will and Melia planned to marry, all other projects were dropped and the men of the co-op appeared everyday to get it finished.

It was like they were afraid the two might change their minds if much time was allowed to pass.

He'd started the cabin the year before, working on it inbetween all the farm projects. It had been planned with the idea he would be living alone. Therefore, adjustments had to be made. The size was expanded to be a rectangle 35' wide by 25' deep, generous by most standards. The hand pump was moved inside so the water could be drawn into the old porcelain sink he'd bought from Clay Mathieson. It was not a piece that would bring bad memories. In fact, he doubted if Melia would recall the old basin that had been part of the laundry. The bedroom took up one end; a tiny parlor separated it from the kitchen on the other end. The small front porch was the entrance into the parlor and allowed enough room for a rocking chair. The windows were covered by transparent oilskin that allowed diffused light to slip into the house. During winter months, shutters covered the windows to keep out the cold.

Helping each other was what the close-knit hill people were noted for. It was the cement that kept them together. Raising a house or a barn was so routine that it could be done in a week. Each day a big bonfire was built where cider and coffee was kept hot, tables were set up where the women could fix and serve sandwiches, and the children did all the chores that required running. Millard was the fastest of them all, hardly able to believe that soon Melia would be his sister. No one remembered to worry about the depression – they only concentrated on the happiness of these two people whose contentment was important to all the dwellers of Boreland Springs.

It seemed more than right that the wedding should take place on the afternoon of Thanksgiving. Rev. Knox waxed long and loud that this was an omen of better times ahead. What could be more auspicious than that the love of these two people be sealed in holy matrimony on such a special day, he asked?

"What's 'auspicious' mean?" Troy Conroy whispered to his older brother Harold.

"Damned if I know."

"I wish we'd had money to buy paint for it," Will said as he carried his bride over the threshold.

"Paint just covers up a lot of flaws. I love it just the way it is."

She lit the oil lanterns while he made a fire in the stone fireplace that formed the back wall of the parlor. She stood in the middle of the little home and felt unworthy of such happiness. But not for long! Melia was ready to take her happiness where it lay – and that was in the arms of Will Hart, her husband -- the man who had opened up her soul to let the sunshine of her youth blaze again.

Kay Meredith

PART THREE

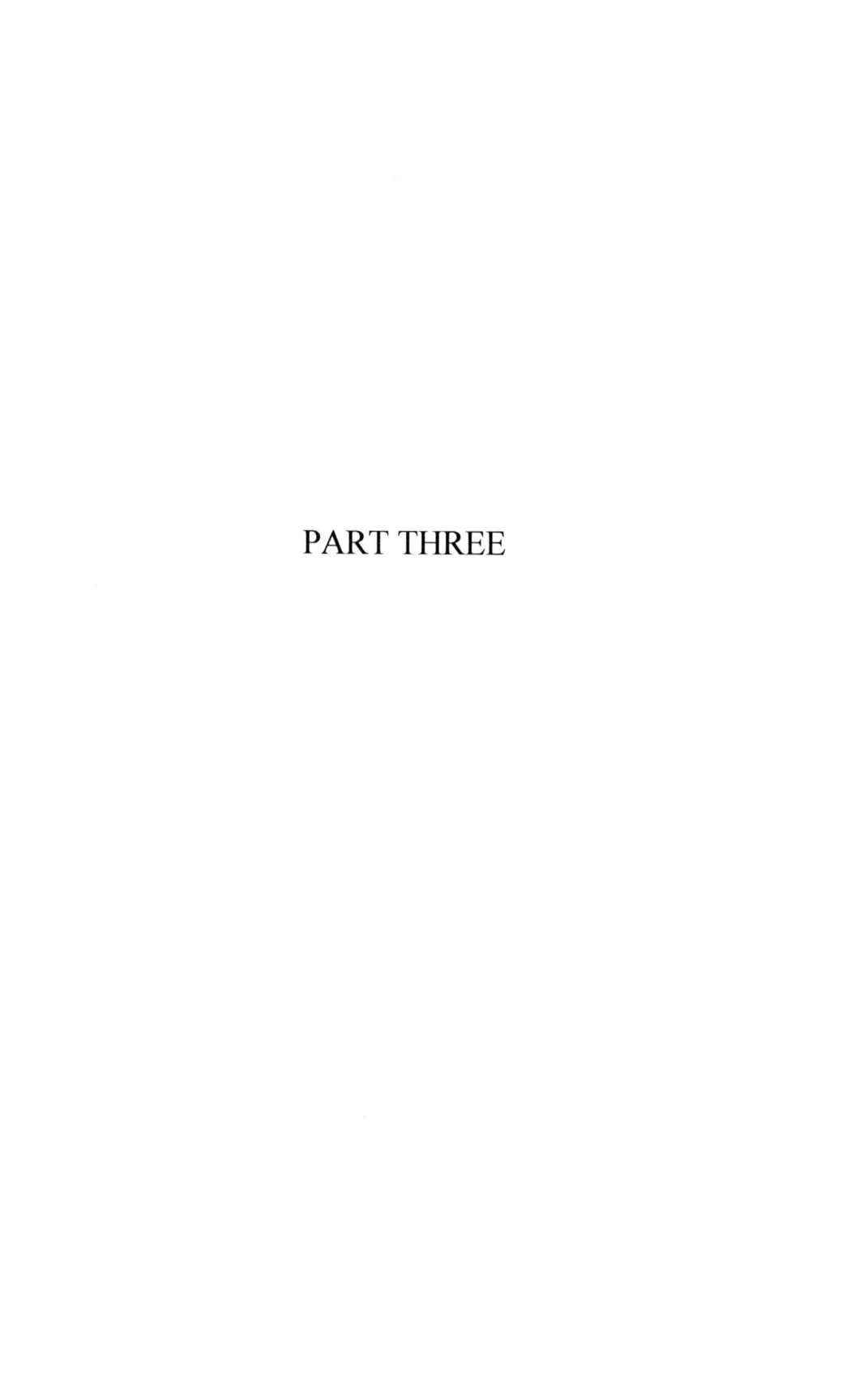

CHAPTER THIRTY-ONE

Spring 1934

The strains of 'Onward Christian Soldiers' floated through the valley around the church. Rev. Knox looked out over the congregation and noted with satisfaction how much it had grown the past three years. His chest was bursting with pride that so many souls had been brought into the fold through the sincerity of his sermons. This Sunday he intended to congratulate them on their Christian living that had brought a slight upturn in the depression. He would entreat them to continue such righteous behavior in the hopes that the recovery would gain strength.

The Harts, Conroys, and Lockharts took up most of the front pews. Lately, Clay Mathieson and his wife, Beth Ann had joined them. Everyone had been glad to see a Mathieson family once again attend church. They all listened in barely concealed boredom as Rev. Knox credited the tiny community of Boreland Springs with the *slight* improvement that had begun to be noticeable all over the country.

"As if we have enough clout here in two tiny counties in West Virginia to affect anything," Melia whispered to Sil as they walked out into the sunshine.

"Don't burst his little bubble," Sil said out of the side of her mouth.

Chris and Will walked behind, discussing the coming planting season. They'd become close friends and the two couples often traded dinners at each others' houses. It had been a happier time than either man had expected. In fact, contentment had added a few pounds to Will's thin frame and Chris had lately mentioned he might need to shed some of his belly.

Sil and Melia gravitated to the edge of the family groups who were coming out of the church and visiting amongst themselves.

"Melia, I'm pregnant."

Melia grabbed her and hugged her hard. "So am I! We'll do it together."

"Just like all the other important things we've done in life."

In November, within days of one another, Melia bore a healthy baby boy and Sil produced a beautiful little girl. Melia and Will named their son Henry Conroy Hart, and nicknamed him Henry C. Sil and Chris named their little girl Elizabeth Anne, in honor of Chris's mother.

CHAPTER THIRTY-TWO

By the spring of 1936, the couples of Boreland Springs had taken God's order to 'go forth and multiply' seriously. The valley resounded with the clamor of a whole new generation of mountaineers – many born of mothers who'd reckoned that by now they would be securely back in an urban setting. However, as the decade plodded toward its end, most gave up hope and decided to make do with the country life they'd grown used to. Mr. Clegg reopened his store to handle basic commodities these new young faces required.

A few residents took time to read the newspapers about what was happening in the world and postulate how it might affect them.

"Says here that Hitler is rearmin' the Rhineland, supposedly to improve unemployment over there." Abner Lockhart was reading the March issue of the 'Grit', a weekly newspaper that carried reports from all over the country and some pertinent information abroad. "Thought Germany was forbidden to do that sort of thing after World War I." He looked at Ruth, who was busy getting breakfast on the table.

She hesitated in her work. "Doesn't sound good to me. As I recall from what I taught Earl in his history work, that was a condition of the Treaty of Versailles."

Earl Conroy, now a sophomore at West Virginia University, frowned over his morning cup of coffee. Hitler is a dangerous man, he thought, as he leafed through the morning paper. The sound of traffic outside his window reminded him of the immediate concern of getting to the men's dorm where he worked in the kitchen. He didn't mind the hard work. It provided the money to pay for his degree in Civil Engineering. The hectic schedule of getting his morning chores finished in time to get to his first class obliterated all thought of an obscure leader in Germany who was apparently breaking some kind of treaty.

"Come, Elizabeth. Help mommy get ready for school or we'll be late." Sil stooped over her cumbersome stomach to help her little toddler put on her shoes. Sil was pregnant with her second child and hoping this time they would have a boy. She knew Chris longed for a son. She'd continued her job as schoolteacher at Pumpkin Knob, taking her little daughter along from the time she was little more than a month old.

Chris looked up from the paper. "Don't like the sound of what this Hitler fellow is doin' in Germany. Givin' those men weapons again can only cause trouble down the road."

Sil nodded but her energies were needed for a busy day ahead that had to be accomplished over an increasing heavy load to carry.

"Interestin'," Will mused as he turned the pages of the 'Grit'.

Melia, too, looked up from putting Henry C's sweater on. "What?" Her brow furrowed as she tried to get a squirming toddler stuffed into his pants. Baby Rebecca Sue was practicing pulling herself into a standing position by holding onto the couch.

"Germany is decreasin' their unemployment by buildin' armament factories that will produce weapons."

"Guns in the hands of the people responsible for the first World War ought to be illegal."

"I think it is," he sighed. "At least it's on the other side of the globe. I'd hate for America to get involved in someone else's war."

Melia's eyes were horror-struck. "My God. I'd never thought of that."

"Let's not go borrowin' trouble," he said. "It's my fault for bringin' the subject up. Germany's too far away to be bothered about us."

Millard Hart gathered up his supplies and headed off to Pumpkin Knob. It was his last year. The only thing on his mind was getting enough education to get a job where the sun didn't burn him to cinders in the summer and the winters didn't frostbite his hands when he chopped firewood. He couldn't wait to join Earl Conroy at West Virginia University. The idea of the United States going to war while not yet finished with a depression and famine was the furthest thing from his mind.

As the years wore on, it was hard to ignore this man called Hitler who was pictured daily in any newspaper one picked up. It became common practice for the customers at Cleggs to stay a little longer and discuss the rumblings of war in Europe. Most had come to buy what provisions they could afford and reckoned a commotion so far away couldn't be of any consequence to them. Still, it was interesting to put forth one's opinion. They'd become more knowledgeable of the outside world and what better way to show this than to offer suggestions as to what England and France should do about a madman in Germany who seemed to be getting ready for a fight. Some weren't quite sure where these countries were located in relation to one another, but one survivor of World War I said they'd better keep an eye on Italy as well.

Other names and pictures began to appear in the local papers as Hitler added followers. Mussolini of Italy came across as a pompous tyrant, threatening that he alone could dominate the world, but was willing to combine his forces with Germany. Japan, a country so remote that it took an atlas and a teacher to locate, was being touted also as a serious threat. In Appalachia it was hard to believe that such faraway lands could be a menace to America.

"Good grief," Ruth exclaimed, causing Ab's brow to furrow. "Hitler's invaded Poland!" He looked over her shoulder and they read the 'Grit' together. "Another world war brought on by the Germans. I knew that man should have had his horns clipped back in '36," he said. Ruth nodded.

"Dammit. It'll be World War II," Will announced as he read the headlines in the 'Grit'.

Melia interrupted feeding Henry C and Rebecca Sue long enough to reply. "Let's hope it stays in Europe." Normally such an announcement would have been cause for a lengthy discussion of how it might affect the United States in general and Boreland Springs in particular. However, two youngsters took all her attention. She made a mental note to talk with Will that night about the situation.

"Hitler's invasion of Poland worries me, Sil. Wars have a tendency to spread... .even across oceans."

She massaged Chris's shoulders gently. "I know. Every History class I ever took attested to that fact.

Before they could carry the conversation further, yelling from the back of the house took Sil forward at a run. "Elizabeth! Stop teasing Roger. He's only two. Pick on someone older, like me!" She disentangled the two from one another. "It's time to get ready for school. I need you both to help me keep an eye on some of the older students."

"Yes, mama," they said in unison, proud that their mother was a schoolteacher and relied on them to maintain order.

She smiled and tousled their curly heads. "Don't know what I'd do without you as my assistants."

"What's a 'sistant', mama."

"A helper, silly!" Elizabeth answered. "Don't little boys know anything, mama?"

"They do when they get a little older. And don't forget, Elizabeth, they get big and strong and sometimes they chase older sisters who've been sarcastic."

"What's sarcastic," Elizabeth asked.

"We'll look it up in the dictionary when we get to school."

Chris watched the trio load up in the old car and head out to school. He wished his mother could have met his wife and children. She would have loved them so much. His father had passed on two years before. He had no siblings and only one elderly aunt. He'd given the farm in Clarksburg to her and her small family. There were no ties for him there. The Lockharts were the family that he held dearer than life itself.

A day never passed that he didn't thank God they'd been born in one of the best places in the country to weather the depression. Life hadn't been easy, but it had been possible to survive without going hungry or losing their land to bank closings. In the interior of the state, where the native population had depended on wages from outside coal and timber firms, suffering and loss was some of the worst in the nation.

Now the fighting in Europe was another cause for concern. It seemed as though nothing could stop the stream of problems that plagued the world. Hitler's continued disrespect for borders or treaties had been a prime topic of newspapers and radio broadcasts for the past three years. Some said it was a matter of time before the conflict spilled across the ocean. Others refused to believe anything so far away could ever affect the United States. Chris had a dull feeling in the pit of his stomach that Adolf Hitler wouldn't let anything so puny as an ocean thwart his relentless ambition.

"What do you think about Hitler?" Millard asked Earl as they walked across campus.

"He's evil and powerful enough to cause us all a lot of grief."

The two young men had become fast friends during their years at West Virginia University. Earl was a year ahead of Millard. Both had decided to get their degrees in Civil Engineering.

"You mean you think the U.S. could get into it?" Millard couldn't digest such an idea.

"Ancient countries like Persia, Greece, and Rome conquered vast areas of the world without mechanized vehicles. Sending troops across the Atlantic wouldn't be much of a challenge for a country that's been building arsenals and fighting vehicles for years."

Millard stopped in his tracks. "Do you think it'll be soon?"

"Hell, Millard. I'm not certain it'll happen at all. Just get busy and pass your exams, will you? Get your thoughts on a career – not a war."

Kay Meredith

CHAPTER THIRTY-THREE

By 1940, drought, depression, bank closings, and the dust bowl were overshadowed by the war in Europe. Sorrowful pictures, taken in the 1930's of people who'd lost their jobs, their homes, and their hope, were replaced by photos of Hitler's relentless march across Europe. German forces had no mercy for those they conquered. It was evident that the Nazi's had no intention to negotiate with anyone – the sole agenda was complete domination of Europe and Asia.

Americans held their breath and lived in dread of the same fate they saw across the sea. No one believed President Roosevelt could keep the country out of the conflict. Waiting and wondering where the invaders would strike sped up the aging process of everyone who had been dealing with the depression for a decade. Now they worried that their children would be called up to fight. Elderly folks wrung their hands in despair, fearing that in their final years they would be sent to 'poor houses' while the children they'd expected to care for them would be engaged by the government in a war effort.

On December 7, 1941, it was no longer 'someone else's war. The attack on Pearl Harbor proved to the world that the planet Earth had become as small as a continent when it came to warring nations on the move. Fear was replaced by fury in the United States. There was no need for conscription – lines of young men, some too young to be accepted, stood ready to enlist to defend their country.

Boreland Springs was no exception. Before anyone could stop them, Earl Conroy and Millard Hart were the first to join up. They were soon followed by countless other young men between the ages of seventeen and twenty-five. Not all passed the physical and age requirements, but too many did. By the middle of 1942, few men young enough to marry or strong enough to farm could be found in Boreland Springs. Labor was left to the women and young married men with families.

Farewells were said privately. This was not a time for festivities – only national pride. Mothers, sisters, and wives hid their tears behind soggy hankies. Fathers with teenaged sons who'd signed on for a war on foreign soil choked back their tears, thumped their offspring on the back, and gruffly told them to 'kill them Germans and git home soon as possible'.

Every house was enclosed in a cloak of misery. The Lockharts, Conroys, and Harts gathered together for an evening of prayer the night before Millard and Earl were due to leave by train to Wheeling. No one knew where they would be sent from there.

Sil stifled her tears as she tried to explain to her students what was happening. The little ones couldn't understand why their older relatives had gone off in a uniform to fight.

"Who are they fightin', Missus Nelson?"

"Will they be away for a long time?"

"Are the Germans mean folks?"

The questions never stopped. There were no answers that made any sense. How does one explain why men in far-off lands can hurt us here in Boreland Springs? Sil wondered about that herself.

Many of the older boys couldn't wait to sign up and go off with their brothers to fight an army in Europe that now had its sights on the United States. Nothing she could say, such as their families needed them at home, changed their minds. "Before this is over there may be no young men left in Boreland Springs," she said to Chris one night after a particularly trying day.

He held her close. "Nobody has the spirit to work in the Co-op either. All they can think about is what may be happening to their sons. Yesterday, I tried to spur them into producing more food to help in the war effort. I'm hoping things will go better today."

Melia got busy re-organizing the WCTU. She was not one who could sit idly by and simply worry. Things had to be done. Radio announcements had been made that bandages would be needed. Victory gardens must be planted, and a monthly gathering should be organized to keep the spirits up of every family in Boreland Springs. The projects were endless. Melia was relentless. She listened to the radio to learn what was being done throughout the rest of the country – and what could be done with the limited resources of Boreland Springs.

She gathered up Elizabeth and Roger and took them with her as she patrolled the hills and valleys delivering baskets of food to the elders, taking medicine to anyone who was sick, and making a weekly trip to Cleggs to pick up necessities for some of the residents who had neither the time nor vehicle to make the trip. Roger gathered the eggs and Elizabeth helped make beds. Both children enjoyed traveling with their mother and they wanted to do more so she wouldn't get so tired.

Will planted extra vegetables so the 'healthy baskets', as they were called, would be full of fresh, nutritious food. The entire Hart family became a familiar sight throughout the community, doing whatever was needed to make things easier to bear. Rev. Knox preached to a full church every Sunday and was dazed when he saw more husbands in attendance than in any of his previous twenty years of spreading God's word.

Home made candy, cakes, and cookies were sent off to sons who missed their homes more than they thought they would. The folks of Boreland Springs covered their sorrow by keeping a constant connection with their loved ones who had gone off to fight for their country.

Kay Meredith

CHAPTER THIRTY-FOUR

February 1942, West Virginia University

    Professor Alonzo Hebert looked out over his freshman class of Political Science majors who'd signed up for his course in writing about politics. It was mostly women since most able-bodied young men had enlisted in the armed forces. This did not fill him with much enthusiasm for it was the men who had the tenacity to research the improprieties of politicians, government agencies, utility companies, etc., to make public officials accountable for their actions. He reckoned it would take a lot of ingenuity on his part to mold a group of tough political sentinels out of so many pampered young ladies. He sighed and called the roll. It was time to ask them in what area they wished to specialize.

    At the end of the period, he was stunned. They all wanted to be war correspondents – even the flat-footed men who'd failed the physical for active fighting! Chronicling the crimes the Nazis were committing on humanity needed to be recorded for future war trials. Not a brain among them, he groused. Doubt if they know what a foxhole is. Too ready to get into a conflict where excitement and high ideals soon descends into death and carnage. They've no idea they can be shot before the first word is written. "I think I've just the assignment to at least teach them how to sift through confusion to find the truth," he whispered on his way to the library.

    In early May he stood before them with his announcement. "Class, here is your project for the summer. I'm giving it to you now so you can begin to make arrangements for travel and lodging." They eyed him curiously. "You will each be assigned to research and analyze an unsolved crime which has occurred somewhere in this state after the turn of the century. Most are obscure, but often violent, offenses where the evidence has been lost or never recovered in the first place. Your job is to define whether or not you think the state prosecutors were thorough and fair in their actions."

    He looked into their faces where curiosity had been replaced by amazement. "I can see you didn't expect to be sent on a difficult mission on your vacation. . . ." He took a few deep breaths. "Well, that's what reporting a war is all about. Ferreting out the truth on *all* sides of an issue in an efficient manner – by that I mean you get the information and have it on the wires the same day it occurs! Your personal thoughts on the subject, what's right or wrong and all that, are irrelevant. That's left to historians." He let that sink in. "This will be scant preparation since in wartime you work during holidays, bad weather, and while dodging bullets."

Their faces reflected shock. "You *do* know that war correspondents go along with the fighting forces to the front?" Silence. "You can't get a factual account by sitting in some cozy hotel far from where the fighting takes place."

Uneven breathing spread through the humid room. Nervous glances looked out the smoky windows onto the manicured campus. Prof. Hebert reckoned they were having second thoughts. Good, he thought. Maybe we can get back to a class that concentrates on bringing politicians into line instead of sending these young people to certain death on a battlefield.

"Your assignments will be posted on the bulletin board in the lobby. Should anyone like to change their focus from becoming a war correspondent, let me know by the end of the week."

Without giving them time to think, he inundated them with class work concerning grammar, research, and points of view. By the end of class they were out of breath, confused, and more than a little bit scared. It hadn't been the glamorous and lofty presentation they'd expected. Every student thought his or her intentions should have been highly praised as an important auxiliary part of the war effort.

Pamela Whitney McNeil listened with interest. It made sense to her. To practice unearthing obscure facts in unfriendly terrain and lost information was a good place to begin learning to be an objective and unyielding journalist -- without the distraction of conflicting forces making it a dangerous exercise. She looked forward to seeing where her task would take place.

Throughout the course, Prof. Hebert had watched her closely. Pamela was the only serious student in the bunch and he was curious to see how she would react to the assignment. It did not surprise him to see acceptance and excitement reflected on her face. She was the only daughter of a prominent attorney in Clarksburg. He and his wife, Gloria, were never far from contact with the faculty. Within a week of her arrival, they had improved her dorm room and changed her roommate to one who didn't smoke.

She was not spoiled, however, as demonstrated by her attitude that was polite, thoughtful and inquisitive. Her attire was simple: sensible shoes and tweed skirts accompanied by wool sweaters in subdued colors that complimented her honey-colored hair that was pulled back with heavy barrettes. Her strong facial features were softened by milk-white skin that was touched with a hint of rose on her cheekbones. She wasn't a delicate creature. Rather, she was tall and lanky – what Prof. Hebert considered the outdoor type. He'd been captivated by her startling blue eyes that offered a window into a character that was straightforward and candid. Perhaps I'm just getting old, he thought, as he perused the rest of the class. She's one of many attractive young things – she simply has a better mind.

He exhaled slowly. "You will have one week to complete your work. The manuscripts are to mailed back to me by June 15th." He smiled inwardly at the sighs of relief that there would still be a summer to enjoy after all. How ironic, he mused. To think they're worried about a vacation while planning careers that will eliminate the niceties of life and place them in hostile countries.

Pamela and her friend, Ardis Hatcher, went together to see where they would be spending a week of their summer vacation.

"Hell," Ardis moaned as she looked at her post. "I've got to go all the way down to Bluefield." She was talking to herself. Pamela looked over her shoulder. "In 1919 a man was hung for horse-stealing then declared innocent when another man made a deathbed confession. I've got to research the culpability of the court that convicted him and demonstrate how I would bring attention to the matter to recover funds for the family of the hung man." She wrung her hands. "Where on earth do I begin?"

Jeff Umbaugh laughed. "I'm to investigate the 1929 stock market crash with ensuing shenanigans of state politicians whose influence saved a bank where most of their savings were invested. That should be interesting."

"Where do you go, Pamela?"

"Seems I'm supposed to look into an unsolved shooting which happened in a luxury mineral springs spa located between Parkersburg and St.

Marys. The name of the hotel was Boreland Springs Resort and it was the owner's son who was killed. No one was ever brought to justice for the crime." She chewed her lower lip and read further. "Doesn't sound very important to me." Her face drooped in disappointment.

"Don't be discouraged, Pam." Ardis wanted to take away the frown from Pamela's pretty face. "It might turn out to be interesting."

"Remember that when you're down there in the middle of nowhere trying to find a plausible reason why the state should be held responsible for making restitution to the family of a man wrongfully executed."

They laughed together. It was only a week. In 1942 it was easy to pass off crimes committed so long ago, forgetting that the people who were involved suffered as deeply as any they would write about in the future. They were young.

It was only June and Sil was already sweating. "What will I do when July gets here," she said to herself. Chris was out with the men on the never-ending job of farming. Elizabeth Anne and Roger Wayne, now seven and five respectively, were fighting over ownership of a shovel. They'll gladly give it up when they get big enough to actually dig a ditch or hoe a garden, she thought darkly.

"Stop that right now." She was out of patience. Sometimes she wished there was no such thing as vacation for children under the age of six. They should be made to stay in school so summer work and a semblance of vacation could occur for the adults. Of course, since she was the schoolteacher, the strategy wouldn't help *her* very much. "Roger, go out to the garden and dig a row for us to plant some beans. Elizabeth, it's time for you to learn how to knead bread."

She was stopped in the midst of this sorting out of bored youngsters by a knock on her door. "Just a minute," she yelled then turned to her children. "Try to keep quiet and busy while I see who's here." Both nodded agreeably, satisfied with the outcome of the dispute.

She wiped her brow with the hem of her apron and tried to tuck her hair back under the kerchief around her head. She pulled the door open.

"Charity!" she exclaimed. She leaned heavily into the doorframe as if someone had forcibly shoved her. One hand covered her mouth as if to take back the words.

The young woman facing her grabbed Sil by the elbow and helped her to the porch swing. "No, M'aam. My name is Pamela McNeil. I phoned last week to see if you could help me with some research in the Boreland Springs area, remember?" Sil nodded but was still speechless. "I got your name from the Extension Service in Parkersburg. They said you'd be the best one to talk to." Sil was gradually getting her breath back. "Are you alright? Do you need a drink of water? Should I go for help?"

"No," Sil exhaled slowly. "You reminded me of someone else there for a minute. I'm fine now. Come on in." She escorted Pamela inside and cleared a space on the couch for her to sit.

Pamela explained about the assignment her college professor had given all the students as experience in researching controversial crimes that had happened long ago. Most of the class thought it was his way of finding out how dedicated they would be when it came to finding out the facts under the worst circumstances.

"You see," she went on, "we all want to be war correspondents. I've a feeling Prof. Hebert doesn't think many of us have the determination and ability to give up our comfortable lives." Sil nodded throughout the explanation, still trying to regain her equilibrium. "Most of us are girls. The fellows in the class are the ones who failed their physicals for active service and this is one way they can face adversity for their country."

Sil looked into the face of this beautiful young woman who was the spitting image of Melia at that age, except for the eyes, which were so like Wyatt Mathieson's. Idly, she wondered why anyone who didn't have to would want to travel to a foreign land and face bullets with a camera and pen. But more than that, Sil railed against Fate who had placed this child, who could pass for the offspring of Melia and Wyatt, in their midst. She struggled to regain her composure. I need to add something to this conversation, she thought, or look like the biggest fool in Boreland Springs.

"What an admirable aspiration. What do your parents think of you going away?"

"They're not thrilled. They hope I'll change my mind or perhaps the war will be over by the time I graduate." She laughed self-consciously. "I haven't mentioned that I'm taking classes throughout summer so I can finish early. I don't want to miss the opportunity to see up close what will probably be the most significant war of this century. . . .or certainly in my lifetime." Pamela's eyes were filled with the allure of dedicating herself to such a grand plan.

Sil remembered her own imposing ambitions at that stage of her life. "Where do you live?"

"I'm from Clarksburg. My father is an attorney there and wanted me to major in law and become his partner one day. I've no desire to work inside musty offices and boring law books. I want to be out doing something for mankind."

"And you feel being a foreign correspondent would fit that need?" Sil had lost her apprehension of the girl she'd come to think of as Charity. The teacher part of her took over with all the curiosity that caused her to probe the minds of students. She glanced at Elizabeth and Roger to make certain they were still quietly at their chores.

"Yes, M'aam. Our citizens need to know the truth about the slaughter Hitler is committing. It will give us more resolve to defeat such a demon."

Sil smiled discreetly. She was having trouble being called 'M'aam' but reckoned she fit the age group Pamela's mother had taught her should be so addressed. "You can call me Mrs. Nelson, if you like. . . .since we'll be spending lots of time together this next week."

Pamela nodded.

"Where are you staying?"

"At a small hotel in Parkersburg. However, it doesn't take long to drive here in my little coupe. Just tell me when it's convenient for you to talk to me and I'll be here."

"Might as well start tomorrow. What sort of information will you want?"

"Circumstances surrounding the crime; where it happened; motive; witnesses; family members; feelings of the community as to who the perpetrator was, and other people I can interview about what happened. Anything you feel pertinent."

"That's a lot of information for one week."

"I know, but that's the rule. Prof. Hebert wants to see how efficient and concise we can be at gathering facts and reporting them in a timely fashion. Our manuscripts must be mailed by June 15th latest."

"I see."

"And of course he'll expect photos of the crime site."

"But the hotel burned to the ground."

"I know. However, I must supply pictures of what's left of it and the springhouse. Those will have to be accompanied by interviews with anyone who lives on the premises now. I did some preliminary research and learned that a son, Clay, still resides there. I must talk with him. At his convenience, of course." She added the last when she saw the look of astonishment on Sil's face.

"But I can supply all the facts you need and introduce you to many of the folks who worked there. Wouldn't that be enough?"

"I'd run the possibility of getting a failing mark. . .or at the very least getting a low score. Our professor is a wily fellow and will have done his own investigation. If I were to omit such an important part of this shooting investigation, I would surely fail!" Her face screwed up with concern. "Is Clay Mathieson ill or something?"

At the sight of Pamela's distress, Sil gave up her reluctance to such a meeting. "No, Pamela. I'll phone him up this evening and set a time for the interview."

"Thank you so much, Mrs. Nelson. You're kind to help me probe into something that happened so long ago. Gads! I wasn't even born yet!" She laughed with relief. "Now, I must go. You have work to do. Here's the number of the hotel and my room number." She pulled out a card with her home address on one side and wrote the hotel information on the other.

Sil accepted the card from Pam's outstretched hand and once again struggled to maintain her balance and composure. "What an unusual bracelet that is," she said. "It almost looks like a baby's locket remade to fit your wrist."

"You're absolutely right," Pam said with pride as she looked tenderly at the tiny locket like the one Sil had given Melia as Charity's first baby gift. "It was given to me by my birth mother." She looked into Sil's eyes. "I'm adopted, you see. My adoptive parents wanted me to know how much I was loved by my real mother. Her decision to find a better home than she could provide was evidence of her selflessness. I wear it always to remind me that I have three of the most wonderful parents in the world!"

"How wonderful of them to be thoughtful. Do you ever wonder about your mother? Or father?"

"Sometimes. I understand that my mother never told my father about the pregnancy, which is a bit sad, don't you think?" Sil nodded. "There are times when I'd like to meet them, if only to see what they look like. However that information was withheld by the agency that handled the adoption." Her eyes were downcast for a moment. "But my father tells me to treasure the past that brought me to them and look forward to the future full of love from them. I was born to a mother who loved me enough to give me a good future with adoptive parents who love me more than if they'd borne me themselves. What more could I want?"

"Nothing," Sil answered breathlessly. "Can you be here around eight in the morning?"

"Absolutely!" It was one of her favorite superlatives.

Sil fell in love with Charity all over again. *I must make it through this week without letting Melia see her. There's no denying who she is. And even though the facts are a bit skewed as to who gave the baby Charity the locket, it's good to know the McNeil's were concerned that their daughter be happy with her background.* "I pray to God that Clay sees no resemblance. He was never around her much as I recall," she whispered. "Elizabeth! Roger! It's time to carry biscuits to daddy."

CHAPTER THIRTY-FIVE

The house nearly shook on its foundation next morning when Pamela hurried in with her boundless enthusiasm. "I'm really excited about this, Mrs. Nelson. Now I'm certain I want to be a news correspondent."

"You might want to reserve your opinion until after you see how much information you can squeeze out of these hills about a subject that tore them apart in 1924. Folks hereabouts rarely tell strangers much about what goes on here. Even after it happened, the investigators had no luck at learning who might have done the shooting – and for what reason."

"Maybe now that so much time has passed more people will be willing go talk."

"Perhaps, but few of the locals were on the scene, only the staff working that night. It was mostly guests who arrived immediately after the shot was heard. I've arranged for you to go to St. Marys and talk to Brian Paige, the man who did most of the investigation."

"Wonderful! We can all go in my car. There's room in the back seat for Elizabeth and Roger." She looked at the two wide-eyed children. "Would you like a ride in my car?"

They jumped up and down, squealing with enthusiasm. They made so much noise that the yard cats ran for cover and the chickens stopped scratching for grain momentarily. Sil was amazed that Pamela remembered the children's names. Unusual for such a young girl so caught up in her plans for a glamorous career.

Brian tried his best to answer all Pamela's questions. It had happened so long ago. While it had galled him at the time, he'd finally given up ever discovering who shot the gun that killed Wyatt Mathieson. He'd put it in the back of his mind, and stored his meticulous investigative reports in dusty, dog-eared files. Life had changed much in little St. Marys during the past eighteen years. More crime, much of it prompted by folks left homeless and hungry during the depression, kept him constantly on the run. No time to worry about the death of one young man in 1924, for God's sake! He couldn't even remember much of the details now.

Pamela was undeterred. She was determined to get as much information as she could from this man. He had been the first investigator to arrive at the crime scene. His information would validate her report. After much hemming and hawing, her jovial personality won out. He handed her the papers that detailed all his trips, whom he'd talked to, and what he'd found out. Brian had too much work on his agenda that morning. He decided to give this young woman the yellowed files about a death nearly twenty years ago at a hotel that no longer existed. It wouldn't hurt anything to let her have a look and get her out of his thinning hair.

"Hope you come up with some ideas," he said to Pamela, trying to recall when was the last time he'd had that same look of expectation to solve the world's problems.

"Thank you, sir. I'll return these at the end of the week."

He gave them a tired nod and returned to the paperwork that covered his desktop. He looked forward to an assistant. City counsel had promised to put that in the budget for the coming year.

They stopped at Brooks Ice Cream Parlor before returning home. Sil spent most of the way home wiping melted ice cream off her rambunctious offspring. Going to town and having a treat was almost more than they could bear without jumping right out of the back seat. "Don't worry about the drips, Mrs. Nelson. The seats are leather...everything wipes off easily."

Nevertheless, Sil was nervous about soiling Pamela's shiny car. She was glad when they pulled up in front of their house. Pamela helped her extricate the two sticky youngsters and take them inside for a good face washing. "Tomorrow morning we go to where the Boreland Springs Hotel used to stand and meet Clay Mathieson," she announced to an exuberant Pamela.

"Absolutely fantastic! This afternoon I'll study the papers from Mr. Paige." She kissed Elizabeth and Roger and sailed out the door.

Sil wondered if she'd have the energy to last a whole week with someone with so much vigor. I'll need to sleep for a month, she smiled, remembering when she and Melia were that full of endless enthusiasm.

The once splendid driveway up to the hotel site was rutted and dusty. Sil tried to listen to the stream of dialogue Pamela was saying, but she was engulfed in a storm of memories. The carnage that had happened nearly twenty years ago surrounded her as if it had occurred only yesterday. She was dizzy, recounting the terrible explosion and the blood that covered the springhouse that night. The inside of her head reverberated with the weeping of the guests who saw the body of Wyatt Mathieson, blown away below the waist. And finally, the memory of Melia's anguish at being pregnant with Wyatt's child – the girl who now sat beside her! Sil thought those recollections had been tucked away in a part of her brain that was closed forever. She was wrong. She gasped and covered her eyes.

Pamela nearly ran the car over the hill. "What's wrong, Mrs. Nelson? You look like you've seen a ghost?"

Sil smiled weakly. "I have."

"Shall we turn around?"

"No, Clay's expecting us. I'm alright now."

At the top of the hill, where the impressive hotel used to look out over the valley, no visible sign gave evidence that it had ever been there at all. Sil was amazed. She got out of the car like she was in a trance and walked to where the porch had been. She knelt down and dug into years of undergrowth gone wild. "This is where the steps were," she mumbled to herself. Pamela watched in fascination as Sil clawed further and found bits and pieces of the old foundation.

"Nothin' much left, is there?"

Pamela looked up and saw a man in his mid-thirties walking toward them.

"No, Clay, there isn't," Sil answered as she stood up. "But at least there's enough to be found so I know it wasn't all a dream."

"More like a nightmare, I'd say. Livin' here all these years since, watching Mother Nature cover it all up with weeds, wild flowers, and a new stand of trees has helped me put my own mess at the back of my brain like the old foundation. . .concealed as long as I don't go diggin' too deep."

"I thought I'd done that, too, until I drove up the lane. The old sights and smells knocked me off balance for a minute. Gave Pamela a scare, I think."

Clay looked inquisitively at the tall girl standing quietly by, waiting to be included in the conversation.

"Good grief. I left my manners at the bottom of the hill!" Sil exclaimed. "Clay, I want you to meet Pamela McNeil – the girl I told you about last night." Clay nodded. "She's been assigned by her college professor to investigate the mystery of Wyatt's death. I'm hoping you can help her. She wants to make a good grade. . . .it's a requirement to get into his class about becoming a war correspondent."

He looked at Pamela more closely. For a fleeting moment she seemed familiar somehow. Her eyes were such a brilliant blue. . .like Wyatt's. He shook the notion out of his head and addressed the next thought he'd had. Why would such a lovely girl want to put herself at risk by reporting about the atrocities of war?

Seeing disbelief on Clay's face, Pamela laughed gleefully. "I know. You want to know why I'd want to write a report while in the midst of fighting."

He nodded.

Her face became serious. "Our gallant young soldiers need to be chronicled. Many will die, others will be maimed, a few will return. Someone has to write their story."

Sil was stunned. She hadn't realized Pamela's beliefs were so pure and unselfish. Underneath the laughter of a privileged young woman beat the heart of a warrior in search of the truth. She looked at Clay, who also seemed to be struck dumb.

"So, where do we begin?" Pamela asked, unsure why the two adults were speechless.

Clay was the first to be jarred into action. He took her by the elbow. "Let's go to the carriage house which I transformed into my home after the fire. My wife, Beth, will have some cool lemonade ready."

"That sounds great! I'm thirsty enough to drink a gallon."

Affair at Boreland Springs

Back to the college freshman, Sil thought with relief. The contemplative Pamela unnerved her. Made her think of a past she wanted to leave behind forever. And *my* role only played out on the edge of it all! What must it be like to be Will or Melia and live with the reality of the shooting and all the lives that were so cruelly affected?

She listened dully as the conversation flirted around her consciousness. Every now and then she caught a word or two but felt no need to respond. This was Pamela's meeting. She sipped her lemonade as Pamela asked endless questions about how it happened: what was the motive; who might have done it; were there any witnesses? On and on – all the things they'd asked themselves back then. Clay patiently answered them all, but there was little of value in the words.

Finally, she put her pen down, frustration written in her furrowed brow. Her voice was filled with disbelief "So, you're saying nobody saw it happen, no one knew whom Wyatt met at the springhouse, no one knows why he was there that late to begin with, and afterward no one knew anyone who would want to kill him?" She paused then looked him square in the face. "Did someone come in and kill him just for the hell of it? If so, how did they know he'd be there?" To her young mind such a scarcity of answers was not to be believed. "Somewhere there has to be somebody who knows what happened. Were local people questioned?"

Clay smiled thinly, surprised at her impassioned outburst. "It was a long time ago. Even now local folks are tight-lipped about unpleasant incidents. The authorities tried the best they could but there was no one coming forth who could say for certain what had happened." He was entranced by her eyes – and something else. Her hair reminded him of someone too, but he couldn't find the name in his memory. He shook his head. "I was only sixteen then. No one included me in any of the details. I'm only telling you what little I know."

"Forgive me, Mr. Mathieson. I was thoughtless. It must have been a terrible time for one so young."

He laughed. "You're forgiven. Just try not to insist I give you a full account." He looked at Sil. "I can show you where it all happened but have Sil take you to Melia Hart. She was here that night too and might able to tell you more."

"Wonderful." Her sunny smile and expressive superlatives took away the feeling that she was conducting an inquisition.

Sil smiled with admiration. This child will make a great investigative reporter, she thought. So passionate – just like her mother. She gasped. God, I can't let Melia see her. Why did Clay have to make that suggestion? Melia will know her own daughter in a heartbeat. Maybe she'll forget he mentioned her.

Footsteps coming from the carriage house intruded into the interview. It was Beth, carrying the lemonade, followed by Roberta Mathieson. Sil panicked. Roberta might see the similarity between her dead son and a girl who worked for her long ago too. Sil stood up abruptly. "Clay, I'm due to take Pamela down to see Mrs. Mac, then on to Cricket Mathews. We should probably leave now." She forced her voice not to quiver.

Everyone looked at her like she had two heads. "For God's sake, Sil," Clay exclaimed, "the lemonade just got here and Beth's brought a plate of her sugar cookies. Mrs. Mac and Cricket can't be that impatient. Also, I'd planned to walk around and show Pamela what's left of the tennis courts, stables and where the springhouse used to be."

Pamela nodded so hard that her heavy curls bobbed like broken springs. "This is the most important part of the investigation, Mrs. Nelson. I need pictures and a feeling of where everything was located. At the very least I must prove I've been thorough at collecting the facts, few though they may be."

Roberta was approaching the group. She walked with a cane but her figure was as straight and petite as when she was young.

"Of course, you're right, Clay," Sil conceded "Why don't you two start on ahead while I visit with your mother. I haven't seen her for ages."

"Can't we have some lemonade first?" Pamela asked plaintively.

"Start on where?" Roberta Mathieson asked. She was looking at the ground, picking her way carefully over the uneven footing. "I'm slow, but I'd love to go for a walk around the old place. The ghosts from this part of my life are buried in the rubble up there." She pointed to the remains of the foundation. "I no longer get a clutch in my chest when I think of those long ago days." She smiled into Sil's apprehensive face. "Can I hold onto your arm for support?"

"Of course, Mrs. Mathieson. We'll lean on each other."

"Mother, this is Pamela McNeil. . .the girl I mentioned to you last night. She's here to do a college paper on the shooting. Are you really up to listening to all that?"

Roberta turned to face the newcomer. For an instant she had the daunting feeling she'd seen the girl somewhere before. Her eyes are so like Wyatt's, she thought. And that marvelous head of hair is very familiar. "You're such a pretty one," she said looking Pamela in the face. "Clay mentioned you'd be here working on some paper about the shooting back in '24."

"Yes M'aam. It's an assignment due back to our professor by June 15th for those who want to be accepted into a class for writing as a war correspondent. There are about twenty of us and our projects are located throughout the state and cover various crimes. Most are vague and all are old, making it necessary for us to develop our skills to ferret out the truth."

"Truth?" Roberta's eyes squinted, trying to forget what the truth was when Wyatt was killed. She was forever thankful that illegal moonshine was never linked to the Mathiesons' and that John died before he could take revenge on Eugene and Will. It had taken many years before she'd absolved herself of the relief she'd felt when he'd perished in the fire. He'd been bound to bring death and destruction to even the score for Wyatt. At least in the end, it only involved himself and his hotel.

She recalled that on the day following the shooting it was like a blanket of silence had descended over Boreland Springs. Everyone had a pretty good idea of *why* it had happened but the identity of *who* did the shooting was up for discussion. While there were those who boasted privately they knew who shot the twelve-gauge, it was a fact that no good could come of passing this information on to the authorities. They felt as I did, Roberta mused. The tragedy was bad enough without bringing investigators in to put people in jail and make it worse!

She looked up from her reflections. Everyone was staring at her. "Did I miss something?" she asked.

"Pamela was just answering your question about 'truth'," Clay answered.

"Forgive me, child. My thoughts tend to wander at times. Could you say it again if I promise to listen?" Her eyes twinkled at her loss of attention.

Pamela smiled in return. "Of course. I was saying that our professor will be looking to see if we've done our research. For instance: did the authorities do a thorough job of investigating; or did they pre-suppose who the killer was and try to find someone who fit the bill rather than search for evidence linking him to the crime."

"Does that really happen?"

"More than we'd like to believe. . . .but usually only the poor are caught in such a trap. Prof. Hebert figures this sort of project will give us good practice on reporting both sides of a military conflict."

Roberta nodded absent-mindedly, still mesmerized by the beautiful girl with the analytical mind. "I've no doubt you will be good at this." She sighed heavily. "I wonder if you or your parents know how much danger you're putting yourself up for. Are they prepared for the possibility of losing you in such a conflict?"

"They try to understand why I want to do this. In all honesty though, they pray nightly that I'll change my mind."

"It's a terrible thing to lose a child," she whispered. The others strained to hear. "I think I will decline the walk, Clay. Go on without me."

"I'll stay with you, Mrs. Mathieson." Sil settled herself in the grass. "I've done my share of tromping over these old hills, too."

"Call me Roberta, Sil. It's time." Her mouth was pinched and she narrowed her eyes as she watched Clay and Pamela drop out of sight. "So familiar," she mused again to herself. "Never thought I'd see those eyes again." Roberta seemed unaware of Sil and Beth. Her face took on a faraway look. Several minutes went by as she rummaged through her brain for forgotten images.

"Your friend, Sil? She worked upstairs for Cricket. What was her name?"

"You mean Melia Conroy?"

"Yes. Pamela's hair reminds me of hers. . . .so full and curly."

"I think that's the style now, Roberta."

"Could be. Very attractive." Her voice was quiet "I hope she fails the paper."

"Why?"

"She could be killed, that's why!" Roberta was shaking. "At this age she has no judgment as to what's the best for her to do. She has no idea the sorrow her parents will suffer if she doesn't come back."

"I'm certain reporters aren't allowed in the middle of heavy fighting," Sil went on, trying to soothe the distressed woman.

"It must be those blue eyes of hers," Roberta was whispering again. "I couldn't stand the thought of them dying." A mourning dove called in the distance. Roberta looked up. "Where is she from?"

"Clarksburg. Her father is a lawyer and her mother is active in charitable organizations there. She's their only child and obviously the apple of their eye."

"An only child?"

Sil nodded.

"Such a shame to have only one. Thank God I had Clay. He's been a godsend."

Clay kicked the weeds away from what was left of the stone that surrounded the springs. The floor had warped years ago and gradually floated away during spring flooding. He waved his arm to encompass the meadow that lay around them. "Hard to believe now that once this was a well-manicured place where we had picnics, played horseshoes, and drank smelly mineral water," he said dryly. "Over there, under those oak trees, tables and benches were placed so the guests could sip tea or lemonade to take away the taste of the mineral water, which wasn't all that appetizing. Always wondered why anything that smelled like rotten eggs was considered to be healthy."

Pamela looked around in awe. A long time ago the killing that occurred in this very place where she was standing must have shaken guests and locals to the bottom of their bones. Yet she'd learned nothing to explain why it might have happened. She watched Clay walk around, hands in his pockets, feet kicking away debris, and shaking his head at how quickly opulence can disappear into the soil.

"Surely, you knew something about why your brother was down here late at night, Mr. Mathieson. Such a meeting doesn't occur out of the blue – it's usually part of a routine." She placed her pen above the pad, ready to write down his answer. "You could give me your thoughts. Won't affect anything now and I'm just a college student, not part of any official inquiry."

He looked up from his musing and laughed. "Tryin' to practice your ability to 'get at the truth', are you? Well, you're right. Won't hurt to give you a hint of what some folks wondered about back then." She held her breath. "Yes, I did know there was a late night meeting at the springhouse every week. Sometimes Pa went but he'd turned it over to Wyatt for the summer. Problem is, it had always been on Wednesday, never Tuesday. That was the big difference."

Several minutes passed. Pamela was impatient. "That's it?" she said. "Just that it happened on Tuesday instead of Wednesday?"

"Yep. And before you ask, I never did know who arrived to meet with Pa or Wyatt on those nights. . .or why for that matter."

"Surely you had suspicions?"

"Nope. Pa considered me too young to be included in such information. I knew that would happen when I got older. I'm certain there were staff at the hotel who might have known. For that matter, mother knows. However, I insist you don't put her through more agony. She's answered enough questions for two lifetimes."

Pamela nodded. "But you'd be agreeable to my asking local folks why it might have happened and who could have committed the crime?"

"Yep. But I'll warn you that from the minute Wyatt was found the entire community developed a serious case of memory loss."

"That's withholding pertinent information!" Pamela was horrified.

"Maybe. But hard to remedy when even the parents of the deceased said they had no knowledge of 'why' or 'who'."

"According to my research, this is a region known to do a big business in bootlegging. Could that have been the cause?"

"Could have been. Or possibly an argument over a woman. . .Wyatt was known to be active with the local girls. Families around here don't put up with the upper-crust taking advantage of young women with big promises for a night of enjoyment. More than one murder has been committed by a furious father or brother when a female member of the family has been dishonored"

"You mean. . ."

"I mean, Pamela, it could have been any number of reasons. Only Pa, Ma, and the fellow who shot the twelve-gauge knows for certain who did it and why." He shoved his hands deeper into his pocket and looked into the horizon. He felt defeated. This was not a place where he came often – too many hurtful memories. "Lots of folks had their suspicions, but no one actually saw it happen. The gun was never found. There was never enough evidence to bring a case against anyone." He turned back to her. "Might as well get on back up to the others. You could learn something else when Sil takes you to meet Cricket and Mrs. Mac."

Pamela put her pen and pad away knowing her interview with Clay was over. She felt like an archeologist – knowing somewhere beneath this earth she stood on and the minds of the people who live in this valley lay the answer. In either case, she didn't begin to know where to start digging. Being an investigative reporter wasn't going to be as simple as she'd expected.

The voices of Clay and Pamela floated up and across the meadow, companionable and relaxed. "It must have been next to impossible for your mother to bear such a thing," Pamela was saying. "Then for her to lose her husband not three years later. No wonder she wanted to return to her family in Philadelphia." She angled a glance at the young man walking beside her. "What made you stay?"

"It's my home. I was born here. I never had a desire to go to a fancy school and work in an office. Leaving because Wyatt and Dad were gone would have meant I'd have lost my home in addition to my father and brother."

"Glad you stayed?"

"Yep. It's peaceful workin' on the land among neighbors who've known me since I was in diapers. Married a local girl, and when my kids are old enough to go to school Sil will be their teacher. Mother visits often so they get to know her."

They were nearly back to the carriage house. Roberta looked relaxed, Sil was sipping her lemonade, and Beth was bringing out more cookies. Clay breathed a sigh of relief.

"Come sit beside me please, Pamela," Roberta extended her hand. "One day I hope my granddaughter is as lovely as you." She looked at Clay's five-year-old daughter. "I think Penny will look a lot like Pamela, especially the hair and eyes, don't you?"

"Ask Beth. She's better at that stuff than I am." Clay was tired from all the walking and talking. He wanted to keep his answers short. Besides, it was good practice for Roberta to speak with her daughter-in-law. She'd been unhappy when he'd married Beth Ann Moore, a local girl with an honest heart but only an eighth-grade education. Roberta had always considered herself tolerant with those less fortunate, but that didn't go as far as letting one marry into her family!

When Clay went against her wishes and married Beth Ann anyway, it was a year before she visited them. When the first grandchild arrived, however, they saw her more often. And in the process, she'd begun to talk with Beth. She found the woman to be thoughtful, a good mother, and she loved Clay more than anything. In light of all the unhappiness that had befallen Clay so early his life, Roberta reckoned he was due for a patch of contentment. I'll not be another thorn in his side, she decided, and supported the growing family with her love as well.

Pamela settled herself beside Roberta.

"Tell me about yourself. So fascinating – you wanting to be a war correspondent. Didn't realize girls were interested in that sort of thing."

Roberta studied the girl as she launched into an enthusiastic explanation of why she wanted to be a war reporter; all her friends did too. It was the best way to honor the brave men who were fighting for freedom. Roberta became immersed in the serious words of this girl whose face tweaked the edges of her memory.

I can't let this happen, Sil thought, as she watched Roberta get sucked into a likeness she thought she saw. "This time we absolutely have to leave."

She stood up and offered her hand to Pamela. "Come, child. When I was young and late for either Mrs. Mac or Cricket Mathews, they chewed me out til my ears were flat. I've a feeling they'll reckon I'm still young enough to need a good talking-to for being late."

Everyone laughed. Before Roberta could object, Sil guided Pamela into the car and they were off in a cloud of dust and lots of earsplitting goodbyes.

Mrs. Mac and Cricket were neighbors, so they were both sitting on Cricket's porch swing when the little coupe drove up. Introductions were made and Pamela took the seat next to the swing. Sil sat on the top step and leaned against the banister. She had explained to the two older women what Pamela would be asking them about.

Pamela pulled out her tablet and pen and got down to business. "Do either of you have any idea who might have wanted to kill Wyatt Mathieson?"

Their faces were expressionless – as was normal when strangers were about, even a pretty one. "Such a clamish day," Mrs. Mac said as she pulled out a big hankie from her dress pocket. Cricket nodded and picked up a fan.

Pamela feared her abruptness might have offended the ladies. She started over. "I apologize for being so fast with my questions. It's just that I've asked the same ones over and over with so little results. I was hoping the two of you could be the most help. And since I know you've got families to feed, I should get right to it." Her eyes pleaded with them to speak their minds. "Could you say if there was anyone who came to mind when you heard Wyatt Mathieson had been shot?"

This time at least, the two women made a stab at looking like they were trying to remember. "Cain't recall nobody I thought about. It was such a terrible night that all anyone thought about was gettin' that poor boy out of the springhouse." Mrs. Mac looked at Cricket. "What about you, Cricket. Did you have a notion of who mighta done it?"

"Cain't say that I did either. Most of us was helpin' poor Roberta to bed. Then we had to clean up all that blood." Her little round face screwed up with revulsion. "Wasn't nothin' much left of him below the waist, you know."

Pamela blanched at the thought. "There was blood stains all over them beautiful doors."

Pamela shook her head in sympathy, hoping this action would get them off the subject of all the gore. "After the funeral, did anyone leave the area?" She looked at them expectantly. "You know, that could be a clue. Someone's killed. Someone leaves."

Cricket sucked on a hollow tooth, then spoke. "Too far in the past. I don't remember who came and went five years ago, let alone nigh onto twenty!"

Pamela turned her eyes on Mrs. Mac.

"My memory is as bad as hers -- what with the depression and all, most folks don't care what went on in the twenties."

"Did you ever hear anyone say the shooting of Wyatt and the hotel burning down might be connected?"

Both women shook their heads.

Pamela put her pen back in her purse and closed her tablet. "Thanks so much for your time, ladies. Even though there isn't much you can tell me, can I take a photo of you so my professor will at least know I tried."

They laughed self-consciously and smiled without opening their mouths – too many teeth missing or blackened with decay. Even older women didn't want to show a flawed smile in a picture that was going to be seen by a professor in a big university. Pamela snapped several to be sure at least one came out clear. She sighed and looked at Sil. "Guess we'd better get back up the hill." Sil nodded and followed her down the path to the car. Within minutes they were bumping their way back up to Horse Neck.

"Spittin' image of Wyatt," Cricket said, as the little car faded from sight

"Yep," Mrs. Mac answered. "Little bit of Melia in that hair and face, too."

Cricket sucked her hollow tooth awhile. "None of our business."

"Nope," Mrs. Mac answered. They kept on swinging and tucked that bit of information into the back corner of their minds, along with the rest of what they thought about that black night in '24.

CHAPTER THIRTY-SIX

"I'm going to fail, I just know it! Nobody can remember anything." Tears glistened in Pamela's eyes and it threatened to become an all-out bawl. "Or they just won't tell. Either way I'm going back with nothing." Her nose reddened. "What about that friend of yours Clay mentioned. Could we talk to her?"

Sil's heart nearly stopped – but her wits returned in an instant "There were so many of us that summer. None of us paid much attention to anything other than getting our work done and collecting our wages on Friday. We rarely saw the Mathiesons. They were the busiest of all, making sure their guests were always satisfied." She glanced at Pamela who was blinking hard trying to keep her tears under control. "Why don't you go to the newspaper in Parkersburg and look up the accounts of what happened," Sil suggested. "I recall the findings were well recorded and factual."

"I suppose I might as well," she answered. "Although from what I've gleaned, those reporters probably didn't get much more than I have." She sounded defeated.

"In any case, there are bound to be long streams of sentences, which are more than you got from Cricket and Mrs. Mac. It'll look good in your presentation."

Pamela let out a hoot. "You're the best, Mrs. Nelson. Can't be down in the dumps around you."

Thank goodness her moods change as fast as a spring rain, Sil thought with a grin. She's easy to divert. Give her a few years though, and she'll be as relentless as a bloodhound. "I'm a teacher. Research, using published papers which usually contain lots of 'fluff' when the facts are thin, comes naturally to me."

"Why didn't I think of that?"

"You will when you've been at it awhile."

The sun was dipping low in the horizon, giving some relief from the heat by the time they stopped at the Lockharts to pick up Elizabeth and Roger. Pamela's little car was covered with dust, inside and out. Sil ran in, kissed her mother on the forehead and thanked her for caring for the toddlers, then hustled them out to the car. She tried to make their haste seem natural. Chris will be hollering for dinner, she explained to Ruth. In truth, Sil didn't want her mother looking at Pamela and noting her uncanny resemblance to Wyatt and Melia! She'd had enough of that for one day. The children were lulled to sleep in the rocking motion of the car. Chris's vehicle was already parked in the yard when they drove up the lane.

"I'll be spending the next two days in town then, Mrs. Nelson. But I'll come back on Friday to say 'goodbye'."

"See you then." Sil and her children waved until the car was out of sight.

"She's such a nice girl, mommy. Will she come back and visit?"

"Only to say 'goodbye' on Friday, love,"

"But I want to marry her!" Roger wailed.

"There will be plenty of young men wanting to marry that one, I think. You'll just have to pick someone else."

"I don't want anybody else." The child dropped into the dirt and became limp as a rag doll when Sil tried to lead him forward. He sat, entangled in his dusty arms and legs, trying to squeeze some tears from his eyes.

She covered a smile with her hand. "You can sit here and be sad, I suppose. But Elizabeth and I are going in to share a piece of cherry pie with daddy." Elizabeth looked at him contemptuously then turned and walked with her mother toward the porch.

"Wait for me. I want some pie too."

Sil spent the next two days in a dither. She relived the past eighteen years as though they were yesterday. The shooting; Melia's pregnancy; Will and Eugene leaving; the fire and John Mathieson's death. They went on and on, these memories. Her concentration was so askew that at one point Chris asked her, had she started the 'change'? She mumbled something about being behind in her class schedule, and still needed to collect vegetables for Melia's baskets.

The appearance of Pamela, who took them all back to the past while she walked among them in the present, was no little matter. What's the right thing to do? Sil asked herself over and over. She ticked off the facts as she saw them: Melia is at peace with her loss; Will no longer feels guilty over his action; Clay has found his place in the world; Eugene doesn't even remember it; and Pamela (Charity) landed on her feet, happy, cared for by doting parents -- completely unaware of her ties to the community of Boreland Springs. Why not leave it at that?

There are lots of reasons 'why not' her conscience niggled. This young woman forms the hub of all the principal players of that drama years ago. Furthermore, don't you have a responsibility to Melia to let her know the whereabouts of her first child? Clay didn't make the connection, Roberta isn't sure, and while Mrs. Mac and Cricket thought they smelled a rat, they will never reveal their feelings, even at the WCTU meetings. You are the only one who can sew the two rough edges together.

Her shoulders felt heavy from the weight of so much contradiction. Her mind wouldn't let her be. I could introduce Pamela to her blood family and shatter the tranquility that will soon be wrecked by the war anyway. Do any of us deserve to relive that muddle while in the midst of the terrible worry of losing our sons and daughters in Germany? Can I let it lay in the rubble of the hotel where it belongs? Does Melia deserve to be upset again by knowing her daughter is so close yet still unattainable? Should Pamela's world be turned hindside-to, forcing her to divide her attention between Melia and the McNeil's? Would she want to know her half-brother and sister?

God, what a headache! Mom always says to sleep on such problems, and when you wake up, He will have provided the answer. I might as well try that since nothing else seems to help. The shrill jangling of the phone brought her out of her stupor. It was Melia.

"Sil. Haven't heard from you all week. Anything wrong?"

"No, just been trying to keep up with the kids, get ready for canning, and keep Chris from starving to death."

"I know what that's like," Melia agreed with a laugh. In the background Sil could hear her two children fighting over something. "Hey, can you and Chris come over tonight. We'll roast a couple of chickens. We need some time to sit down without having to stack hay or haul water."

"Sounds good. Chris likes your chicken better than mine. I'll bring the pie."

"See you tonight, then. Got to go and get that hammer away from Henry before he clobbers Rebecca."

The dinner led them all to a state of reminiscing. They talked about the previous decade with all the suffering and how it now seemed to be receding into the past in the face of war. The suffering of the thirties, and now the forties, had relegated the twenties to the forgettable past. Most of the conversation concerned the fact that so far none of the boys from Boreland Springs had been killed in the war. However, many mothers worried that the government was just slow to inform parents of deaths and injuries – that maybe there had already been losses that had not yet been reported.

The raucous frogs began their evening song, and in its discordant and uneven rhythm their feeling of well being was lost under an ominous cloud. No one wanted to talk about what might happen down the road. However, there had been some news that week.

"We heard from Millard and Earl on Monday," Melia said with a slight catch in her throat.

"Where are they?" Sil's voice was thready. It had been a difficult blow to the Harts and Conroys when their two youngest signed up. Will, Chris, Melia and Sil had heard their parents speak of the carnage of the First World War and they were well aware that going off to fight was not something to be taken lightly. But no one could convince this generation to wait awhile before making such a choice.

"Still in boot camp in Kentucky. But, due to their education, they've both been notified they will be assigned to the Army Corps of Engineers."

"That sounds better than fightin' in trenches," Chris said, hoping that was, indeed, the case.

"Except that engineers often precede the fightin' forces who need bridges and roads to get to where the combat is." Will's shoulders slumped. "And they're not normally prepared to defend themselves since supervisin' construction is their primary duty." It was still hard for him to believe his youngest brother was old enough to go fight in a war somewhere on the other side of the globe.

The air became troubled – full of fears no one wanted to mention. What could anyone say? There's no safe way to go to battle. No guarantee that *your* loved one will return. West Virginians were patriotic people when push came to shove. For all their distrust of the government they believed in fighting for one's country. But in Boreland Springs the war was now in their own backyards and ambivalence ripped their principles to shreds. It made them ashamed that their hearts wanted victory for the Allies but not at the expense of *their* sons and brothers.

They sat mulling over these anxious thoughts until a screech owl brought them all out of their reverie with a start.

"Time to gather up the kids and get on home," Chris said and picked up Elizabeth Ann. Sil nodded and bundled up little Roger.

Will and Melia followed them out to the car. The goodbyes were said listlessly. No one could muster the enthusiasm for more.

Kay Meredith

CHAPTER THIRTY-SEVEN

Pamela bounded into the house like a whiff of fresh air. "Elizabeth! Roger! I've brought chocolate!"

The floor shook as each child tried to reach her first. Sil hurried after trying to put Roger's shirt on as he ran. He kept pulling out of her grip. In an instant the house was full of laughing children and adults. She's better than a song, Sil thought, as Pamela put a small chocolate into each tiny hand. "We'll save the rest for later," she said and placed them on a shelf well above the reach of greedy arms.

"I've come to say 'goodbye' and to thank you for your hospitality." She gave Sil a hug that left her gasping for breath. "Brought you a small token of my appreciation." She handed Sil a rectangular box about six inches deep.

"Now, you didn't have. . ."

"Shush. Just open it, will you?"

Sil carefully untied the grosgrain ribbon that secured an expensive paper wrapping depicting scenes from eighteenth century England. This must have come from Tiller's, she thought, the most exclusive shop in town. The box itself was special, embossed with the store emblem. She'd never had such a beautiful package to open. When she raised the lid, facing her was a photo of herself, Chris, and the children that had been snapped as they had all walked hand-in-hand up the path to the house. A smile lit up her face. She softly encircled the edges with her fingertips. "It's beautiful," she breathed. "Something I've always wanted to have done, but just never seem to get around to it."

"I took it when you weren't looking. Those are always the best."

Sil looked up at Pamela. "You bring so much happiness into our home. I'll miss you."

"I'll miss you and the brood, too," Pamela returned with a bit of irreverence. "Don't know what I'll do without sticky fingers to wipe." She eyed Elizabeth and Roger who fell laughing to the floor.

Underneath the picture was a hand knitted table runner, the color of eggshell and intricately designed with cherubs. "This is too much," Sil objected. "Your mother must have something as precious as this."

"She does. And she'd say you earned this one, putting up with my loud mouth like you have."

"I'll miss that loud mouth."

It was time. They hugged each other, knowing they'd made a special connection that may have only been for a week but would be remembered for a lifetime. The children cried a bit, until Sil promised another chocolate that afternoon. Pamela walked out to her car that had been washed sometime during the previous two days. In the next few minutes Pamela would leave, taking with her those blue eyes and lanky frame, so unnerving to some in the community.

Sil was sweating. She must say something. But what?

Her thoughts were interrupted by another colossal hug that took the words from her mouth. "I'll never forget this week, Sil. I hope one day we meet again." She turned quickly and got into the car.

"Pamela!"

"I never say 'goodbye', Mrs. Nelson. Too hard." She threw the words over her shoulder and put the car in gear.

"Wait!" Sil yelled and ran after the slowly moving coupe.

Pamela stuck her head out the window. "What?"

Sil stopped so fast that her ankles nearly turned. Her mouth was dry. Her tongue felt twice its size. It took time to form the words that would change so many lives once again.

Pamela was waiting – her brows arched and foot resting lightly on the accelerator.

Sil's breath escaped her chest in one great gulp. ". . . . .Just wanted to wish you luck with the paper."

"Thanks!" Pamela smiled, waved, then turned back to face the road ahead. In an instant, she was gone.

The three watched until the rumble of the engine was but a hum in the distance. The affair at Boreland Springs dissolved into the dust churned up by the exhaust from Pamela's little car. Sil turned the children around and they went back into the house for a piece of chocolate.

END

About the Author

Kay Meredith

Kay Meredith's previous published writings have all been non-fiction works concerning the training, competing, and schooling required at each level of competitive dressage (an Olympic discipline founded on the science of mounted warfare). This is Ms. Meredith's first novel. She lives in Raleigh, North Carolina.